Veteran

City Streets Trilogy, Book Two

This is a work of fiction. Similarities to real people, places, or events are entirely coincidental.

VETERAN

First edition. November 1, 2020.

Written by Susanne Perry.

Also by Susanne Perry

City Streets Trilogy
Runaway
Veteran

For my brothers, Jim, Glenn and Tom... veterans all.

"All war is a symptom of man's failure as a thinking animal."

John Steinbeck

"Never think that war, no matter how necessary, nor how justified,

is not a crime."

Ernest Hemingway

Chapter One

Sitting at his office work station, Dylan Colby grew impatient. He glanced at the corner of the screen. At least the time display didn't disappoint. Nearly time to call it a day. One last meeting and his workday would be over. But this meeting wasn't going to be an easy one. He regretted that it had to happen, but it was time. He must be very clear about that. His focus returned to the screen. Satisfied with the final notations, Dylan saved his changes then attached the documents to an email. He selected "Send" before he could change his mind again.

This meeting would be the last time he'd waste effort on this particular endeavor. Futile interactions were an expense he could not afford. There simply were too many others requiring his attention. Their past conferences had not been noted on the office calendar and neither was this one. They had agreed on this at the onset. They arranged to meet at the end of the work day at one of a few select locations which included his office. Except for Dylan, the office was empty. Quiet, dark, and cavernous. Like a tomb.

Dylan stood, stretched, and reached for his water container on the desk. He wanted to see the matter finished. Then he could head to the gym. *Where the hell were they?* Tardiness irritated him nearly as much as excuses. There would be some bullshit excuse which would serve to steel his resolve to be done with it. His after-workday-workouts helped to purge the frustration from his psyche as well as from his central nervous system, of this he was sure. *God,* he prayed, *please let me be on the treadmill within the hour.*

Engaged in his thoughts, Dylan headed to the break room to fill his water container. He boasted an enclosed work space in the back of the office because of the nature of the business conducted there. Private it was, but a distance from the kitchen, the entrance, even the men's room. Not even a window nearby. But he liked the location of his workspace. He thought of it as his inner sanctum. Street lights illuminated the perimeter of the vast office space, but the interior was encased in blackness. He liked it this way. On evenings when he was still working when the cleaning crew arrived, he disliked that they turned on all the lights. Time to stop working and turn the place over to them, he told himself at those instances. At least they were efficient.

The street remained wet from rain earlier in the day and the temperature hadn't been warm enough to dry the puddles that formed. Light from the windows reacted to movement, catching Dylan's eye. As he returned to his office, he glanced at the clock deciding to wait only five minutes more. If they didn't show he'd have to deal with it another time. What a colossal pain.

At the doorway to his office, a force grabbed him from behind in a strong and vicious embrace that pulled him backwards and off his feet. Before he could register any reaction, Dylan felt a sharp knee punch to the groin. He would have doubled over with pain and nausea but his upper body was restrained. Incapacitated, Dylan became a rag doll as strong, gloved hands grasped his head on either side. In one quick motion, the hands twisted his head to the left, quickly separating the occipital bone at the base of the skull from vertebrae protecting the spinal cord, irreparably damaging soft tissue. Dylan fell to the floor of his office, dead.

The killer retrieved the metal water container from the floor where it landed during the attack. Stepping over to Dylan's desk, gloved hands used the water container as a cudgel, smashing the monitor, the CPU case, the keyboard, even the router. The killer surveyed the damage to the office, glanced at the body of Dylan Colby, then left. The cleaning crew would arrive shortly.

Chapter Two

Liz's cell phone buzzed next to her head. The vibration annoyed her. After a few seconds, she realized in that vigilant, cop part of her brain what it was she was hearing. Her eyes opened. *Damn it. Why is it I never get a call on the nights I can't sleep? Why do the calls come only when I'm out for the count?* Liz had been sleeping on her stomach which was her usual position when she was in deep slumber. She reached and felt firm back muscles. Mike was asleep next to her, snoring softly. He was lying on his side, facing away. *Good. I may be able to get up without waking him.*

She slipped out of bed, picked up her vibrating phone, and headed for the living room. She pulled silently on the bedroom door. She saw that the caller was the department dispatcher. Liz had assumed that already. No one else called at this hour. Then she realized it wasn't late. She and Mike had had an early dinner and turned in soon after, exhausted after a long day. *Are we getting old? In bed, sound asleep at the shank of the evening?* It happened more often than it used to.

Mike Dwyer was the manager of Avalon, a temporary shelter for homeless families and single women in Columbia City. As budgets for social services waxed and waned, Mike often assumed responsibility of small, grant-funded resources for folks on the street. It was relentless work, trying to help more people with less. Mike was better at the work than most because his heart was in it. And the truth was that his schedule was kinder than hers. A cop for fourteen years, promoted recently to Lieutenant, Liz's schedule was unpredictable. Columbia City, directly across the big river of the same name from Portland, was home.

"Liz Jordan," she said as she answered the phone.

"Lieutenant, Detective Connors asked us to notify you," explained the dispatcher. "He's on site at the scene of an incident. He's got it under control but his hands are full or he'd have contacted you himself. He's requested that you meet him there."

"Send me the address," said Liz, trying to sound more awake than she actually was. She hoped she sounded less bitchy than she felt.

"Just did, Lieutenant. You should have it now," answered the dispatcher.

"Yes, got it, thanks. Inform Connors that I'm on my way." Liz ended the call and glanced at the address. She didn't know what was housed at the address but she knew it was downtown. Connors was Detective Kyle Connors. Except for his family and close friends, everyone called him Connors.

Liz returned to the bedroom. Mike was still asleep under the down comforter. She studied him sleeping for a few seconds and contemplated. *What was he to her, exactly? A best friend, yes. A boyfriend?* She hated that word. I mean, what was she, sixteen? *Her significant other?* Mike was most certainly significant. She thought the world of him. They had been best friends since college. Their friendship had become intimate at various intervals over the years. The current interval of intimacy had been going on for a while. They were happily compatible and comfortable together.

The most recent development was spending most nights at Liz's. Mike had his place but it was easier to stay at Liz's to take care of the kids. Without any time to dwell further on the relationship definition, Liz stole quietly into the shower.

As Liz stepped out of her shower, she smelled coffee. *Crap. I woke Mike.* She regretted that she woke him but the coffee smelled great. Freshly ground French roast. Her favorite. She dressed quickly in jeans and a Washington State Cougars hoodie. When called to a crime scene at an odd hour, you get Casual Liz. She grabbed her shoes and headed to the kitchen.

Mike was sitting at her breakfast bar. His expression was cheerful considering he'd been awakened from deep slumber. He managed a smile, walked over to the coffee maker and poured a cup. He handed it to Liz and sat back down.

"Thought you'd want some coffee," he said. "Hope you don't mind if I pass. I'm going back to sleep. At least, that's my plan. But who knows? I'm assuming you got a work call. Any idea what's going on?"

Liz sipped her coffee. "Connors asked me to meet him at an incident. The address is downtown. That's all I know." Another sip of delicious coffee. It was strong and hot. "Must have a reason for requesting my help but I won't know what that might be until I get there." Liz was irritated about having their rest as well as their routine interrupted and was making an effort to hide it. The coffee was helping. "Thank you for the coffee, by the way. Sorry I woke you."

"You're welcome. It's okay, Liz, but you need your sleep too," said Mike. "Making lieutenant was supposed to mean you'd have fewer of these night calls. Connors must think it's a hairy one if he wants you on the scene this early in the game."

"That's what I'm thinking," Liz answered, putting on her shoes. Her promotion to lieutenant a few weeks earlier was still in the transition phase, at least in Liz's mind. She was still getting used to having a team of detectives, murder cops, report to her.

Liz and Connors had worked together on some ugly cases and she expected to be briefed each morning regarding incidents to which her team had responded the previous night. They could request her help or expertise at any time and she would have to get used to that. Connors had made the call, so it must be a bad one.

"Where are the boys?" Liz asked.

"They took over the bed after you got up. They'll be mad when they realize you've left for work," Mike told her, shaking his head.

"Well, they'll be okay. Besides, they won't care that I've gone when you climb back into bed," Liz said, joking. "I'll tell them I'm leaving. Would you mind feeding them?" Liz asked, as she headed to the bedroom to say goodbye and retrieve her service weapon and shield from the safe in her bedroom.

"Of course, they'll eat. They always eat," answered Mike.

The "boys" were Liz's cats. Eddie and Little Kurt were both adopted as tiny, starving strays. Liz brought them home after finding them abandoned when she was a rookie officer in uniform. Eddie was named for Eddie Vedder of Pearl Jam fame, Liz's favorite band since high school. Little Kurt was the namesake of the late Kurt Cobain from her other favorite band, Nirvana. Liz was proof that you can take the girl out of the grunge scene but grunge lives forever in the soul of the girl.

Liz gave each of her cats a snuggle. She stroked Eddie's calico fur and rubbed behind Little Kurt's orange tabby ears. She whipped her blonde hair into a ponytail, slapped moisturizer on her face, and returned to the kitchen with her shield and service weapon. Mike was pouring coffee into a Dutch Bros. travel mug. "Here's a cup for the road," he said. "By the way, Marjorie called earlier," he told Liz. "She wants to meet for dinner. She'll be in town for a few days."

Marjorie was Mike's mother. He always referred to her by her given name and used "mom" only to her face. Liz had wondered why but she had never asked. She chalked it up to the quirkiness she enjoyed about him. Liz reached for the travel cup Mike held out in her direction. Thinking about Marjorie and not wanting to meet Mike's eye, she stared at the coffee mug. She placed it on the breakfast bar next to her badge and gun. "Your mom's going to be in town?"

"That's what she says. Some buyer's event." By Mike's facial expression you'd think he had delivered bad news to a colleague instead of telling a friend his mother had requested a visit. Poor Mike. "Anyway, I can go alone. If your schedule's too busy."

Schedule was an unknown factor since no mention was made of a particular date. *Tread carefully,* Liz advised herself. "Dinner would be nice," said Liz while still avoiding eye contact.

"It would be nice, especially with you there to help me make conversation," Mike said with a sleepy grin. "I'll let you know what evening works for Marjorie. I'd like to have you join us...but I know it's hard to commit when you're working a case. Let's wait and see what's up with Connors."

It wasn't that Liz disliked Marjorie Dwyer. She merely had nothing in common with her. Marjorie had been a corporate buyer of women's high fashion apparel since Mike was a child. Liz had nothing against fashion, per se. She was just very pragmatic about it. Liz placed value on appropriate, professional dress during work hours, but off the clock her chosen ensemble was a tee shirt and yoga pants. Or jeans and a sweatshirt if the occasion demanded more thought be given to what one was wearing.

As for her fashion sense, Liz appreciated that quality garments lasted longer and fit the form better than less expensive pieces. She knew her best colors and even had a few favorite go-to labels. But Liz disliked shopping and viewed Marjorie as a woman who had devoted her professional life solely to fashion, which Liz considered vain. Whenever she was around Marjorie, she felt that her value was assessed by her couture, or lack thereof. What was she supposed to do? Apprehend perps in stilettos and a pencil skirt?

"You're staying here with the kids?" Liz asked Mike, hoping that he would stay but not wanting to sound like she expected it of him. As she asked, Liz walked over to the sink with her coffee cup. She drained it, rinsed the cup, and put it in the dishwasher. Clean as you go was her method for housework.

"Yep. I'm too beat to drive to my place," he answered, rubbing the back of his neck. Mike stood up. He looked exhausted, thought Liz to herself and again she was sorry that his rest had been interrupted. "I'm going back to sleep, hopefully until morning," he told her between yawns. "I want to be home in time to run before work and I've got no gear with me. If you make it back here before dawn, wake me."

"Let's see what time that might be before I make promises. You know how these things can go. I hope you get some sleep," Liz told him, regretting that she had to leave. Sleep sounded good to Liz too but duty called. "Thanks for hanging with the kids," she said, with a hand on each side of his face. She pulled him close for a kiss. She smiled at him, thankful that he was okay staying with the kids. She also smiled from relief that she had an excuse not to have dinner with his mother if she was needed on the job.

Sidearm in place, Lieutenant's shield visible, Liz put a department windbreaker over her hoodie and picked up the travel cup of coffee that Mike had prepared for her. She was off to find Connors at the address downtown.

Chapter Three

Heading out into the cool, damp evening, Liz was grateful for the hooded sweatshirt. At least the rain had stopped. She entered the address into the vehicle's GPS. The location was identified as the main facility for the Community Services Office. There were three other branch offices in Columbia City. They were distributed at different locations throughout town for the convenience of clients, most of whom used public transportation. The address downtown was the largest and busiest office.

For the residents of Columbia City, the Community Services Office was the place to apply for a variety of resources, from food stamps to housing assistance to vouchers for clothing, fuel, or energy assistance. *Apply* was the key word. Applying for help didn't mean qualifying to receive anything.

Liz wondered what had occurred at the CSO that prompted Connors to request her presence. The place had an atmosphere that could become unpleasant due to the dire straits in which some of its visitors found themselves. But as she and Mike had discussed, she wouldn't know until she talked to Connors.

For half of a second, Liz considered pulling into Dutch Brothers, her favorite stop for coffee. She glanced at the travel cup she had already drained. The cup was decorated with a little blue windmill and tulips and the DB logo. In the cool, wet evenings of the Pacific Northwest, Liz craved hot, strong coffee. She reconsidered and resisted the urge for more caffeine. She reminded herself that it was late in the evening and she may choose to sleep at some point in the next few hours. If she was lucky.

Liz pulled into a parking space in front of the building. She approached the entrance and was about to identify herself to the female officer standing sentry when she was interrupted.

"Lieutenant," said the officer beating Liz to the punch. Liz recognized her but didn't know her well. Her name tag identified her as Officer Castillo. "Connors is waiting for you. He's in the back of the office. Marsh will direct you to him." As Castillo spoke, she waved over another officer. Liz nodded her assent, aware that Castillo stood sentry at the building entrance and was unable to leave her post. She followed the young officer called Marsh and entered the building.

She found Connors standing with a group of three people. Two women and a man, they were dressed in uniforms labeled Sparks Janitorial. Liz approached, made her presence known, and asked, "Connors, what have we got here?" Connors beckoned Liz to the side, telling the three he would return shortly, asking them to remain there.

"Lieutenant, we have a male victim. He was discovered by the cleaning crew. He's been identified as Dylan Colby. He was on staff here. His job was to process applications for assistance. I'm trying to figure out when the last of his colleagues left for the evening. Shouldn't be too difficult as they use monitored key cards." Connors looked at the notes he was holding, glanced around the office, and continued, "The last co-worker to leave may be of help." Liz and Connors shared a look, both thinking the same thing. The last to leave may have seen something. They may have been the last person to see the victim alive. Or the last coworker to leave the building may be the killer.

"What else does the crew have to say?" Liz asked, motioning in the direction of the cleaning crew.

"According to the janitors, Colby worked late into the evening quite often. He was still here working alone in the office a couple of times a week when they arrived. They didn't know him by name. They usually arrive here between 6:30 and seven. It's a nightly gig for them. They got here at quarter of seven, according to the entry code."

Liz pointed with an incline of her head to an area with enough activity to indicate the crime scene. "I'll head over. Fill me in on other details as you learn more."

Crime scene specialists in sterile, gauze garments were busy gathering evidence. With care and respect, they went about their work. Liz couldn't mistake the draped figure lying on the floor of the office. She looked around the work space of the deceased, absorbing detail. Someone had done a job on Colby's office. There wasn't a way to tell if anything was missing but Liz supposed it could have been a robbery gone bad. The computer equipment seemed to have taken the brunt of someone's rage. Taken the brunt, that is, other than the victim.

A pathologist from the medical examiner's office was making a preliminary examination as required at the scene of a suspicious death. As it happened, this particular pathologist was Liz's least favorite person in the entire world. *My-*

ers. *Why did it have to be Myers?* She stopped her eyes from rolling, tried to minimize her reaction.

Liz took a breath. *Just be cool,* she told herself, hoping to keep the disgust from her face and out of her voice. "Myers, Detective Connors requested my presence on site. What can you tell us?"

Myers was crouched over the body. He did not look in Liz's direction. A few moments passed. Liz wondered if Myers was ignoring her deliberately. She knew that the feelings of disgust were mutual. Truth be told, Myers didn't like Liz any more than she could stand the sight of him. It was a long story, the tale of their feud, and neither of them talked of it.

As she was about to nudge a reaction, Myers acknowledged her presence. He looked up at Liz for a quick second then returned his gaze to the victim. He gently covered the dead man's face with the drape. "Lieutenant," said Myers, addressing Liz only by her rank. "We've determined that the deceased is Dylan Colby, aged twenty-six years. It appears that he died from a traumatic injury to his cervical spine but we will know more for certain after we can be more thorough."

Myers paused and looked at Liz. He looked around what had been the dead man's place of business. Myers stood up and addressed his remarks to Liz. "I'm not seeing an indication of other injury or trauma from my rudimentary field exam. I can tell you he has been dead maybe two hours, placing time of death at about 6:30 p.m. this evening. And I can tell you he didn't do this to himself and it wasn't an accident."

"So, he didn't fall, you're saying. This man didn't trip or suffer a seizure of some kind due to a medical condition." Liz hesitated, then added, "I realize you'll have a more complete picture after a full autopsy but at this point you think he was murdered?"

"May I continue, please, Lieutenant?" the pathologist asked.

Liz felt herself grow impatient but she did her best to quell the urge to strike. "Yes, of course," she said and for good measure she uttered a quick, "Sorry. Go on."

"The cervical spine is a housing of sorts, which contains the spinal column at the back of the neck. The bones are intricate, almost delicate in design. They are also strong and flexible. That's what allows movement of the head in many directions." Myers demonstrated what he was describing by moving his head back and forth, up and down. The pathologist crouched again near the dead man. Looking toward the victim under the drape, Myers shook his head slightly. He placed one hand on his own knee, the other rested gently on the dead man's shoulder. "Dylan Colby's cervical spine was forced into a position which nature did not intend. And it would have taken considerable strength to do it."

"Then your best assessment at this time is homicide," repeated Liz. "Any detail you can guess about the killer? Height? Left or right-hand dominant. Anything at all?"

"Probably male or a tall, strong female. Someone as tall or taller than our victim. Possibly right-handed but I'm not certain and I'll tell you why. Lieutenant, as I said, this would take strength but it would also take a certain degree of knowledge, even training," explained Myers. "This man's life was ended with precision. That kind of expertise doesn't confine itself to a dominate hand. This man was executed. By someone trained to kill."

Chapter Four

"Executed? Do you mean you think this was professional?" Liz asked. "Like a paid hit?"

"I can't speak to the motivation behind this. That's up to the investigative skills of you and your detectives to discover. I can address only the method, of how and when he died, of possible weapons. That's my function," said Myers. "I will look very closely, of course, but I doubt there was any weapon used other than two strong hands. Also, I suspect death was instantaneous." Myers stood up and said, "I've done what I can here. Find me if you have other questions. And let me know when I can have him moved." With that remark, Myers turned and walked away, the dead man at Liz's feet.

Liz found Connors. "I got statements from the three janitors," Connors said. "The fellow wanted to work his shift. He said he needed the hours. We told him no one could be on site unaccompanied as it was a crime scene. Both of the women left a while ago. They were in no condition to work anyway. Contact info for them is in their statements."

"We may need to talk with them again. Connors," began Liz, "Myers suspects a traumatic neck injury, like a twist, is what killed him. And further along that vein, Myers thinks this was a quick kill, pulled off by someone who knew what they were doing. Trained."

"Huh. Really," said Connors. He had a look on his face that Liz couldn't read. "Colby's boss is in the employee break room. Her name is Ms. Hamilton. Cheryl Hamilton. She arrived a few minutes ago. The cleaning crew called her after they called 911. They're a contracted service but they report to her on this job. She wants to help."

"You want *me* to talk to her? Connors, tell me something. I'm not grasping why you need me here. I mean, I'll help in any way I can. But you have things under control. Was there some specific reason you thought I should be here?" she asked him directly, her hands held out in his direction.

"I don't know, Lieutenant. Maybe, but nothing I'm ready to share. Just a hunch and a weak one at that. Maybe nothing," Connors answered, shaking his head. Liz noticed he was glancing around the room, obviously avoiding looking at her. "No evidence of forced entry. If anything is missing, we may not know for a while. Too many employees to talk with. Colby's office was certainly a target. Nothing else seems to have been disrupted in the building."

"Okay. Just fill me in as soon as you can. Nothing is ever nothing. Or something like that," she said rolling her eyes. "Anyway, you know what I mean, Connors?" said Liz. "Let's see what Colby's boss can tell us. Check in with crime scene specialists. Myers wants to move him."

Liz found the break room. Officer Marsh was standing near the doorway. After making eye contact with Liz, he nodded and indicated a woman sitting at a round table bordered by a half dozen chairs. She was a slight woman in her late thirties or early forties with dark, curly hair of medium length. Not wavy hair, mind you, but curls that women with straight hair covet and pay big bucks to sport. Liz was no expert but she guessed the woman's curls were a blessing of nature and genetics.

The woman was sitting with a tissue in her hands. She wore an expression of concern but did not appear to have been crying. She was sad but in control of her emotions. The word that came to Liz's mind was *fortitude.* There was a younger woman sitting next to her, mid-twenties, wiping tears with tissues that she tried to wring and fluff. The younger woman clenched and unclenched her fists nervously, the tears continuing to come. Both women sat motionless except for nervous fingers.

Liz extended her hand. "I'm Lieutenant Jordan. Detective Connors asked me to speak with you. Are you Ms. Hamilton?"

The woman looked up at Liz as the words registered. "Yes, I'm Cheryl Hamilton. I manage operations here. I'm Dylan's supervisor," she paused mid-sentence then added, "I was." The corrected statement served to upset the younger woman. She wiped her eyes as tears welled up again. Ms. Hamilton motioned slightly in the direction of the younger woman beside her. "This is Lily Simons, our front desk receptionist. We were attending a community meeting together when I got the call."

Liz nodded in the young woman's direction as an acknowledgement, and said to them, "I am sorry for your loss. You both knew Mr. Colby rather well, I assume. I'll need to talk to each of you but I'd like to speak with you first, Ms. Hamilton."

The two women nodded their responses. "Of course," said Ms. Hamilton, "and please, it's Cheryl. She turned her attention to the younger woman beside her. "Lily," she said to the receptionist as she placed a hand on the young woman's arm, "wait in the lobby while I talk with the Lieutenant. Have a cup of coffee while it's hot."

Cheryl stood and stepped to a cabinet. She removed a cup. Lily was dazed but followed the older woman's lead. She stood, walked over to the coffee maker, and taking the cup from Cheryl's hand, poured a cup for herself.

At the mention of coffee, Liz noticed that the kitchen held the aroma of really good brew. She'd had a cup before leaving her apartment and sipped another on the road, but it smelled good enough that she nearly swooned.

"Coffee seemed like a good idea," Cheryl explained, grateful for the comfort of the hot beverage and for the routine of preparing it. "When the officers said we were cleared to use the kitchen, we made a pot. Can I get you a cup, Lieutenant?"

"Yes, thank you," Liz answered.

"How do you take it?" asked the woman. "My guess is you like it black."

"Yes, I do. That's the only way to have coffee, in my opinion. How did you know?"

"Just a guess but I'm usually correct. I have good coffee sense." She walked over to the doorway of the kitchen and closed the door. Liz heard the definite strains of New England, maybe Boston, in the woman's voice. The accent was always pleasant to her and reminded Liz of the Kennedys and Red Sox baseball at Fenway.

Cheryl poured two cups of coffee and returned to her seat at the table. Liz took a seat and a sip of her coffee. It was very hot and the taste was even better than the aroma. Liz guessed either freshly ground Arabica or possibly Sumatra.

"I do enjoy good coffee," said Cheryl as she sipped from her cup. "Life is too short to drink bad coffee." The impact of the off-hand statement uttered under the present circumstances occurred to her. Her face fell. "Oh, my goodness. I can't believe I said that. I'm so sorry, Lieutenant. It's just all such a shock. Please, what would you like to know?"

Liz took out her small notebook and pen, explained that she would be taking notes. Cheryl nodded her assent. Liz began her questions by asking, "How long had you supervised Mr. Colby? And how long had he been employed here?"

Removing a file from a leather messenger bag, she opened it and began to peruse. As she studied the information, Cheryl was visibly impacted by the reason for the inquiry. Her hands were shaking ever so slightly, her voice tinged with emotion. "When the officer said he'd have questions for me, I thought to grab Dylan's personnel file." She looked for specific notations, fingers hovering as she found them. "He was hired a little over two years ago. Had been in his current position as a processor since his hire date."

Liz noted the information. "Could you describe for me what his duties were?"

"He was one of several processors in this office. Basically, they review applications for assistance and process the paperwork generated by that review. Dylan's job was to determine eligibility and approve assistance from a variety of options. The simplest case may be a client needing temporary nutrition resources for their family, what we used to call food stamps. Or a client may request energy assistance only once a year in the middle of winter."

Cheryl paused to take a sip of coffee. The warm beverage seemed to steel her nerves and she continued. "On the other end of the spectrum are clients needing regular help regarding a variety of services, from long-term subsidized housing to help getting their bills paid on time. The majority of our clients are somewhere in between."

"That sounds like social work," said Liz, reflecting on the assessment of Colby's duties. "Was that his area of training?"

The woman thought for a moment, fingers interlaced, hands near her face, and elbows set on Colby's personnel file. "Not exactly. The requisite experience for the position is in accounting. Because we are disbursing state funds, the legislature requires that eligibility and approval for assistance be determined by staff certified in basic financial software."

"The job must have required him to interact with disadvantaged folks on a daily basis," Liz stated. "How did he handle that kind of situation? And more importantly, how did clients interact with him?"

"Dylan was very good at his job, Lieutenant. He held a graduate degree in Public Administration. His undergrad was in Economics. He was highly qualified. Yes, it can get stressful. You're correct that our clients can be challenging. Sometimes they're at the end of their rope. Dylan was very good at spreading resources to assist as many people as possible in the most efficient way. He had a definite knack for it. With his background, you'd think he could be impatient or judgmental but if he was, I never witnessed it."

"How many applicants for assistance did Mr. Colby encounter in a week?" asked Liz, wondering if the number, whatever it might be, included a client angry enough or desperate enough to kill him. But Liz told herself it was early to move in any certain direction. *Be patient. Let the evidence speak,* she reminded herself.

"It varies. A fair guess would be fifty to sixty. With paperwork for another hundred or so on his desk."

"Do you recall him having a particularly testy encounter? Recently or a while ago? Anything at all that comes to mind?"

Cheryl looked at her coffee cup and took another sip. She slowly stood, walked over to the pot. "A warm up, Lieutenant?" Liz declined. Cheryl topped off her cup and sat back down. "It happens once in a while. Usually clients are careful to stay under the radar. Most seem to feel that drawing attention or causing a problem will hinder any help they hope to receive. It can be a demeaning process. We try to be aware of that. And we have to consider our safety."

"A few days ago, Dylan had a man in his office," Hamilton said. "Their conversation got a little heated but when I asked Dylan about it, he was vague, said he forgot it even happened. I wasn't here at the time but Lily was here. I heard about it later which is policy, to inform supervisors. Receptionists don't miss much, you know. Lily could tell you more."

"Okay, thank you for the information," said Liz. "There was some effort put into damaging Mr. Colby's computer. We'll need to retrieve whatever we can about what he had been working on, correspondence, records, etc. Detective

Connors is reviewing keycard access and we need to talk with the last of your staff to leave the building today." Cheryl nodded her assent. "The last detail I need from you is regarding Mr. Colby's emergency contacts. Did you know his family?"

"His mother lives here I believe, although I haven't met her. But she isn't listed as his emergency contact." She looked through the file, turning to a specific page. "His emergency contact is Jayson Abbott. He was Dylan's partner. They were to be married in a few months," she said with a sigh. "This is so, so sad."

Liz wrote down the contact information for Jayson Abbott, knowing that very soon it would be her responsibility to inform him that someone he loved was gone. "We will try to release the scene as soon as possible for your staff to carry on with business, but to be honest, that depends on the crime scene specialists. It can take some time. Possibly days."

"We have other offices, Lieutenant, and they are all on a network. We'll provide services from those locations as long as we have to." Cheryl hesitated, then asked, "Will you be talking with Jayson? And what should I tell our staff?"

"For now, tell them what you know. Dylan Colby is dead and it appears he died here in the office. Let them know that investigators will be talking with them. Our initial impression is that Mr. Colby was specifically targeted and it doesn't appear to have been a robbery. We doubt that anyone else is in danger but we can't be sure of that. There will be lots of questions especially when you have to relocate them to other offices temporarily," stated Liz. "As for specifics, try to limit conjecture. A good response is usually that we don't know a lot yet. Because we don't. And yes, either myself or Detective Connors will handle notification."

"I certainly don't envy you that task." Cheryl sighed, then added, "Jayson is a nice man."

Liz handed Cheryl her card and told her, "I'm sure we'll be in touch but if anything comes to mind that you think is important, please call me. You'd be surprised how often people remember things later. It's tough to think clearly so soon after the death of someone you know."

Liz stood up, coffee cup in hand. She walked to the sink, rinsed the cup out of habit, and placed the cup there. "I'll go find Ms. Simons. Thank you for the information," Liz said as she shook Cheryl's hand, "and thanks for the coffee." Cheryl nodded, took a breath. She reached for a tissue and deposited it in the trash. Cheryl walked to the sink with her cup and placed it there. Liz left the break room, closing the door behind her.

Chapter Five

Liz found Connors in the lobby. He had been talking with Lily, the receptionist, and was finishing up the documentation of her statement. They were seated behind the reception desk. As Liz approached them, Lily looked up at the Lieutenant. The young woman's demeanor was similar to what Liz had noted in the kitchen, but she seemed to have turned the corner from shock and disbelief to a calm sadness. Connors acknowledged his Lieutenant's presence by interrupting the interview to bring her up to speed.

"Lieutenant Jordan, this is Lily Simons. She is the receptionist here," said Connors. Lily continued to look at Liz with wide eyes but didn't say a word. This was a common reaction during investigations. Mostly shock due to the circumstances but with a touch of fear. Liz used a calming approach whenever possible with interviewees. It was the only way to get any substantial information out of them in a hurry. Unfortunately, information had to be the priority over kindness when there was a killer to apprehend.

"Ms. Simons and I were introduced earlier. We appreciate you waiting here, Lily. I'm sure you're ready to get out of here but the more we can learn early on, the better," Liz explained. "You and Mr. Colby were colleagues, but did you know him aside from work? Were you friends?"

"Yes, we were friends. Dylan and his partner, Jayson are both friends of mine," she told them. "Actually, I've known Jayson since high school. He's going to be devastated. Poor Jayson." Lily looked ready to well up and cry but she kept the tears at bay, asking, "Will you be the one to tell him? About Dylan?"

"Yes, and we'll be in touch with him soon. If he's a close friend, maybe you'll want to be available," suggested Liz. "But first, I understand that you may have some information about an incident involving Mr. Colby and another man, is that correct?"

"Y-ye-yes, I told Detective Connors about it," Lily said. "It happened one morning about a week ago."

Liz needed more detail. "Did you know this other man? Do you know why he was here to see Mr. Colby? Was he a client?" she asked Lily.

Connors jumped in with what he had learned from Lily already. "It looks like this man was not a client. According to what Lily has stated, Lieutenant, he came here to talk with Mr. Colby about someone else. Like he was advocating for someone."

"Like a caseworker? He was here in a professional capacity? Did he have identification with him?" Liz asked, trying to make sense of it. She alternated eye contact between the two of them, hands placed on the counter above the receptionist's desk. Liz was eager to gain some ground but when she realized she was firing off questions with impatience, she stopped herself.

Connors kept silent and nodded to Simons with an outstretched hand, urging her to explain. "He wasn't a caseworker," she said, shaking her head slightly. "I'm pretty sure he was a homeless guy. And it wasn't exactly an argument. They didn't yell at each other. It was as if they were...I don't know, just really irritated. Neither seemed very happy to see the other."

"Lily," asked Connors, "why do you think he was homeless?"

"He was dressed like he spends a lot of time outside," Lily told them, remembering the physical details of the visitor. "Layers of clothes. He wasn't dirty but he wasn't really groomed either. His clothes were kind of old. He had a backpack with him."

As she talked, Lily gestured towards her own garments, her hair and face, and indicated a backpack carried on the shoulder. "He didn't check in with me. He came into the lobby and stood by the wall. He was only here for a few seconds. Before I could ask him if he had an appointment, Dylan came into the lobby and waved at him to follow him back to his office."

Liz glanced at Connors, then asked, "And you didn't catch a name?"

"No," said Lily with another shake of her head, "and it's unusual for me not to get a visitor's name or see ID. That's what I was telling Detective Connors. The man followed Dylan to his office but Dylan didn't wait for him, you know? Dylan walked quickly back to his office with the man following him from a few steps back. Dylan was angry but he acted like he didn't have a choice. Like he wanted to get it over with. Neither of them raised their voice but they weren't friendly and they didn't sound friendly."

"Were you able to hear any of what they said to each other?" asked Liz.

"No, not specifically. Just the tone, their expressions," she answered.

Liz continued with questions. "How long did they talk? How long was the man here?"

"I think only a few minutes. The man walked out on his own. In a hurry, too. Angry. Dylan didn't walk him back to the lobby, which is the norm. Workers normally escort clients out to the lobby. That way reception knows the staff person is free, like removing the busy alert on their phone. Dylan didn't mention it to me later," she said, "and I didn't ask him."

"So, when it was documented by Ms. Hamilton, did she get a name?" Liz asked. She suspected she knew the answer but wanted to hear it from Lily.

"Well," said Lily cautiously, "I asked Cheryl if she got the man's name from Dylan. She said Dylan didn't know the man's name either. That really seemed odd to me because they acted like they knew each other."

"Lily, would you recognize this man if you saw him again?" asked Connors.

"Yes, I would recognize him. He reminded me of my Uncle Randy. He was a Gulf War vet, too," Lily told them.

"What made you think this man was a Gulf War vet?" Liz asked, her words coming slowly, measured.

"His backpack. It's dark brown leather. Worn soft from years of use. My uncle has one real similar. And he had a patch on it that said where he served, just like Uncle Randy's."

Liz and Connors exchanged a look, eyes locked for a few seconds. There was only one man known to them who carried a backpack of that description.

Chapter Six

Connors and Liz wrapped up their chat with Lily and the young woman retreated to the break room to join Cheryl. The specialists responsible for gathering crime scene evidence were making headway but were far from finished. Hamilton had assisted Castillo and March with securing entrances and exits. All keycards were deactivated except a few in police possession. Notices were posted that the building had been deemed a crime scene. Myers was still there, fuming because the deceased hadn't been cleared to be moved to the morgue.

Jordan and Connors needed to talk. The description of Colby's mystery visitor, and especially the backpack he carried had troubled them. Moving to a private corner they shared their thoughts.

"Connors, I've seen one backpack in my life that meets that description. You and I both know it," Liz began. She tried to be calm. The investigation demanded that, but it was proving difficult. "The man who visited Colby, the man Colby may have known, according to Lily, was Ty."

"I guess it's possible, Lieutenant," Connors said. "But it's got to be a coincidence. There must be a number of backpacks like that out there." But Connors looked doubtful.

Ty Phillips was well known in Columbia City's homeless community. A leader of sorts, respected by many of the folks on the street, Ty had been a resource to the police in the past. He was not an informant. Ty would consider that practice to be an invitation to bad karma. But he had provided a conduit, a connection, between street folks and law enforcement on a few occasions. Liz and Connors knew and trusted Ty, as well. But they knew he fought some big demons. He didn't have a permanent residence and was very private about his situation. Ty had helped out at Brooks House, the men's shelter, for long enough that he had earned a level of trust, especially with other vets. And Ty had a special friendship with Mike Dwyer.

"What do you mean, a coincidence?" Liz asked, trying to keep her voice down. "What's going on, Connors? What is it you're not telling me?" Liz demanded to know and by the tone of her voice, she wanted to hear it now.

"Before you arrived on scene, there were a couple of street kids out front near the entrance. They were waiting at the bus stop across the street. We asked them if they'd heard or seen anything." Connors hesitated before continuing. He was anxious, his breathing accelerated. He took a moment to wipe his face with his hands. "They said they saw Ty on the street. They know him. They're sure it was him. This was a few minutes before the cleaning crew arrived."

"Is that why you requested my help on scene, Connors? Because Ty was seen on the street?" asked Liz in disbelief. "Anyone walking the street is a suspect now?"

Connors inhaled, thought about it, then answered. "The main reason I wanted you here was the timing of the whole thing. The kids at the bus stop called out to Ty and he didn't turn around. They said he seemed to be in a hurry," Connors explained. "And now, finding out from the receptionist that Ty may have paid a visit to Colby's office a few days ago, that they may have known each other enough to get into it about something. I don't want to miss anything, Lieutenant. And it's not looking good for Ty." Connors hesitated, shaking his head in disbelief. "We know him. I can't believe he's involved in this."

"Well, shit," said Liz, exasperated. "Yeah, I understand. It's not like I don't have a personal connection to him myself. I would have done the same thing and called in more eyes and ears." Liz turned slightly to look over her shoulder. Myers and his assistants from the M.E.'s office moved the gurney with Colby's body from his office to the front entrance.

"We need to talk to Ty as soon as we can find him. That may not be easy depending on where he is right now. Gary at the men's shelter may know." Liz paused for a beat, then added, "Mike talks with Ty fairly often but I doubt Mike would know where to find him."

"Ty usually turns up at Avalon on his own schedule, Lieutenant, when he wants to talk with Mike," said Connors, and Liz agreed.

"And we need to notify Jayson Abbott that the love of his life is dead." Liz sighed as she looked toward the M.E.'s van that was pulling out into the street. "I'll notify Abbott. Connors, you head over to the men's shelter. Maybe Ty's there. Find out about Ty's whereabouts for the whole evening. With any luck maybe we'll learn he was there serving dinner and it wasn't Ty that was seen from the bus stop. I have Abbott's address. I'll be in touch when I leave his residence. Maybe he can shed some light on this. Maybe something was up and Colby mentioned it."

Liz and Connors left the scene of Dylan Colby's death in the hands of Officers Castillo and Marsh and headed their separate ways.

Chapter Seven

Liz got to her vehicle and put Jayson Abbott's address into the GPS and pulled into traffic. With her phone connected to the vehicle's Bluetooth, she directed a call to Mike's cell. She wasn't worried about waking him. If he was sleeping, he'd have left the phone's alert on silent. That was his habit.

The call went to his voice mail. "This is Mike. It's your call. Tell me what I need to know." Liz smiled as she heard his voice and remembered the cut-and-dried greeting.

"Hey, it's Liz. I'm leaving the scene now. It's bad. A suspicious death. On my way to notify next of kin. I'll connect with Connors about a few things after so I don't have an ETA as to when I'll be home. If you wake up and I'm not there, call me. Love you." Liz disconnected from the phone call and settled in to the drive.

Her imagination began to run wild, with thoughts of Colby and that he may have been acquainted with Ty. She hated to think that Ty could be involved in Colby's death. Liz had not seen a side of the man that indicated a proclivity toward violence. He was a private person and Liz did not know him well enough to have discussed his personal struggles with him. She had long suspected some degree of post-traumatic stress resulting from his military deployments. Liz may not know Ty very well but Mike certainly did. He and Mike had shared much together including their shared struggle to maintain sobriety. Liz thought of what Mike may know of Ty's past but she also reminded herself that Mike respected Ty's privacy. If Ty didn't share, Mike wouldn't ask.

Liz's thoughts rested on Mike and how he would react if Ty became a suspect. He'd have a harder time believing Ty was involved than she would, than Connors would. Connors could be talking with Ty at this very moment. Liz decided to believe that Connors would discover solid evidence that Ty was not involved. As any cop knows, the evidence is key.

The voice GPS informed Liz that she was near her destination. Within a few minutes she pulled up to the curb in front of a newer townhouse in an older part of the city. The neighborhood would appeal to young professionals who no longer needed to rent but didn't want to spend their time or money maintaining expensive landscaping. There were retaining walls, landscaping with low shrubs and bark, and a few of the original old trees near the street. The home was a triple-decker with a small footprint and a very small lot. The first floor looked to be comprised of the entry to the residence and a double garage, topped by two other floors of living space.

Liz made her way to the front door and rang the bell. She heard a man's voice and footfalls on steps approaching the door. As the door opened, a man looking to be in his mid-twenties asked, "Why didn't you come in through the garage?" He stopped short when he saw Liz. "Oh. Hello... can I help you?" He asked, as he glanced past Liz to the street, trying to figure out who she might be.

Remembering she was dressed in jeans and a hoodie with her department windbreaker, she must look like the drug squad, she thought. Liz had her shield out and identified herself. "I'm Lieutenant Liz Jordan with the Police Bureau. I'm looking for Jayson Abbott."

Immediately stunned, the man struggled to respond with, "I'm Jayson Abbott. What's this about?"

"May I come in, Mr. Abbott?" asked Liz.

"Of course." Jayson backed away from the door, allowing room for Liz to enter. There was a short hallway from the entry, leading to stairs and a door Liz assumed opened to the garage. The young man indicated the stairs, saying, "Let's talk up in the living room."

Liz followed him up the flight of stairs to a comfortable living space with a small sofa, two upholstered chairs, an ottoman, and a built-in media wall that conserved space. Liz took note of a few small pieces of framed artwork. She noticed a framed photo of the young man before her and a smiling image of a living Dylan Colby.

"I'm here about Dylan Colby," began Liz with a calm voice.

He started to offer Liz a seat but upon hearing Dylan's name, he stopped short. "Why? Has something happened?" He was wary already, having Liz at his door and then inside his home. When Liz mentioned Dylan Colby, his reaction went from concern to fear.

"Let's have a seat." Liz knew what was coming. She had delivered devastating news many times. It never became routine. It always felt like the first time.

"No, no, please, just tell me, just tell me," he pleaded. He allowed himself to sit on the sofa. Liz took a seat near him on one of the upholstered chairs.

"I'm sorry to inform you that Dylan Colby is dead. He was found in his office this evening. It appears he was killed there. I'm so sorry for your loss."

"Oh, no. Not Dylan. This can't be true." Instinctive reflexes brought one of Jayson's hands to his face, the other he held palm out to Liz as if to stop the words. Tears instantly forming. Palpable sadness.

Liz waited a few moments as the news sank in. She stepped over to the kitchen and poured a glass of water, then returned to her seat in the living room and offered the glass to Jayson. He accepted it but his eyes did not meet hers, his focus alert but not aimed at anything.

"He didn't meet me at the gym tonight. We meet there almost every evening. When I heard the bell, I thought it was Dylan and he'd forgotten his keys. When he didn't show and didn't call to tell me, I knew something was up...but not this."

Jayson sipped water and placed the glass on the end table. He was saddened and shocked but dealing with it as well as could be expected. "What happened? When did this happen? You say it was at the office?" His senses returning, he was asking questions. The psyche was demanding the basic details. In Liz's experience, this is how the human brain processes information that the human soul finds hard to accept.

"He was found in his workspace at the office, yes. The cleaning crew found him when they arrived around 6:45. The crew called 911 then alerted Dylan's boss, Ms. Hamilton. I'm guessing you're acquainted with her." Abbott nodded that yes, he was. "When Ms. Hamilton arrived at the scene, she was accompanied by a young woman named Lily Simons. She mentioned she's a friend of yours." He looked Liz in the eye as the name registered. He nodded yes, again.

"How did Dylan...how did he die?" he managed to ask, choking back his sadness.

"We are looking into it. It appears he was attacked after work hours. My colleague, Dr. Myers, a forensic pathologist, will have more information for you soon."

"Attacked? By whom?" he asked, eyes wide in disbelief. "Was it a robbery?"

"We're going to do everything we can to answer those questions for you. We haven't ruled anything out at this time. We need as much information from you as possible. Could you answer some questions for me? It may help us," Liz offered.

"Of course. Anything. You said your name was Lieutenant Jordan? Did I hear that right?"

"Yes, I'm Liz Jordan. I'll leave you my card so you can contact me. You said you were waiting for Mr. Colby at the gym. That was your routine. Do you recall what time you arrived? What time you left?"

Jayson looked at Liz, realizing she was asking him where he was when Colby was killed. "We sign in electronically. I was there from about five-fifteen until about six forty-five. I stayed later than usual. I thought Dylan would show." Liz was sure that the gym would have closed circuit cameras. They all did. She made a note to check.

"You knew him better than anyone. How had Dylan seemed to you lately? Did he share any concerns, especially regarding his work at the community services office?"

"He was fine. Busy, but fine," he said, shaking his head. "Everything was normal. We both tend to be consumed by our work. I'm a certified financial planner. I manage retirement accounts for a firm here in town. We were at opposite ends of the financial spectrum, you could say. Dylan and I made it a point to reconnect at the end of our work days. That's why the gym together is part of our routine."

Jayson sighed and took another breath before he continued, his references slipping between present and past tenses. Liz knew the change would take time. He sat very still except for his right hand, which alternated between covering his mouth and grasping his throat. "We're planning to be married in a few months. In Cabo." His fingertips supported his forehead as his eyes were hidden for a moment of privacy when he mentioned the celebration that wouldn't be happening.

Liz waited a moment, then she asked, "He hadn't told you about anything in particular that he was concerned about regarding work? He never mentioned colleagues or clients that come to mind in that way?" Jayson shook his head. Liz continued. "What about in his personal life? Anything that he was threatened by? Any recent arguments with neighbors? Friends? No issues of that sort?"

As the question registered, he looked at Liz with wide eyes. "Do you think someone Dylan *knew* attacked him?" he asked, not wanting to believe it. "No, no," Jayson answered, still shaking his head, hand over his mouth except to speak.

"We don't know yet, except that the attack occurred inside the office when he was there alone," was all Liz could say.

"Dylan wasn't the most patient guy, but it was more about efficiency than expectations of others. He didn't like waste, whether it was time, money, resources, whatever. But he was very accepting of differences. I've known him for six years. We met in college, both economics majors. I used to say it was amazing to me that he was so tolerant of others having grown up in that home." Jayson paused and looked up at the ceiling, eyes rolling. "Oh, shit. I'll need to contact his mother."

"We can handle that for you, if you would rather," suggested Liz.

The young man considered the offer for a moment but declined. "Thank you...but no. I should be the one to tell her," he told Liz with a sigh. She was impressed he was so thoughtful of Dylan's mother.

"You mentioned the home Dylan grew up in. How were his relationships with his parents?"

"His father died a couple of years ago. Doug was a nice man. They got along well. Close." A hesitation. "His mother, Erica, can be pleasant but there's a superficial quality to her. She is accepting of us, as a couple, of Dylan as a gay man. But her acceptance grew when having a gay child became more en vogue. It always seemed to me that she was more pleased by the accolades for being an accepting parent than for actually being accepting." Jayson stopped speaking, thoughtful for a moment, then continued. "I'm so sorry for that. It sounded awful. Erica will be crushed by this. Dylan was an only child."

"No reason to apologize," Liz told him. "I appreciate your honesty. I know this is difficult. Can you tell me how they got along, Dylan and his mother?"

"Mostly, there were no issues. He made it a point to be in touch regularly, mostly to keep Erica from complaining that he didn't call and visit. His job was their issue. She thinks that he wasted his education on a dead-end job. She thought he should be doing big things at the government level." He interrupted himself, consumed by thoughts mired in grief. "Erica just couldn't get it. Dylan had a long-range plan. He liked his job, but it was a means to continue to learn about public administration, responsible allocation of public funds. His plan was to make a name for himself on his abilities not just his background. Erica's father was a former mayor. She thought that fact alone gave Dylan the credentials he needed."

Interesting, thought Liz, but she didn't comment. "Thank you for answering my questions. You'll need someone here with you. Is there someone you'd like me to contact? Ms. Simons was concerned about you. She couldn't contact you herself before we talked. But maybe we can get in touch with her now, if you'd like."

"It's probably a good idea. I'll call her," he said as he reached for the cell phone on the end table.

Liz walked over to the large window opposite the kitchen. She gazed outside and listened as the young man briefly spoke with his friend. She was impressed with his strength. "Lily said she'll come right over. I told her you were still here."

"Would you like me to stay until Lily arrives?" Liz asked. "It's really no problem."

"No, it's okay. She's only a few minutes away," he answered.

He's doing okay, Liz thought. But it's shock more than acceptance. Liz decided to make her exit slowly.

Jayson walked Liz down the steps to the door. She offered him her card and made sure he knew he could contact her at any time. "I'll be in touch when we know more from Dr. Myers." Liz hadn't once used the words morgue or coroner. "You won't need to identify him. But if you wish, you'll be able to see him."

He thought for a second. "Yes, I want to see him." Jayson looked at the card in his hand. Tears had formed. "Goodnight, Lieutenant," he said. As they shook hands, Lily pulled up to the house. Light rain had begun to fall.

Chapter Eight

A few blocks north of the community services office where Colby had been murdered was an area known as The Beau. The Beau encompassed a distinct area bordered on one side by Beaumont Avenue, from which the area got its name. Every large city has an area like The Beau and Columbia City was no exception. Whether such areas are called ghetto, slum, the bad side of the tracks, or socio-economically-depressed neighborhoods, there are certain conditions that factor in: old, ugly buildings that define urban decay, a few small businesses that try to survive, people without much to occupy their time, and people who live in a state of panic or resignation. Some folks are happy to call one of those old buildings home, but there are others who cannot claim even that.

Brooks House, otherwise known as the men's shelter, was a longtime center of activity and resources in The Beau. It was called the men's shelter because as long as there were beds available, single men could sleep there for the night. When the weather was bad in the winter and early spring, it became a warming shelter and crammed in as many people as possible after sweeps were completed of the nearby doorways. Women and children were sheltered overnight at Avalon, the shelter managed by Mike Dwyer. Brooks House provided help in other forms, as well. Folks without a permanent address could send and receive mail, do their laundry, take a shower. It was a hub for community-donated items and bus passes. Anyone could get a hot meal at Brooks. The big, commercial kitchen prepared and served three meals each and every day.

Connors headed straight to Brooks when he left the scene of Colby's death. He was hoping to find Ty there. Ty was a fixture at Brooks. He helped keep the guys in line. He helped keep the shelter clean and orderly. He was a resource for homeless men trying to get their bearings or needing someone to listen to them over a cup of coffee. If the man wasn't there, Connors was hoping someone at Brooks would know where he was. Connors was on a mission to find out where Ty had been all evening. Once he had accomplished that, Connors told himself, he and his fellow cops could move on to finding the person responsible for Colby's death.

He pulled over and parked in a spot near the bus stop half a block from Brooks, called in his location, locked up, and headed down the street. Connors was well known on the street as a straight-up cop who didn't cause you trouble if you weren't causing any for somebody else. Connors had not taken more than a few steps before several of the street guys welcomed him. He gave a high five to one, got a fist bump from another, and heard a couple of guys ask, "Hey, Connors man, how goes it?"

The entry to Brooks, with stone steps and a big double door, felt like entering the vestibule of a church because that's what the building originally had been. The city had purchased it twenty years earlier from the Lutheran Synod when the congregation wanted to move to the safer, east side of the city. The big building was the perfect place for the services provided there.

The fellow who ran Brooks was named Gary Burgess. Having come of age in the bay area near San Francisco, Gary had embraced the counterculture of the late sixties to the hilt. When he was granted conscientious objector status during the draft, Gary's conservative parents promptly kicked his ass out. After surviving on the streets of The Haight for a few months, Gary spent a couple of years at Cal Berkeley studying art. But his heart wasn't in it. He was too preoccupied with helping his friends find something to eat or get over bad acid trips. Then the guys started coming home from Southeast Asia. He vacillated between fury at what had happened to so many of these men and an intense sadness for them. Soon he was the guy who knew how to help. Now in his sixties, Gary resembled a thin Santa Claus with wire-rimmed spectacles, longish gray hair, and a gray beard. Gary was the most socially conscious man one could hope to meet, but he was savvy. He kept his back to the wall.

Connors approached the office when he saw Gary at his desk, then realized he was overhearing a phone conversation. "No, that's not right," Gary was saying with a shake of his head, index finger of his free hand pointing in the air although the person on the phone couldn't see it. "I'm telling you if you had mail it would be in your locker. Remember that only you can open your locker." Pause. Gary saw Connors, waved him in. "Wait. If you're looking for wired funds, it's not delivered as mail. Check with the cash place. They handle wired funds." Another pause. "Yep. No problem. Take it easy, man." Gary hung up the phone.

Gary and Connors shook hands. "What the hell happened uptown? I heard you were asking questions." Gary didn't miss much, and the buzz traveled fast in The Beau.

"Yeah, there's been some trouble. Can't say much at this point. I'm looking for Ty. I'm hoping he can help. Is he around?"

"He is," said Gary, "He's in the dining room, I think. A meeting just ended. Grab some coffee, Connors; you look like you could use it. Anything I can help with?"

Connors tried to be respectful about imposing himself at Brooks. He knew he was the rare cop who had the advantage of being accepted there. Usually in casual street clothes, service weapon and shield under a loose over-shirt, he didn't attract too much attention. Until he needed to.

"Maybe in a while. Thanks, Gary." *Hopefully, you can confirm Ty's story that he was here*, thought Connors. "Okay if I go back?"

"You bet. I'll be back there in a few minutes," Gary replied with an easy demeanor. "I usually scan the room after meetings in case anyone needs anything." Twelve-step meetings in the homeless community could indicate a need for anything from the ER, a bed in treatment, or just a place to clean up or sleep for the night.

A short hallway opened into a large room that at one time may have been the fellowship hall with its proximity to the kitchen. A half-dozen cafeteria-style tables were placed to one side, an area with folding chairs in a circle to the other. One of Gary's staff, most likely the counselor who led the meeting, was talking with a man Connors did not recognize.

Nearby, with another fellow, was Ty. The two men folded and stacked chairs.

Ty was like so many other veterans who had returned home changed. As a young man, Ty had been friendly, open, and communicative. Three deployments later he had become a very different person. He had tried to leave the anguish behind, but the task had proved too much, the damage too severe. From what Connors knew of the man, many of the coping methods Ty had tried had been self-destructive, adding to his problems. Ty saw Connors approach and greeted him with a discreet nod of his head. Connors noticed nothing in his manner that would indicate he was concerned to see him. "Hey, Ty. How you doing?" Connors greeted him casually.

"Doing okay. Yourself?"

"I'm okay. I'm going to get a cup of coffee. You got a few minutes?" With others in hearing distance, Connors was careful not to sound like a cop asking for information. Even though that's exactly what he was. Best for everyone if he stayed under the radar.

"Sure. Give us a few," said Ty, as he and the other man continued to deal with folding chairs. Connors ambled over to the big coffee urn. He grabbed a ceramic cup and used the push spout to fill the cup with hot coffee. A couple of holdovers from the meeting recognized Connors and nodded their acknowledgment. Connors took a sip of coffee. He always expected shelter coffee to be shitty. Usually he was pleasantly surprised. The shelters brewed so much of it that the coffee was often fresh. And the folks tended to make it strong.

Taking a seat at one of the tables, Connors looked around. There were a few people sitting together in small groups, in conversation. Many had a cup in front of them, coffee or water. Steam rising would be the indicator as to which. The dining room was the only community area to speak of and the room was off limits during meetings. When the meeting ended, people made their way back in. After the evening meal, the only available fare was either coffee or water until breakfast.

Chairs folded and stacked, the fellow helping him departed, and Ty filled his own coffee cup. He picked up his brown leather backpack with the Gulf War insignia. He walked over to the table and took a seat opposite Connors, placed the backpack on the bench seat next to him. Ty didn't say anything for a few moments. He took a deep breath, exhaled, took a deep draw on the cup. He set the cup down on the table but his fingers stayed around the handle. "What can I do you for?" Ty asked.

Connors chose to get right to it. "Do you know a man named Dylan Colby?"

Ty looked thoughtful, almost pensive. He took another sip, then answered, "I know of him. I'd say there's a difference."

"What do you know of him, Ty?" asked Connors, using Ty's words, watching for signs of stress or evasion. Hard to watch for, because with his background and the lifestyle he led, the man was a master of becoming invisible.

"He works for the CSO. He's one of those bureaucrats who decide who's desperate enough or meek enough, depending on which way the wind blows, to warrant some help. Why?" Ty still had not looked Connors in the eye. But that was pretty normal for many of these guys.

"Dylan Colby was found dead in his office this evening. It's looking like someone wanted him that way. You were seen in the area and you know we have to ask, so can you tell me where you were?"

Ty sipped his coffee. He appeared to be thinking intensely about what Connors had said, what he was asking. Ty raised one hand to his neck. He reached back with both hands and grabbed the edge of the hood on his sweatshirt, pulling it up over his head. He brought palms together in front of his face like he was praying, and looked Connors square in the eye. He reached back and put the hood back down. He shook his head, sipped coffee and said, "Well, shit. He was found in his office? You're thinking he died there?"

"That's what it's looking like, Ty. The timeframe we're interested in is from five o'clock until six forty-five this evening."

Ty looked at his coffee cup then up at Connors. He averted his gaze back to the cup, took a sip. "How did he die?" Connors noted the tenderness with which Ty made the inquiry.

"Not sure," answered Connors. "M.E. will know more soon." Ty and Connors looked at each other for a quick moment, both men knowing that wasn't entirely true. "Where were you?"

"You said I was seen in the area. That's not out of the ordinary. Where else would I be?" Ty wasn't being a smart ass, as the question could have sounded to other ears. From Ty, it was a legitimate question. He continued. "But okay. I was at the diner on Main earlier. Left before five for a meeting at the church across the street. I was supposed to meet someone, but they didn't show."

"Did you stay for the meeting? Does anyone know you there?"

Ty was not happy about being asked questions, but he was particularly not pleased about having to explain the details of his sobriety support.

"Well, I did attend the meeting. I didn't talk. Not sure I was noticed. Didn't know I needed to be. I was there for someone else, like I said, but they didn't show." Ty straightened his back which served to pull his upper body away from the table, as well as from Connors. "And no, I won't tell you who I was supposed to meet. You know that."

"Where'd you go after that?" Connors asked Ty.

"Meeting was 'til six. Then I walked up Main Street. Sometimes after meetings I walk. Think." Connors knew that Ty had been sober for many years and had helped others into recovery. He knew that Ty still attended meetings sometimes.

Connors was figuring out in his head that if Ty was uptown until six, it was doubtful he could have walked to the CSO and been seen by the street kids at the bus stop before six-thirty. It was at least a two-mile walk. If he was at the meeting until six, that is. "When did you get here, to Brooks?"

"I've been here since seven, maybe a little later. Had a bite to eat then helped set up for the meeting at eight o'clock." Connors quickly figured that Ty's whereabouts were unaccounted for between six o'clock and seven-fifteen.

Possibly longer if no one could remember him at the earlier meeting from five until six.

"When you were walking between the meeting uptown and when you arrived here at Brooks, did you stop anywhere? Did you talk to anyone?" Connors was hoping to narrow the amount of time in question. He hoped he didn't sound like he was grasping at a straw. But that's how he felt.

Ty reached for his cup, picked it up and drained it, then said, "The park. I went over there for a bit. I sat at a table, had a smoke."

"Did you talk to anyone else?"

"I didn't," Ty said as he shook his head. "No one around that I knew. I saw a couple of dudes asking for spare change near the bathrooms. Didn't know 'em."

"Okay, Ty. Thanks." Connors switched directions. "When you were walking up Main past the CSO, did you hear anyone calling out for you? There were a couple of kids at the bus stop who said they saw you and called your name. They were surprised you didn't even turn around."

Ty thought for a minute, shook his head. "Hell, Connors. My hearing isn't great anymore. It may have happened, but I didn't hear anyone call out to me."

Connors nodded, then said, "There's only one more thing to ask you about. The receptionist at the CSO thinks she saw you there last week. She remembers your backpack. Described you and the pack pretty well. Were you there having a talk with Colby?"

Ty looked at the backpack. His fingers rested over the patch that signified his unit in the Gulf War. He silently nodded his head that Connors was correct then added, "Yep."

"Under the circumstances, the man being dead and all, you want to tell me why you were there? What you talked about?" Connors was trying to keep the sarcasm out of his voice, but it was becoming difficult.

"I was there. Briefly. I talked with him," he conceded.

"The receptionist said it didn't sound too friendly, Ty. Maybe you'd better tell me what the conversation was about."

Ty shook his head. "I won't tell you that. It was nothing anyone needs to know."

"Look, Ty. The man's dead and you were seen with him and it wasn't a routine visit. Then you were seen in the area around the time he was killed. You gotta tell me more than that," Connors implored.

"I hear you, Connors. And, yes, I had a talk with him in his office. It's no one's business but mine now. I was near the office earlier. There's nothing I can do about that. I won't deny it and there's nothing else I can tell you. But I know I didn't kill the guy."

Chapter Nine

As they finished talking, Connors asked that Ty check in with him. Ty promised to be in touch. To remind himself of what he needed to follow up on, Connors checked his notes. He would be making several calls to verify what Ty had told him: the diner uptown and the church across the street, the five o'clock twelve-step meeting, the guys at the bus stop, and the staff here at Brooks.

Some pieces of Ty's story he couldn't confirm because Ty wouldn't divulge all the details. Who had asked him to attend a support meeting with them and then didn't show? How well had he and Colby known each other? What had they talked about in the CSO? Connors thought it odd that Ty Phillips, a man well known around The Beau, could sit in the park and claim to see no one he knew. In a park frequented by homeless folks and street kids.

Connors stopped by a table near the kitchen where Gary was talking to a few people. *I may as well get to it*, Connors told himself. He asked Gary if he had a moment and they stepped to the side of the dining room. "What's up, Connors?" he asked him. Gary didn't ask what was up with Ty, but this didn't surprise Connors. He knew the man well enough to know that if he wanted to know what was up with Ty that he'd ask the man himself.

"Can you tell me if you know what time Ty arrived here at Brooks earlier this evening?" Connors kept a flat affect, but looked Gary in the eye. He looked back at Connors, knowing this was important because Connors had his cop face on.

Gary folded his arms over his chest; spread his feet a bit further apart. Still looking at Connors, he said, "Ty said 'Hey' when he walked in. Said he wanted to grab a bowl of soup before setting up for meeting. Dinner was put away at seven-thirty. We keep it available later on meeting nights, but you know that. That puts him here before seven-thirty."

"Thanks, Gary," said Connors, then decided, "One more question: do you know a man named Dylan Colby?"

"Don't know him. Never met him. Heard of him." He looked around the dining room of the shelter he managed, then added, "That particular young man has made it difficult for some of the guys around here. Especially guys in treatment or looking for work. The hoops they have to jump through are endless anyway, you know what I mean? Sometimes they need a break, just one thing to work in their favor. It can make all the difference."

"Yeah, I know. I've seen it," Connors agreed, nodding his head while he surveyed the room.

"Most of these men have been their own worst enemy their whole adult lives," explained Gary. "Throw combat into the mix, alcohol and drugs to forget, add a layer of adjudication on top. It sucks and most blame only themselves. Anyway, word is Colby is a tough egg. Why are you asking about him?"

"He was found dead this evening. Appears to have been killed in his office. Between five and six forty-five."

If Gary was shocked by the news, he hid it well. "Are you suspecting one of these guys? Are you seriously suspecting Ty

Phillips?" Gary's questions registered more shock than the news about Colby. Especially the questions about Ty.

"At this point, we are establishing a timeframe," he said. "I'm clearing whomever I can. Just getting started. Thanks, Gary. I'll be in touch if I need to ask you anything else."

"Well, you be damned sure to do that, Connors." Gary dropped his volume a bit, adopted an even more serious tone, and added, "Keep me in the freaking loop, okay? I don't have to tell you that surprises aren't popular down here."

As Connors said, "I will, Gary. I will," his phone rang. It was Liz.

Chapter Ten

Connors answered the phone with, "Lieutenant."

"Where are you?" she asked.

"I'm just leaving Brooks," he answered. "Next of kin notified?"

"Yes. We talked a while. He took it as well as can be expected. Has an alibi for the time of death. He was at the gym and knows we can verify. He was actually waiting for Colby. It was their routine. Sounds pretty solid. And he wanted to call Colby's mother himself. Wasn't looking forward to it but wanted to be the one to tell her. Lily Simons arrived as I was leaving." Liz took a breath. "Did you find Ty?"

"I did. He accounts for his evening before five o'clock and he had been at Brooks since seven. But pieces are going to be hard to confirm."

"Why?"

"Ty won't say who it was he was supposed to be with from five to six. He claims to have been at a twelve-step meeting but the person he was meeting there didn't show. He won't say who stood him up," said Connors. "Plus, he admits to having met with Colby last week in the CSO, but won't say what they talked about."

"Huh. Okay," said Liz mulling over the information from Connors. "Let's call it a night, Connors. It's late and we can't do much until we hear from the lab and the M.E. Bright and early, okay? Let's get started before eight."

"Okay, Lieutenant. Uh...can I ask what you're going to say to Mike?"

"You know as well as I that I can't tell him very much. I'm going to ask him some questions and try not to sound like I'm interviewing him." Liz took a tired breath, sighed. "Officially, if it comes to that, you'll step in. If we need a statement from him, that is. But I'd like to know if Mike knew Colby. Maybe he can shed light on this."

"Well, good luck with all that. Goodnight." The good luck was offered because Connors knew that Mike would defend Ty. Mike had known him quite a long time. Connors thought about the man he knew as Ty Phillips. He thought about the tough life he led, but some of it wasn't of his choosing. Ty kept to himself, didn't cause problems and he was well-known as an advocate for folks on the street. And he had helped the police on more than one occasion.

"Yeah. See you at eight, Connors," said Liz. "Get some rest." Liz hung up the phone and started for home. Her thoughts rested on Mike. When she left the apartment, he had asked her to wake him when she got home, if he was still there. Knowing the man, she would bet he was still asleep in her bed with Eddie and Little Kurt curled up close by.

Liz lived in the third-floor apartment of what had once been a large single-family dwelling. Her home was just north of the city center in an older, established neighborhood. What she most enjoyed about living there was that the small, rear-facing balcony overlooked the track and football field at Columbia City High School. The area was quiet and private. Quiet, that is, except for the seasonal excitement generated by high-school sporting events. Liz was athletic and had been raised to be a football fan, so she enjoyed hearing the kids compete. She occasionally ran on the track. The neighborhood was quiet tonight. Rain fell just heavy enough to hear the drops hit the asphalt.

Liz made it home, parked, and was up the stairs in a matter of minutes. She would know instantly if Mike was there. If he wasn't, Eddie and Little Kurt would hear her and meet her at the door. But if Mike was there sleeping, they wouldn't be bothered to leave his side. She quietly opened the door to her home. No cats greeted her. She locked up and left her shoes by the door.

Had she been alone, Liz would have been tempted to stay up for a while after a late evening on the job. She would have had a snack, sipped a brew, and listened to music to unwind. But with Mike there, she wanted nothing more than to enjoy curling up with him and the kids. And Liz knew sleep was in order. She was looking at a long, full day ahead.

As she locked up her service weapon and shield and readied herself for sleep, she thought about Dylan Colby. She reviewed in her mind the conversation with Jayson, the dead man's partner. Then Liz thought of the victim's mother, Erica Colby. Either Liz or Connors would be talking with the woman soon. She remembered the conversation with Cheryl, Dylan's boss and with Lily, his friend and colleague. Liz thought about Ty and how Connors mentioned some hiccups in his statement.

Liz was concerned. But she was suddenly very tired. Not a sound or a stir had emanated from the bedroom except for the deep R.E.M. sleep breaths of Mike and the two precious cats. Liz climbed into bed. Eddie and Little Kurt adjusted, barely expressing any annoyance. Glad for the reprieve, she would talk with Mike in the morning. Her last conscious thought was that Marjorie Dwyer was to visit soon. She sighed and thought, *Oh, shit.*

Chapter Eleven

Liz awoke alone in her bed. She stretched and looked at the clock on the bedside table. Realizing she had slept later than she had intended, she rolled out and walked to the living room. Instead of Mike, she found the cats perched on opposite ends of the back of her sofa. They meowed when they saw her. She walked over and gave them each a stroke. They moved their bodies up toward her hand as a returned greeting.

Heading to the kitchen, she saw a note on the breakfast bar:

Up at five. Too early to wake you after your late night.

Kids ate breakfast. Coffee ready to brew.

Talk later. Love M.

Liz enjoyed the tone of the note for a few seconds. Then she remembered that she really had hoped to talk with Mike about Colby. And maybe about Ty. *Crap*, she thought. She needed to be the one to mention the case and the circumstances that may, or may not, involve a man he knew and respected. Mike wouldn't appreciate not hearing it from Liz. If tables were turned, she would want to hear it from him.

Grabbing her phone, she called Mike. It went to voice mail. She didn't need to leave a message. A missed call from her at that time of day would let him know she was up and had thought to call. He was either in the middle of his morning run or busy getting ready for work. She looked at the time. She needed to do the same. Liz flipped on the coffee, glad that the weather was dry, at least for the moment.

Forty-five minutes later, at precisely seven fifty-five a.m., Liz walked into the precinct. Two detectives were ready to review their respective cases with her. She let Connors know he was on deck. After a few minutes to orient herself, she called the detectives in, one after the other. Liz thought of it as managerial juggling. She met with them each for about twenty minutes, then called Connors into her office. "Please tell me you got some rest, Connors. I'm going need a lot of focus out of you today."

"I'm good to go. Here's what I've been up to, Lieutenant: I talked with the last two coworkers to leave the CSO yesterday. Neither of them noticed anything suspicious or out of the ordinary. They both confirmed it was normal for Colby to be in the office late, that he was often the last to leave. I'm ready to review security footage too."

"Okay. Has anyone checked the other workstations? Anything else missing or damaged?" Liz asked.

"We're escorting them in, one at a time to check. So far, nothing missing and no other damage. Obviously, Colby was targeted. And Lieutenant," said Connors after a pause, "we got a call from Erica Colby. She wants to see her son."

Liz nodded. "Talk to Myers. It'll be up to him when that can happen. Then let Mrs. Colby know. Here's the contact information for Jayson Abbott." Liz opened her notes, turned to her lap top, clicked a few keys, and sent the information to Connors' desk. "Call Abbott first. He may want to see Colby by himself first. He should have that option. And let him know Mrs. Colby's been in touch."

"Will do," answered Connors. "Also, I will request forensic and pathology reports as soon as they're ready. I checked with the lab. They are working to eliminate prints. Easy to do with CSO staff. As state employees, all prints are in the system."

"Sounds thorough." Liz's office phone line rang. She looked at the time. It was her captain. "This call is from upstairs, Connors. I need to take it. Keep me in the loop," she said as Connors left her office.

Liz picked up the phone. "Yes, Sir," she said. Liz listened attentively and responded, "Of course, Sir. I'll be up directly."

Sir was Captain George Miller, a thirty-year veteran of the police force to whom Liz reported. *Up* was to the third floor of the building where Miller's office was located along with all the other brass. Liz and other lieutenants under Miller's command were often summoned to provide information or answer questions about current investigations. Miller was a straight-up cop, he knew the job as well as anyone, and he wasn't inclined toward bullshit. But he didn't like surprises. That meant if there was something he needed to know, it was best he heard it from you.

Forgoing the elevator, Liz went up the two flights of stairs and entered the third-floor corridor. She walked towards Miller's office and caught the eye of Clarice, Miller's venerable administrative assistant and gatekeeper extraordinaire. Clarice was on the phone, explaining that the captain was not available at present but she would relay any message. As she explained this to the person on the other end of her call, she waved Liz into the inner office where Miller awaited her presence.

Although expected, Liz knocked on the doorframe nonetheless. Upon receiving the captain's permission to enter, she walked in and closed the door behind her. Captain Miller was seated behind his massive desk. The desktop was remarkably organized and free of clutter. Miller was a large, African-American man in his sixties. He wore a graying mustache and kept the same tight buzz cut since his days as a Marine. If his wire-framed reading spectacles were not perched on his nose they were in his shirt pocket. Miller wore a crisply pressed dress shirt and an expensive tie. His suit jacket hung on a chair nearby. Liz noticed the light indicating an incoming call flash on his phone, but the phone did not ring. He did not want to be disturbed so calls were being routed to his voice mail or being handled by Clarice.

Liz stood and waited to be addressed. Miller indicated the visitor's chair, and said, "Have a seat, Lieutenant." in Liz's world an underling would not presume to take a seat in the presence of a commanding officer without having been directed to do so. Liz thanked him for the consideration and sat down.

Miller met Liz's eyes briefly with a half nod of his head and hint of a smile as a preamble, then began. "I've been reviewing the notes of the incidents to which our units responded over the last forty-eight hours. The Colby death, the state employee at the Community Services Office; it appears that Connors took the call. Why did you respond, as well?"

"Connors requested my presence, Sir. Public building, lots of employees and clients in and out of the area constantly. He expected it to be a tough scene to secure. I think he made the correct call requesting a senior officer be dispatched."

"According to Connors' notes, there has been a person of interest already identified. Ty Phillips. Do you think he's your man?" Miller's hand went up to stop Liz from responding immediately. "Before you answer, I know of this man, Phillips. I know he's been a help to us regarding other incidents in The Beau. I know there's a connection between Phillips and Mike Dwyer." Miller let those statements hang in the air for a moment before he continued. "So, I need you to think carefully before you answer. But if anyone knows that the evidence alone is what we use to determine suspicion, you certainly do. What is the evidence telling us?"

"As you read, Sir, Phillips was seen in the CSO with the victim days prior to his death. They appear to have been acquainted. Phillips advocates for people on the street occasionally. Colby could be tough about granting assistance at times. But that's mostly conjecture. What's more important is that Phillips was seen in the area at the time of death." Liz laid out the details with matter-of-fact precision.

"Was he the only one in the vicinity?" asked Miller.

"We're trying to determine that and if anyone entered or exited the building within the time frame," Liz answered, again with precision.

"About his statement to Connors; it sounds like Phillips can't verify his presence elsewhere during the time in question. Is that correct?"

"He may be able to divulge further details as well as identify witnesses to support his alibi, but," she paused for a second, "he's choosing not to do so." Liz thought about how close she had come to referring to Ty by his first name. In her own defense, Liz had known the man as Ty for so long. But she must tread carefully.

"I see the preliminary from forensics is calling COD a sudden forced motion of the head. The military trains select operatives in skills such as that. Phillips is a Gulf Vet. Did he receive special forces training?"

"Sir," said Liz. "I believe that he may have. It's not information I know for certain. We'll need to confirm."

A veteran himself, Miller was pensive as he continued. "This man Phillips has had a difficult time. If I remember, he doesn't have a permanent residence, has wrestled with addictions, maybe flashbacks. On the other hand, he serves as a volunteer and is able to advocate to some degree for others on the street. He makes use of his VA benefits."

"Those statements are true to the best of our knowledge, Sir," confirmed Liz, wondering where the conversation was headed.

"Then why won't he help us confirm his whereabouts if doing so supports his alibi? What's he hiding?" Miller spoke with force. He asked the question as if he really wanted to know.

"I can't answer that. My guess is that he's protecting another individual. The man battles his demons and like so many of these men, the way he lives is never completely by choice. One thing I've learned about Ty Phillips is that he's fiercely loyal," said Liz.

"Too loyal to aid in his own defense, if it comes to that?" Miller paused. The captain was thinking to himself as he rubbed his chin between his thumb and index finger. Miller began to shake his head slightly as if he was hearing something he just could not believe. “Lieutenant, it's possible he has no further details. If there are no indicators that lead to anyone else as a person of interest, then we go with the evidence linking Phillips. I expect Connors to gather what he can and continue to dig. But if this looks to be headed in Phillips' direction, it's a done deal. When you're satisfied, make an arrest. Is that clear?”

Liz felt a sting to her integrity and she did not like the feeling. “With all due respect, why would you feel the need to tell me this, Sir? If the evidence supports a warrant for an arrest, then that's what happens. If a person of interest declines or is unable to confirm their alibi, then they have no alibi. We can't ignore the facts no matter who a person is connected to.”

“True. And that can suck. But that's the job. It's called equal justice, as you know. Keep me posted. And we won't have another conversation of this nature regarding this case, will we?” Liz knew that Miller was implying that if she couldn't do her job because of her personal feelings for a suspect or his friends, he'd take her off the case as supervising officer. She wasn't going to let that happen. Hell, no.

“No, Sir. That won't be necessary.” Liz stood and took her leave. She left Miller's office without noticing whether Clarice was at her post or not. She was too worried about Ty and about Mike. But someone was responsible for Colby's death and Liz was sure as hell going to find out who it was.

Chapter Twelve

Liz was downstairs in her office, about to tag Connors when he appeared at the doorway. He knocked on the open office door. The look on his face told Liz the news wasn't good. "Have a seat, Connors. Tell me," she urged the officer.

"I talked with Myers. They got started over there early. Jayson Abbott is headed over soon. He told Myers' assistant he'd have friends drive him. Myers will have the report on Colby completed in a few hours, but he's maintaining the initial assessment of a sudden neck twist by someone with strength. Myers thinks they wore gloves by the impressions, but no fibers of any kind have been found. It wasn't an accident, it took a certain know-how, and death was quick." Connors looked Liz in the eye and waited for the nod of her head before he continued. "Doesn't look like he was drugged or had ingested anything in a few hours. Myers guesses Colby was taken by surprise. No indication he had a chance to defend himself."

"All right. We'll wait for the full M.E. report. What about the crime scene unit? Anything from them yet?"

"Prints in Colby's office have been determined to belong either to him or other staff at the CSO. We're reviewing security cameras. Clear footage of Ty Phillips when he was in the building last week." Connors checked his notes and continued. "He was in the building for eighteen minutes, including the time he waited in the lobby. What's weird is that we haven't found any footage of anyone who is unaccounted for entering or leaving the building after four p.m. yesterday."

"What do you mean, no one unaccounted for?" Liz asked him. She was determined to dig deeper. "Absolutely everyone picked up on the security camera is either on staff, a client, or had business there?"

"It's true, Lieutenant." Connors was uncomfortable about continuing but forged ahead when Liz's expression and tone said he'd better keep going. "I've looked at the layout of the building. There are public restrooms near the lobby. I think Colby's killer may have slipped in and hid in the restroom. It's possible."

Liz looked at Connors, clearly not wanting to believe it. "Even if that got them in, how would they get out of the building? Wouldn't they be stuck without a way out?"

"The back of the office has a crash door. It's right around the corner from the break room. It serves as a fire exit. Exit only but no entry. There's no key lock and the steel door will lock from the outside when it closes. The alarms are remote and aren't set until the janitors leave," explained Connors. "The fire exit leads to an alley. The alley leads in two opposite directions. And the security camera behind the building isn't working."

Well, hell. Isn't that convenient? Liz spent a moment thinking and one of her thoughts was that she desperately wanted some strong, fresh coffee. She remembered the great brew Cheryl had served the night before. She stood up, took off her suit jacket and hung it on the chair back and said, "I need coffee, Connors. Check in with the guys that said they saw Ty. The guys at the bus stop. Check into the diner and the recovery meeting at the church uptown. I need to know as soon as possible if we can verify Ty's whereabouts."

"Okay. Will do. Just one more thing, Lieutenant," said Connors as he noted the calls he'd be making. "Myers is clearing the way for Erica Colby to see her son as soon as the autopsy is complete. He figures by early afternoon. I assumed you'd want one of us to be there."

Liz remembered the dead man's mother had called earlier. She thought about the comments Jayson Abbott had made regarding Erica Colby and her relationship with her son. "We should talk to her together, Connors. Call Mrs. Colby back. Ask if she'd like an escort to the morgue. Let her know it would be no problem. Tell her we'd appreciate talking with her."

Connors nodded and left the Liz's office. Liz grabbed her favorite Dutch Brothers mug and headed to find coffee. The pot in the staff break room looked okay. Liz took a sniff. She decided it was worth a chance. Liz filled her cup and took a sip. It wasn't bad. Fairly fresh, decent roast. Drinkable.

Liz walked into her office and heard the buzz of her cell phone ringing on vibrate. The screen told her it was Mike. She picked up the phone and answered, "Hey, there," she said. "Long time, no see."

"You were supposed to let me know when you came in last night. I must have been sleeping deep," Mike said. "I didn't hear you."

"You were. So were the boys. I was exhausted when I got home." *And I had a lot to think about.* "How are things going over there?" asked Liz about Mike's morning at the family shelter.

"It's a big day. We have two families moving out. A family with four kids going into a mobile out near the highway. You know the place." Mike referred to a mobile home neighborhood known to service providers as The Trailer Park from Hell because the owner made a fortune renting to people with few options. The trailers were ramshackle at best and maintenance was a joke. "It's a dump but it's big enough and it's cheap. They're pretty excited."

"What about the other family?" Liz asked.

"They're heading to stay with family. They've worked at it but just couldn't pull it together in time. I've given them additional time. Twice. I can't justify more than sixty days with the waiting list we have."

"That sucks," Liz said, because it did. She knew Mike hated to do it.

"They have a place to go. I've told them after a few weeks with family, if they aren't settled, they can come back if there's a room. They have one child. Mom's working but Dad's having a harder time finding something. Hold on for a sec." Liz listened while Mike took a step over to his office door and closed it. "And news is buzzing about the guy at the CSO. A lot of folks down here knew of him. I'm guessing that was the call you got from Connors last night. Colby, right?"

"Yes," she answered, "the Colby case. What are people saying?"

"That they either thought he was okay and they're sad or they didn't like him at all, in which case they're not all that sad. Depends on whether he was helpful to them or not. It is sad, though. He was a young guy. Hate to see it. I've actually met Colby myself. On a few occasions," he shared.

"That's not surprising, considering what business you both were in. When was that?" Liz asked. She was trying to sound normal and not like an investigator.

"Oh, let's see...over the past year, two or three times. At those damned information meetings. You know the ones, where those of us in services try to tell the county how strapped we are and the county tells us how there's no money. Then, what do you know? They find some."

"We're trying to talk to people who knew him outside of family and co-workers," Liz told Mike. This wasn't an untruth. "What did you think of him?"

"Smart. Efficient. A numbers person. I got the impression he appreciated the practical side to budgets, as documentation for work delivered." Mike paused for a moment then added, "I got the feeling he had a privileged background. I'd stake my life on that. I can usually tell."

"How so?"

"In how he spoke, dressed, etc. He made an effort to tone it down. He may have been advised not to look too advantaged working for an agency helping people who have nothing. But he couldn't quite pull it off. The country club attitude and the smell of the Ivy League don't fade."

As Mike explained his assessment of the dead man, Liz was amazed that he sounded so matter-of-fact, without an iota of judgment. Almost clinical. His tone changed when he said, "The couple with the baby that is moving in with family? Colby could have been a little easier on them."

"What do you mean? It's Colby's fault they can't get a place?"

"Not exactly. She wanted to earn her GED before getting a job. The guy is on probation. They're both pretty young. There's a children's admin case requiring him to do alcohol counseling and drug screening. He couldn't meet all the requirements and do twenty hours a week work search too. He asked to be exempt from work search for a few weeks. Colby wouldn't approve it. I think it might have helped. She quit the GED program and took a fast food job so one of them would be working. Colby didn't see the logic in that."

"Maybe Connors should talk to them. Is he an angry guy?" Liz asked.

"No, he's a kid. But they worked with Colby, if that's the perspective you want," added Mike.

"Okay, I'll mention it to Connors. I should get busy," Liz told Mike. "I don't know what time I'll be out of here."

"I'm heading back to my place after work," Mike mentioned, "unless you need me to feed the kids. Marjorie arrives this afternoon. I'll probably visit with her after she gets settled. She still plans on dinner with the two of us one evening this week. I'll keep you posted. Did you remember?"

"Yes, of course, I did." *That doesn't mean I'm looking forward to it.*

"...and I had a weird conversation with Ty earlier," Mike said. The statement caught Liz off guard even though she had been thinking of the situation with Ty. "He stopped by for a cup of coffee. Said Connors came by Brooks last night. Asked him about Colby. What was up with that?"

"We have to talk to anyone who knew him or saw him recently. Like the kid on probation. We had reason to think

Ty knew him and he was in the area." Shit. Liz needed to watch what she said.

Mike was quiet for a moment. "Well, sure he knew him. At least he knew of him. You're telling me Ty was in the area when Colby was killed? Then maybe he saw something that can help."

"Yeah, maybe. We're hoping someone can. Sorry, but I do have to go. Let's talk later."

Mike hesitated for a moment again. "Yep, I know. See you later." Liz heard the call disengage. Had she sounded odd to Mike? He knew her so well. There was no bluffing with him. *Shit, shit,* she thought as she put the phone down.

Chapter Thirteen

Liz returned calls and managed paperwork for the rest of the morning. Her tasks often were interrupted by thoughts of her conversations with Connors, with Captain Miller, and with Mike. Was she handling this investigation with the same approach she'd use if she did not know the people involved? Liz needed to be sure. Her integrity was at stake but other factors were more important. She and the crew were responsible for finding Colby's killer.

At close to midday, Connors popped into the doorway of her office and knocked. "I've got updates on the Colby case, Lieutenant. If you've got a few minutes."

"I do. And I've got something to run by you. But you go first." Liz gestured to the visitor's chair and Connors took a seat.

"A server at the coffee shop confirmed that Ty was there until just before five. She identified him from a recent picture. I was able to reach the couple at the bus stop. Both are definite, without a doubt it was Ty they saw walking near the CSO. And I confirmed the time. They were waiting for a transfer," Connors explained. "They aren't happy if their word gets Ty in trouble. I convinced them the important thing for everyone was telling me the truth."

"Okay, Connors. Anything else?"

"The recovery meeting did take place from five to six at the church across from the coffee shop. But no one remembers seeing Ty there," he told Liz. "He may have been. They just don't remember seeing him. We can't confirm where he was between five o'clock and seven p.m. when he arrived at Brooks."

"We can't confirm unless he chooses to help us," Liz added. "And help himself."

"I spoke with the M.E. Myers completed the autopsy and his report is in the system for your review," said Connors. "Death was the head snap. No drugs in his system. No other injuries. According to Myers, Colby was fit enough that he would have been able to defend himself. No defense wounds so Myers' take is that he was ambushed and taken out quickly. Like by someone trained to survive hand-to-hand combat."

"That was his initial assessment at the scene. Myers is experienced and he's a pretty smart pathologist. He's an asshole but he's smart," said Liz as her thoughts digressed to her dislike of the man.

"And Lieutenant, we can't find anyone else who was around. No one saw or heard anything," Connors said.

It was clear to Liz that he had tried repeatedly to find someone. Anyone. Liz knew that Connors needed to bring Ty in as a person of interest. It would soon approach the point of an official interview.

"We need to talk to Ty again. And we'll have to ask about his military training. There's no way around that. And he won't want to talk about it," Liz told Connors, who nodded because he knew this to be true.

"What did you have for me, Lieutenant?" asked Connors.

"Mike says there's a lot of chatter about Colby at Avalon today. There's a young family moving out. They were Colby's clients and didn't have the best of experiences. It might be worth a chat."

Connors looked at Liz like she had thrown him a life line. As he made a note, Liz said, "I don't have a name, but Mike does. And I don't know how long they'll be there."

"One last thing, Lieutenant: I'm driving Erica Colby down here at two p.m. to view her son's remains in the morgue. It's set with Myers. I knew you wanted to be there."

"Yes, I'll be there. And it would be a good idea to catch the folks at Avalon. Can you grab a bite and then head over there? I'll be at the morgue waiting for you when you arrive with Colby's mother." Liz looked at Connors and stated emphatically, "And if you learn anything that points us away from Ty, I want to know."

"You got it, Lieutenant." And off he went.

Liz sat collecting her thoughts for a few minutes. She should eat something but decided on more coffee. Just as she made that decision, there was yet another knock on her office door. Liz looked up to see Assistant District Attorney Jackson Powell. "Hello, Lieutenant Jordan. I'm hoping you have a few minutes."

It wasn't unusual for Powell to visit the precinct. A sharp ADA, he worked closely with investigators. Serving as the court representative for the department, Powell, known as Jack, was their go-to guy for issuing warrants for arrest or obtaining a judge's signature on a search request. More often than not, Jack would be the state's attorney prosecuting defendants brought to trial following the department's efforts. It was, however, unusual for him to drop in unannounced. The suspicious side of Liz's psyche made her mental defenses rise but she was able to quell them. At least she hoped that's how she appeared.

"Sure, Jack. Come in and have a seat. I'm getting a cup of coffee. May I bring you one?"

He took the seat Connors had vacated. A few years older than Liz or so she guessed, Powell had a tall, slender build. Blonde turning slowly gray. He was always impeccably dressed but Liz found that to be the standard with most barristers. Liz knew him to be a brilliant attorney who never breached protocol. Showing up unannounced wasn't exactly a protocol breach but it was unusual. To Liz, this meant something was up.

"No, thank you. And I just need a moment of your time. I'll be out of your way shortly." A busy man, Liz heard him to say. He preferred that she wait to retrieve her coffee so he wouldn't have to wait for her and waste his time sitting there. "I was upstairs at a meeting with Captain Miller. He mentioned the Colby case."

"Okay," Liz answered. *Would I be suspicious having this conversation regarding a different case?* she thought, but didn't know the answer. "What could he have mentioned?" she asked. "Connors has barely begun looking into it."

"That's not what I hear. Seems there's been a degree of inquiry already. And I know that Connors pulled you in early. That tells me things are moving along."

Liz detected a compliment but didn't dwell on it. She was not one to thrive on that sort of attention. In her experience most compliments indicated an ulterior motive was lurking.

"Yes," she confirmed with reserve. "Connors called me in at the scene. He was concerned about securing the evidence. There were quite a few people to interview. Plus, with it being a public building, it was reasonable to need my back up."

"You have a person of interest. A homeless man. The evidence is solid. Why are you waiting to make an arrest?" Powell asked. Liz noticed that the detail about a person of interest also being homeless was significant to him. She knew that Powell was tough on crime, more so than was required for his job. Liz remembered that on more than one occasion, Powell's rhetoric was downright ugly especially when prosecuting a defendant who could not afford decent counsel.

"We are not waiting for anything other than providing due diligence in working the investigation," Liz responded, careful to measure her choice of words and tone of delivery. "There are details to consider. Timeframes, data, and alibis. Jack, you know as well as we do that it's a mistake to rush ahead and draw conclusions."

"I understand, Lieutenant." He was being professional with her, but Liz picked up on the slightest tone of impatience. "I've reviewed details. Even from my chair, it looks solid. Make an arrest or provide the people with a very good reason for not doing so."

She felt pressure and didn't like it. "Jack, we will make an arrest or we will provide a very good reason for not doing so within the next few hours. And one last thing: I don't work for you. But you're welcome to assist us anytime you'd like to take this on." Liz was steamed. She knew that's how she sounded but she didn't give a shit. "If you have nothing further, I need to get back to it. We have an appointment with the deceased's mother at the morgue in a couple of hours. Want to tell us how to handle that part of the job?"

Liz stood up. Powell followed suit and stood up, as well. "Well," he said, as he adjusted his suit jacket and smoothed his tie. Powell's tie cost more than most homeless people have to live on for months. "I'll let you get that coffee, Lieutenant." He gave her a nod of his head as a farewell gesture and left her office.

Chapter Fourteen

Leaving the precinct, Connors headed to the street. He took a minute to grab a hot dog and a soda from a vendor half a block away. He ordered the dog with "the works" and enjoyed every bite. Standing in the street, no rain in sight, Connors could almost pretend it was summer if the day had been a little warmer.

He headed to the car for the short drive to Avalon, the homeless shelter. He hoped to talk to the young residents that were moving out. Connors thought of Ty. He wondered where he might be spending his day. Maybe at Brooks, maybe in the park. Connors hoped Ty was somewhere nearby in case he was needed for questioning. Connors wasn't happy with himself for thinking in those terms. He hoped it did not come to that.

Connors got along with most of the folks on the street. Mainly, they respected him because he was fair. Also, they knew he would try to help whenever possible. Especially if they had children. He thought back to an old case, the case of the death of Leah Bishop. He knew that if the police hadn't been assisted by folks living on the street, it probably wouldn't have been solved.

As he pulled in across the street and down a short way from Avalon, Connors called in his location. He was in street clothes but it didn't mean the residents wouldn't make him for a cop. Hell, he might even run into people he knew. If he did, he'd be glad that they were off the street, even if only for a few weeks.

He walked past the large sign out front with the names of the facility and the agencies responsible for running it. There was an older minivan in one of the front parking spaces, packed to overflowing. He approached the double entry with its interior set of double doors. The lobby was empty except for one woman. She was sitting in a chair studying a chart that may have contained bus schedules. The woman looked up at Connors and briefly made eye contact. She didn't react as though she recognized him, but her expression became veiled nonetheless.

The woman may not have known Connors, nor did she know he was a cop. But she certainly knew that he didn't belong in a homeless shelter. Connors gave her a half smile and a nod of his head as a greeting. The woman responded with an almost half smile of her own and resumed looking at her chart.

As Connors started to hit the button on the wall to alert staff that a visitor was in the lobby, Mike came through the double swinging doors that led from the dining room. He was accompanied by two adults, one male and one female, and a host of young children. The family was surrounded by bustle and was clearly excited and happy.

Mike saw Connors and he didn't seem surprised to see him at the shelter. Mike wasn't surprised by much. "Hey, it's Connors. Come here," he said to the adults, "you should meet this guy. He's a good one for you to know. Ali, Matt, this is Connors. He's a police detective. If you need a cop for any reason, he's your guy." Connors shook hands with the fellow, then with the woman. "They're moving into a mobile on the north end of town with their four kids." Connors picked up on Mike's inference. *Shit,* he thought. He knew the place.

"It's a dump but it's a place. The locks are strong," Matt mentioned, speaking to Connors. The comment told Connors that he knew it was a shitty place to live.

"Yeah, it's a dump but we've cleaned it up. And the washer and dryer work," said Ali. "We've got four kids. That's a dream come true."

"How old are your kids?" asked Connors, hoping that at least one was school age. The elementary school serving that neighborhood did a nice job of assisting families. The principal was active in community efforts and the teachers were especially sensitive to the families. One of the teachers at the school was a close friend of Connors' by the name of Pete Denucci. He had known Pete and Kelly for years. He thought of Kelly, an outreach worker assisting folks living on the street. Again, Connors thought back to the murder of Leah Bishop. Kelly's help and her knowledge of the streets had helped find Leah's killer. Kelly and Pete expected the birth of their first child any day.

Ali was speaking. Her voice brought Connors back to the present. "Our oldest is seven. She's in second grade. Then another girl who's five and a four-year-old boy. Youngest is this guy here. He's two," Ali said proudly as she indicated the toddler in her arms. "Maya, our oldest, wasn't thrilled to change schools but since she met her new teacher, she's been good with it. His name is Mr. Denucci," she said, naming Connors' buddy, Pete.

"I hope she has a great year there. It's a good school." Connors took out a card and handed it to Matt. "Let me know how things are after you get settled. It's nice to meet new families in that neighborhood but it can be hard to make the rounds." *It can be hard because they don't stay long, get evicted, or they end up in jail or in treatment,* thought Connors.

"I will," said Matt. He looked at the card then at Connors with a nod of his head. "Okay, we got to go. Got to unload the van while the weather holds out and Ali has to work at five. I wanted to be at home our first evening there," Matt told them. "Thanks for lunch and the care pack of provisions, Mike. And thanks for this, he said to Connors with the card held out in front of him.

Mike and Connors walked out with the family to the packed-up van. They watched them get everyone buckled in and waved goodbye as they drove off. Mike and Connors stood for a bit. Connors figured he would let Mike enjoy the moment watching a sheltered family head to a home of their own. Sometimes it wasn't a matter of finding a home but of keeping it. All too often Mike waved goodbye wondering if families would be back at Avalon in a few months or a year. It could be due to skyrocketing rent or loss of a job, hard to tell. Each situation was different.

"So, I guess you're here to talk to the kids I mentioned to Liz," Mike asked Connors while they were still outside. "The ones that worked with Colby at the CSO."

"Yes," Connors answered. "If they're still here. Do you think they will be okay with talking to me? I need to ask them questions anyway but it's nice to know how they might react."

"I know you need to talk to them. They're okay with it. If I thought they'd have a problem I wouldn't have warned them. I know the drill. Come on. They're packed up. Waiting for a ride."

Connors followed Mike back into the building. The woman with the bus schedule was still sitting there. "Are you doing okay, Mary?" Mike asked her.

"Yep. I'm good. Heading out to the bus in a bit," Mary answered, looking up from the paper that held her attention. "How you doin'?"

"I'm fine, thanks. I'll be out back if anyone's looking for me," Mike told her. Connors followed Mike through the doors leading to the dining room. The dining room contained several cafeteria-style tables but only one appeared to have been used for the midday meal that had just ended. There was a woman in the kitchen straightening up and two other adults were cleaning the table and the chairs used for lunch. A young man was caring for two young children nearby.

"How many for lunch today, Ava?" Mike asked one of the two adults cleaning the room. Connors realized she was a shelter staff member he had met some time ago.

"Fifteen with Ali and Matt's gang." Ava told him as she continued to spray and wipe the large table.

Mike and Connors headed out the side exit of the building. There was a large covered area, a picnic table, several benches, and assorted riding toys for children of various ages. Parents were allowed to smoke on the periphery while keeping an eye on their little ones. A young woman with short, spiked blonde hair sat on the ground attending to a toddler. Thin and pale, she was dressed for being outside. Dark eyes were made up to look more dramatic and she had several piercings. The toddler looked sturdy and chubby, as if height had not caught up with girth. The child was warmly dressed, as well.

Connors took the small child to be a boy. He looked to have had spaghetti for lunch as his face was a bright reddish-orange. The toddler looked in Mike's direction and started to head toward him on his short legs. The young woman reached for his hand and stood up, keeping him near her. She smiled when she saw Mike. She had no expression as she looked at Connors.

There was a young man nearby. He was securing boxes tightly with twine. There were two large duffle bags and several tote bags stuffed with items. A car seat was next to the tote bags. The young man was slight of build but appeared to be wiry and strong. He was wearing a dark hoody of an indistinguishable color on top of layers. He wore jeans and a ball cap turned backward was pulled down over longish brown hair. He glanced over in their direction when the woman stood to attend to the toddler.

"Danny, this is Kyle Connors," Mike offered as an introduction. "I mentioned he might be coming by to talk with you. Connors, this is Kim and the little dude is Ian. Kim, can Ian go inside with Ava and me for a few minutes? While you and Dan talk to Connors?"

Kim, the young woman, looked from Mike to Connors. Her expression was impossible to read. Apathy. Maybe distrust. Distrust veiled as apathy, which was common. Kim glanced at Dan before answering. "Sure. That'd be okay. It'd be good if Ava got him to sleep. My brother won't be here for us for at least an hour."

Mike got Ian to follow him back inside which wasn't difficult. The toddler obviously knew and trusted the shelter manager. Danny quickly finished up with the boxes and gestured to the benches under the covered porch. Connors extended his hand to Danny. The young man shook the detective's hand and sat down. "Do you mind if I have a smoke?" he asked. Pack in his hand, he waited for Connors' assent before he removed a Marlboro.

"Not at all," said Connors, taking a seat on a bench.

"I'm getting a cup of coffee while it's hot," said Kim as she glanced back and forth between Danny and Connors. "Do you want some?" Kim's question was directed at Danny. He nodded yes, and she said she'd be right back.

"We can get you a cup too, if you want," Danny offered. "It's not bad coffee, although I ain't real picky."

"I'm good for now, but thanks. I've had Mike's coffee before and you're right, it's not bad." Connors noticed that Dan seemed a little wary of him but not overly so. It was the reason for Kim's reaction to his presence that he couldn't determine.

Connors decided to dive in. "You knew Dylan Colby in a professional capacity. Is that right?" Danny took a drag off the cigarette and nodded that he had. "And you know he died yesterday evening? Apparently in his office?"

"We heard about it," he said. Danny paused for a moment, looked at the burning end of the cigarette. "I didn't especially like the guy but I don't wish anybody dead." As he said that, Kim approached carrying two cups of coffee and sat next to Danny.

"Can you tell me how it was working with Colby?" Danny started to respond to Connors' question, but Kim was quicker.

"It sucked, that's how it was," said Kim. She sipped her coffee. Danny looked at her, clearly unhappy that she had shared her distaste for having been Colby's client. "Danny, let me tell him," she begged. When Danny didn't respond, Kim took it as a sign to continue. "We've had our bad times, but we're both trying hard to get our ducks in a row. For Ian. For us." Kim was irritated but trying to keep her cool. Frustration seeped out of her voice. The apathy in her affect had been replaced with ire. "Danny had to turn down a job. It was only part time, but it might have turned full time. Colby could have requested a delay on other stuff if he'd chosen to."

"Sorry to hear that. What was the job?" Connors watched as Kim looked to Danny, allowing him to answer.

"My cousin runs a tavern. He likes to serve food right up 'til closing. I've done diner work. If it had worked out, I was gonna take over the janitor's shift too. Not ideal but the hours would have worked for us 'cause Kim had school in the mornings." Danny took one last drag, snuffed out the cigarette then picked it up and placed it in a receptacle high enough off the ground to be out of the reach of children.

"Not a bad gig for a guy with a family," said Connors. "What was Colby's objection?"

"First, he thought my cousin was full of shit. He said it wasn't a 'bona fide offer of employment' even though Billy signed off on it. It wasn't under the table or anything, man.

Then he tried to say it wouldn't be healthy for me, 'cause I'm in recovery," he explained.

"Danny doesn't drink. He never has. Doesn't like the taste," added Kim. "But Colby didn't believe him."

"My drug of choice was pills, not booze. The job with Billy would have allowed Kim to stay in school 'cause I'd be around to care for Ian. Anyway, Colby wouldn't let me off work search. Twenty hours a week to keep our assistance grant. With NA meetings and random UA's to prove I'm clean, there aren't enough hours in the day. All those services except the NA meetings are before five."

"Who ordered the UA's?" asked Connors.

Danny hesitated before he responded. He seemed to be deciding if Connors was worth the effort of being honest. Danny decided he was. "I was already on probation for possession of a controlled substance. From before Ian was born. I had one freakin' slip up." He looked at Kim with eyes full of apology. The expression she responded with was full of empathy and she urged Danny to continue. "I was out of my head one night. It was over a year ago. I was watching Ian." "He was asleep in his crib," Danny shared, "I just wasn't myself. I wasn't thinking. I forgot he was in bed and I left to meet a buddy."

It was Kim who picked up the story from there. "All hell broke loose," she calmly explained, looking from Connors to Danny and then back at Connors again. "Don't get me wrong. It kind of needed to. Children's Admin stepped in 'cause he'd left Ian alone. He went back to jail for a few weeks. His PO actually went to bat for him."

"Who's The PO?" asked Connors, wondering if he knew the probation officer Danny was taking about. And why in the hell they would go to bat for a guy on pills who placed his infant son at risk?

"Her name's Sue. Sue Skinner." It was Danny who answered after he and Kim shared a glance. "She's pretty tough but she's been straight with me. The deal was that Sue went out on a limb for me and I knew it. I wasn't going to let her watch me screw up again."

Connors wasn't acquainted with a PO by that name. But it wasn't all that surprising. There were several offices and people working in positions of that kind came and went. "Can you tell me where you were yesterday between five p.m. and six forty-five?" As Connors asked the question, Danny and Kim shared another glance with each other, and a look of concern clouded both their faces.

"Are we suspects? Do you think we had something to do with Colby's death? Because we didn't." For a second time during the conversation, Kim sounded a little agitated.

"I don't have any reason to think that, Ma'am. But when we investigate a suspicious death it's best to rule out what we can as early as possible so we don't waste time." *And it helps to know who doesn't have an alibi,* thought Connors.

"Kim was at work until five," he said as Kim nodded slowly in the affirmative with her eyes on Connors. "My color came up so I had until six p.m. Ian was with Kim's mom while I went in." His "color coming up" meant the random daily draw for urinalysis yesterday was for his color group. Danny had to call in before noon to learn whether or not he was required to produce a urine specimen for analysis. If he didn't show before six, it was a missed UA. And a missed UA is a dirty UA.

"I had this week's check-in with Sue at four fifteen. I went by for UA right after, maybe four thirty. I met Kim when she got off at five. We took the bus back to her mom's," said Danny.

"What time did you get back to Kim's mom's house?" Connors asked him.

"Five-thirty, I'd guess. Then we came back here to finish packing our stuff," said the young man.

Connors' quick calculation was enough to figure out that he could confirm their whereabouts for the period in question. He asked one other thing. "And the two of you had Ian with you when you left Kim's mom's house at five-thirty and came back here to Avalon?" They nodded. "What time did you get here?"

"It was before six 'cause dinner was still being served," said Danny. All the details were verifiable and there wasn't time between the events to have been at the CSO. Plus, Connors doubted these two could have killed Colby between five thirty and six o'clock with an active toddler in tow.

Connors nodded. He recorded the information, then he asked, "So, where are you guys headed?"

"We're staying with my brother," answered Kim. "They don't really have room. They have three kids. But that's where we'll be until we get a place. Or can get back in here."

Connors confirmed where he could reach them, if needed, and jotted down contact information. He thanked them for their help and took his leave. Connors went inside the shelter to find Mike and let him know he was leaving. It was time to head over to Erica Colby's home to pick up the bereaved woman so she could view her son's remains.

Chapter Fifteen

After Powell left her office, Liz sat for a few minutes and tried to remember the last time she felt an investigation slip this far out of control. Would it have been better for everyone, especially Ty, if Connors had not requested her help at the scene of Colby's murder? Liz was angry and that wasn't helping get things back under control.

If Ty didn't kill Colby, and Liz strongly doubted that he did, someone was responsible. And instead of being free to focus on other persons of interest, Liz and her decisions were being scrutinized because of her connection to Mike and his friendship with Ty. At the same time, with the evidence they had, if she neglected to investigate Ty as a suspect, the ramifications would be just as bad. In Liz's mind, she and Connors were between a hard place and a rock. But her unenviable spot paled in comparison to what the law may have in store for Ty.

Liz checked the time and figured she had long enough to read Myers' report before heading out to meet Connors when he arrived with Erica Colby. Accessing the justice center data system, it took a few keystrokes to pull up Myers' assessment of how and when Colby died:

Subject is identified as Colby, Dylan, aged twenty-six years. Height is five feet, eleven and one-half inches. Weight is 167 lbs. The subject was in good health prior to his death. BMI, skin, muscle tone, hair, and nails all within the normal

range. Toxicity report found no positives for either prescription or illicit drugs or alcohol; there are no defensive wounds present; no indication of illness, infection, condition, pathology or prior injury that may have contributed to death.

Cervical vertebrae surrounding the spinal cord at the base of the occipital were separated by manual manipulation causing lethal damage to muscular and skeletal systems. This damage in turn caused autonomic failure of electrical impulses regulating cardiac, circulatory, and respiratory function. Severe injury to the upper prolongation of the diencephalon indicates damage sufficient enough to have rendered death almost immediate.

Summary: Cause of death was an arrest of the necessary functions of respiration and cardiac systems due to severe damage to the medulla oblongata. Respiration and cardiac function ceased, followed closely by brain function. The deceased may have been conscious and aware during his last few moments as heart and respiration ceased. The subject was unable to defend himself due to the initial response of the muscular paralysis or disconnect with neural pathways enabling large muscle groups.

Liz reread the summary of Colby's last few moments. She reached for the phone and dialed the morgue. Myers picked up on the second ring.

"Medical Examiner, Dr. Myers."

"Myers, it's Jordan. Do you have a minute? I just have a question or two after reading your autopsy notes regarding Dylan Colby."

A few seconds of silence were followed by a deep sigh. Upon hearing Liz's request, Myers conveyed an impression of having been unexpectedly bothered and was now required to summon as much patience as he was able. His response to Liz was similar to how she would react if Eddie or Little Kurt crapped on her carpet and she discovered it by stepping in it.

"What is your question, Lieutenant?" Was Liz imagining it or was there a slight attitude as he spoke the word *Lieutenant*? Was Myers mocking the fact that Liz had earned a promotion? Liz didn't have time to be annoyed. *Rise above it,* she counseled herself, but it was difficult to ignore Myers. Their mutual disgust had eased somewhat but was still healthy. Or unhealthy depending on your point of view.

"Your notes say that Colby may have been cognitively aware in his last few moments. Do you mean that he felt his heart stop and knew he couldn't breathe? I'm not asking to be morbid. I want to understand what happened to him."

"It's impossible to know definitively. I have every reason to think that in the way this man's fatal injuries were inflicted, he may have been aware, only for a few seconds. For two or three seconds before Dylan Colby died, he may have experienced the excruciating pain of sudden heart failure. He may have felt as though he were suffocating. And at precisely the same time." Myers paused for a moment as the meaning of his words impacted Liz. "Mr. Colby's death was immediate but may have been preceded by a few moments of extreme pain and torment. That's precisely how select groups of military personnel are trained to kill. Fast and deadly. And inhuman." Myers' disgust was not aimed at Liz as he spoke. Liz thought about Dylan Colby's last few moments. Myers' voice rousted her attention. "Is there something else, Lieutenant?"

"No, Myers. Sorry. And thank you for your help."

"I believe you are accompanying Detective Connors when he arrives with Mr. Colby's mother, is that correct?"

"Yes, I'm heading your way soon. Myers, we're not telling Erica Colby about the last few moments of her son's life, are we?"

"Lieutenant, no mother should have to hear that. I'm sure you agree. And she'll never read this summary if I can prevent it. It would haunt any parent."

"I agree, Myers. And I'm on my way." As Liz ended the call with Myers, she was chilled to the bone by the way this young man's life was ended. And Liz was infuriated that his death was intended to be so cruel. She grabbed her jacket and headed out.

Chapter Sixteen

When Liz entered the wing of the justice center that housed the morgue, more commonly known as the medical and forensic department, she was struck, as always, by how calm and innocuous the area appeared. The bland and unassuming décor was in consideration of people visiting the place. If you found yourself here it meant only one of a couple of things and neither were good: either you were there to identify a family member who may or not be dead, or you already knew a family member was dead and you were there to view their remains.

Liz saw Connors standing in the waiting area situated to one side of the lobby. A woman stood near him who looked to be in her mid-forties. Petite and small in stature, she was blond and fair. The woman wore an expensive-looking wool coat with a fit that suggested it may have been tailored. She carried a Coach handbag and wore a pair of Kenneth Cole boots. Liz's initial thought was that Marjorie, the fashion buyer, would approve of the ensemble. Rude. Liz scolded herself for thinking in those terms as she approached. She nodded at Connors, made eye contact and extended her hand as she said, "Mrs. Colby, I'm Lieutenant Liz Jordan. I'm so sorry for your loss, Ma'am."

Erica Colby turned slightly, as if in slow motion. Several inches shorter than Liz, even in high-heeled boots, the woman had to look up. She held her gaze for a brief moment and Liz detected almost no facial expression of acknowledgement. The woman took Liz's hand, lightly grasping and barely shaking it. "Thank you, Lieutenant." Liz may have been insulted by such a reception under other circumstances but she had learned long ago to never pass judgment on the bereaved. They rarely behaved as themselves. Nor should they have to concern themselves with convention or courtesy.

"We've checked in with Myers and the staff," said Connors. "We have a few minutes to talk before they're ready for Mrs. Colby." The three of them took seats on the nondescript sofas in the waiting area. Erica's affect was flat and strangely subdued. Her eyes were clouded but it didn't appear that she had been crying. Liz wondered if she had been medicated, either by a physician or her own doing. Liz knew enough to refrain from quick judgments of the emotional condition of others. Snap assessments, unless necessary, caused mistakes and Liz tried to avoid making them. She would check in with Connors as to his initial impressions of the woman's demeanor.

Erica sat motionless and silent. It was Liz who spoke first. "Mrs. Colby, can you tell me when you last talked to your son?"

She sighed before speaking. "A few days ago; before the weekend." No further detail was forthcoming. Often family members used the opportunity to talk about loved ones in the most routine way possible. Discourse was helpful to form impressions and get information. But Dylan's mother wasn't interested in talking. At least not with Liz. Maybe Connors had been able to get her to speak more readily. Hard to tell.

"How was your son doing at that time?" asked Liz. "Did anything seem odd or unusual? Did he mention anything or anyone specific that was of concern to him?"

"I'm his mother, Lieutenant. I'd be the last one to know about anything troubling Dylan."

With that statement, Liz thought she noticed a brief chink in the armor, but it was illusory and faded quickly. "Jayson would know better than I. Detective Connors said you've spoken to Jayson. But, of course, you have because that's how I received the news. Jayson came to my home last night. He told me about Dylan."

Erica went over these few details slowly and quietly as if to remind herself of how recent events had unfolded. No emotion, affect remained flat. Liz wondered again about medication. It was a gut feeling and not terribly reliable given the situation.

"Is there anything you can tell us about your son's job or his work environment? Anything significant about his colleagues? His clients?"

At this, Erica didn't hesitate, and Liz detected the first spark of emotion in the conversation. "My son was wasting his time in that ridiculous position. With his education and acumen for finance and management, he should have been involved in more important work. Honestly, assisting with services to the needy. Those very services might have been better administered if Dylan had pursued a position in city government. That was his calling, regardless of what others thought."

Erica stopped talking and took a breath. Her eyes were on her hands resting in her lap. Manicured fingers held a handkerchief which she handled loosely. No tears to wipe away.

"Dylan did not need the experience of administering 'direct services,' as he defined them to me. He would have been as capable as his grandfather. My father had been in public service. Now it's all such a waste."

"Did you know any of his colleagues, Mrs. Colby?" asked Liz, trying another tack.

"I met a young woman once. Apparently, she worked in that office with Dylan. Her name was Lori...or Lani...I really don't know," she responded with a wave of her hand as if the idea of her son's having colleagues at that level was unimportant, even absurd. "I believe she was a friend of Jayson's. He could tell you."

"I'm guessing you refer to Lily, the receptionist. We have spoken with her. You didn't meet other coworkers of Dylan's? Maybe his supervisor, a woman named Cheryl? She spoke very highly of your son and the work he did."

"No, I was not acquainted with anyone else. Why would I have been? I had no occasion to visit his office and it was certainly never suggested." Dylan's mother paused for a moment, then continued. "I had so hoped he'd realize his potential and leave that place." Her words came down on her abruptly and cruelly as she heard herself say them. Erica took a deep breath and straightened her posture, eyes straight ahead. The gestures — breath, posture, focus, performed in one swift motion— relaxed her and helped her regain her composure and control. It was as though those gestures were a combined reflex she had relied on for many years.

Erica turned to Connors, who sat quietly letting Liz speak with her. "I do hope you'll still be going in with me, Detective Connors. To see Dylan."

"Yes, Ma'am. I will. If that's what you'd like." It was clear to Liz that her presence was neither expected nor desired.

"Oh, yes," she implored as she patted Connors hand with an air of familiarity. "Please. I appreciate you helping me through this."

Liz and Connors shared a look and it was Connors who spoke. "Jayson Abbott will be here soon. He wanted to speak with you for a moment, Lieutenant. And he wanted to be here to drive Mrs. Colby home."

"Yes, we need to talk about arrangements," Erica told them. "For Dylan's service."

"Before you leave, Lieutenant, May I have a moment?" Connors asked Liz as he stood, then directed his attention to Erica. "Please excuse us for a brief minute, Mrs. Colby. I'll be right back." She nodded and gave Connors the slightest smile, almost out of habit.

Liz and Connors stepped away to the lobby area. "I talked to the fellow at Avalon. His name is Danny Jones. He and his girlfriend had no love for Colby, but the timing isn't right for them to have been involved. I need to check in with his PO. A woman named Skinner. He met with her yesterday. Between that meeting and the UA he provided, I don't see him as a possible suspect. And the girlfriend was at work, although I will confirm."

"Sue Skinner? I know Sue," Liz told Connors, as she thought about the probation officer. "Red hair. From Australia originally. I'll check in with her. We need to confirm

Jones' story anyway. Connors," said Liz as she lowered her voice and took a glance around, "We need to bring Ty in for official questioning. As a person of interest. If we follow protocol to the letter, and I have to, especially with this case, that means you and an officer handle it. Find Castillo. And ask Castillo to change into street clothes." That was the one of two concessions Liz would make. She wasn't going to have Ty Phillips brought in by uniformed officers. "One more thing, Connors. No cuffs." That was the second concession.

Connors agreed to the plan to bring Ty in for questioning as Jayson Abbott appeared in the entry corridor. He approached slowly and extended a hand to Liz and then to Connors and glanced over in Erica's direction. He reached into the breast pocket of his jacket and pulled out a small item. "I was hoping to see you, Lieutenant. I found this in Dylan's desk at home. It's a thumb drive. It contains files with financial data. I've been studying them all morning and even as an accountant, I'm not sure of all the information they contain. I can tell you they involve a reconciliation, a balance, if you will. But some of the details are beyond my expertise. Looks like public domain to me. I thought you should have them, even if they are meaningless. A good forensic accountant should look them over. I'm sure your department has someone they use."

"Yes, we do. And thanks for bringing it to us, Mr. Abbott." Liz instantly thought of Miles Carey, the best financial investigator she knew. Miles could track funds down to the last corrupt nickel.

Liz had no way of knowing what was on the device, but now was not the time to slip up on chain of custody with items of evidence. She withdrew from her coat pocket one of the small, plastic evidence envelopes she always carried. Using a tissue, she dropped the tiny storage device inside. Jayson affixed his signature on the duplicate label that served as a seal. Liz signed the label and handed him one copy as a receipt. She then sealed the envelope with the adhesive side of the label with both signatures visible.

Jayson watched Liz with interest. When the reason for her protocol occurred to him, he placed the receipt in his pocket and nodded to Liz. He excused himself and headed to the waiting area. He took the seat next to Erica. He placed an arm around her shoulder, and she seemed to take comfort in his presence.

The door to the viewing area opened and Myers stepped into the lobby. Liz and Connors looked over at the same time, recognizing the medical examiner. Neither Erica nor Jayson knew who he was and the surprise was evident on their faces. Connors stepped up to handle the introductions.

"Mrs. Colby, Mr. Abbott, this is Dr. Myers, our chief pathologist."

"I'm sorry for your loss, Mrs. Colby, and my condolences to you, Mr. Abbott," offered Myers as he shook their hands. It was the first time Liz had witnessed Myers with bereaved relatives. She was touched and surprised by his sensitivity. She hadn't suspected he had that much compassion. Liz had certainly never been the recipient of his goodwill.

Myers briefly looked in Liz's direction and offered one quick nod of his head in acknowledgment. "Lieutenant," was all he uttered.

Liz had a thought. "If you could excuse us for just a moment, Mrs. Colby, Mr. Abbott. I need a quick word with Detective Connors and Dr. Myers," explained Liz as she motioned for the two men to follow.

When they were a reasonable distance way, Myers asked with exasperation. "What could possibly be important enough to take us away from this viewing, Lieutenant? These people want to get this over with. I've had to keep them waiting long enough and we're finally ready for them."

Connor looked decidedly uncomfortable but had the good sense to stay quiet. He glanced back and forth between Liz and Myers.

"I think it best if I head back to the office, Myers. Mrs. Colby has asked Connors to be here with her. She seems comfortable with him and she has Abbott here for support, as well. It's not necessary for me to be here. This isn't a party." Liz turned her attention to Connors. "Do you agree?"

"I do, Lieutenant. No reason for both of us to be here and you have other details to look into."

"Myers, I'm not neglecting everyone by excusing myself. In fact, the opposite is true. I'm actually taking Mrs. Colby's feelings into account. That's all." Liz sounded defensive. She heard it in her voice. Myers had that effect on her.

Myers looked over at the grieving pair. He looked back at Liz, the petulance oozing out of him. "Fine. Far be it from me to question your priorities, Lieutenant. Detective Connors, the family is waiting." Myers left them and joined the waiting pair.

Liz directed her attention back to Connors. "I'll see you back at the precinct and I'll get in touch with Sue."

“Yes, Ma’am,” said Connors and took his leave, rejoining Erica, Jayson, and Myers. Liz left to return to the office.

Chapter Seventeen

Liz entered the precinct and made it half way to her office when a uniformed officer intercepted her. "Lieutenant Jordan, I was about to call your cell. Captain wants to see you immediately. He's been looking for you."

"Right. Thanks." Liz turned around, walked to the elevator, and went up to the third floor where the brass spent their days.

Clarice was at her desk. She put a hand up signaling that Liz should wait. Clarice picked up the receiver of her desk phone and hit one button and said, "Sir, Lieutenant Jordan is here." After the slightest pause, she said, "Yes, Sir." Clarice replaced the receiver then said to Liz, "You can go in. He's been waiting for you." Clarice dropped her voice to a whisper and added while looking at Liz over the top of her glasses, "and he's not in a good mood. Sorry."

Liz locked eyes with Clarice for a moment but uttered no response. She knocked and entered the Captain's office, closing the door behind her. As always, Liz waited to be invited to take a seat. The invitation, however, was not forthcoming.

"Lieutenant Jordan, I understand you spoke with ADA Powell earlier today." It was a statement, not a question.

"Yes, Sir, and I understand you and ADA Powell had a conversation, as well." Another statement. No question. "I believe it was regarding the investigation into the Colby death. You've made your feelings about the investigation clear, Sir. Connors and I are actively pursuing leads. May I ask what could possibly have come up since you and I last spoke together?"

He looked at Liz. His expression was unreadable, but Liz felt a tumult coming. She could feel it in her gut. "Yes, Jordan, I talked to Powell. About other matters but we touched on the Colby investigation, not that my conversations are any concern of yours. But here's the deal. I looked into the military record of your person of interest. Did you know that Phillips was part of a special ops team in Iraq? I'm talking about an elite group trained to go in silently and quickly neutralize any threat they encountered. He's been trained in combat survival including deadly force. And I've read the M.E.'s summary."

"No Sir, I didn't know the specifics of his training, but I suspected as much. I know it now, thanks to you."

"Have Phillips' whereabouts for last evening been verified? Have you discovered others in the vicinity that present alternate theories or whom you suspect may have, or could have, committed this crime?"

"The answer to both questions is no, at this time."

"Then, unless I'm missing something big, you are to see that Ty Phillips is charged for the murder of Dylan Colby." The captain was adamant. "And let me remind you, Lieutenant, you are the supervising officer on this case. Connors is the lead. He chose to ask for assistance from you as his commanding. You need to be taking a step away from the front line on this one."

"Sir, Connors is bringing Phillips in for official questioning as a person of interest. I agree it's come to that. But an arrest is premature, in my opinion. There are other leads being investigated. And to be honest, I'm feeling pressured by an assistant district attorney to make an arrest when I don't feel we're at that point." Liz paused, made a show of clearing her throat, then added, "Sir."

"Lieutenant, for your information, the only pressure you're feeling is from me. We have more than sufficient evidence to make an arrest and I'm not pleased at needing to point that fact out to you. This man is a veteran of our armed forces. He served our country. No one feels worse than I do about our suspicions. But the evidence is incontrovertible. A veteran, yes, but this is also a homeless man living on the margins. He could disappear faster than you can snap your fingers. You know it and I know it."

Liz did not respond. *Shit*, she said to herself. *He's right.* She would never suspect Ty of disappearing, at least not permanently. She was aware, however, that Mike and others in the community had mentioned that once in a while, weeks would pass without Ty turning up. No one seemed to know where he spent his time away. *Shit, shit, shit.*

"I want this man held, Jordan. Do I make myself clear?"

"Yes, Sir. It'll be done within the hour."

"Good. You're excused. And have Connors keep me informed." The captain returned his attention to paperwork on his desk before Liz turned to leave his office. As Liz stepped out and walked to the elevator, Clarice was no longer at her desk. Liz returned to her office feeling decidedly alone.

Chapter Eighteen

Liz made it back to her office. She closed the door, removed her jacket, preparing to sit down and gather her thoughts. It was happening, after all. Liz was tempted to call Mike and let him know what was going down. *Damn it!* She wanted to but Liz knew that was a huge breach. *Screw it.* She owed it to Mike to let him hear the news from her. She picked up her cell phone and dialed Mike's. His voice mail picked up. "Mike, it's me. Call me as soon as you get this. It's been a crap day and it's going to get worse. Just sharing. Love you."

Liz hung up the phone. She remembered the evidence envelope in her pocket. Feeling for the small bag, she retrieved it. She held it in her hand, studied it through the plastic with curiosity. She placed it on her desk. There was one other call she felt compelled to make. She should know better but in her heart of hearts Liz knew it was the right thing to do. Again, she was breaching protocol, but she needed to do this. There was one person Liz knew she would want in her corner if she ever got into trouble. Before she talked herself out of it, Liz punched the number using her cell phone. After two rings, a familiar voice answered with the greeting, "Harrison and Gilliam Law Office; how may I help you?"

"Hi Lynda. It's Liz. Is Diana available? I just need a moment."

"Oh, hello, Lieutenant. She just finished taking a deposition. She might have a minute. Let me check. Can I ask you to hold?"

"Of course."

"Thank you." Liz was on hold for maybe thirty seconds, just long enough to ask herself, *Shit, Liz, what are you doing?* But she knew what she was doing. And she knew why. Whether anyone else would agree with her actions, anyone like her captain, was another matter.

"Hey, Liz. What's up? Haven't seen you in ages. Are you calling to invite me out for a well-deserved cold one after a shitty day?"

"Diana. Thanks for taking my call. I know you're busy. First, you need to understand that this call isn't happening. When I tell you what's up, you'll know why."

"Okay. You have my attention." Liz heard the court-appropriate voice come into play. The voice that Diana used when questioning witnesses on the stand.

"You remember Ty Phillips, don't you? Helps Gary and the staff at Brooks House? Mike's buddy?"

"I do. Gulf War vet. He kept a lot of heads cool during the investigation last year into Leah Bishop's death. It was a scary time downtown. Especially for folks in The Beau." The case had been especially significant to Diana because she had known the young woman as a client and as a friend.

"Ty is going to need representation. I know if you consent to help him, you'd probably agree to take the case pro bono. But I want to help with the expenses."

"We'll discuss that later. When is this happening, Liz? Can you tell me the charge?"

"Soon, very soon. Within the hour. Ty is going to be arrested for murder."

"Are we talking about the death at the CSO yesterday evening?"

"We are."

"Okay." Liz heard a sigh from her attorney friend. "If you're doubtful about culpability, Liz, why are you arranging counsel? Why is he even being arrested?"

Liz took a second of caution to consider what she should say before she responded. She was so far out on a limb now that she decided it was too late for prudence and forged ahead. "The evidence points in Ty's direction. He may be able to offer some additional information that could help clear him, but he refuses. You know how these guys are with their code of honor. My guess is he has what he believes is a very good reason. I haven't talked to Ty personally. Connors did. We're having a hard time believing he could do this."

Diana was silent for a moment, then she said, "If he accepts my representation, I'll take it on. I'm leaving here in thirty minutes. Is that soon enough? You might want to look surprised when you see me."

"Yeah, I think you're right about that. I appreciate this, Diana. I have tried but haven't been able to reach Mike. He doesn't know about any of this mess. If things here get sticky, I may have to ask you to call him. I was hoping he could hear it from me."

"Probably better that I tell him for you. Maybe he can meet me at the justice center."

"Thanks, Diana. I owe you a beer. Actually, I owe you several."

"Yeah, you do. Maybe later. Have to go." With that, Diana ended the call.

Liz took a deep breath, thought about what she had done by calling Diana. The impropriety of alerting an attorney to an imminent arrest was clear to her. It may be grounds for discipline, maybe even dismissal. Her thoughts fell to Ty Phillips, the calm, decent, homeless veteran who advocated for everyone but himself. Liz considered him to be someone for whom she could take a chance. At some point, Liz and Mike would be having a face-to-face about Ty's situation and Liz wanted to be able to tell Mike that she went the extra mile. Even if she couldn't tell anyone else.

Remembering another task that needed to be done, Liz picked up her office phone and rang a number. "Probation services," was the greeting at the other end.

"This is Lieutenant Jordan at Metro. Is Sue Skinner in her office?"

"One moment. I'll ring her desk. If she's there, she'll pick up, otherwise it'll go to voicemail," explained a voice teetering between efficiency and a lack of concern.

Liz waited while the call was forwarded. She heard two rings, then a familiar voice with an Australian accent said, "Skinner."

"Sue, it's Liz Jordan."

"Oh, Hey. Where have you been? I haven't seen you since before the promotion. I was happy to hear of it, although it was long overdue. Not that anyone asked me what I thought."

"Thank you, Sue. Means a lot. How are things going for you?"

"Good. There's rarely a dull moment." Sue laughed and then added, "When you think you can't be surprised any longer, someone surprises you."

"I'm hoping you have a few minutes. I need to ask you to confirm some information."

"I try to always have ten minutes for anyone who needs it. If I like you, you may get twelve or thirteen minutes. If you annoy me, you're lucky to get seven or eight. What is it you hope I can confirm?"

"Whereabouts of one of your guys. Name is Danny Jones. He claims he was meeting with you yesterday."

"Yes, we met yesterday. He linked his weekly with me and his UA. His color was up. I'm checking my contacts, hold on." Liz heard a couple of keystrokes. "Dan was here at four-fifteen. Why are you asking? Please tell me it's nothing I need to know."

"A case worker at the CSO was killed yesterday. You probably heard. We asked Danny and his girlfriend about their involvement with him. We don't suspect either of them, just wanted information. But we want to cross all the t's, you could say."

"I heard about the death last night. Colby. The young man created difficulty for Dan and for no real reason. Why do some in social services have to make things harder for people just because they can? I would think they have enough to keep themselves busy."

"Maybe Colby had his reasons," answered Liz. "I'm guessing his job wasn't easy."

"No, it wasn't. And I don't make excuses for people. I think you know that. Let me say something about Dan

Jones. He was at fault. No doubt. He violated probation because he used. But the worse of it was leaving his baby unattended when he was out of his head. That mistake scared him badly. Here's the thing: Dan could have lied and said his girlfriend's mum was caring for Ian. But he didn't lie. He was mortified by what he'd done. He took responsibility for his actions. That's why I spoke on his behalf."

"What did Colby do to make things rough for him?"

"Danny needed a job! It's a condition of his probation. He had a chance at work that may have become full time. The girlfriend could have stayed in school. Colby didn't want him working in a pub, but Danny doesn't drink. It made no sense. I called Colby myself, tried to get him to reconsider. Did no good."

"What did Colby tell you?"

"Just bullshit about the original drug charge. I told him that should be my concern more than his. To be honest, I think the recovery issue was a touchy one for him. Struck a nerve."

"A nerve, as in, he had personal experience with recovery? Do you have reason to think Colby had addiction issues in his past?"

"I can only say it seemed to be a trigger for him. At least this time. I've had fellows on his caseload before. That particular issue hadn't caused a problem with anyone else."

"Okay, thanks," said Liz, as she jotted down what Sue had said.

"You're welcome. Let me know if you need anything else. I'd actually like to help," the probation officer said, sounding very sincere. "Keep me in the loop about Danny. He's a good kid. I know you'll take a close look. You're tenacious. What is it you people say? About a hungry animal?"

Liz thought for a few moments, drawing a blank. Then it occurred to her what Sue was referring to. "You mean 'like a dog with a bone'?" Liz asked.

"Right, right. That's it," she said, recalling the American simile.

"I don't know. Maybe your hungry animal is a better description."

Chapter Nineteen

Connors accompanied Erica Colby throughout the viewing of her son's remains. And Jayson Abbott, who was to have been her son-in-law, was there. Myers may have been irritated that Jordan wasn't present, but Connors didn't really want to know. He avoided stepping into their on-going feud. He tactfully stated that Liz had been on site to assist with the interview of Mrs. Colby prior to the viewing. He made it clear that as the lead detective on this investigation, it was his duty to keep Liz, his supervising lieutenant, apprised of all developments.

Erica was more comfortable in the company of men. Connors felt certain of it. He wasn't a trained psychologist, far from it, but he was an astute observer of people. He couldn't base his assessment on anything in particular except that the grieving mother had quickly developed a rapport with him and had formed no such connection to Liz. *Grief can interrupt one from engaging or connecting with others,* thought Connors. Was that it or was it something else? And why had she latched on to him? *Maybe he reminded her of the son she had lost*, he thought. Whatever the reason for the disconnect, Connors was sure that Liz had felt it and that was why she excused herself. Regardless of how Myers felt, Connors considered Liz's actions respectful.

Along with Officer Castillo, Connors headed to Brooks House. He had had a conversation with Ty at the shelter just last evening although it seemed as though ages had passed since then. Connors and Castillo were both in street clothes and Liz had made it clear that Ty was not to be restrained by cuffs. Connors believed that Liz's concessions were not to afford special treatment for Ty's as much as to avoid causing a disruptive level of agitation in a community ripe for it.

With dozens of men at Brooks, some easily excitable and many at their wit's end at any given time, sparks of discord had been known to ignite tense situations. If Connors felt that he, Castillo, or anyone was at risk, he would have to rethink their approach. But he seriously doubted it would come to that. Connors had a job to do and he summoned his unemotional cop persona to execute. He wasn't happy about finding Ty and bringing him to the station, but it was his job.

They parked close to the entrance and made their way into Brooks House. They stopped by the office, as Connors had the evening before. He wanted to check in with Gary, but Connors didn't see him. They made their way into the dining room. Thankfully, it was pretty empty at the moment, just a few people sitting at tables, nursing coffee cups. Good. But that would change as the dinner hour approached.

Gary was sitting with Ty at a table near the kitchen. The two men were talking and drinking coffee. Connors and Castillo approached the men at the table, as casual as possible without taking a seat. It was Gary who spoke first.

"Connors, what brings you to my place again so soon and with a buddy, too." He looked at Castillo and added, "It's Castillo, right?" as he held out a hand to the female officer. Castillo accepted his hand with a nod and they shook hands.

"Hey, Gary. We need to talk to Ty," said Connors. He didn't respond and Ty didn't say a word. Connors watched as Ty took another draw on the coffee and put the mug on the table.

Ty looked at Connors, looked him deep in the eye, then fixed his gaze on Castillo for a moment. "Nice to be able to get out of those blues once in a while, huh, Castillo?" said Ty. His comment was lighthearted, almost friendly, but the tone in which it was delivered was reserved.

Before Castillo could say anything one way or the other, Ty added, "My guess is we aren't going to be talking here this time. Am I right?"

Connors leaned a bit closer, creating the illusion of privacy. "Ty, we need you to come down to the precinct for questioning as a person of interest in the death of Dylan Colby."

Having said this, Connors sat down. He was directly across the table from Ty, Gary to his left. Castillo stood behind Ty and a step or two away. "I know you have information that would help you out of this situation," Connors told Ty. "I'm asking you, right here and now, to tell us what that is so we can verify your whereabouts yesterday and clear you."

With a steely regard, Ty looked at Connors and answered, "I'm not going to do that. I can't help you. You can stop asking."

"Then, damn it, Ty, we have no choice. Car's outside. You can bring your stuff or entrust it to Gary. I can't tell you when you'll be back."

At this juncture, Gary joined the discussion. He spoke calmly but firmly. "If Ty has information that he could use to help himself and he's choosing not to share it, then my guess is he has a good reason. That can only mean a couple of things: either he's respecting someone else's right to privacy or Ty believes that the person he's protecting needs to take responsibility and Ty won't interfere with that." Gary continued, but he now spoke only to Ty. "You have your reasons and I have to respect that, man. I'll do whatever I can to help."

Ty nodded his head slightly at Gary. He placed both hands on the table and stood up. "There's just a couple of things in my pack I want with me. I'll leave the rest here with you," he told him. "Let's do this then," he said to Connors and Castillo with resignation. "I won't cause you any concern. I know you're doing your job. If anyone understands that, I do."

They turned around as they heard steps approaching from behind. The four of them looked up to see Mike Dwyer walking toward them and he looked pissed off as hell.

"Well, at least I made it down here in time for the show," he said with a voice full of sarcasm. Mike then spoke to Ty. "Let me know what I can do. You know I'll help in any way I can, brother." Mike turned to Connors. "Connors, you know this is a big crock of horse shit. You know that as well as I do." Mike stepped toward Ty, but then he turned to face Connors, raising his hands as one does to give up, and said, "You have a job to do, I get it. But Jesus freaking Christ!"

"Yeah, it sucks, Mike," said Connors firmly. "I know it and Ty knows it, too. Let's get out of here before folks start arriving for dinner."

Connors saw Ty start to turn around with his back to him and place his hands behind him. "No, Ty, that's not necessary. You're a person of interest at this point and coming in to assist the investigation of your own accord." He and Castillo shared a look and Castillo gave Connors an almost imperceptible nod of accent. "We're not placing you under arrest." *And fuck 'em if they don't like it,* Connors thought to himself.

Mike placed a hand on Ty's shoulder. "And I've got an important message for you. Diana Harrison is meeting you downtown. It's all been arranged. No discussion," Mike told his friend with resolve.

Chapter Twenty

Connors and Castillo were able to get Ty into the car without attracting attention. The few people in the dining room watched but kept their thoughts and comments to themselves. There was an older couple sitting outside in front of Brooks. They were consumed enough in their own private drama that they weren't interested in what was happening to anyone else.

Arriving at the precinct, Connors and Castillo entered with Ty through a side door and made their way to an interview room. "Can I get you water or something? Have you eaten today, Ty?" asked Connors when they sat down.

"No. I'm good." Ty took a moment to clear his throat. He didn't look panicked, just uncomfortable. Being in the police precinct usually had that effect on people. His demeanor had begun to waiver. His calmness at Brooks may have been an effort to keep the situation cool and controlled for everyone.

In his mind, Connors reviewed what he knew of Ty: he was a Gulf War veteran, he had experienced homelessness for a very long time, and he had very few trusted friends. Ty was known to those in the community and to the network of providers who help them. He had struggled with addiction in his past but as far as Connors knew, had stayed clean for many years.

Connors thought of others whom Ty had helped who were trying to get clean or stay clean. He had been a support for a young man named Malachi and the fellow had turned things around. But Ty had some deeper issues, as well, probably post-traumatic stress disorder stemming from his military service. The PTSD, at whatever level, was a factor in Ty's life and made the homelessness less of a choice and more of a result. Connors knew confinement might be rough. He'd seen it before in veterans dealing with trauma.

"Okay, Ty. I'm recording our conversation. And I'm required to inform you that other police personnel may be observing. I'm not giving you the Miranda warning because you aren't under arrest, but anything you tell me is part of an official record. Do you understand?" As Ty started to respond, there was a knock on the interview room door. It opened and Diana Harrison entered the room.

"Good day, Detective Connors. Good day, Mr. Phillips. I've been engaged to advocate for Mr. Phillips should he feel the need for legal counsel. Do either of you object to having me sit in on this interview?" Diana took a seat. It wasn't likely that Ty would object to having counsel present. And since Ty agreed to the interview, it wasn't likely Connors would protest. "Mr. Phillips, may I assume that you are agreeing to my presence here and will allow me to represent you, should it come to that?"

"Yes, Ma'am," answered Ty.

"Thank you for that statement of intent to engage me as counsel, Mr. Phillips." Diana directed her attention to Connors. "And just to review, Mr. Phillips is being questioned regarding his knowledge of the death yesterday evening of Dylan Colby, correct? And at this time, Mr. Phillips is a person of interest only and is not under arrest?"

"Yes," said Connors, as he began recording. "That is correct. Persons present are Ty Phillips, Diana Harrison, Counsel for Mr. Phillips, and Detective Kyle Connors."

"Mr. Phillips, how were you acquainted with Mr. Colby, the deceased?" asked Connors.

"He worked in the CSO. He processed applications for help." Ty answered matter of fact with no emotion.

"Did you know of him in any other capacity?"

"I did not," responded Ty, still succinct.

"You were seen at the CSO a week before Colby's death. It's been stated by witnesses that you spoke with him in private. Why were you meeting with him?"

"I was there. I talked with him about assistance for a mutual acquaintance."

"You didn't have an appointment, Ty. Who were you there to discuss with Colby?" Connors didn't think he'd get an answer, but asked anyway. Hoping.

"That's not important. It has nothing to do with his death," said Ty, sticking with his story.

"We can't take your word for that at this point, Ty. I think you know that," said Connors.

"Detective Connors," said Diana, putting an end to Connors' statement with a fine point. "Ty says he didn't know the man outside of their work-related contact. It's not up to Mr. Phillips to provide you with Mr. Colby's client list."

Connors changed his tack. "Let's talk about yesterday. You said when we talked before that you had coffee uptown until just before five. The waitress at the diner remembers you. When you left the diner, you went across the street to the church because you had promised to attend a support meeting with someone. You stated that the person did not show up, is that right?"

"That's right."

"The coordinator at the meeting can't confirm that you attended. You may have, he says, but you didn't sign in, and you aren't known there so you weren't recognized. Showing your photo, Ty, did not help."

"That's probably true," Ty nodded, not offering anything helpful.

"You stated that you stayed for the meeting but did not speak or share. And after the meeting, you walked down Main Street and sat in the park for a while. Did you talk to anyone?"

"Not that I remember." Ty paused and stifled a laugh. "If I could do it again, I'd be sure to."

"When you were walking up Main you went by the CSO, correct? Do you know what time that would have been?"

"Not off the top of my head. Must have been about six-twenty or six-thirty."

"Did you hear anyone shout to you? Shout your name?"

Ty thought for a moment, searching his memory. He rubbed the whiskers on his chin with one hand, eyes recollecting. "Not that I recall. Didn't see anyone I knew. There was traffic on the street that may have muffled anyone yelling. I was deep in thought and wanted to get further downtown."

"How long were you in the park?" asked Connors, trying to establish the timeframe.

"Not long," Ty answered. "Just passing time."

"Where did you go when you left the park?" asked Connors.

"To Brooks," Ty responded to the question quickly. "I had volunteered to set up for the eight o'clock meeting."

"But you had just attended a meeting at the church uptown. Why would you attend another?"

"Mr. Phillips can attend as many support meetings as he chooses. Is that really a valid question?" asked Diana, interrupting.

Ty glanced in Harrison's direction, waved his hand nonchalantly and answered. "I wasn't attending the meeting at eight. Just setting up."

Connors took a deep breath, gathering his thoughts. He began to speak with a slight shake of his head, as if delivering news he didn't want to deliver but had no choice. "Okay, here's the deal, Ty. We can't verify your whereabouts between leaving the diner and arriving at Brooks. That's a period of time between five and seven-fifteen."

Staring Connors in the eye, Ty said nothing, head straight, jaw set.

"That's been determined as the period of time during which Colby died. And you have no alibi for your whereabouts and you were seen in the immediate area," stated Connors.

"Are the details regarding Ty's whereabouts at the time of death the only reason for your interest in him?" asked Diana.

"No," answered Connors, continuing to look directly at Ty. "There's also the matter of your visit to Colby's office last week. The situation was out of the ordinary in several respects."

"All right. You've established those points," conceded the attorney, then she asked, "Anything else?"

"Yes," answered Connors, directing his gaze to Diana. "There's the manner of death. Colby was killed by someone with training in how to inflict a death blow with their bare hands." Connors redirected his focus to Ty and continued. "Ty, you served in a Special Forces capacity that provided training in that level of assault, correct?"

Diana was silent but contemplative, eyes fixed on Connors. Ty, chin resting on clasped hands, elbows on the table, slowly closed his eyes.

"Yes, that's correct," he stated. "Unfortunately. I wish to hell I hadn't been."

"Ty, I urge you to refrain from providing any more information at this time," Diana told him, her hand raised between them as if to fend off further response. Then she directed her response to Connors. "There are any number of former servicemen trained to defend themselves in the manner you describe."

"This attack was not in defense. Many who have served are trained in the tactics I've described. But Ty is the only one placed in the vicinity." Connors' voice was quiet and resigned, as if he didn't want to believe the facts as stated. "And we cannot verify he was elsewhere at the time Colby died."

Connors leaned in close, almost begging, "Ty, I ask you again; will you provide anything else or can you direct us to corroborating witnesses who can verify where you were when Colby was killed?"

"No," answered Ty.

"Even if it means we have to put you in a cell, Ty? We really don't want to do that," pleaded the younger man. "You're not giving us a choice."

Ty was steadfast. He made no response.

"Detective Connors," said Diana, "I'd like to speak to my client in private."

"At this point, I'd say you'll have that opportunity, Counselor," agreed Connors. But he was exasperated. Then he paused, not wanting to continue but it was inevitable.

"Ty Phillips, you are under arrest for the murder of Dylan Colby. With counsel present, your cooperation up to this point is duly noted. From this point on, you have the right to remain silent..."

As Connors read the Miranda warning, Ty sat next to Diana with his hands clasped and eyes straight ahead.

Chapter Twenty-one

The interview of Ty Phillips was observed from the other side of a large mirror that was actually a one-way window looking in. Present on the opposite side of that window were Liz and Powell, representing the prosecutor's office.

As Connors ended the interview and placed Ty under arrest, Powell leaned over and flipped off the speaker that had allowed them to listen to the proceedings in the next room.

"It's a solid case, Lieutenant. We both know that. The evidence presented by Detective Connors supports it," Powell said, as he gestured toward Connors in the other room. "Mr. Phillips is unable to dispute any of it." He explained his beliefs to Liz with confidence and a tinge of arrogance. He began to place papers into his briefcase and glanced up at Liz. Powell's head was tilted to one side and in a jaunty tone he added, "And all was stated with his counsel present."

Powell was correct in theory, and Liz knew it. She didn't want to believe that Ty had murdered Colby, but she could only base her doubts on what she knew of the man personally. And she was the Lieutenant in charge of the investigation that had led to Ty's arrest. She had to be careful in how she responded.

Liz and Powell had been standing side by side as they watched and listened through the glass. Needing some personal space, Liz took a step away, which was all the space the small room afforded. Her arms had been crossed but she waved one hand toward the window as she spoke.

"He's protecting someone," said Liz calmly, stating the obvious. She recalled the confidence in Powell's voice and wanted to avoid sounding concerned. But concerned, she was.

"Well, if that's true, maybe he's protecting himself, as well. Have you thought of that? Instead of this mystery person helping to clear Mr. Phillips, maybe finding this person would only support our case. Maybe they were present at the time of the killing," Powell speculated as he closed his briefcase and affixed the clasps. "But it hardly matters. He was seen in the vicinity. He's been trained to inflict the kind of physical damage that killed Colby. And he lied about knowing him and arguing with him. And that, Lieutenant, brings us to motive. Placed with means and opportunity, we have the blessed trinity necessary for legal prosecution." His confidence was now upgraded to full-blown arrogance.

Liz didn't like arrogance. She felt her jaw clench, her gut got tight. Dealing with Myers had the same effect on her physically. And she didn't like what was happening to Ty.

"I was here, Jack. Remember? I stood next to you and heard the same interview you did. But thank you for the interpretation." Liz knew the comment sounded belligerent. She exhaled audibly. With no furnishings in the limited space other than the small surface that held the prosecutor's briefcase, Liz leaned and placed her hands on the wall below the window, bracing herself.

"You are right, the evidence points to Ty," Liz agreed. "But neither of us can deny that he's protecting someone. Someone who knows something about Ty's actions last night. Just suppose for a moment that whatever this person knows proves to clear Ty. If that's true then the person who killed Colby is still on the street. And as for motive? Colby didn't make a lot of friends while doing his job. We haven't begun to uncover enough about him to know why someone might have wanted him dead."

Liz pushed back from the wall, hands landing on hips. She turned to face Powell knowing that her voice held an attitude of contempt. "And you know as well as I that with an arrest made, department resources won't support continuing the investigation." Liz let the idea hang in the air between them that this was exactly what the prosecutor wanted.

Powell stopped, hand on the door. He turned to look at Liz with impatience which he quickly replaced with pleasure. "That's true, Lieutenant. But don't bet on there being someone out there who can support Ty's innocence. The man has his problems but he's no fool. If he could help himself, he would. And my bet is he's not going to help us." He walked out of the room.

As Liz watched Powell stroll out of the observation room, she was livid. And for the first time in her career, she hated the job she loved.

Why was Powell so intent on talking the easy route with this case? Or was her impression the result of her friendship with Ty and her feelings for Mike? The evidence did support charging Ty with Colby's murder. She couldn't deny it. But the evidence also supported the fact that Ty was protecting someone. But to what end? Could this knowledge hurt Ty's case or help him?

Soon, Ty would be processed, the grueling routine formally placing him in custody. He would be searched, fingerprinted, relieved of his personal belongings and clothing. He would change into jail-issued garments. Liz knew it was demeaning by design. For a brief moment, Liz remembered her phone call to Diana. Liz's call brought the attorney here to be present for Ty's interview. Liz had taken a huge chance, a risky chance. But she didn't regret it.

Liz figured that following a meeting with Diana, Ty would be placed in a cell. A cell. Few words conjure up more dread for the average person. Liz was usually elated when she was able to jail a suspect. But in this instance, she felt anxious, worried. When the other prisoners in the pods caught wind that Ty was a traumatized vet held on a murder charge, Liz hoped the mystique may serve to keep them at a distance.

It wasn't Ty's physical safety that concerned her as much as his mental health. As highly functioning as he was compared to some guys on the street, Ty had his struggles. Shadows in the man's past had kept him on the margins for a long time. Mike's theory was that for some of the men on the street, their freedom was more important to them than a home, a job, family. It was freedom and a life of solitude that kept the demons at bay more than anything else. Liz hated to think of Ty having to handle that loss.

Chapter Twenty-two

When Liz reached the corridor outside her office, she remained deep in thought until she saw Mike waiting near her office door. There were chairs nearby along the side of the corridor but he stood, waiting. Liz looked around the squad room. Most of the department had met Mike but whether they knew of the connection between Mike and Ty, she wasn't aware. *Damn it, anyway*, she thought. *What's done is done, and we need to talk.* When she approached, he stepped aside to allow her entry.

"Have you been waiting long?" Liz asked, trying to sound conciliatory.

"Not all that long but I don't have much time. I need to get back," Mike told her, meaning he was needed at Avalon.

She stopped for a brief moment at her office doorway and looked into Mike's eyes. She hoped to get a read on his thoughts. Mike returned the eye contact. His expression was one of anger that Liz sensed was aimed at the situation and not at her. She felt for him but doubted she could say anything to ease his concern. They entered Liz's office and she closed the door behind them.

"How's he doing, Liz? And how can this be happening to him?" Mike asked her, his expression still angry but his voice heavy with concern.

"Ty's doing as well as we'd expect. I haven't talked to him although I observed the interview. He seemed to be all right." Liz watched Mike react with a small amount of relief as she answered the first question.

"Please, Mike, sit down for a minute," she suggested. "As for how this happened, the evidence links Ty to Colby. They were seen together and it wasn't a friendly exchange. Ty didn't tell the truth about knowing Colby. And witnesses place Ty in the area at the time of death. Plus, he's being stubborn about helping himself."

"What do you mean?" Mike asked with brow furrowed, clearly not understanding.

"We can't verify that Ty was elsewhere at the time Colby was killed although he claims to have had nothing to do with his death. He says he was meeting someone uptown at a five-p.m. support group but they didn't show. He says he slowly made his way back downtown. He refuses to say who he was meeting. Ty says he was in the park for a while but didn't see anyone he knew or talk to anyone. Have you ever known Ty to hang out in the park and not run into someone he knows? We can verify that he was at Brooks after seven p.m."

Liz felt words tumbling out of her mouth, an avalanche of information that, piece by piece, had led to Ty's arrest. She knew she was speaking fast, reviewing the facts as much for her own understanding as sharing them. She looked at Mike. He'd been listening intently, his body language indicating full alert.

"I believe his story but there's no way to support some of it, Mike. Connors and I think that Ty's protecting someone at his own expense. Why would he do that? He's never talked of family. Do you know of anyone that he's close to? Close enough to risk his freedom to protect them?"

Mike began to process the information but he was clearly perplexed. After a few moments to think, he shook his head, eyes fixed on Liz's. "I know the man better than a lot of people, but we only know what a person chooses to share. If there's someone Ty wants to protect my guess would be it's a fellow vet who's going through a rough patch."

Silent for a moment, then Mike added, "Gary would be the one to talk to about it. He sees more of what's happening with the guys than anyone. He's going to respect Ty's choice though. He made that clear when Connors and the other cop brought Ty down here. But it might be worth a conversation."

"Mike, listen," Liz said with her fingers splayed on her desk, shaking her head. "Connors and I are investigators. Our role is to gather evidence until an arrest is made. Once that happens our job is essentially finished. At this point, we turn the case over to prosecutors. When cases go to trial, our testimony is usually in support of the prosecutor's case. Yes, there are questions I would like to have answered and more evidence may be out there, but my hands are tied. I don't like it but that's the system." For the second time that afternoon, the job she loved had left a bad taste in her mouth.

"The system, huh? Give me a damn break, Liz." Mike spoke calmly but his voice was filled with disgust, his words full of indictment. "You know that Ty didn't kill anyone. He's the definition of a soldier turned pacifist. Your 'system' asked more of him than he could give and he's been unraveling at his own seams ever since."

"I know all that, Mike. And I believe it to be true. But we can only use the evidence we have. If Ty has any information that could help his case, he needs to share it with Diana. She's his advocate. If it had been up to me, I'd have delved deeper into Colby's business dealings, his personal life, and his family. My sense is there's a lot going on in those areas."

As Liz spoke, she remembered the thumb drive with the financial reports Abbott had brought to her at the morgue. She recalled the odd interaction with Colby's mother. Liz didn't mention those points to Mike, but she added, "The fact that he was killed in his office and a mess was made of the place should be significant to someone. But it's out of my hands."

"You can just step aside? I know you better than that, Liz. We learned that there is no justice without the truth while we were both still pups. That's why you made that call to Diana." Mike sat forward as he spoke, his index finger pointed at Liz.

Liz had been staring at Mike, the conversation becoming increasingly uncomfortable. She averted her gaze when he mentioned her call to the attorney. Liz looked down at her desk again feeling heat rise to her face and emptiness in her gut. Yes, she made that call and Mike's mention of it reminded her that she had taken a huge professional risk. But she saw it as an act of conscience instead of duty.

"Diana is the best attorney I know. And she's a friend. I knew I could trust her and it was the best I could do for Ty. I knew Connors and I would have to step away if he were charged," she explained, her heart beating rapidly. Mike's tone had put her on the defensive. Liz found herself in that mode often as a cop but never with Mike. It was unsettling, to say the least.

"Of course, you can trust her," said Mike. "That's why she called me. Diana's official story is that I'm the one who informed her that Ty needed counsel. At least she can make her own decisions. Diana can do what she believes is right without having to appease 'the system.'"

"What's that supposed to mean?" shouted Liz. "Now you see me as a sellout? I don't have a choice here, Mike. I'm not a defense attorney. I don't argue cases, advocating for persons charged with crimes. We build the best possible case according to the evidence. And I answer to a captain who felt we'd completed our job." Liz felt like a traitor trying to protect her honor. The previous night, the case, tension with her captain, stress of dealing with Powell; it was all taking a toll. Getting shit from Mike was the last straw.

Mike didn't answer with another jibe but he didn't apologize either. He was quiet for a few moments then he cleared his throat as a preamble and asked, "Will Ty be allowed visitors?"

"I can think of no reason why he wouldn't. You can request a visit at the custody desk, but it'll be tomorrow afternoon at the soonest. If you see him, please encourage him to help himself. And maybe Gary would be willing to try," Liz said. "And Mike, when you see him, could you please give Ty my best? I really don't think he deserves this. I would hope you'd know that."

Mike stared at Liz, chewing his lip, but made no reply. His response was a half nod of his head. He waited another moment or two, then said as he stood up, "I need to get back to Avalon. And I want to call Gary at Brooks. They were pretty shaken up over there once they heard Ty was in custody. Gary felt he'd better stay on site. I promised I'd let him know what was happening."

Liz stood up and came around the side of her desk. Parting company from the privacy of her office, it should have been comfortable for them to exchange some small show of affection. But neither of them felt affectionate. Mike was concerned about Ty and wanted a target for his ire. Liz was angry and on the defensive. She knew her voice had raised and she was trying to calm down. She didn't know what to do with her hands so she put them in her jacket pockets. Mike moved closer to the door and further from Liz as if he needed physical space between the two of them. Liz saw the tension in his jaw. She felt tense, awkward, wanted to look him in the eye but hoped to avoid expressing her anger again.

Liz wanted to ask if she'd see him later, but before she could find the words, Mike stopped and turned halfway back in her direction.

"Shit, I almost forgot to tell you. Marjorie is planning on dinner with us tomorrow evening. The timing sucks but that's par for the course," he said sarcastically. "She's at the Hilton with the rest of the trade show folks. She likes the restaurant downstairs so I guess we can meet there. I'd like you to be there but it's up to you."

"Of course, I'll make it if you want me to join you. I said that last night."

"We'll see, but who knows? You may have another big case land before then." His words could have been taken as a slam, but Liz knew it had happened on occasion.

Mike turned and opened the door to Liz's office. "I'll see you later," he said with disappointment dripping from the phrase. He turned and walked away.

She watched as Mike walked down the corridor. The tension between them was like sandpaper on her heart. *I have a job to do and I did it,* she tried to tell herself. Liz was a believer in following evidence to solve cases. But nothing about this case felt solved to her. Too many questions, too much still unknown about Colby and why he was killed in such a brutal attack.

Mike had asked her, "So, you can just step aside?" No, she guessed, in good conscience, she could not. And Mike was right, they both knew that there is no justice without truth. Liz would need to uncover the truth and find justice for Ty, and more important, for Dylan. And she'd have to be very careful doing it because someone dangerous was betting against them.

Chapter Twenty-three

For the first few minutes after Mike left, Liz sat alone in her office, deciding what to do next. *I need to get my perspective. Talk to someone neutral,* she thought, *someone who isn't a cop*. She could barely believe her luck when Kelly Denucci stopped at her office door.

"Hello. Mind if I sit down? If you have a few minutes." Kelly managed outreach services for persons experiencing homelessness. No one knew the community better than she except, of course, the people living on the streets. At the moment, Kelly was very, very pregnant with her first child.

Before Liz could respond with *Yes, yes, sit. How are you doing?* Kelly had managed to lower herself into the nearest chair.

"I saw your office door open and hoped you'd be in here. I need a few minutes before I walk down to the car," Kelly replied. "Pete drove me over."

"You look great. It's nice to see you."

Kelly glanced at Liz with an amused expression. "Thanks, Liz, I appreciate that even though I look like a beach ball and we both know it. Nice to see you too. I've been 'in office' since last month. It's like being on a deserted island."

"When do you start maternity leave?"

"I plan to work until I go into labor. Could be tomorrow, could be two weeks."

"What the hell are you doing here? This is no place for someone in your delicate condition."

"Following up on paperwork, nothing major. We like to keep law enforcement informed about efforts for outreach to people on the street. Then we can say 'we told you so'. I'm trying to tie up loose ends before I'm out for a few weeks—and I don't feel very delicate."

"I was just wishing for someone to talk to other than a cop, and here you are," Liz told Kelly with a half-hearted smile.

Kelly seemed to read Liz's thoughts. "The Colby case, right? Pete and I heard about his death when Connors cancelled their weekly basketball game last night. It's sad. And word got around fast on the street that Ty was held for questioning."

"It's a bad situation, Kelly, certainly for anyone who knew the victim but also for those of us who know Ty." Liz thought about what she could share. "I feel like this case is a runaway. It's hard to explain but nothing about it feels right. I'm not trusting my objectivity. Do you know what I mean?"

"I think I do. People in your life don't like what's happened. You don't like what's happened," she answered, as she waved a hand at Liz's words. "Neither do I, for that matter. I'll never believe Ty could have done this. But I realize you're a cop and you're doing your job and you answer to higher-ups. As for Colby's family, I've met them. His parents, that is. At a civic event for the outreach grant. The father died some time ago. Doug Colby was a nice man. He wasn't condescending. He seemed genuinely interested in the work we do."

Liz remembered her initial conversation with Jayson Abbott. He had mentioned Dylan's father with fondness.

Jayson had shared that there were issues with Erica and upon meeting her, Liz had formed a few impressions of her own.

"I met the mother today. At the morgue. Rough way to be introduced to someone but it wasn't the first time. What do you know about her?"

"Erica? She was civil when we were introduced. She knew I was involved with implementing the grant so she wasn't interested in conversing with me." Kelly stretched her lower back by widening the space between her knees and pushing her abdomen forward, making it seem even more enormous, which was hard for Liz to have imagined. Kelly's hands rubbed her stomach, one hand on each side. Liz watched, fascinated that there was a tiny person inside.

"The woman was very well put together. It was as if she wanted to be appreciated for that alone," said Kelly, thinking back. "Have you ever been introduced to someone and felt that they silently calculated how much you paid for what you were wearing? I'm sorry, I know how that sounds, but displays of wealth annoy me. I've worked for too long with folks who have next to nothing."

Liz nodded in answer to Kelly's question, thinking of how Marjorie always assessed her outfit. But at least it was the woman's job.

"I'm interested in your impressions of Erica because I met her under unusual and very sad circumstances. I'm wondering what she's like typically. Did she seem introverted? Quiet or withdrawn?"

Kelly thought about Liz's question. "Quiet, yes. Subdued, maybe...but more like selective. When we were introduced, she was more interested in Pete than in me. Not a big deal but enough to notice. Pete and I joked about it later after we'd left. I would bet she remembers my husband, but I doubt she'd remember that she and I were even introduced."

Interesting. Kelly had noticed that Dylan's mother had appeared to be more comfortable in the company of men. Liz hadn't taken the woman's behavior personally and she didn't know if it might be significant. But there might be more going on than grieving the loss of a son.

Liz remembered Erica's demeanor and how she had wondered if she'd been on medication. Liz had another thought. "Was it a social event? Was she drinking?"

"It was the kick-off event for the grant. Everyone had a glass in their hand just to be polite. I couldn't tell you if she was drinking a little or a lot. It was a couple of years ago. At the time I didn't know who her son was or that he and I would interact professionally."

"This helps, thanks. There are so many questions about Dylan that I'm still curious. About his family, for one. His work, for another. Is that the only time you were around his parents?"

"The father, yes. I've seen Erica from a distance at other similar occasions but we haven't spoken again. Her father was Bill Adams. Adams was mayor for about ten years when Erica was a young girl. She and Doug had dated since they were teens, I guess."

Bill Adams. Liz certainly did know that name. It was all over City Hall and the Justice Center. William "Bill" Adams had been a bastion of conservative local politics. These were the days before the Cold War ended, when Eastern Europe was still considered an evil empire. And Bill Adams had been Dylan Colby's grandfather.

Liz reviewed in her mind what she knew of Dylan, adding the information she had learned from Kelly: he had been educated in economics and public administration. He had come from a wealthy, politically connected family. Wanting a career in public service, he had wished to experience the field from the ground up. Dylan hoped to gain empirical knowledge instead of relying on his family's connections or his grandfather's legacy. His mother had shared that he was wasting his talent and training. What about Dylan's father? Liz wondered where he might have weighed in on the subject of his son's career. Liz also wondered if it was the politics, the legacy, or the family's affluence that the young man had most rejected.

Liz left her thoughts for later and returned to her conversation with Kelly. "Bill Adams. Sure, I know the name," she said. "Any cop in this city would, but I confess to not knowing much of the man beyond the basics. I'd heard that Erica's father had been mayor but hadn't known it was Bill Adams. I'd also heard that Colby's family may have come from money. Dylan himself had given the impression he wanted to play that down but maybe his mother enjoyed, even exploited the affluence. Did the father, Doug, come from money?"

"I don't know. If I had to guess, I'd say no," Kelly told her. *It shouldn't be too difficult to find information about Doug Colby,* thought Liz.

"Thanks for the information, Kelly. And for listening to me. I won't bore you with my problems any longer. But I have another question on a totally different topic."

"Shoot," said Kelly.

"As it happens, I'm having dinner with Mike and his mother tomorrow evening. You're an old hand at this sort of thing. Any words of wisdom?"

Kelly laughed, her huge belly bobbing up and down at an alarming rate. "That sounds like fun since I know how much you enjoy the woman's company. Give her a break, Liz. After all, she raised a pretty great son."

"Yes, I guess she did," said Liz. She didn't want to mention it to Kelly, but Liz worried how much more strained things might be between she and Mike by dinner tomorrow.

"Besides, maybe you'll enjoy yourself. Have a glass of wine for me." Kelly carefully hoisted herself out of her chair. "I need to get going. I'm moving slowly and if I sit any longer my feet will inflate like balloons."

Chapter Twenty-four

Kelly said she'd say hello to Pete and Liz promised to try to enjoy dinner with Mike and Marjorie. They parted company agreeing that Kelly would be more comfortable when the baby arrived, but she may never sleep again. Kelly closed the door to Liz's office on her way out.

The evidence bag containing the thumb drive Jayson Abbott had given her sat on her desk. He had mentioned that he made sense of some of the data but didn't really know what the files involved. Glancing up from her desk, she assured herself of privacy. Picking up the small plastic envelope, Liz looked at the device with curiosity and started to open the seal. She stopped herself. She considered what the law required her to do with this device and the data that may be stored on it. But could she determine what was required without knowing what it was?

Normal protocol would have been to log the item into evidence, have it analyzed, and turn it over to the District Attorney. But Liz decided that normal protocol had gone out the window on this investigation. She wasn't going to turn the thumb drive over to Powell and his office without knowing what was on it.

Glancing up at the closed door again, her curiosity won out over her better judgment. Liz opened the sealed envelope and removed the thumb drive with a tissue. She removed the cover from the small device in the same fashion and studied it for a moment. *That was useless effort, using a tissue,* she thought. As soon as she broke that seal, it was tainted. *Screw it, I've gone this far.* She inserted it into the USB drive on her computer. Liz could see that there were several files and that they were large. Opening one file, she recognized data that resembled a spreadsheet but looked unlike anything she'd used in her limited experience with financial documents.

A thought occurred to Liz: she'd had the thumb drive in her possession before Ty's arrest so she could explain her actions by saying the analysis had already been in the works. Liz picked up the phone and dialed Miles Carey. The phone rang a third time and Liz thought the call was going to voice mail. Instead she was greeted by a live person stating, "Financial Investigations, Carey."

Liz didn't know Miles all that well. They were about the same age and he had been with the department for a few years. She wasn't sure of his training or background. She rarely saw him in person and when the occasion arose, it had been for conversations in his office with his attention directed intently on a computer screen. None of that mattered to Liz because he was the best at following any money trail. Miles believed that numbers never lie. Nor can they hide from him forever.

"Miles. It's Liz Jordan. I know it's late in the day, but I have something I'd like you to look at."

"Hi, Liz. What have you got?" Miles spoke in a pleasant but clipped voice. Fast, efficient. Liz heard keystrokes in the background.

"A thumb drive. I'm looking at data. A spreadsheet maybe. Lots of accounting codes, I guess. It's a big file. There are a few files on this device and no titles or names that I can decipher."

"Where did it come from?"

"The case Connors picked up last night. The deceased's partner found it and had no idea what it was, but he thought it might be significant."

"Okay. No problem. When do you need it?"

"Soon, of course. And Miles, I should tell you there's already been an arrest made. The victim worked as a benefits processor for the county."

"Okay...do you have a feel for what this is? Is this personal data or public?" Liz could hear the interest in Miles' question.

"The partner works in finance so he's familiar. He thought it looked public."

"If it's regarding public funds, the data is subject to disclosure. Meaning it's already out there somewhere. They're on a thumb drive, huh?"

"Yes," Liz answered.

"That's curious; an odd way to store them," said Miles.

"Why is that odd?" Liz asked him.

"Well, there's no need. If these are public, they're on a secure server, accessible to anyone authorized whenever they need them. And storing on a thumb drive is not especially safe. Thumb drives can be damaged, lost. If it's important data, why risk it? I'll reserve judgment, but my guess is it's a copy."

"Okay. Makes sense."

"Upload the files to the department server. I'll access them there. Name the files 'Jordan' and number them. I'll find them by date. Keep the device in a safe place, Liz, but the files, whatever they are, will already be safer after you upload."

"Great. Thanks, Miles. And if anyone is interested, I put you onto this earlier today, okay?"

Miles didn't respond for a few moments, then he said, "I can say we talked earlier, in person. I'd have no idea when you put it on the server for me. Could have been anytime. Does that work for you?"

"That works. Thanks, Miles. Get back to me when you can."

"Yep." And with that, Miles and Liz ended their call.

Liz uploaded the files from the thumb drive to the department server as Miles had requested. She noted the time stamp but it was out of her control. She removed the device from the drive and studied it as she held it in her hand. Liz placed the cap back on the thumb drive and returned it to the evidence envelope. She placed it in the bottom drawer of her desk, locking the drawer.

Connors, thought Liz. *I need to connect with him.* Had Connors found anything pertinent in Colby's work correspondence? There must be a reason why his office equipment had been damaged. Someone wanted to destroy evidence. Liz hadn't exactly destroyed evidence, but the irony didn't escape her. But whoever had damaged the equipment in Colby's office wanted to hide something. Liz hoped they hadn't been successful.

On the other side of the corridor from Liz's office was a large, open area that housed the squad room, the workspace for the detectives. It was handy that Liz could see from her office which detectives were in-house. Looking across the corridor now she saw only a few members of the team, which was unusual. She headed out of her office to look for Connors. She wasn't sure where he was, but Liz was tired of sitting at her desk so she welcomed a reason to get up and walk around. Liz asked the detectives, busy at their desks, but they hadn't seen Connors either.

Walking back to the kitchen where the coffee maker was kept, she considered having a cup. But coffee didn't sound appealing. That was unusual, too. Liz spent a few minutes completing mindless tasks as a sort of therapy. She emptied the dregs from an old pot of coffee and cleaned the glass decanter. She straightened a few items in the cupboard and wiped down the countertop. Better now, she told herself. Now to find Connors. As she turned around, Connors entered the kitchen.

"Lieutenant, you're looking for me? I had a couple of messages to follow up on when I got back from booking." Connors sounded normal but the stressful events of the day had taken their toll on the young detective. His color was bad, like he'd eaten something that hadn't agreed with him. His hair looked unkempt and he needed a shave.

"I wanted to see how you were doing, Connors. And I wanted to ask how it went in booking."

"It went well, considering I arrested someone I know and respect. Ty was more worried about me. He seems to think the whole thing will resolve itself with no effort on his part." Connors sat down at the break room table. "When I left to head back here, he was processed and Diana Harrison was waiting to talk to him."

"Good," Liz answered, nodding, as she pulled a chair out for herself and sat down. "I assumed that he and Diana would talk soon. Ty will likely be arraigned tomorrow. I doubt he'll be released on bail."

Connors was tired and keyed up at the same time. He ran his hands over his head, rubbing his buzz cut for the lack of anything else to do.

"This is over for us then? We leave it to the attorneys now and wait until we're called to testify? This all seems rushed, Lieutenant. Too many questions unanswered."

Checking to see that the two of them were alone, Liz assured him she felt the same way. "But there are other cases to work, too. And I can't keep you out of rotation for taking new calls. We're accountable for how we spend our time."

"Right, Lieutenant. I know."

"I'm looking into a few of those questions, Connors, but I have to be careful. I've already been put in my place on this case, by Miller himself." Liz continued, speaking with a direct tone. "But to be honest, I don't like the way Powell has approached it. He went over our heads and had a conversation with Miller before we could finish our investigation. I've not known him to do that before. Why now? Why this case?"

"I don't know. I don't get it," said Connors, shaking his head.

"Miles is looking into the data on the storage device that Abbott found. And I learned some interesting details about the Colby family by talking to Kelly." Liz paused for a moment, then added, as explanation, "She happened to stop by. She's looking pretty uncomfortable."

Connors stopped and took a deep breath, the relief of a different topic registered on his face. “I haven’t seen her in a week or so, but Pete’s excited. You remember he teaches second grade.” Connors rubbed his face. When his hands moved away, he revealed a grin. “His students gave him a ‘new daddy’ party.”

They enjoyed the respite of talking about Kelly and Pete’s expected baby for another minute before Liz brought them back to the reality of the Colby case.

“Connors, do we know anything yet about Dylan’s current workload? Was there anything pertinent on his computer?”

“I talked to IT. They’ve had his office equipment since last night. Anything on the hard drive was lost, but in time, they can tell us everything he had accessed online within the last week or so. The server stores that info. They can also retrieve any emails he may have sent.”

“Okay, Good. We’ll have to wait and hope there’s something useful. You should head home and get some rest. We can both keep our ears to the ground on this tomorrow. Like I said, there is much we don’t know.” Liz checked for privacy once more, then added, “And I want to know why you and I are the only ones who have noticed.”

“Okay, Lieutenant. Thanks, and I’ll see you in the morning.”

When she returned to her office, Liz thought about what Kelly had to say, and she was curious about Dylan’s father, Doug. Turning to the computer, Liz googled Doug Colby. She found several men by that name in various places so she narrowed the search to Columbia City, Washington. There were three references to the man.

The first was an obituary dated a couple of years earlier for Douglas M. Colby. A native of Columbia City, he had attended Green Mountain High School, east of the city, where he'd been active in student government and sports. Doug Colby was an alumnus of Lewis and Clark College. He had been a partner in a local development firm and supported various civic organizations. He was survived by his wife, Erica Adams Colby and son, Dylan, of Columbia City.

Second was a reference to a website for The Adams Company, a development firm of which Doug Colby had been a managing partner. So, Dylan's father had managed a company named for his wife's family. And the family had been involved in politics as well as in developing local properties. Their son had been educated in finance and public administration but had resisted joining the family business to gain experience in social services. Interesting. Perusing the company's website further, Liz noted that Erica was a member of the Board of Directors.

The last reference that came up in the Google search for Doug Colby led to a series of local newspaper articles detailing business information pertaining to The Adams Company. The articles were dated over the past decade and included information about the establishment of a corporation, the ownership divisions by percentage, and something about a corporate division that had impacted the way their business was handled.

Most of the financial jargon was way out of Liz's area of expertise but she was able to discern that there were no indications of any malfeasance. The business dealings had been covered by the financial desk of the local paper and the documents were public. Liz noted the name of the reporter who had written the articles. John Morrissey. She thought she recognized the name although she didn't read the financial pages too often. She sent the website's link and an email to Miles, asking that he review the articles about The Adams Company.

Liz's cell phone rang. It was Diana calling. As anxious as Liz was to hear from the attorney, she knew she couldn't expect the news to be good. Liz thought of Ty and the charge against him and felt an instant weight in the pit of her stomach.

"Diana, I was hoping to hear from you. What's happening over there?" asked Liz, dreading the reply.

"Things are moving along, I guess you'd say. How soon are you leaving for the day? I want to talk but not at your office."

Liz checked the time. It was later than she'd thought. She was glad Connors had gone home. "I can leave soon. Where do you want to meet?"

"How about your place? I'm tired of public places and it will be easier to talk. I'd like to talk to Mike too, if he's around."

"My place it is. The kids will like seeing you." She waited a moment, then Liz told Diana. "I don't know if we'll see Mike. It may just be us."

"Okay, I can find him later. I'll bring food. See you soon," said Diana as she hung up.

On impulse, Liz called Mike. He hadn't mentioned his plans for the evening and she wanted to check in because normally he would be at her house. The call went to voice mail.

"It's me, Mike. I'm heading home. Diana is coming over. She asked to talk but didn't want to meet here. I'm hoping you'll join us. If we don't see you, give me a call later, okay? And let me know what time for dinner tomorrow. Bye."

It was a friendly message, she told herself, but no "love you," as she usually ended her calls.

Entering her apartment, Eddie and Little Kurt met her at the door, meowing and circling her ankles. "Hey, guys. I know you're ready for food, too." She bent to pet the cats, comforted by the softness of their fur.

Liz stood and surveyed the third-floor apartment where she made her home. She wasn't much for interior design, but she had attempted to make her home comfortable. The boring brown of the sofa was highlighted by bright red throw pillows. Framed prints on her walls were few, small, and subtle, each with special meaning. The tall scratching post stood near the sliding glass door with cat toys strewn nearby. The place felt oddly quiet and empty because Mike wasn't there and she realized she was feeling sorry for herself.

Liz put fresh food and water out for the cats. She locked her weapon in the gun safe and changed into an old, comfy tee shirt and sweats. Diana would be in her work clothes which sounded uncomfortable, but it couldn't be helped.

Thinking about the Colby case, her thoughts settled on Erica. The woman had come from privilege, the daughter of a former mayor. She had married a young man she'd known since high school and they'd had a son together. Erica must be in her mid-forties, making her ten or so years older than Liz. There was a similar age gap between Mike and Ty. They did not have a traditional kind of friendship but the men knew and respected each other. Besides, what's more traditional than friendship, of any sort? Mike and Ty could have open, lengthy conversations. They'd had similar struggles with sobriety. And each was committed to advocacy for folks in need of help.

Under what circumstances could Liz and Erica have been friends? What commonality could have brought them together? Liz didn't come from an affluent family, but like Erica's father, her parents had been in public service. Liz's mother and father had been public school teachers. Retired now, her parents still lived in the town where they had worked and raised their family. Her mother occasionally substituted for teachers on leave.

They had raised Liz to respect knowledge, honesty, and responsibility. Material possessions were considered temporal and you couldn't judge someone by where they lived, where they worshipped, or what they wore. A person's actions and the way they treated others were more important gauges of character. What Liz had learned of Erica said she had been brought up with importance placed on different things.

There were many reasons why the two women may not have been friends but common ground had brought them together, nonetheless. Their lives had intersected due to the tragic death of Erica's son at the hands of another. And Liz was committed to finding the person or persons responsible. She was convinced that it was someone other than Ty.

Liz turned on music and was greeted by Nirvana's "Come as You Are." The song made her think of Mike. It was one of his favorites and it reminded Liz of the tension between them. She pressed the advance button to play the next CD in rotation. She heard the first few bars of "And it Stoned Me" by Van Morrison and decided it better fit her mood.

Pouring a glass of water for herself, she then placed a second glass on the countertop, ready for Diana. She checked that beer glasses already were chilled in the freezer and, as always, they were. There was a decent bottle of red, if Diana preferred wine tonight, but it was unlikely. Liz would bet that the bottles of cold, Dead Guy Ale in the fridge would be her choice.

Liz picked up her water glass and carried it into the small living room. Looking out the sliding glass door, she realized the weather had been dry most of the day. She decided to leave the door open and enjoy some fresh air, careful to close the screen so as not to tempt the kids to wander out. The track and football field below her balcony were vacant of activity.

She hadn't heard from Mike and was tempted to call him again. She wanted to speak with him. She didn't like the way they had left things at her office. Secretly, Liz wished that he would call and apologize for acting like she'd betrayed Ty simply by doing her job but she was too irritated to admit that this was her feeling, as well.

Liz heard a knock and stepped over to open the door for Diana. As she opened the door, she was surprised to see Mike standing there.

"Hey," she said. She was so relieved to see him that she could have cried but she was too stubborn to act like it or to tell Mike that that was how she felt. "I left you a message. Didn't want you to worry about the kids since I was coming home. How are you?"

"I'm fine. I saw the call but I didn't check the message. I should have, I guess. I wasn't sure when you'd be home and I usually feed the kids in the evening. I came by to check on them, then I saw your car downstairs." Mike bent over to pick up Eddie as the cat curled himself around Mike's ankles. He carried Eddie to the sofa and sat down.

Liz reluctantly joined them on the sofa. Little Kurt found her lap. She sat with her feet tucked under her legs, feeling self-conscious.

"Diana is coming over. She wants to talk and didn't want to meet out somewhere. You should stay and hear what she has to say. She's bringing food. I'm sure there will be plenty."

"Thanks, maybe. I'd like to know how Ty is doing, hear Diana's take on all this before I try to see him tomorrow. He's not as tough as you'd think. I'm worried."

"Well, I'd like it if you were here. Diana wants to talk to you anyway. And to be honest, I'm not happy about the conversation we had in my office. Maybe we can clear the air later."

Mike didn't say a word for a minute. He stroked Eddie's fur. Liz wasn't sure he had heard what she said. Without looking at her, he responded, "That not a good idea, Liz. I think it best if we agree to not talk about it."

"How can we not talk about it? You all but said I was responsible for Ty's arrest. That stung, Mike."

"You're not responsible, but the system is, Liz."

"I get that. Really, I do. I consider Ty a friend and I'm worried about him too." Liz could feel the ire rising as she spoke. "It can be hard to have confidence in the justice system when someone you know is suspected of a crime. As it's hard to wait for justice when someone you know has been victimized. We have to believe that the system will prevail in their favor."

"You are a part of that system. You want me to understand but I can't do that."

Liz was stunned. The surprise turned to anger and sarcasm. Liz crossed her arms. "You're holding me responsible for Ty's arrest? It must feel great to work in a profession that's flawless. I suppose if there's a family sleeping in their car tonight, we can blame you?"

"That's a ridiculous comparison. We do the best we can, but we can't help everyone.

"Then why can't you understand that we're doing our best?

"Because when we come up short it's due to a lack of funding. Ty's arrest feels like a hushed-up, rushed-up, wrap."

She wanted to tell Mike that she had the same feeling, but before Liz could respond, there was a knock at her door. She knew it was Diana. The timing of things lately had been terrible and it was starting to get on Liz's nerves. She moved

Little Kurt from her lap and stood up, stepped toward to the door but waited to open it.

"I'm sorry about the timing here. I want us to talk this out but you're probably right, that we won't resolve anything. But I want you to stay. Hear what Diana has to say. Maybe it will help. Have some food."

Mike didn't say anything. Liz had one hand on the doorknob. She held her other hand out palm up, indicating that she was waited for a response. Mike was irritated but nodded his head in agreement.

Chapter Twenty-five

Liz opened the door for Diana, who carried a large pizza box on one outstretched hand and held a small bag at her side in the other.

"Sorry it took me so long. They were swamped. I got a large New York-style that I think is still hot and a Caesar salad." She looked in Mike's direction and said, "Oh, good. You're here. One less phone call for me to make. I need your input."

"Hey, Diana. Thanks for picking up dinner. What do we owe you?" Mike asked as he removed Eddie from his lap and helped Diana with the carry-out.

"You owe me nothing except one of the beers I'm hoping Liz has in the refrigerator."

"I'll get one for each of you," he said as he placed the pizza on the breakfast bar then walked toward the kitchen.

Diana took a seat at the bar and flipped open the cardboard lid revealing the New York-style pie. Taking the salad out of the bag, she opened that container, as well.

"Dinner is ready. Let's eat," she said.

Diana had traded her suit jacket for a fleece pullover. Her pencil skirt had been replaced with exercise pants and she'd switched out her heels and hose for running shoes and socks.

"You look comfy. Did you hurry home to change?" Liz asked her as she placed plates, forks, and napkins on the bar.

Diana shook her head. "I keep clothes in the office in case I can get in a walk or a trip to the gym. Or an impromptu pizza dinner with you."

Liz's tiny place had no dining area other than the little breakfast bar for two. Mike insisted that Diana and Liz sit at the bar. He stood on the other side of the bar in the kitchen where he was able to face them. They were glad for the food but their minds were not on the meal.

"I spent an hour with Ty after booking," Diana began. "He wanted you to know that he's doing okay and he's allowed me to share some details with you, 'Whatever you think is appropriate,' he said. He's asked me to try to arrange visiting privileges for you, Mike, and for Gary, his friend from Brooks House." Diana paused for a sip of beer. "That should be easy enough. Connors hung around the booking area long enough to talk to several of the custody officers. He left word for them to call him immediately if Ty has any problem with anyone. But Connors didn't want Ty informed of that."

"No, he wouldn't," reasoned Liz, munching on salad. "Better for the officers, for Ty, and for Connors, too."

"I'm also requesting that the required health evaluation be completed by a physician of Ty's choosing from the VA," continued Diana. "Ty says he's familiar with a doctor there and I have the call in already." Liz and Mike looked at each other, nodded their approval.

"This is good to hear, Diana," Mike shared with her. "Like I told Liz earlier, he's not as tough as you might think. I'm glad to know Ty has you to advocate for him."

"Anyone under arrest is entitled to a legal advocate. And the man seems pretty tough to me," responded Diana, before she took a bite of pizza.

"It will be good for Mike and Gary to be around. They can monitor how he's handling being inside," mentioned Liz, to which Mike and Diana agreed.

The pizza and salad quickly disappeared. They moved over to the living room. Liz and Diana sat on the sofa while Mike found a spot on the floor. Each of the women had opened another Dead Guy Ale, Mike sticking with his water.

"Here's where 'we', meaning Ty and myself as his legal representative, need your help," Diana was clearly speaking to both Mike and Liz, alternating her focus. "Ty will be arraigned tomorrow morning. It would be good to see friends and community people there. As for you Liz, this is an odd situation. You're responsible for the investigation and you supervise Connors, the arresting detective. You and Connors would normally attend arraignments in support of the prosecution."

Mike bristled, attempting to hide his disdain by returning to the bar to clear away dishes and discard trash from their meal. Liz glanced his way but quickly sighed and returned to look at Diana. The attorney either didn't notice the tension or had decided it wasn't her business.

"That's true," she said, "normally, an arraignment is a confirmation that we've done our job and apprehended a suspect. I'd rather not attend, to be honest. My presence isn't necessary. And even as the arresting detective, Connors wouldn't be required to attend until some point in the future." Liz alluded to the idea that Connors may have to testify.

"That's what I'm saying, Liz. Professionally, if you attend in support of the accused, the department will hang you out to dry. If you don't attend, the press, the public, certainly the ADA's office will notice and wonder why. You can claim to be dealing with other pressing matters, or you don't have to comment at all." Diana took the opportunity to pause for effect. "Your statement may be more profound if you and Connors are not in attendance. Neither of you are vested in the prosecution's case here. Connors has made that clear. And that's why you called me earlier, isn't it?"

Liz nodded at Diana's words. She looked at Mike, hoping he realized that she was trying to support Ty. He wasn't making eye contact and his perception of things was hard to decipher.

"And I agreed to keep that detail between us," Diana promised her, once again.

"I appreciate it," responded Liz, "and I still believe it was the right thing to do."

"It was, Liz. Ty accepted my counsel so he agreed with you, as well. Okay, let's look at the points in evidence. Ty was seen at Colby's office. The two men knew each other. Ty admits to that." Diana held up one finger, reviewing what she knew with precision. "It's been alleged that Ty was seen in the vicinity." The second point ticked off with a second finger. "Ty was trained by the military to kill in the way Colby died. Jack and his team will use that fact, I guarantee it." Diana tapped on a third finger. Then she held her hands out in front of her, holding up both pointed index fingers. "But the biggest problem for Ty is he can't or won't prove that he wasn't there."

Diana turned to Mike. "That brings me to an urgent request of you." Diana spoke with precise words and a succinct manner, her hands out before her in supplication. "I suggest you do everything you can to convince Ty to help himself. He seems to think he can wait this charge out without being more forthcoming. I disagree. I've reviewed the evidence that supported his arrest. Ty needs an alibi for the time of Colby's murder. I've told him how I see things. I sense that he understands but not to the point of wavering. He needs to hear it from people he's placed his trust in for a long time. Like you."

Mike listened to what Diana said. Then he studied his water glass for a moment before he drained the glass of its contents. "If it comes to it, he'll reconsider without any input from me or anyone else," Mike assured them. "He's stubborn but he's not a fool. He won't risk his freedom."

It occurred to Liz that Powell had made a similar statement about Ty after he and Liz had observed the interview. That Ty had his troubles, but he wasn't a fool or something to that effect. It was eerie hearing Mike use nearly the same phrase, but she wasn't going to mention it.

"You know the man better than I and I hope you're correct. And there's one other thing I want you to know," Diana said. "I suggested to Ty, and he has agreed, to a mental health evaluation."

"A psych eval?" asked Mike. He was surprised by the idea and his response was thick with suspicion. "Why? Do you think he's unstable? Ty agreed to this?"

"Yes, Ty agreed," she assured him. "And actually, I think he's stable and rational." Diana took the time to address Mike's suspicions calmly and carefully, wanting him to understand. "I know of several psychologists we could enlist but Ty wanted to go a different route. There's a licensed counselor he knows and trusts who leads recovery meetings. I've got a call in to him."

"As for Ty's stability, "Diana continued, "I also believe he's compassionate, too compassionate to have committed this crime. It will be strategic to have a mental health professional attest to that. A mental health evaluation is for Ty's protection, too. I want to know if this ordeal has had an adverse effect on him. The system owes him that much."

"Yes, it does," said Liz, speaking her mind before Mike could weigh in.

Mike and Liz looked at one another. Finally, it was Mike who spoke up. "I see your point, Diana. If Ty agrees, it could help him in the long run. And you're right. The system definitely owes him that much."

Liz had been wrestling with herself whether to share about the files on the thumb drive that she had asked Miles to analyze. Then she thought of the network information from Colby's computer, and the details about the Colby family. She opted to be vague in case it all proved to be nothing.

"There are a few details that Connors and I are waiting to hear back about, items from the scene and from Colby's home. Anything discovered will be added to the case evidence." Liz turned to Diana. "You and the ADA would be notified, but I can try to give you a heads up. If anything comes out of it, let's hope it's good news."

"Sounds good, Liz," she said. Diana checked the time on the smart watch she always wore. "Well, boys and girls, we've had enough fun for one evening. I should get out of here. I want to be ready for tomorrow morning." Diana stood up. She started to carry her empty beer glass into the kitchen.

Liz stopped her. "Let me take that for you, Diana. You've done enough," Liz told her as she took the glass from Diana and stepped toward her kitchen. "Dinner was great. Stop by anytime," she joked.

"It beats cooking after a day like this, Liz. Thanks for letting me camp here for the evening. I needed to run things by the two of you and we needed privacy and comfort." Diana gathered up her things and said goodnight. Mike and Liz wished her good luck in the morning.

Mike was lying on his back on the living room floor with Eddie and Little Kurt circling around his head and jumping over his chest. His only movement was his right hand, slowly stroking fur. He had started the music again and Liz could hear the notes of a familiar song as she did a quick survey of the kitchen. Mike had taken care of most of the cleaning up, as he usually did.

Liz joined him in the living room. She sat on her sofa and hugged a throw pillow, feet on the ottoman, soothed by the music of Morrison's "Moondance." Liz had been listening to Morrison since she'd been a child in her parent's home and sometimes no other artist fit the bill.

"Thanks for starting the music again. It's one of my favorites, you know."

"Yep, I know. I decided it's not a good night for anything too raucous," he answered, rolling onto one side so he could see her as they talked.

"I'm glad you stayed to talk to Diana. She has Ty's trust. And it sounds like she believes him. Do you think you can convince him to tell Diana who he was meeting yesterday?"

"I don't know, Liz. I'll talk with him but I won't press him to reveal something he feels strongly about keeping private. That's why we're friends. I respect him."

"Mike, we're talking about his life. His freedom. Who is worth that?"

"Only Ty can answer that question, Liz."

They listened to Morrison together for a few minutes, Mike playing with Eddie and Little Kurt. Finally, Liz tentatively asked a question that had been on her mind.

"Did it bother you that Diana and I were drinking beer?"

"Nope," he said rolling back onto his back. "It's been a long time. It doesn't even look appealing anymore," he lied. Truth was, it always looked appealing but he wasn't going to confess that to Liz. Sometimes he thought about going to meetings again, on a regular basis, not just on his anniversary dates.

In Mike's experience, most people assume that folks in recovery attend meetings on anniversary dates for the congratulations. The truth is anniversary dates can trigger a drink or drug use. Some folks either test themselves or they feel the urge because the drink or the drug is heavy on their mind that day. The memories can create a "slippery spot" or they serve to steel the resolve to stay sober. Mike had felt it himself and had seen it happen with others in both ways.

It was hard to explain to anyone who hadn't been through it. But this was Liz's home and he still considered himself a guest here. "You didn't even know I was going to be here until I showed up. I don't want you to adjust what you want to do because I'm here."

"Well, would you tell me if it was an issue for you?" Liz asked.

"Yes, probably," Mike told her. But he doubted that he would.

"So, what's the plan for tomorrow with your Mom? What time should I meet the two of you?" she asked Mike, as Little Kurt, wandered over to the sofa to demand her attention.

"About six o'clock. When I suggested that we'd meet her at the restaurant at her hotel, she insisted I pick a local place. 'Somewhere you and Liz go', she said. I hated to tell her that we don't eat out much and when we do, it's burgers at Callahan's, which she would hate."

"How about UnderBar? You know, the place that's modeled after a thirties speakeasy," suggested Liz. "The food is good. It's comfortable. And it's fun. I think she'd like it."

"UnderBar, it is. I'll see if they'll reserve a table for three. And please feel free to have a drink with Marjorie. It'll be fine," he said, knowing his mother would order a cocktail anyway.

"Great. And let me call," Liz told him. "I know the owners, Kurt and Kendra. I'm sure they'll save us a table."

"Dinner with a cop in a speakeasy. Sounds like a fun time," he laughed as he slowly climbed up from the floor. "I have to go, Liz. I need to run in the morning. I'll try to catch Gary tonight. Maybe he can attend Ty's arraignment with me if he can get away from Brooks."

"Okay," she said, "but you know I want you to stay. The boys do, too."

"Thanks, but let's talk after the arraignment." Mike grabbed both of her hands, pulled Liz up off the sofa, and kissed her. "And I'll see you at six at UnderBar with Marjorie in tow."

It has started to rain lightly. Mike stepped outside into a drizzly night and said goodbye. Liz locked the door behind him. She had hoped he would stay but wasn't surprised that he felt the need to go. It had been a rough day and a few minutes of solitude to collect her thoughts would do her good. Solitude, that was, except for her cats. Van started singing "These Dreams of You," and as she listened, Liz really wished Mike had stayed.

She turned off the music, shut down the lights, and she and the boys went to bed.

Chapter Twenty-six

When Mike left Liz's, he sat in his car for a few minutes, thinking. He wanted to talk to Gary. The man might be at home and Mike would hate to bother him. But if Gary knew it was about Ty, he'd want to be bothered. Mike could go home and call Gary, have a conversation, and go to bed at a decent hour. But the static electricity in his head told him sleep would be a hard sell. Mike wanted to talk to Gary in person and he wanted to know how the guys at Brooks were handling things.

Pulling out his phone, he punched in the number to Gary's cell. No answer. Instead of leaving a message, he decided to try Brooks House. After a few rings, the call was answered and Mike was greeted by the voice of Gary's assistant.

"Brooks House. This is Wyatt."

"Wyatt. It's Mike Dwyer. Is Gary around?"

"He's here. It's been a busy evening. Lots of questions about Ty. Lots of confusion. What can I do for you, Mike?" Wyatt was busy. Mike could hear noise in the background, but Wyatt still managed to sound genuine.

"Will Gary be there for another half hour? I want to catch him before he leaves. I could be there in just a few minutes."

"Come on down, Mike. I'll tell him you're on your way."

It was a short drive to Brooks House from Liz's, shorter than it would have been from Mike's place, and he arrived within minutes. There were benches out in front of the shelter and as usual by this time of the evening, the benches were full of guys sitting and waiting for beds. When the weather was bad and the beds were all taken, they could sleep in the dining hall. It was hard on the older men but it was better than sleeping outside, although some of the guys would do that anyway.

As Mike walked up to the entrance, he knew several of the men who were waiting and they said hello or waved to him. Most held paper coffee cups in one hand and unlit cigarettes in the other. If they wanted to smoke, they had move down the block, away from the entrance. But doing so would lose them their place in line.

Heading inside, Mike could make out the unmistakable voice of Sam Cooke belting out, "Bring it on Home to Me." He approached the office on the left. He saw Wyatt leaning over a table, going over paperwork with an older man who was struggling to hear him. When he saw Mike, he offered him his hand, and said loudly, "Excuse me for just a second, Rollie."

"Hey, Wyatt," said Mike, as he shook his hand. Mike looked at the older man whom Wyatt was helping and said, "Sorry to interrupt," but the fellow just nodded his head and Mike doubted that the man realized he'd spoken to him.

"How are you, Mike? Gary's in the dining room. He said to come on in. He'll be free in a few minutes." Wyatt looked at Mike a bit more closely and asked him, "So, really. How are you doing?"

The question made Mike wonder if the static he felt might be visible on his face. He tried to relax and answered, "I'm doing all right. Thanks. I'll let you get back to what you're doing."

Man, but Sam could sing, Mike thought. Gary didn't have music on at the shelter every evening. Too many memories for some of the guys, too many regrets. Often the regrets led to disagreements, even altercations. But on some occasions, Gary felt the need for tunes was worth the risk.

Mike found Gary seated at one of the cafeteria-style tables with a group of men, several of whom Mike knew he had met before. They were each listening intently while one of the men, whom Mike thought was named Merlin, was speaking.

"It just ain't right, man. You gonna take the time to go to meetings and then lie about it? Nah, nah. If a man's messed up, he's messed up. If he's clean, then he's clean."

"Anyone's welcome to attend a meeting depending on their own needs and choices," Gary said. "And folks are free not to attend meetings, unless it's required for some reason. It's a matter of conscience."

"I hear you. I know it. But we choose what we share about ourselves. I respect a man for keeping what he knows of another man's business to himself. That's all I'm saying." Heads at the table were nodding in agreement with Merlin's words.

Mike thought the conversation sounded like a discussion of community rules for twelve-step meetings, but as he had just arrived and had not been part of the conversation, he wanted to be respectful and hung back. Gary saw Mike and waved him over. "Guys, I appreciate your thoughts. Thanks for sharing. I need to talk to Mike before I call it a night. Take care and I'll see you another time."

After a few fist bumps and high-fives, Gary extricated himself from the group. "Let's talk in the office," he told Mike. "There's still coffee, if you want."

"Thanks, but it's too late for me. I won't keep you long. I know it's been a long, damn day."

They walked back up to the front of the building. Wyatt was still trying his best to talk with Rollie, who couldn't hear him. Wyatt managed to sound caring and patient which was remarkable, considering that he was practically shouting. Mike followed Gary into the office and sat down. Gary took his seat behind the huge, steel desk that resembled a battleship.

"Wyatt is trying to help Rollie with paperwork to get him a hearing aid. It's enough that the poor dude can't hear but his glasses are broken so he can't read either. One thing at a time, right, man? At least we've got him off the street for a few nights."

"Yes, I agree. One thing at a time. Anyway, Gary, I wanted to talk to you before tomorrow. I had a conversation with Diana Harrison earlier. She expects Ty's arraignment will be in the morning. She thinks it will help if we can be there as a show of support. Any way you can make it?"

"Absolutely. I'll be there," answered Gary with conviction. "Any word on how he's doing?"

"Sounds like he's okay. There are some requests for services for him to ensure he's looked after. Diana has requested that you and I be able to visit him as soon as possible. She also wants us to try to reason with him about coming up with an alibi."

"I hope it doesn't come to that, Mike. Ty's a reasonable person but he will do what he feels he has to do. Especially now that the political landscape is redefining itself."

"Political landscape? What does that mean, Gary?"

"I take it you haven't seen any local news this evening. Am I right, my friend?"

"No, I haven't. I was meeting with Diana and Liz. What's up?"

Gary reached for his smartphone, scrolled a bit, and found what he was looking for. He handed the phone to Mike.

"You need to see this. Just hit play." Gary had cued up a news video.

Mike focused on the small screen and pressed the play button. The opening frames were of Assistant District Attorney Jackson Powell at a podium.

"Are you kidding me? Please tell me the asshole didn't hold a press conference about Ty's arrest."

"Not specifically. It's worse than that, Mike. He's announced he's running for mayor. He intends to run on a 'Tough on Crime' platform. And since he blames what he calls 'the homeless element' for the crime rate, he wants the folks off our streets. I guess no one's told Powell that they're their streets, too."

Mike stared at Gary, not wanting to believe what he was hearing. He kept his ear close to city and county politics so he usually knew which way the wind was blowing. His job and the services it provided had survived a change in course many times. But he knew this couldn't be good for Ty's case.

Mike returned his focus to the screen of Gary's phone just in time to hear Powell's pitch:

"Columbia City has been plagued for long enough by people who refuse to help themselves, people looking for handouts, who survive by working the system. Business owners in the downtown area are forced to move their stores and offices elsewhere because they can't ensure their clients and customers won't be accosted. The homeless element in our city is out of control and has served to drive our crime rate through the roof. Our social service workers, professionals trying to help these people, are no longer safe in their own offices after hours. One young man was recently attacked and killed. My name is Jackson Powell and I say enough is enough. With the support of many of the concerned citizens of Columbia City, I'm announcing my intent to be your next mayor and I will work to change the deplorable situation on our streets. Thank you."

"The son of a bitch is using the Colby case as a springboard for a mayoral bid," Gary said as he shook his head in disgust.

"And what could be better than seeing that a homeless man is charged with the crime?" Mike said, as he rubbed his hands over his eyes like he wanted it all to stop. "He'll have every reactionary idiot jumping aboard."

This was bad news for the homeless community in general, but especially for Ty. The timing was bad and Mike knew it. The static electricity in his brain had not abated. Mike asked Gary to send the news link to his phone. He didn't want to wake Liz with this sorry turn of events but she would want to know of it in the morning.

The two men shared their outrage over Powell's announcement for a few more minutes. They agreed that his candidacy was bad enough but the rhetoric he'd chosen was just plain mean. They were both exhausted and decided to try and get some rest. They agreed to meet up in the morning to be present when Ty was arraigned, then they said goodnight.

No men sat on the benches outside Brooks when Mike left. They'd either been assigned a place to sleep at Brooks or had moved on to another option. Or maybe no option at all. Mike walked through light rain to his car. After he climbed in, he started the engine and blasted the defroster. Mike sent the news link to Liz's phone. He glanced down the block and saw the flashing neon sign outside Mo's, a tavern that had been in operation for a long time. The light was distorted by the rain and the intermittent wipers on the windshield.

Mike stared at the sign for a minute or two. He remembered what it looked like inside the place, what it smelled like. The electricity was still there and it was making him sick to his stomach. He gripped the steering wheel with both hands, took a deep breath and exhaled. He dropped the car into gear, signaled, pulled out onto the street and drove himself home.

Chapter Twenty-seven

Getting ready for work the next morning, Liz gave extra thought and effort to the routine. She wanted to be presentable for dinner that evening with Mike and Marjorie. She wouldn't make it home to change unless doing so was absolutely necessary. It wasn't her style. To her mind that would be a waste of time and effort. She selected a light brown jacket with trousers, a black blouse, and had even added a necklace with an amber stone. Liz told herself she was going the extra half-mile for herself, not for Marjorie. But she knew it wasn't the truth.

After putting extra food and water out for the boys, she gave them each a cuddle and was about to head out. She wanted to call Mike to say, "Good morning." He was probably out for a run. It wouldn't be unusual if he didn't pick up, but the recent strain between them had her overthinking and was making her defensive. She had decided against making the call when she saw she had a message from Mike. She opened the text and realized it was a video link. Why would Mike be sending her a link?

It took Liz about ten seconds to understand why.

"My name is Jackson Powell and I say enough is enough. With the support of many of the concerned citizens of Columbia City, I'm announcing my intent to be your next mayor..."

What a smug, arrogant asshole! He had this in the pipeline when he went over Liz's head and talked to Miller. Liz watched the video a second time. She was no less angry but she listened more closely because she was less stunned.

No wonder he was so delighted after the observation of Ty's interview. He figured Ty's arrest would be icing on his cake. What a shit bag.

Liz thought about forwarding the video to Connors but she doubted he had missed the news. She planned on speaking to Miller as soon as she could arrange it. She wanted to know if her captain had known this announcement was coming prior to Ty's arrest. She wanted to believe he didn't and that he was as angry as she was. But she wasn't sure of it.

Liz's phone rang. It was Diana.

"Have you seen this news?" Diana shouted when Liz answered.

"Yes, just now. What's this going to mean for Ty, Diana? Can Jack get away with the timing on this?"

"Oh, I've no doubt that the timing is exactly how he wanted it. How it plays out will depend on the judge. This could go well for Ty, if the judge wants another ADA assigned. We'll know more after arraignment."

"And speaking of the arraignment, I'm going to be there. I want to hear this son of a bitch try to turn the tragedy of a young man's death to benefit his own political gain."

"Well, I can't say I blame you. I won't attempt to draw attention to you directly, Liz, but I plan to vigorously advocate for my client."

"Do what you have to, Diana. Don't worry about me. It's my choice. Do what's best for Ty. We'll talk later."

Liz ended the call, grabbed her things and headed out the door.

Arriving at her office, Liz saw Connors at his desk, busy with a phone call, but he looked up when she walked in. Two other detectives on her team flagged her down, needing to review their cases with her. Craving coffee, she promised to be with them shortly.

Liz made a quick call up to Clarice in Miller's office. He wasn't available to meet with her until that afternoon but she was given time on his calendar. *Good*, she thought.

Arraignments started at ten o'clock. Liz checked the online docket to see Ty's place in the stack. She would have time to grab coffee and talk with her crew, then connect briefly with Connors before heading over.

Half an hour later, two detectives left her office with a game plan regarding a case. Liz took one last sip of coffee before she called to ask Connors if he had a few minutes. He was at the office door in seconds. Liz was right. Connors had heard the news. He sat down but he was far from relaxed. Connors body exuded energy and his expression told Liz he was ready for a fight.

"I can't believe this, Lieutenant. ADA Powell wants to run for mayor so he can clean up crime, which he blames on street people? What's his plan regarding crimes against people experiencing homelessness? Does he realize how easily they are victimized? And he announces his plan the day a homeless man is arrested for murder?"

"It is hard to believe, even from an arrogant shit like Jack," Liz agreed. "First of all, I want you to be aware that I'm talking with Miller later today. This is clearly inappropriate, at best, if not a blatant political ploy. And second, I'm attending Ty's arraignment. I'm heading over there in a few minutes. I know you're busy but if you want to go, I won't tell you not to. Not under these circumstances."

"I can be of more help to Ty here, Lieutenant. I'm working with the IT analysts on Colby's records. Besides, until I catch a new case, I'm staying on this one. And if I attend his arraignment it would be difficult for me to appear neutral."

"I understand, Connors. You're probably right about your time being better spent. Let me know what you and the analysts discover. There's got to be something there. Why else would Colby's workspace have been trashed?"

Connors stood up and turned to leave but he sensed that his Lieutenant was not ready to excuse him. He hung back, waiting. Liz stared at the young officer for a few moments, her thoughts mixing with the uneasy feeling in her gut. She was waiting for the thoughts to form into something she could express without sounding paranoid.

"Watch your back, Connors. Just the fact that you're still looking into records may raise eyebrows."

"Thanks, Lieutenant. I will."

"This case has taken an even stranger turn now, Connors. It was weird already. But to use a murder case like this? I realize it's been done before, but why wouldn't an ADA with political aspirations wait until he had a win? Wouldn't it make more sense to have that in the can and use that to your advantage?"

"Those are valid questions, as I see it. It would be nice to answer some of them." With a nod of his head, Connors left Liz's office and returned to his desk.

Chapter Twenty-eight

By the time Liz arrived at the courthouse on the other side of the justice center, the courtroom of the Honorable Clayton McCarthy was packed. This was a boon to Liz as she wanted to slip in to a seat in the back of the room and observe without drawing attention to her presence.

Defense attorneys came and went as their clients were arraigned on their individual charges. Liz recognized three assistant prosecutors from the District Attorney's office. They each would step up to the counsel's table as cases they'd been assigned were called, charges noted, and defendant's pleas entered. One of the three prosecutors was Jack Powell.

Diana was seated in an area reserved for those attorneys serving as defendant's counsel. Liz would have been unable to catch her eye even if she'd wanted to. Seated in the row directly behind the defense counsel's table sat Mike and Gary along with others Liz recognized as advocates from the homeless community but whom she did not know by name.

Within a couple of minutes, Liz watched as an officer led Ty to the defense counsel's table where Diana had just taken her place. Liz didn't have the best view but Ty looked like any man his age would look if he were in jail and about to be arraigned on a murder charge. He was dressed in a bright orange jumpsuit with CCDOC, for Clark County Department of Corrections, emblazoned on front and back.

Unshaven and uncombed, Ty's grooming supplies had probably been nothing more than soap and a toothbrush. Liz was struck by the thought that a homeless man could look even more destitute in jail than on the street. But it wasn't just his physical condition but Ty's frame of mind that Liz was witnessing. Liz noticed that Ty reacted with thanks when he saw Mike and Gary. The men each placed a hand on Ty's shoulder as a show of support. Ty turned around to face Judge McCarthy. Diana leaned over slightly, placed her hand on Ty's arm and whispered briefly in his ear.

"Case 186775," called the bailiff, not to anyone in particular, and handed a folder of documents up to Judge McCarthy. "*The People vs. Tyler Phillips*. The charge is murder in the first degree."

Judge McCarthy opened the folder and perused the documents before him.

"Is counsel for Mr. Phillips present?" inquired the judge, eyes still on the documents.

"Your Honor, Diana Harrison, representing Mr. Phillips."

Upon hearing Diana's voice, Judge McCarthy looked up from the documents. He looked in Diana's direction and nodded, seemingly in approval.

"And for the prosecution?" asked McCarthy.

"Jackson Powell representing the People, Your Honor."

Judge McCarthy looked over at Powell, in much the same way as he had studied Harrison when she identified herself, then said, "Proceed, Mr. Powell."

"The People charge that Tyler Phillips assaulted the deceased, Dylan Colby, at his place of business and that the assault was premeditated and resulted in Mr. Colby's death," stated Powell.

"Mr. Phillips, do you understand the charge against you?" McCarthy addressed Ty directly.

"I do, Your Honor." Ty answered with a clear, firm voice, just loud enough to be heard in the back of the courtroom.

"And you have engaged counsel, I see?"

"I have counsel, Your Honor."

"And how do you plead, Mr. Phillips, to the charge leveled against you?"

"Not guilty."

"Mr. Phillips, may I assume that you have conferred with Ms. Harrison regarding your plea of not guilty and she supports your decision?"

"Yes, Your Honor," stated Ty.

"May I address this charge, Your Honor?" inquired Diana. She sounded calm and matter of fact, obviously expecting to be granted the chance to speak.

"Yes, Ms. Harrison," replied McCarthy, interested in what she had to say. Liz was confident that the judge would give credence to Diana's remarks because of her competence. There were a few judges that might condescend to gender, but McCarthy wasn't one of them.

"I wholeheartedly support my client's plea. But, it's important to state at the onset that not only was the police investigation into Mr. Colby's death rushed to a conclusion that cast suspicion on my client, but the People have chosen to hurry along with that suspicion to the exclusion of any other possibility."

Diana spoke directly to McCarthy, but as she said the words, "the People," she turned and indicated Powell with an undeniable contempt in her voice.

"Mr. Powell, what is your response to Ms. Harrison's claim?"

"My response, Your Honor, is that the evidence will support the timeliness with which the investigation was completed. The swift competence of our law enforcement officers shouldn't be regarded as a problem."

Liz cringed at Powell's remark, guilt and regret poking at her conscience. Judge McCarthy didn't like the rhetoric either. He glanced down at the prosecutor.

"Mr. Powell, that's quite a statement. You'll have plenty of opportunities to congratulate law enforcement, but it's not time to gather endorsements yet. And we all still have our jobs to do."

Ouch, thought Liz, although she enjoyed the dig. McCarthy had made a stinging reference to Powell's announcement that he intended to run for mayor. Judge McCarthy seemed particularly brittle toward Powell and Liz doubted she was the only one who noticed. Liz waited for Powell to respond with some comeback but before he could say another word, McCarthy moved things along.

"Are the People requesting remand?"

"Due to the seriousness of this charge and the brutality of the attack on the victim, absolutely, Your Honor."

Diana jumped in. "Mr. Phillips has no prior record of violence or any other conviction, for that matter, Your Honor. He's never been arrested before. Never before been charged with a crime. He's a veteran in good standing of our armed forces. And he's a respected and valued member in his community."

"Excuse me, Your Honor, but what community would that be?" asked Powell. "Does Ms. Harrison expect this court to support bail for an unstable, homeless man charged with a capital offense? And assure us that he'll appear for trial before the bench? The very nature of his circumstances speaks to his ability to disappear into the streets." Powell paused and then started to chuckle, as if in disbelief. "How could the court possibly allow his return to his home, when he doesn't even have an address?"

Judge McCarthy's jaw clenched. He glared at Powell. His voice was steady and firm. "Mr. Phillips is so charged and will be held in custody pending trial. Ms. Harrison has requested medical and psychological examinations. Both shall be completed at the court's expense." Angered, McCarthy raised and rapped his gavel with one quick blow. "Court is recessed for one half hour. Counsel, I will see you both in chambers. Now!"

McCarthy stood and descended the bench, robes flowing. He had collected the documents regarding Ty's charges and took them with him. Custody officers began to secure defendants and return them to the holding area. Most of the attorneys wore expressions of surprise that quickly turned to annoyance at this unexpected delay in their carefully timed routines. One of Powell's colleagues, a fellow ADA, actually raised his arms as if to say, "How dare McCarthy impose this inconvenience! Who does he think he is, anyway?"

On the other hand, Diana wore an expression that would be hard to read if you didn't know her well. Liz, however, could tell that the attorney was pleased. Powell looked satisfied with himself the way an obstinate teenager looks when they get into trouble for misbehaving, but having enjoyed themselves, decided the punishment was worth it.

Diana and Powell, ignoring each other, made their way to Judge McCarthy's chambers. A knock on the door was returned with McCarthy's abrupt demand that they enter. McCarthy was hanging his judicial robe on a wooden hanger. He focused on Powell as he placed the hanger on a hook and sat down behind his desk. He didn't offer a seat to either attorney, instead giving in to his fury immediately.

"Since when does an officer of the court request denial of bail because the accused is homeless? And then to laugh about the man's homelessness? In open court!" McCarthy pointed a finger at Powell. "Bail is granted or denied depending on the seriousness of the charge and any former convictions, not the economic circumstances of the accused."

Powell began to speak but McCarthy put a hand up and said, "No, no. I want you to hear me, Jack, so listen up. I will not allow grandstanding for your own purposes in my courtroom. I would think you'd be smart enough to know that. You will not make this case an extension of your campaign to be elected mayor. Homelessness was not the cause of this young man's death."

"But Your Honor, homelessness *is* an issue of this case. The problem is pervasive and..."

"Save it for the campaign, Jack," taunted Diana. "Or I'll file an injunction against you that my client's right to a fair trial is hindered by a prejudiced perception of his circumstances."

"It's not a perception; the accused is homeless. He lives on the streets, Diana."

"Regardless of his circumstances, he has a right to a trial based on evidence, and that right shouldn't be impeded by a prosecutor's political aspirations."

McCarthy listened to their brief exchange, then he intervened.

"That's enough from both of you. Ms. Harrison, there will be no references to Mr. Powell's candidacy for mayor during this trial."

The judge was silent for a moment, deep in thought. He was staring at Powell when a brilliant idea seemed to occur to him. "Ah, okay, I get it now." The judge wagged a finger as if the action helped him to formulate his words. "I couldn't figure out why you'd announce your candidacy now when it would better serve your campaign to wait and have the win under your belt. But you actually *want* to make this trial about the homeless. You *want* to blame every unfortunate person on the street for a man's death. You're planning to be removed from the case so you can claim that even the courts are out of control when it comes to crime and homelessness."

Hearing McCarthy's words left Diana speechless. Powell looked embarrassed but not like he'd been accused of anything untoward. "Your Honor, with respect, that's ridiculous."

"Ridiculous? Yes, it would be ridiculous if I let that happen. I'll tell you what; you are going to try this case, Jack. And I'm going be vigilant about keeping politics, prejudice, and fearmongering out of it. This verdict will not be decided on a municipal ballot. You will try this case on the evidence alone. And for your sake, Jack, I hope you don't have another arraignment before me today." McCarthy stood up, indicated the exit from his chambers, and concluded the meeting with, "Now, if you'll both excuse me."

Chapter Twenty-nine

By the time Judge McCarthy had ordered the recess, Ty's arraignment on the murder charge was a done deal. Mike and Gary were waiting to visit him and were told they would be allowed to visit him together. They had half an hour to kill.

Liz caught up with them in the lobby outside the courtroom and offered to buy coffee. Mike was surprised to see her. He looked tired and readily accepted the invitation. Gary was as pleasant as ever, for which Liz was grateful. She expected cold shoulders from folks who knew Ty. Or maybe that's what her conscience made her believe she deserved.

"I didn't think you were planning to be here," said Mike. His surprise had been replaced with curiosity.

"I changed my mind after seeing that piece-of-shit video. I'm glad I didn't see it last night. I may have had nightmares." Liz tried to sound amused as she greeted Gary and shook the man's hand.

Liz had met Gary on a few occasions but she didn't know the man well. She was aware that his background in social services dated back to the Civil Rights Era and that he was well-respected locally. Mike thought of him as a mentor and that was recommendation enough for her. Liz was also aware that he was a close friend of Ty's and she was glad to see him there.

The small café area in the courthouse basement had some of the best coffee you could ask for but it was the cinnamon rolls that were famous. Patrons picked up the scent of cinnamon and freshly baked pastry as soon as they stepped off the elevator at the basement. The rolls were baked every weekday morning and were the size of saucers. Neither Gary nor Liz could resist having one but Mike passed.

"At least Gary's having a treat with me so I don't look like a pig. You're the one who runs all the time, Mike. I'd think you'd be able to splurge a bit with some glorious calories," teased Liz, between bites of syrupy cinnamon, warm dough, and puddles of creamy white frosting.

Mike responded with a half grin. "Enjoy it, Liz," as he saluted her with his cup of coffee. Liz studied Mike. She knew that the last couple of days had been difficult for him. He looks tired, she told herself, but there was something else. Pensive, she decided. They needed some alone time to talk together about things other than this case. At least in her view, that's what they needed. Their routine had been interrupted by current events and they both needed to get things back on track. Her thoughts made Liz feel selfish but it was the truth.

"This is good stuff, Liz. Great idea," offered Gary as he took another scrumptious bite. "Makes me wish I could take one to Ty. He does like his pastry. Anyway, how did he look to you, Mike? He seemed okay to me, but, man, it was hard to see him in a jumpsuit and cuffs."

"That it was," he said to Gary. Then he turned to Liz. "So, you enjoyed the little news clip? You should know that it came from Gary, here. That's how I found out that Jack had announced his candidacy for mayor of our fair city."

"It was a surprise," she said, after a sip of coffee.

"His rhetoric is offensive," Mike said, his words snapping with venom. "Someone ought to tell him that being mayor means he's mayor for homeless people, too. I'd like to inform Powell that scores of people without a permanent address work and pay taxes, and many are even registered to vote."

"Go for it, Mike," urged Gary, with his coffee cup almost to his mouth. "Seriously. I'll back you up." He sipped his coffee. "And he used the word 'unstable' to describe Ty. This Jack Powell fellow should hope to be as stable as Ty."

"It was Jack's timing that pissed me off," Liz shared with them, between bites of cinnamon roll. "Announcing a run after Ty's arrest and before he's even arraigned? I should watch what I say but I need to get this off my chest. This case has been stinky from the beginning and I've suspected that's been by design. I'm going to try to figure out if the source of the stink is just Jack's political plans or if police command is involved."

"Command? Why would police command want to see Ty held for a murder?" It was Gary who was asking. "What would they possibly gain from this?"

"The only thing we should gain is a conviction, if we do our job the way we're trained, and if and when the verdicts come through. That's all we should ever gain from an investigation. Look, I respect Captain Miller. He's a good man. But I know that Jack spoke with him before we were told to conclude the investigation and arrest Ty." Liz thought for a moment. "That in itself isn't unusual. Normally, we're working toward the same end. For all I know, Miller may have been given bad information, or info may have been kept from him." Liz shrugged. "He may have been pressured. I don't know. But I'm going to ask a few questions. I'm meeting with him later."

"Sounds pretty bold, Liz," said Gary with a lilt in his voice. "Give it to The Man, my sister!" He enjoyed the small show of rebellion enough to raise his palm for a high five, which Liz returned with joy.

"You think this sounds bold, Gary? You have no idea how bold our Liz can be. That's what I love about her." Liz's face reddened at Mike's words. When he leaned over and kissed her, she was stunned. Mike rarely kissed her in public, especially while she was on duty.

Liz was embarrassed by the gesture but she was amused enough to laugh. "Okay, that's it. I've got to go. Must I remind you that I'm a cop? Show a little respect, please."

"Respect? Hell, Lieutenant Liz," laughed Gary. "You're my new hero."

Mike looked at the time. "All right, Gary. We're on deck at the jail. Let's go see how he's doing. Now that things are moving along with this train wreck, maybe he'll have something to tell us about the other night."

Liz knew that Mike had alluded to a possible alibi for the time Dylan was killed and she hoped he was right. But it was Gary who responded with, "I wouldn't bet on that happening, man."

As the three of them walked back to the elevator, Mike remembered dinner with his mom. "See you at six, Liz. Don't forget. You're going to call about a table."

Chapter Thirty

When Liz returned to her office, the detective's squad room was buzzing with activity. Phones were ringing; people were talking, even shouting, at times. Keyboards were clicking away. Liz saw civilians sitting with officers, giving statements regarding crimes or complaints that were under investigation. The energy was intense and showed on the faces in the room.

Liz had three phone messages plus a written note waiting for her on her desk. The note was from Connors, stating that he had made progress with IT on their victim's correspondence. Notes were in the system case file for her review.

The first phone message was from Miles Carey, asking for a return call. The second was Clarice, confirming her meeting with Captain Miller. No return call to make on that one but Liz stuck a note on her monitor to remind her. She planned to head upstairs ten minutes early.

The third message was from Erica Colby. Liz listened to the message twice. The voice sounded small and distracted by grief, but the woman clearly wanted to talk to Liz.

"Lieutenant Jordan, this is Erica Colby. (Hesitates) ...I need to talk with you as soon as you are able to call me. (Hesitates again) ...A terrible mistake has been made and I...don't... know who else to speak with about it. It's very important. Thank you, Lieutenant."

Erica ended the message by leaving her number. Liz noted the slight catch in Erica's voice that often accompanies grief or illness, the effort required under the circumstances to express oneself. Maybe that catch is from being emotionally spent, exhausted, or just having cried your eyes out with sorrow.

At any rate, Liz would return Erica's call shortly, but wanted to clear the deck of these other chores first to better give the grieving mother more of her attention. She would be as quick as possible. Checking the time, she figured it was late enough in the morning that someone would answer at UnderBar. She dialed the number with her cell phone. The call was picked up on the second ring.

"UnderBar, this is Kurt." There was much activity going on in the background: reggae music, the echo of large, empty pans being manipulated, a water faucet running, and what sounded to Liz like a commercial refrigerator slamming closed.

"Kurt, it's Liz Jordan."

"Hey, Liz. Hold on, I'm in the kitchen. Let me go out front."

Kurt sounded happy to hear from her and Liz was just as thrilled that he had been around to answer the phone. In her mind, she thought of the proprietor as Big Kurt to differentiate from Little Kurt, the cat she had named for Cobain. But she had never addressed him as such to his face and doubted she'd ever have the nerve. Liz was excited to show the place to Mike and even to Marjorie. She was sure they'd enjoy it.

"How are things? What can I do for you, Liz?" It was much easier to hear him now. Faint strains of UB40 remained in the background.

"Things are well. Tonight's kind of a special occasion. Mike's mom is in town. Would you be able to reserve a table for the three of us?"

"For you, Lieutenant? Anything. What time, my dear?"

"Will six work?"

"You bet. Six, it is."

"Great. Thanks, Kurt. She'll love your place. Don't worry if Mike and his mother, Marjorie, arrive before me. I will try to be on time, but it may be one of those days."

"Not to worry. I'll be here after four. Have him ask for me. It will be nice to meet him. We'll make sure you are all well taken care of. You keep those streets safe for us."

"We try. See you this evening."

"We'll look forward to it. Thanks," and Kurt ended the call.

Great. That was done.

Liz logged on to the computer system and found Connor's recent entry:

IT confirms the following actions occurred from the victim's workstation:

Files from ClarkCountyWA.gov were downloaded and saved onto a portable storage device three days prior to damage of hard drive. This action is significant b/c deceased had not previously downloaded files from the gov server.

Forty-eight individual client account files were accessed and thirty-nine of them showed changes were saved over the last two days prior to

damage to the hard drive. These actions referred to requests for assistance that were approved/authorized.

Twelve emails were sent in the 24 hours prior to the damage to the hard drive. Nine were responses to emails. Three were initiated emails, one of which was sent within two hours of estimated TOD. The last sent email contained two attachments. IT is working to retrieve text of email, recipient's name and IP address, and attachments.

Well, now. That's all interesting. Good work by Connors and his buddies in the IT division. Liz could make sense of Connor's notations, although she didn't understand the methods used to retrieve it. She would bet that the portable device mentioned was the thumb drive given to her by Dylan's partner, Jayson. And the storage device was locked in a drawer in Liz's desk.

Picking up her office phone, Liz punched the extension for Miles. He picked up as soon as the line rang.

"Liz? You're calling from your office?" Miles sounded excited, eager.

"I am."

"Great, then you can speak freely."

"Have you found something, Miles?"

"Yes, and it's odd. That's the only way to describe it. You were correct, the files are public. They're balance sheets, basically, detailing how funds intended for services are received and from what sources of revenue, and then how the same funds are allocated."

"Okay, so what makes it odd?"

"It's the streams to which the funds are allocated. Many are easy to track, like housing, ongoing medical; those are the big ones. Then there are discretionary lines; food banks, emergency medical, children's programs, etc. But a few are coded instead of designated as line items in the county budget. It's hard to explain. The question is why are they coded? The easy answer is they were coded to hide the expenditures."

"Hide them? Like stealing the money, Miles?"

"No, the accounts aren't being stripped. It's more like the funds have been re-routed, funneled elsewhere. I take it you'd like me to keep digging and find out where they landed?"

"Yeah, yeah, please, keep at it, Miles. And I want to know why the data was significant enough to our victim, a public assistance processor, to download the files to a thumb drive and store it at home. IT says that he downloaded something to a portable storage device a day or two before he was killed. Can you confirm it was this info? Is there a way to date it, or something?"

"Not on the thumb drive itself, because it's not on a system or a server. It's just a free-standing storage device. But the files might match what was downloaded. And you said IT has that action dated."

"Okay, thanks a lot. This is a great lead."

"You're welcome. I'll be in touch. Bye, Liz." And with that, Miles was off the line.

Chapter Thirty-one

When they left Liz, Mike and Gary had made their way over to the jail for their visit with Ty. They had each been through the routine before but it irritated them how long it took and how tedious the process could be to get in to see someone at the jail. They were each signed in and their IDs verified. Then they waited. Their personal items were checked and locked up. They waited in another area. Then they were searched for contraband and waited a few minutes more. They understood the need for security but it seemed like the waiting was endless.

A burly custody officer named Peterson, according to his name badge, took them to a large room that resembled an indoor picnic area stripped of any gaiety. Gray linoleum floor, tan walls, no windows. Metal tables were bolted to floor. Each table was surrounded by four metal stools, also bolted down securely. Between visiting hours, the room was used for meals. The underlying scent in the room may have been eggs and toast but the smell was overpowered by the odor of disinfectant. The atmosphere was similar to what one would notice in the dining rooms in either of the shelters managed by the two men. The similarity was not lost on either of them. It was a good use of space.

Several of the tables were occupied by incarcerated men sitting with visitors, conversing quietly. At one of the metal tables sat Ty, waiting for them. Mike and Gary approached him, each clasping Ty's hand in turn, bringing it to their chest as they held it, a heartfelt gesture of support in an environment where a hug was forbidden.

Mike studied Ty as they each took a stool. He'd only been able to discern a quick impression of how he was doing when he saw him in the courtroom. By all appearances, Ty seemed all right. There were no outward indications that he'd suffered blows or been roughed up. As Mike had noted earlier, he was clean but unshaven, still wearing the orange jumpsuit. It didn't surprise Mike that Ty looked tired and anxious at the same time. Jail and a murder charge could do that to a man.

"How are you, Ty? Are you holding up okay?" Gary asked, as soon as he sat down across from him.

"I'm doing okay. Except that I haven't slept. Reminds me of being in the VA. Only worse."

"Well, I'm sure the folks at the VA would be pleased to know you think jail is worse," responded Gary, trying to sound normal and lighthearted.

"Does me good to see you, Ty," Mike told him. "What do you need? What can we bring you?"

"Toothpaste would be much appreciated. Something to read maybe. London or Steinbeck, you know, something descriptive enough to distract. All I've seen in here is newspapers. No thanks."

"You got it," Mike said with a nod. Then he leaned forward and asked, "Have you heard any news about the district attorney that's prosecuting your case? The one from your arraignment, named Jackson Powell?"

Ty shook his head slowly, then asked Mike. "Heard anything like what?"

"He's announced that he plans to run for mayor," Mike explained with a serious tone. "He thinks there are too many homeless people and it's causing too many problems downtown."

"Can't say I disagree. But I'm guessing we'd have differing ideas of how to remedy the situation."

"I've got this guy pegged as a fearmonger, and a mean one," Mike told him, remembering his own anger at watching the news clip. "He sounds like he wants to put folks on buses and haul them out of town, like they have no rights, like that would solve anything."

"No. That just moves their problem somewhere else. I've tried it," agreed Ty. "Doesn't work."

Mike and Gary shared a look, but it was Gary who spoke next.

"He's going to use this case, Ty, your arrest and that young man's death, to advance his ugly agenda. It's the timing, man. It can't be a coincidence."

Ty listened to Gary's words, then sat back a little with his hands gripping the side of the shiny table.

"You think they're hanging me out to dry? Using me as a scapegoat for some fascistic bullshit because I'm on the street?"

"It's looking that way," confirmed Mike. "Liz says the investigation was rushed. Too many unanswered questions. She's still looking into things, she and Connors. And Liz doesn't trust this prosecutor." Mike paused for a moment. "She sends her best to you, by the way. And she doesn't think you deserve this."

Ty looked at Mike, obviously touched by his words, then he closed his eyes and covered his face with his hands for a few seconds.

"Look, you didn't kill that fellow Colby," Gary began, "but this reactionary politician and his base of freaked-out followers are going to let you take a fall because it will advance what they want to believe. And you're letting them succeed because the cops haven't heard your alibi."

"Gary...," began Ty. But Gary was on a roll. He raised a hand and stopped Ty before he could say another word.

"Just let me finish, Ty. You weren't involved, but someone did kill that guy. You owe it to him to do what you can to see his killer brought to justice. Whoever you're protecting, for whatever reason, it's not worth a killer getting away with it. It's not a matter of personal standards. This is cosmic, man. Bigger than all of us."

"I hear you." Ty looked Gary in the eye. He looked over at Mike. Then Ty nodded his head and sighed. "And you're right, if I don't provide an alibi, a killer goes free. It's not just about me providing an alibi. But I made a promise and I don't take that lightly. It's just that...this goes back a long way."

As Gary and Mike were sitting with Ty at the jail, Liz was ending the call with Miles about the financial records on the thumb drive. Curious about what Miles had discovered, Liz hoped to hear more from him soon. She had a gut feeling about it and wondered in what direction the data would point. Liz took a few minutes to process what she had learned from Connors' notes regarding the progress with IT. Liz thought, and Miles had agreed, that the data was linked.

Dylan may have left them a significant piece of evidence which his partner, Jayson, had suspected was important.

Liz checked the time. She gauged that she had sufficient time to return Erica Colby's phone call and still have plenty of time to grab lunch, tackle some paperwork and make it upstairs on time for her meeting with Miller. And Liz was hoping she may hear back from Miles by that time.

She punched in the number left in the message. After three rings, the message recorder picked up. Liz listened as a mechanical voice told her she had reached the correct number and could leave a message.

Liz identified herself, said that she regretted missing the call, and would be happy to talk at any time. She started to leave her cell phone number when Erica picked up.

"Lieutenant, I'm sorry but I'm screening my calls. I just can't...talk to anyone now and the phone keeps ringing. But I really must speak to you. I...I hope you can help me."

"I'll certainly try. What's this about, Mrs. Colby?"

"I was informed that the police have charged a man in connection with Dylan's...death." Erica's speech pattern was stalled, many starts and stops. Unsure? Untrusting? Or as simple as a grieving woman attempting to express herself? "Are you still looking into it...to what happened to Dylan, Lieutenant? I am hoping you are, you and...Detective Connors."

"Yes, your information is correct, Mrs. Colby. We have sufficient evidence to have leveled a charge against a suspect. They were arraigned earlier today. That's where I was when you called, actually. I do apologize. I had assumed you had been notified of our progress on the case."

"Arraigned? That must mean... it's really happening... I just don't know what to do!" The woman was frantic, her voice full of distress. She seemed a very different woman than the one Liz had encountered previously. She was on the verge of panic and had begun to cry. Liz heard the tears cloud the woman's words.

"Mrs. Colby, you're obviously upset. If there is any way I can help you, I will. Why don't you tell me what is concerning you?"

"I'll...I'll try. I so wish Doug was here," she said, referencing her late husband. "He would know how to handle this." Erica paused, tried to recover some of the poise and control she had displayed when they had first spoken. "There must be something I can do."

"Would it be better for you if we spoke in person?" Liz offered. Then she remembered the level of comfort the grieving mother seemed to have had with Connors. "I can come to you...unless you would rather have Detective Connors give you a call." Liz was hoping this option would prove more acceptable. It wasn't that she didn't want to be helpful but Liz suspected Connors' demeanor, as well as his gender, might be a better fit. Then she reminded herself that Erica had chosen to call her in the first place.

The woman hesitated to answer. Liz gathered she was thinking about what to do. "Would you mind terribly? I would very much appreciate that. When would you be able to come, Lieutenant?"

"Now. I can come right now." To hell with lunch and paperwork.

Within a few minutes, Liz had the address and had left word with dispatch of where she was heading. She was familiar with the part of town to which she was going; upscale homes in established neighborhoods. Most of the interaction the department had had in this part of town was with private security unless something major occurred. Which was, of course, the case here.

Liz reviewed to herself, the details of the brief phone conversation. The woman's son had been killed. A suspect charged and arraigned. Erica had specifically mentioned that a party had been arrested and charged. She had contacted Liz regarding some "terrible mistake." Something had happened that had upset her greatly and she felt compelled to try to remedy the situation. Did it involve the comments she had shared with them while waiting at the morgue? Maybe it concerned Jayson, her son's intended, grieving his own loss. Hopefully the woman's distress had nothing to do with her experience at the morgue. The last thing Liz wanted to deal with was a grieving mother's problem with Myers. If that was the case, she wished already that she'd let Connors handle it.

Liz recalled all she could about their encounter the previous day and she was still mystified as to why Erica would want to contact her. But it really didn't matter. Liz would try to help and if she couldn't help maybe she could learn something useful.

Arriving at a gated entrance, Liz identified herself and was informed by the guard that Erica had told them of her pending arrival. Liz was directed to take the avenue ahead to the right and the Colby residence would be the sixth driveway. She'd know it by the huge willow in the front.

The home was large but not palatial, more modest than expected. Liz wondered if they had moved to smaller accommodations when Dylan had left home or if Erica had made a change after her husband had died. Brick, two-stories, with a covered double entrance, nicely landscaped with a detached two-car garage. Liz parked and made her way to the front door. The scents of freshly trimmed shrubs and assorted greenery floated in the breeze. The street was amazingly quiet. No pets, no children, not even another vehicle that Liz could see. No one enjoying a stroll before the next rain shower.

She rang the bell, hearing the deep two-toned bong from inside the house. Liz couldn't help but notice the wreath which has been placed near the front door, the traditional sign that the inhabitants of this home were in mourning.

Erica answered the door herself. She was just as put together as when Liz had seen her at the morgue, but her ensemble was casual, comfortable. Not a hair on her head out of place, not the tiniest smudge on her carefully made-up face. But the emotion coming from her eyes was different. It wasn't intensity Liz saw. It was as though control had slipped from her grasp.

"Lieutenant Jordan, please come in. I'm so relieved that you were willing to come here." Liz stepped inside and Erica closed the door behind her. The house was decorated in a style which Liz assumed might be called traditional classic with old, expensive, heavy pieces. There were several large plants in huge pots. The hallway smelled of eucalyptus. Natural light greeted her but Liz couldn't have said where it came from.

"Let's talk in the library," she said, and Liz followed the woman down a small, central hallway to a room on the left. "Can I have Wanda bring you something, Lieutenant?"

"Coffee would be nice, thank you."

"Of course," responded Erica as she stepped to a small intercom on the wall. She picked up a receiver, much like a phone, and said into it, "Wanda, uh, yes dear, could you bring coffee for the Lieutenant and myself to the library. Yes, yes, thank you."

"Please sit with me, Lieutenant." She had presented the controlled version of herself as she answered the door and requested coffee for them. Perhaps the domestic details had served to soothe her, because as they entered the library to sit together, her distress returned.

They took seats in matching wing chairs, upholstered in a dark paisley, set at an angle from each other. An oval table was positioned between them. A tumbler sat on the table. It held a drink. Erica lifted the glass to her lips, taking a small sip of the amber liquid. The fingertips of her other hand rested on her temple.

"I hope you'll excuse me. It's early but I've been plagued by a terrible headache that only a few sips of brandy can relieve."

"No apology necessary. This has been a difficult time," empathized Liz, noting to herself that she'd been correct. The woman was self-medicating.

"Lieutenant, you said on the phone that it's true, that a man was arrested for, for hurting Dylan." She was careful not to use the words kill or murder to describe what had befallen her son. Sometimes, Liz knew, that could take time.

"Yes ma'am. It's true."

Erica took a breath. Her eyes closed. When she opened them, she asked Liz, "Is his name Phillips? Ty Phillips?"

"It is, yes."

She became more distressed and Liz was surprised at hearing the woman refer to Ty by name. Liz was quickly intrigued, not able to guess where the conversation might be going.

"Lieutenant, Ty Phillips would never have hurt my son. I would swear to that."

"Mrs. Colby, are you acquainted with Mr. Phillips?"

Erica didn't look Liz in the eye but she wasn't avoiding eye contact either. Liz felt that for a moment, she had almost forgotten Liz was seated next to her. The woman's gaze rested nearby but not on anything in particular. Her eyes began to squint ever so slightly as if remembering an event and then she made an effort to widen them again to push the memory away. Erica sighed and calmly answered, "Ty Phillips was my husband's best friend. I've known him for nearly thirty years."

Chapter Thirty-two

Sitting at the metal table in the jail visiting room, Mike and Gary listened to Ty's story, that by his own assessment, went back a long way.

"Doug Colby and I were pals. We went to high school together. Doug, Erica, and I ran around together. We were part of a bigger crew but Doug and I were tight. You'll understand it as I tell the tale. I was what you might call his back-up and he was always there for me too. It wasn't a big deal. He met Erica at a party. Doug attracted girls everywhere he went. Anyway, Erica had a lot to drink the night they met. It was the last day of school our sophomore year. A celebration, I guess. We kind of looked out for her and she appreciated it. She let her Dad know that we were stand up guys, trustworthy. We had no idea that her father was our mayor. It wouldn't have mattered if we had, but we didn't. Erica and Doug started dating pretty steady. By the holidays our junior year, they were serious."

Ty hesitated for a brief moment, then decided to continue. "Doug and I had gone into a little business venture, I guess you'd call it. We had a few dozen high-grade cannabis plants up in the woods. Indica. It was an indoor set-up in an old barn on property owned by Erica's dad. We had made some money the year before, to our minds anyway. We were hoping to do the same our senior year. Neither of us were exactly from the privileged class, you know. It was just weed but back then it was a different deal. Medical marijuana was just coming into the conversation and there was sure as shit no legal recreational weed back then."

"No, there was not. There was a whole different attitude back then," said Gary, remembering.

"By the time we were seniors, Erica's dad wanted to help Doug get into a good college, figuring he was probably going to be joining the family. He pulled a few strings and between Doug's good grades and athleticism, the old man put it together for him. Then two things happened almost at the same time: Erica found out she was pregnant and our little weed operation was busted."

Gary and Mike looked at Ty with disbelief, mouths gaping, he continued. "I know. It was hard to believe at the time too. Anyway, we had a feeling the place was being watched and it wasn't going to take long for them to figure out who was using the place and why."

Ty paused for a moment, thinking back. "Doug was my best friend. He had more to lose than I did. We met up one evening to figure out what the hell to do. I told Doug I'd carry the load. He wasn't going to let me do it but he finally relented. I convinced him to let me do it because of the slight difference in our ages. Doug was a few months older than me. He was already eighteen. I convinced him that he would suffer a worse fate than me because I was still underage. By a month. By one stinking month."

"Wow, man. That was one big favor," said Gary, shaking his head.

"Doug and Erica went to her dad and begged him to try to help me out. I don't know if they admitted to Bill Adams that the patch was Doug's and mine. But Bill worked out an armed forces enlistment for me in lieu of the drug charge. All we had to do was shut it down and I kept my head low until my birthday."

"I wasn't happy about the enlistment but I figured it beat jail and I wouldn't have a record. Then six months after boot camp a little operation known as Desert Shield went into effect. I guess you know how that turned out. The screening and tests they had administered indicated I was cut out for some pretty specific operations. Besides, at that level, you go where you are told whether you want to or not."

"Shit, Ty. You were just a kid," said Gary. He covered his face with both hands for a moment, then he moved them and continued. "So many of you kids over the years."

"It broke my mother's heart. She wanted me to stay here and get a job after graduation. I never told her the story and she couldn't understand why I would want to enlist. She thought it was my choice. She died while I was over there, during my second tour. I was deep into special ops by then and they couldn't get in touch with me for bereavement leave. I've not yet forgiven myself for that. Among other things." Ty paused a moment, his thoughts introspective.

"Doug tried to keep in touch. I'd get letters and messages but I guess I resisted contact. I didn't regret my decision and I was happy for them. I tried to tell Doug that I was fine. But I didn't feel like me for a long time. Then came the self-induced numbness to try and run away from myself and the shit over there. Doug and Erica sent me pictures and updates about Dylan."

"Did you ever contact them?" asked Gary. "I'm asking because it sounds like they made quite an effort. You were important to them."

Ty nodded with a sigh. "A few of times over the years. It was hard for me to pretend I resembled the guy they had known. I wasn't him anymore. Then everything went crazy for them when Doug got sick. Dylan was a good kid but he was close to Doug and it was tough on him to deal with the stress. He was in grad school. I knew he was gay. Doug had shared that with me. He was glad Dylan and Jayson had found each other and so was I."

He stopped talking for a brief moment and studied his hands. Then Ty picked up the tale. "Anyway, Erica had liked the drink from the time she was a kid. She hid it well when she needed to. Both of her parents had made drinking a big part of their social scene. Years later when Doug became ill, it was hard on Erica and she relied on the booze. Her alcohol abuse got to the point where she couldn't hide it anymore. Doug got a hold of me. He knew I'd had a rough time of it myself but he knew that I had cleaned up. He wanted to help Erica, but he was too sick by then. He really didn't know what to do anyway. He said he had no right to ask anything of me. I told him he was being a dumb ass. At least that made him laugh. I promised him I would do what I could."

"Three weeks after Doug passed, Dylan found his Mom passed out in her room. She had suffered a bout of alcohol poisoning and almost died herself. Dylan was convinced that she was mourning. Which of course she was, but she was also an alcoholic. Dylan would never admit that his mom needed help to stop. Like a lot of people, his belief was that dependency was a weakness and an addict should will themselves to stop. Like an ill person magically turning off a disease."

Ty's words hit Mike hard. He knew what Ty was talking about. He had lived with addiction himself and it didn't become easier, at least in his experience. He didn't say a word.

"I'd been checking in with Erica periodically since that close call. She knew for a long time she needed help but she wasn't ready. Then Erica got in touch with me last week. She knew she could reach me at Brooks. We talked about meetings. Erica hoped to keep a low profile. In this town, as prominent as her family was, that wasn't going to be easy for her. We decided together to go to a meeting where I wasn't well known." "Dylan found out and he wasn't happy about the plan. He wanted her to go to some rich people spa, like all she needed was a vacation. The day I visited his office that's what we had words about. I told him the last thing his father asked of me was to help his mother get sober and whether he liked it or not, I was going to help if she was ready."

"Why did you talk at the CSO?" Gary asked Ty.

"Dylan left a message for me to stop 'bothering' his mom," answered Ty, looking at Gary. "It wasn't like he was going to invite me to his home. It was the easiest place to catch him, to tell him I wasn't backing off." With that explanation, Ty resumed his story.

"The property where the barn was situated was on a parcel that was willed to Erica when her father died. There's a small hunting cabin still up there but the infamous weed barn fell into disrepair years ago. Doug and Erica let me use the cabin whenever I wanted. I still do. When I need to get off the street or just can't stand the sound of my own voice anymore, I go up there. No plumbing, kerosene lamps. Lots of firewood. It's nearly inaccessible if you don't know where you're going."

Mike and Gary had listened as Ty told them his story full of secrets. Gary had asked a few questions and made comments, but Mike had been silent. Finally, he couldn't stand it anymore. "Do you mean to tell us that you offered to take the brunt of a drug bust for a friend? Why would you do that, Ty?"

He looked at Mike, then at his clasped hands on the metal table. He didn't assume a defensive tone. He reiterated his reasoning calmly because the choice had been his and he didn't regret it. "Because Doug was a good friend, the best friend I ever had, at least up to that point. He was needed here and he had a lot to live for."

Ty had leaned back, hands flat on the metal table with arms outstretched. "You have to understand. Or, I guess you don't have to understand. My prospects weren't exactly inviting. I wasn't going to college. All I had to leave behind was my mom and a few other friends. I was underage. I thought I was looking at a slap on the wrist, a few months in a youth facility. The enlistment wasn't my idea."

"I get that," agreed Gary with a nod of his head. "I get that you wanted to help your buddy, his girlfriend, and their baby on the way. It was a selfless act on your part. And it explains Doug Colby's devotion to you throughout the years."

It was Mike who spoke next. "Gary's right about that. It was a truly selfless act. And I understand that you wanted to help someone address their addiction. No one close to her, not even her own son, was going to help. But please, Ty. Do yourself and those of us who care about you a favor. Please tell Diana what you told us. You won't help Erica Colby's problems by going to prison in place of the person who killed her son."

Chapter Thirty-three

Liz listened to a similar story from Erica in the comfort of the woman's home, not aware that Ty was offering up his tale of the events to Mike and Gary at the jail. The version Liz heard from Erica included the same main points but it was peppered with her own perspectives.

Erica had been in love with Doug Colby from the moment she met him. As Ty had shared, Doug, Ty, and Erica had been part of a tight-knit group of friends from school who had enjoyed partying together. To hear Erica tell it, Doug had been, by everyone's estimation, the shining star and she was determined to be with him. Erica's father had been fond of Doug but did not consider him worthy of his daughter. When it became evident that he wasn't a passing fancy in his daughter's life, Bill Adams used his influence to redesign the young man into a protégé of which he could be proud. Erica explained to Liz, in her own words, that her father had never been able to re-educate Doug out of his social conscience. He had always wanted to support programs for "the poor and the needy," as she referred to them. Liz remembered Kelly telling her about Doug Colby's interest in the work she did on behalf of people experiencing homelessness.

She expressed to Liz how grateful she had been to Ty. Erica knew that his sacrifice had allowed Doug to remain at home with her and their expected son. She knew some of the details of Ty's past including his military service. She supported Doug's efforts to keep in touch with Ty over the years. Liz found it interesting that Erica didn't seem to include her husband's loyal, homeless friend with the faction she considered "poor and needy." Perhaps it was the personal connection. Ty was the only homeless individual with whom Erica had ever been acquainted. Or maybe Erica never realized how deep Ty's problems were.

At this point, the story addressed Erica's drinking problem. "When my husband became ill, he thought I was drinking too much, and I probably was," she stated slowly, her gaze falling to her hands. "Doug wanted me to talk to Ty about it. It was just too much to deal with. Besides, the problem was that Doug was sick, not that I was drinking. But he was very worried. I kept assuring him I would contact Ty. I just tried to ease his mind."

"Did you talk with your son? How did he see things?"

Erica sighed. "Dylan said it was my business. He said if a drink helped me cope, I should have one. But after my husband passed away, I didn't want to think about anything anymore. I drank too much one day, became very ill and was admitted to the hospital. Dylan was very angry that I had let it happen. Jayson, his partner, told me that Dylan was frightened of losing me so soon after losing his father."

Liz listened to Erica talk about nearly killing herself with alcohol as if she had overdosed accidentally on prescribed medication. Liz had seen it before and she had had enough conversations with Mike to know that addiction is addiction. Prescribed painkillers and alcohol can make it easier to ignore a problem for far too long because those substances may be more acceptable. *But Officer, I have a prescription for these pills. But Officer, I only had two glasses of wine. Sure.*

Yeah, right, Liz would tell them, as she put them in the tank and called their families. She could only hope they could be convinced to seek treatment.

"I was embarrassed when I went home from the hospital. Ty came to see me. He said I should not try to handle it alone. He said the problem of addiction was medical. I didn't want to believe him and I was still consumed with grief over losing Doug. But I called and talked with Ty several times over the next few months. He assured me he would help when I was ready. Finally, I was ready. At least I thought I was. I parked in front of that church, knowing Ty was inside waiting for me."

"The five o'clock support group. Ty was meeting you there."

"Yes. I just couldn't go in. I sat in my car for some time. I don't know how long, Lieutenant. Then I drove down the street, past that office building where Dylan worked. I pulled into a spot in the lot near the park. After a while, I saw Ty walk by. He saw me and came over to the car. He asked if I wanted to talk and he got in on the passenger side. He wasn't angry or disappointed with me. Ty said I'd know what to do when I was ready. But he warned me that I should not tempt fate by thinking that I have all the time in the world."

"So, Ty wasn't sitting in the park, as he claimed. He was talking with you in your vehicle. That's why no one he knew saw him in the park before he went to Brooks."

Liz was responding to what Erica was telling her, but the last statement was more for herself, making sense of the events of that tragic evening. The fact wasn't lost on Liz that

Erica was probably talking with Ty at the precise time her son was murdered.

"Yes, Ty was being a friend to me, a friend that I didn't deserve. And he won't say so because he promised Doug that he would help me when I was ready. Ty is an honorable man, a decent man. And if he hadn't been with me that evening, I'd still know he didn't hurt my son, Lieutenant."

"Mrs. Colby, are you willing to testify in court about what you've told me? Will you provide Ty with the alibi he needs?"

"Yes, yes. Of course, I will. Ty has done so much for me. It's the least I can do for him."

Liz looked at her watch. She needed to get back to the precinct and her meeting with Miller. Erica seemed to be relieved to have shared her story but Liz wanted to be sure.

"Thank you for the coffee, Mrs. Colby. And I appreciate what you've shared. Some of it couldn't have been easy."

"Lieutenant, I would have called sooner if I'd known Ty had been arrested. I really must go see him. I think we should talk together."

"You're probably right. I know that your housekeeper is here with you, but would you like me to call Jayson for you? If you need him, I'm sure he'd come over to be with you."

"No, no, I'm all right." Erica hesitated for a moment. "Dylan's service is the day after tomorrow. Jayson and I will support each other through that difficult time. We'd be honored if you are able to attend, Lieutenant."

"I will certainly try, Mrs. Colby. Now, I really must be going."

"Of course, Lieutenant. Let me see you to the door."

As Liz turned to say goodbye, Erica stopped her. She shook Liz's hand.

"Thank you, Lieutenant Jordan. And just one more request. For Jayson and myself. Please...find out who hurt my son."

Chapter Thirty-four

Liz was driving back to the precinct when she realized she had missed two calls from Mike. No messages. She wanted Diana to know what Erica had to say about the evening her son was killed. Liz knew she should document the conversation and share the details with Miller. She wished she had recorded Erica's story but she hadn't guessed that the distraught woman would share new evidence. Liz decided to return a call to Mike. Maybe she could brighten his day with the news.

"Hey. What's up?" Liz said when Mike answered his cell. "How was your visit with Ty?"

"It was informative, Liz. Gary and I told him about Powell's announcement and our thoughts about how he's using Ty's case to help his bid for mayor. He didn't exactly like the idea. He shared with us who he was waiting for at the support group. It was..."

"...Erica Colby. I know," Liz told Mike. "She called me earlier. In fact, I just left her home. She didn't know Ty had been arrested until this morning. She's a messed-up woman and she's in mourning, but she has respect for Ty."

"Gary and I are hoping Ty will share the info with Diana as soon as possible. But even if he doesn't, now that you're aware, it's a different situation, Liz. Isn't it?"

"Well, Ty's been formally charged. The judge could dismiss but that would require a sworn affidavit. That's likely to happen but may take some time. Or the DA could drop charges based on new evidence. But that's not likely to happen."

"What should we do?" asked Mike. He was exasperated, wanting to do what he could for Ty.

"Mike, I need to go through channels. It could screw things up for Ty if I don't follow the process with what was disclosed to me. What you and Gary do with what you learned from your source is your own business. But it will be to Ty's advantage that the same information is related to different people by different sources."

"Maybe I should tell Diana myself," Mike said, seeking a confirmation from Liz.

"If Ty doesn't tell her...yeah, I think you should. Look, I'm almost downtown. I should go. We're set for UnderBar at six p.m. with your mom. I'll be there on time but if you arrive before me, ask for Kurt. He's one of the owners. He's expecting us."

Mike sounded a little unsure, but responded with, "Kurt. Okay, got it. But Liz, please try to be on time. I don't relish entertaining Marjorie in a bar by myself."

When Liz made it to her office, she had enough time to get coffee and check messages. Nothing that couldn't wait, she was relieved to discover. There were no lurking detectives, desperately seeking her out.

She took the elevator up to meet with Miller a few minutes early, exactly as she had planned. On the way up she remembered that she had asked to meet with him regarding the way Powell's announcement could be perceived as impacting Ty's arrest. But things had changed. It wasn't a matter of perception anymore. There was new evidence. Ty had shared his alibi with Mike and Gary. And Erica had corroborated that information.

Clarice was at her desk and for once, she wasn't on the phone.

"Hello, Lieutenant. You are right on time, as always. Let me tell Captain Miller you're here."

Clarice picked up the phone and announced Liz's arrival. She nodded, responded in the affirmative, then replaced the receiver.

"You can go right in, Lieutenant. He's ready for you."

"Thank you, Clarice," Liz told the admin as she walked toward the office door, opened it, and stepped inside."

Captain Miller was not seated at his desk, as Liz expected. Instead, he was on the sofa on the other side of the spacious office. Miller was holding a folder in his hand which he studied intently. He indicated to Liz to take a seat on one of the two chairs opposite from him.

"Thank you for taking time to see me this afternoon, Captain. There have been a few important developments in the Colby case I hoped to review with you."

"If you mean like that son of a bitch Powell announcing a run for mayor? On the coattails of the arrest of a homeless veteran, no less. An arrest which you tried to explain to me had been rushed? Yes, Jordan, let's review a few things."

"Sir, I appreciate that, but you were operating under information that ADA Powell chose to share with you."

"Don't sugar coat it, Lieutenant. When I'm wrong, I'm wrong. Tell me what else we know at this point, because I have a feeling you didn't back off as you were ordered."

"I haven't actively pursued information, Sir. But some new evidence has come to light that should impact the case."

Liz brought her captain up to speed on Ty's whereabouts when Dylan was killed. She conveyed the story as told to her by Erica out of concern for her late husband's dear friend. Liz did not mention the conversation Ty had shared with Mike and Gary. It was best if Miller didn't know she had been made privy to that exchange. He'd learn about it eventually.

Miller was interested in the alibi provided by Erica, but he reminded Liz that this was information that Ty could have offered sooner, possibly avoiding arrest, as well as keeping the investigation active. Liz agreed that he was correct in holding Ty responsible for that. *That's the captain for you; always seeing the big picture*, thought Liz. But she knew he was right.

After Liz shared what Connors had recently uncovered from Dylan's work computer with aid from IT specialists, she confessed to her captain that she had been present at Ty's arraignment. Miller had read Connors' notes in the system already, which didn't surprise Liz. But he hadn't known that she had been present at court.

"Honestly, Sir, I hadn't planned on going. I wanted to stay away from this one. I wasn't comfortable attending in support of the prosecution but didn't want to appear to be in protest either. After I watched the video of Jack's announcement, I felt like I'd been played. I wanted to see how Jack would handle himself in court and I was curious to see how McCarthy would react."

Miller nodded his assent and continued with more questions for his own clarification, about the charges and the arraignment.

But what most intrigued Miller was the public financial data that Dylan's partner had discovered in their home. Liz held her breath, waiting for Miller to question her access to the data. But he didn't ask the question. Liz wanted the conversation to keep rolling forward before Miller's thoughts could circle back.

"The deceased's partner found it? Didn't know how long it had been there? Had never talked with the deceased about it, why it was saved, or why it might be significant?"

"No, Sir. And Mr. Abbott works in finance himself. He admitted to me that he had viewed the files but wasn't familiar with the data. He thought they looked public. That's why he turned it over to us." Liz wanted Miller to be aware that the files were public to begin with, and the thumb drive contained merely a copy, that had been downloaded to the department server for analysis.

Miller sat back, draping an arm across the back of the sofa, deep in thought.

"Okay, Jordan. Thanks for the updates." Liz thought the captain was going to dismiss her, having heard what he needed to know. She was about to stand, ready to thank Miller for hearing her out, when he continued.

"Now, I have something to share with you. I had a couple of odd phone calls earlier today, Bright and early this morning, I got a call from the DA's office, from Kellerman himself, Powell's boss. Our esteemed district attorney wanted me to understand that Jack had been assigned to the Phillips case by luck of the draw. Mind you, Kellerman has never before felt the need to call me regarding ADA assignments."

Waving his hand in front of himself as if to fend off an offensive odor, Miller added, "That call was nothing more than a big mound of cover-your-own-ass bullshit. If Kellerman really cared about integrity, he would have had Jack censured for pulling this stunt. Honestly, pushing for an arrest to set the stage for his own political plunge."

Miller's voice was steeped in disgust and Liz was surprised that he would have shared his ire with her so vehemently. Liz simply nodded so the captain would know she followed his remarks.

"The second caller identified himself to Clarice as Jack Powell. I'll admit I was curious. I was hoping to rip Jack a new asshole so I took the call. Turned out it was actually from his campaign. It was a fellow calling on Jack's behalf, a guy named Xander Rhodes. It's possible Clarice misunderstood him as he identified himself, but that's not likely. This fellow Rhodes wanted a supporting statement from me, as commander of the Colby murder investigation. In addition, Rhodes wanted my view on the city's street crime, the department's difficulty in managing the problem, and how, as mayor, Jack could assist us."

"I've not heard of this guy. He sounds like a shithead lackey."

"Hmm...sounded more like a strategist to me. But, a shithead strategist, nonetheless. He didn't seem concerned about the numbers of homeless citizens victimized by street crime."

"What did you tell him, Sir?"

"I told Mr. Rhodes that he'd been misdirected. That we have a public information officer for him to contact. I added that police command does not issue personal statements and that I believed Powell already knew that. I told him 'Good day,' then I hung up on the arrogant shithead."

"Nice, Sir. I wish I'd been here to hear that," Liz told him, thoroughly approving of the attitude.

"I'm telling you this so you'll know where I sit regarding this case. You are right, Jordan, you were played, and so was I. And I'm sure you can gauge how happy I am about that. We're reopening the investigation in light of new evidence. I'll have a statement issued to that effect. We'll do what we can to have Mr. Phillips released as soon as possible, but it's in the court's hands. And the DA's."

"I agree that's the best course of action, Sir. There's a killer still out there, after all. That fact angers me as much as an innocent man having been arrested because we were rushed to a conclusion." Liz stood up, thanked Miller for his time, and left his office.

Liz took the elevator back down to her floor. On the way, she remembered the previous meeting with Miller when she had been told to back off and have Ty held for Colby's murder. A lesser person would have expected an apology from the captain, but Liz knew that he was steamed about all of it. When Miller admitted he'd been played, that he'd been taken in by Jack's agenda, it was confirmation enough that he had taken responsibility.

She noticed the squad room was scarily calm for this time in the afternoon. In her office, she checked messages, responded to a few requests, and made some notes. She carefully documented the meeting with Erica and notified Miller that this task was completed. *Connors. He needed to know.* Liz sent the officer a quick message to review her recent notes in the system. He would be relieved to know what had transpired. Liz made a mental note to connect with him after dinner to set up a game plan as to where they would go from here with this reconstituted investigation.

Picking up the phone to call Diana, she noticed the time and put it down again. She had just enough time to freshen up and make it to UnderBar to meet Mike and Marjorie for dinner as she had promised.

Chapter Thirty-five

UnderBar was a trendy food and drink establishment located in the basement of a refurbished building downtown. The atmosphere recalled a speakeasy of the nineteen-thirties and catered to local patrons in the neighborhood. The place also had become quite popular for small, intimate special events. They specialized in top-shelf craft cocktails and really good fare prepared by Kendra, the talented chef and co-owner.

The owners were proud to provide a venue to the local arts community. Poets, authors, artists, and musicians were featured on a regular basis. Their game nights and trivia contests boasted brutal competition. Liz had attended a special event they'd hosted to celebrate the anniversary of the passage of the Twenty-First amendment to the Constitution in 1933, making the sale of liquor legal after twelve years of Prohibition. It had been quite a party. For many years, the basement space had been used for court-ordered sobriety support meetings, a fact that could be seen as odd, appropriate, or oddly appropriate, depending on your position.

The place was in the heart of downtown and had a reputation for treating the street community with respect as long as the respect was returned. On one rare occasion, the respect had not been returned, and Liz assisted with a disturbance call. The incident had ended peacefully with no injuries or property damage due, in part, to the kindness and understanding of the owners and staff. And that was how Liz became acquainted with Kurt, the owner, who had been nice enough to have taken her dinner reservation earlier. Liz and the other officers had been impressed by Kurt's humanity and his ability to maintain a cool head under pressure. Liz liked to visit often. And besides, the place had great food and delicious drinks.

Pulling into a parking spot on the street outside Under-Bar was not unusual. Many of the regular patrons either lived or worked nearby. Liz parked, locked up, and walked to the entrance and stepped inside, letting her eyes adjust to the difference in light. She had taken a few moments to run a comb through her straight, dark blond hair. She'd applied a bit of powder to soften her cheeks and the slightest dab of lipstick.

It seemed like ages since Liz had donned the tan suit and the black blouse. She was glad to have made it through the work day without making a mess of herself at a crime scene or by engaging with a rowdy perp. The necklace she wore with the chunk of amber had been a gift from Marjorie, and Liz was glad she thought to put it on. She rarely bothered with jewelry, especially when working.

Liz descended the stairs, which took a ninety degree turn at a small landing at the mid-point. The unmistakable voice of David Byrne singing, "Take Me to the River," the fragrance of herbs and the aroma of fresh baked bread invited her down. At the bottom of the steps, she was greeted by a dark, cavernous room that boasted ten candle-lighted tables. Behind the tables was a mirror-backed bar decked out with a grand assortment of libations, wines, and pull handles featuring microbrews, and every kind of glassware imaginable. Every candle in the room was reflected in the mirror behind the bar as were the dimly lighted sconces on the walls. The only bright light came from the kitchen area to the right.

At a table against the far wall, Liz saw Mike, sitting with his mother. With them was Kurt, being particularly charming. Marjorie Dwyer was smiling at something Kurt was telling her and Mike looked pleased about it. There was a glass of white wine on the table in front of Marjorie and what looked to be club soda in a tall glass with a wedge of lime on the table in front of Mike.

Kurt looked up, noticed Liz approaching and stood to greet her with arms extended.

"Ah, there she is. Our favorite Keeper of the Peace." He took each of Liz's hands in one of his, extending them to her sides, and gave her a quick kiss on her cheek. "How are you, Lieutenant Honey?" he asked with a wink.

"I'm well," Liz answered. "Thank you for fitting us in, Kurt." Then turning to Marjorie, she said, "I tried to make it here before you, really I did."

"So nice to see you, Liz. Michael and I arrived barely a few minutes ago. Kurt was telling us about when he met you and how helpful you were," Marjorie chirped, as she sipped her wine. She was enjoying the attention. Kurt had Marjorie eating out of his hand. Mike looked to be enjoying the show as he stood to greet Liz.

"That's me, doing my best to protect and serve," Liz said with a smile as she gave Mike a quick hello kiss. Mike returned to his seat and Liz took the chair next to him. Mike mentioned that he had stopped to feed the cats before picking up his mother for dinner, for which Liz was grateful. So much had occurred today, Liz thought to herself. She wished they could go home to her cats and her small apartment, change into old, comfy clothes and discuss the events of the day. But this was one evening, one dinner, and it was Mike's mother, after all. Talk would happen later, she hoped.

"No, no. You protect, I serve. What can I bring you, Lieutenant Honey?" Kurt asked, ready to take her drink order.

"I'd like a glass of what Marjorie's having. It looks refreshing. It is a Chardonnay?"

"It is. It's a Willamette Valley Chardonnay. I think you'll like it. It pairs well with Kendra's special tonight, salmon crostini."

"Perfect. Thanks."

"Excuse me then. I'll be right back with a glass of wine for our favorite cop."

"Lieutenant Honey?" Mike repeated with a bemused expression. He was clearly enjoying the moniker because in his mind, Liz was no one's honey.

Liz returned the bemusement with a grin of her own. "Yep, that's what I am around here. They love me. I'm glad to see you were both well taken care of."

"And Kurt didn't seem surprised when I ordered soda," said Mike, still bemused, and inferring that Liz had shared Mike's recovery with the proprietor, which she had not.

"Why would he be surprised? Not everyone drinks. Especially not everyone who enjoys dinner out."

Marjorie took a sip of her Chardonnay, then said, "I can't believe you still aren't having a drink now and then. How could it possibly hurt?"

"Well, here's the deal, Mom. Let's just say I'd rather not. One might turn into a few. Let's move the conversation along, shall we?"

Marjorie rolled her eyes at his remark but acquiesced. Liz was glad that Marjorie was having white wine. Sometimes the pungent scents of red wine, spirits, even beers were hard on Mike. Liz was embarrassed as she remembered that she and Diana had enjoyed beer with pizza at her house the evening before. She had asked and Mike assured her that it hadn't bothered him. But Liz wasn't sure and she resolved to be more supportive of his sobriety in the future. She looked at Marjorie's glass of wine on the table. Mike had asked her to have a drink with his mother at dinner. He wanted Marjorie to be comfortable, and she obviously didn't understand addiction.

Kurt returned with a glass of Chardonnay for Liz, which he placed on a cocktail napkin. He told Mike that he was so pleased to finally meet him and the two men shook hands. Kurt turned to Marjorie and took her hand in his. He was so glad, he said, that she had joined them this evening. Then Kurt turned back to Liz, telling her that Julian would take their dinner order when they were ready. He excused himself to return to the "back of the house," otherwise known as the kitchen.

Marjorie Dwyer had mastered what was known as "aging gracefully." She was as tall and slender as Liz, but that's where the similarity in their appearances ended. For Marjorie, who had worked as an executive in the fashion industry for decades, it was all about appearances. She wore her silver-white hair short and styled into a coiffure that looked effortless, but perfect. Her face was made up with the slightest traces of cosmetics.

She wore a pantsuit that Liz tried her best to study while the woman remained seated. It was comprised of a long, loose collarless black jacket coupled with Capri-length trousers that were full enough through the entire length of the legs to be mistaken for a skirt. Marjorie wore long, deep-blue jeweled earrings, set off by her platinum hair. She was a stunning woman.

Liz watched as Marjorie placed her hands gracefully on either side of her wine glass as she prepared to speak. "Michael tells me you're involved with a difficult case right now, Liz. He says it has social and political overtones."

"Yes, it is and it does. And we've been ordered to reopen the investigation," Liz stated as she glanced over at Mike, wanting to be sure he understood her point. "But in this case, Marjorie, it's warranted."

"I see. But you've been promoted to Lieutenant. You'll be able to delegate most of the required tasks, won't you?"

It was Mike who answered. "It doesn't always work that way," he tried to explain. "And I'm starving. Let's order food."

"That sounds like an idea. The special Kurt mentioned sounds good to me," Liz decided, as Mike waved Julian over to take their dinner order. "And I'd like to hear about your business trip, Marjorie."

"Oh, no, you would both be bored to tears," she said with laughter, but she was probably correct.

The party of three conversed casually over dinner, mostly Mike and his mother catching up on family news. Liz and Marjorie each enjoyed a second glass of wine and Mike had a refill of soda with a lime wedge. After dinner, they had coffee, decaf for Marjorie. Kendra had surprised them by appearing from the kitchen with a small platter of specially selected, tiny pastries, more varied than petit fours. They were each exquisitely done and were delicious. Liz took pleasure in seeing that Marjorie was impressed.

As Mike prepared to pay the check, he looked across the room as two men took seats at a table. Marjorie didn't notice but Liz saw him instantly tense and set his jaw. Mike handed the dinner check and his credit card to Julian. As the server walked away with them, Mike pointed with his lowered head and quietly said to Liz, "I need to get out of here. The place suddenly reeks of entitlement and bias."

Liz turned to look just as Jack Powell and a second man sat down. She did not recognize the man with Powell, at least not from the other side of the darkened room. Liz doubted that Powell noticed her, of which she was glad. If she decided to approach them, she could facilitate a sneak attack, always a cop's preference. If Powell did notice her, Liz would want to approach first or her diffidence would be perceived as weakness, at least in Liz's mind.

"I'll meet you both outside," Liz said, as Mike signed the receipt for dinner and place his card back in his wallet. "I'll only be a minute." She stood up, casually turned and walked over to Powell's table as Mike and his mother were thanking Kurt for an enjoyable evening.

"Well, Lieutenant. Nice running into you," said Powell as he extended his hand to her. Apparently, he had not seen Liz across the room and was clearly surprised to find her standing there.

"Jack, you're a busy guy these days. I'm surprised you could take a time out. But then, there's really no rest for the wicked, now is there?"

Liz's spoke with a smile but she hoped that Jack and his minion would know she had chosen her words carefully. Liz shook hands with the ADA.

"Lieutenant Liz Jordan, I'd like you to meet Xander Rhodes, who has joined my team. He'll be handling public information for my mayoral campaign. I assume that you've heard my news that I plan to be our next mayor."

Liz didn't offer a "pleased to meet you" comment or the like, but simply repeated his name. "Mr. Rhodes," she said flatly as they shook hands. Quickly, almost as a dismissal, she turned to address Powell again.

"Yes, I've heard. Pretty ambitious of you, considering you're still on the county payroll, Jack."

"Not to worry. I can handle it." Jack turned to Rhodes. "Xander, Lieutenant Jordan was in charge of the investigation that caught that vagrant killer. The one I'm going to keep behind bars for the rest of his life."

Rhodes was studying Liz at the same time she was assessing him. He looked to be about Connors' age, a few years younger than Liz. He was of average size with an athletic build, light hair in a trendy buzz cut with some length left on top. He wore a sport jacket of some decent label over a polo shirt, and dark, pressed slacks. Liz could make out wafts of an expensive men's cologne. Rhodes chewed gum with vigor. In fact, he didn't chew the gum; he seemed to be wrestling it. He may have been wearing the aviator-style sunglasses with mirrored lenses before entering the place but they now were perched out of his way. Liz noticed something in Rhodes' manner. Ex-military, maybe, or security. Maybe he just enjoyed politics. But if Xander Rhodes had had the term "self-important" tattooed on his forehead, the message wouldn't have been more obvious.

"Good work on behalf of the tax-paying citizens of our community, Lieutenant. Dangerous characters have taken over the downtown area, I'm sure you agree." Rhodes assumed Liz agreed with his rhetoric before he continued. He really was an arrogant shithead, as Miller claimed. "The kind of swift justice you performed will be expected and appreciated after Mr. Powell assumes office in City Hall."

"Thanks, Mr. Rhodes, but let's not start counting those votes just yet." Disgusted, Liz turned her attention back to Powell. "As for the Colby case, I thought you might have been informed that it's been reopened due to new evidence."

Powell, coy as ever, smiled. But under that smile was the slightest spot of anger, a barely perceptible irritation. "Yes, I heard that. Something about a half-baked alibi. Too little, too late, Lieutenant. And it won't matter. There's enough evidence already to proceed with trial."

"Well, glad to hear it, Jack. I'd hate to have anything as mundane as Truth or Justice interfere with your political aspirations."

Powell stared to respond. He didn't look pleased to have been spoken to in that way in front of Rhodes. Liz interrupted him somewhat rudely which she thoroughly enjoyed. "Anyway, you both have a nice evening. I highly recommend the special."

With that last word, Liz walked up the steps and out of UnderBar to find Mike and Marjorie.

Chapter Thirty-six

Liz and Marjorie said goodnight with a plan to try to visit again before Marjorie left town. Neither of them expected another visit to happen, but out of mutual courtesy, they pretended.

"How did that go in there?" Mike asked, referring to Liz's impromptu conversation with Powell and his sidekick. He had closed the door for his mother who had taken a seat in the front passenger side of Mike's car. They stood on the curb outside UnderBar. Liz was parked a few spaces up the block.

"They're pompous asses, Jack and his buddy Xander. I'll tell you about it when you get to my place. It will help to review with you what we've learned. It always does. Please tell me you're coming over. There's a lot to talk about and we haven't had opportunity to discuss anything."

"I'll be over," he assured her with a nod of his head. Reaching over, Mike put his arms around Liz and hugged. The hug felt good; welcome, needed after the long day. "I'll be over after I drop Marjorie back at the Hilton. I thought to grab a few things earlier so I don't have to go home before work in the morning." He released her from the embrace. "Thanks for the evening. Mom enjoyed it and so did I. Nice idea to come here."

"Hey, you grabbed the check. Thank you for dinner. I'd better let you two get going," Liz told him, glancing at the car where his mother was waiting. "I need to make a couple of calls. I'll try to finish them up quickly."

Mike stepped over to the driver's door, opened it. "No worries. Do what you have to," he said, knowing the calls would be about Ty. "I'll see you soon." Mike climbed in, started the car and drove away with Marjorie waving goodbye to Liz.

Liz walked up the block to her car, unlocked the door, and climbed in. She organized her thoughts as to what to do next. She wanted to connect with Connors, who by now would know Captain Miller had reopened the investigation. She would hope to hear from Miles with more information about the financial documents. Miles worked fast, but Liz supposed it would be at least another day or two for him to make headway.

Ty was still sitting in jail on murder charges. Diana would work diligently to have the statement from Erica offered into evidence as soon as possible and request that the charge be dropped. Liz was angry that Powell referred to Ty's alibi as "half-baked" and "too little, too late." Was Powell making assumptions? Did the arrogant shit realize Ty's alibi was provided by the victim's mother? No, he couldn't have that much information in such a short time. Miller released a statement that he had reopened the investigation due to new evidence but offered no other details. No, Powell was just baiting her. Liz had made it clear to him that she felt the arrest had been rushed and Powell had disagreed. Liz decided that he was just angry to have been proven wrong.

Liz made it home; shed the suit she'd worn all day, opting for her comfy tee shirt and yoga pants. She sat down with the cats close by and placed a call to Connors, who picked up on the first ring.

"Lieutenant, I got your message and reviewed the notes. This is great news." Connors didn't try to hold back his relief. After all, Liz reminded herself, Ty having been seen in the area was what had prompted Connors to request Liz's presence at the crime scene. As much as the early evidence had pointed to Ty, Connors wanted all the stones turned over. And he had been the one to bring Ty in for questioning, leading to his arrest.

"Well, good news for Ty," said Connors quickly. "But Colby was killed by someone and they're thinking they got away with it, Lieutenant. It's interesting that his mother has known Ty for so long, that his father and Ty had been the best of friends."

"It is, Connors. Her whole story serves to make sense of a lot of things. Her background, her attitude about her son's work, her demeanor. And she was very upset that Ty had been arrested for her son's murder. She said she'd never believe he did it and Ty's lucky she had the gumption to call me. So, here's where we go from here."

Liz and Connors developed a game plan. Connors needed to revisit all interviews conducted as part of the investigation, including staff at the CSO, clients working with Colby, people on the street. He would re-examine the evidence from the scene and talk with Myers again in case the pathologist had discovered something else. The fact was that someone had been in Colby's office the night he died. They came into the CSO, killed a man and made a mess of his office, then left again, unseen. They would dive deeper into Colby's correspondence, looking for areas of concern or trouble. Liz would wait to hear back from Miles and hoped it would be soon. Connors ended the call, anxious to get back to work.

Checking the time, Liz called Diana. The attorney picked up immediately and Liz could tell that she was in her car.

"Good timing. I'm just leaving the jail so I have a few minutes. I'm going to have a busy evening, but I don't mind. Motions to file, you know. None of which would be necessary if the ADA dismissed charges. But I'm not holding my breath."

"Did you hear Miller's statement regarding the new evidence? He's reopened the investigation into Colby's death."

"I'm glad to hear it. Ty called my office himself, requesting a meeting. I figured that talking with Gary and Mike caused him to decide to help himself. And Erica Colby? I'd not have guessed that. The story is amazing, so much history and heartbreak. Ty's alibi is not conclusive without corroboration but I can..."

"But Diana, it is corroborated. That's what I most want to talk with you about. When Erica Colby realized Ty had been arrested and charged, she contacted me in a panic. I went to see her. Erica was disclosing virtually the same story to me in her home while Ty was telling it to Mike and Gary at the jail."

"Well, that's certainly casts a different light on things," said the attorney. "How fortunate for Ty. Did you record her version, by any chance?"

"Sorry, I didn't. I offered to visit because she called the office very upset about something. I assumed she was concerned about the investigation or some procedural issue so I wasn't prepared to record. I never imagined she was going to tell me she was with Ty when her son was killed. She agreed to provide a statement, however, to see that Ty is released."

"I'll include those facts in the motion I prepare and I'll inform Judge McCarthy as soon as possible. He'll need to decide whether to have your department take a statement from her or schedule a deposition. Of course, Jack will hear of this, as well."

"Jack knows, but I doubt he knows that the new evidence involves Erica Colby." Liz shared with Diana that she had run into Powell and Rhodes upon leaving her dinner with Mike and Marjorie. She conveyed the tone of the brief conversation and Powell's attitude regarding new information. Liz also shared that she had met Powell's campaign staffer.

"The guy is a creep. He called Captain Miller for a statement this morning. He claimed to be Jack so Clarice put the call through. I wanted to cuff him to a table as soon as he opened his mouth to speak to me."

"That was pretty bold, calling Miller like that. But those political types will try anything. They have no scruples. Most are just lobbyists. Their loyalties change depending on who's paying their salary. Xander Rhodes is the name? I may look into him; see what I can dig up."

Mike arrived at her front door just as Liz was finishing her call. She walked over to open the door for Mike, letting him know she was talking with Harrison. Liz returned to her place on the sofa. Mike sat down next to her. Eddie and Little Kurt swarmed him as a greeting and he petted them in return.

"Connors is back on the case," Liz told her. "We will do our best to keep you apprised of developments."

"Good. Find the person who killed Colby. That's the best thing we can do for Ty right now. And for Erica Colby."

Liz hung up from her call. Sitting side by side with Mike on her sofa, she looked over at him. She placed her hand on his shoulder and enjoyed a minute of watching him play with the cats.

"Diana just left a meeting with Ty. He shared his story about Erica."

"Good. I'm glad he made the decision himself. Gary was pretty convincing though."

"Diana's preparing a motion for Ty's release but doesn't have a timeline. It will depend on the judge and the DA's office. I was going to tell her that the case has been reopened but she'd heard. And I shared that we ran into Jack. Did you get a look at the guy with him at UnderBar?"

"I did. Who the hell was that?"

Liz explained to Mike what she knew of Rhodes, his call that morning to Miller's office, and the details of the short conversation she'd had with the two of them.

"Great," said Mike. "A minion to do his bidding. He sounded like a strategist to Miller, you say. Anything else you know about the guy?"

"Other than his level of pretentiousness?" answered Liz with sarcasm, making Mike chuckle and shake his head. "I know nothing more. But Diana mentioned wanting some background. Between the two of us, we will learn what we can."

Liz snuggled up to Mike. "Enough. I'm not working anymore tonight. I want to know how you are doing. If I didn't know better, I'd almost say you enjoyed dinner with your Marjorie."

"It was a fine evening, thanks to you. She enjoyed herself and that's all that matters."

"Mike, that's kind of you, but that's not all that matters. She honestly does not understand why you don't drink anymore?"

Mike sighed heavily, thinking of how to respond to Liz's question. When he had formulated his thought, he turned to Liz and tried to explain. His hands continued to caress the cats.

"My mother sees drinking as a social nicety, like linens on the table. She's not been around many people who have felt the need to seek help to stop drinking. And no, she doesn't understand addiction. Recovery isn't about getting rid of the drugs, alcohol, gambling or whatever. It's about getting rid of whatever led you to use them. But in Marjorie's mind, alcoholics are the black sheep in other people's families. Go figure."

Liz listened to what Mike had to say regarding his mother's perception of his struggle for sobriety. She nodded that she understood but she thought that Marjorie's lack of support was odd. "I thought you handled it very well, moving the conversation to another topic."

Mike thanked Liz for the compliment, nodded his assent, and continued to stroke Eddie's soft fur.

"How are you doing?" Liz asked Mike. "I've been concerned about you."

"I'm okay. Tired."

"You seem more than tired," Liz told him. "I know you've had a lot on your mind with this damned case and Ty's arrest, but is there something else going on?"

Mike thought of the intermittent static electricity in his gut that for some reason had taken a respite. He hadn't felt the characteristic uneasiness, the grinding, grating feeling, for most of the day. Certainly not as he had the previous evening.

"No, nothing else. Things at the shelter are pretty normal, I guess. We have a full house. No major issues except the buzz about Colby. Marjorie's visit makes for a change in routine. Yes, I'm worried about Ty. Same as you. Same as Connors. Gary, too."

Liz wanted to leave it at that but she added, "You are right, we're all worried. But I'm concerned about you right now, Mike. If there was something else, would you tell me?"

Mike looked at Liz. He came close to sharing with her about the static in his gut, about sitting in his car outside the tavern in the rain. He came close to telling her that he thought about attending support meetings again. He came close but didn't mention any of it. Not tonight, he thought, as he pulled her close and kissed her forehead.

"Yes, Liz, I would tell you."

But Mike was still deciding whether he would or not.

Chapter Thirty-seven

Miles Carey enjoyed his job. His enjoyment wasn't about catching people in their financial misdeeds as much as uncovering the data they tried so diligently to hide in their records. In Miles' mind, it was a simple matter of following money trails—and there was always a trail.

Contrary to what many people thought, even cash had a point of origin. The Digital Age had made it impossible to hide funds forever. At least from the eyes of someone with skills such as Miles, who knew where to look and what transaction markers to look for. Accessing funds, especially overseas, could be a different matter. But Miles was not interested in access. His job was to determine the route the funds had traveled.

Miles had deciphered the information Liz had obtained from Jayson Abbott. He recalled that it had been stored on a thumb drive that Liz now had in her possession. He preferred storing data on the department server. Much more secure, as he had explained to Liz.

Earlier in the evening, he had contacted John Morrissey, the financial reporter with the *Post*. Miles had not met the man, but knew him by reputation. He was a sharp "money guy" who had been researching local businesses for a long time. He had written articles about the Adams-Colby investments and had been asking the right questions for years. The conversation had proved to be of mutual interest and they decided to speak in person.

The reporter suggested a grubby downtown café. Miles could think of a dozen other places he would have preferred, but Morrissey said the place would be deserted by that time of the evening.

He was correct. When Miles walked into the café, he saw one patron in the place. It had to be Morrissey. He was sitting alone at a booth. The man looked to be in his fifties, with short, graying hair, a well-groomed beard. He studied the screen of a smart phone through wire-framed spectacles. A coffee mug sat before him on the table.

Miles approached with an outstretched hand and said, "Mr. Morrissey, I'm Miles Carey. It's a pleasure to meet you, Sir."

"It's nice meeting you, Mr. Carey," said Morrissey, as he gestured to the bench on the other side of the table. "Call me John. Would you like coffee?"

"Sure," said Miles. He looked at the coffee mug on the table and noticed it was old, chipped and stained.

"Another cup, please," called Morrissey to the server who was hovering near the lunch counter. He turned back to Miles. "Thanks for meeting me here. I don't recommend the food, in fact, I don't remember ever seeing the menu. The best thing I can say about the coffee is that it won't kill you. But it's a good spot for a meeting when you want privacy."

The server came over with a second mug as old and ugly as the one Morrissey had in front of him. She placed the mug on the table and filled it from the pot in her other hand. Then she topped off Morrissey's mug. The coffee smelled very strong, but to Miles' surprise it didn't smell old. Miles took a sip. Not the best he'd ever had, but it was drinkable.

"This place is fine," Miles told the reporter. "It was close and I don't want to take up much of your time."

Miles reached for his ID but Morrissey waved it away. "I know who you are. I checked. I've even seen your picture. You said you were working with the investigation into Dylan Colby's death. I was sad to hear what happened to him. I was acquainted with his father and his grandfather. I wish I could help, but I can't imagine what I might be able to offer," said Morrissey as he raised his mug to his lips. He paused long enough to sip his hot coffee. "Anything I know of the family and their business dealings is included in the articles I've written over the years. If you want to read them, I could provide them to you."

"No need. I've read most of them, that's why I called you earlier. As I said on the phone, I'm not a typical detective," Miles explained. "I'm a financial analyst. I'm looking for confirmation more than anything. What I didn't tell you over the phone is that I know that Dylan sent electronic files to you. By email."

When Miles mentioned the files, the reporter's eyes narrowed behind his glasses. But he was careful not to show his hand. "Why would he have sent anything to me? And, if that were true, how would you know this?"

"I'm sure you know the answer to that question," Miles told him. "Just like you, I find answers, uncover data. As to why he sent the files to you, you're a reporter. I believe he sent them to you to protect the information they contain."

"And you think Dylan was killed because of that information?" asked Morrissey.

"Yes, of course, he was," said Miles. "I think you know it, too. That's why we're sitting here."

Morrissey was thinking as he glanced around the café, deciding how to proceed. "What is it you'd like me to confirm for you, Miles?"

Miles looked around the place, but here was nothing to see. "I think Dylan had been in touch with you before he sent you those files. Did he send the files to support what he told you?"

"He did," answered the reporter with a sigh, "And yes, we had talked. Several times."

"Did he mention anyone to you? Anyone he was suspicious of?" asked Miles.

Morrissey shook his head. "I don't think he was ready to go that far quite yet."

Miles nodded and asked, "When are you planning to go public with this?"

"Soon," Morrissey said. "But first, I need to better understand the data."

"I've researched each file thoroughly. I can tell you everything you want to know, but not until after the investigation into Dylan's death is concluded."

"Do you have a suspect?" asked Morrissey.

"Are you asking as a reporter?"

"I'm asking because I knew of the young man. I believe he was trying to do the right thing."

"I can only say that we're pursuing leads," Miles answered. "But I have a question for you: when I'm able to share what I know about the files, will you tell us about your conversations with Dylan?"

Morrissey thought for a few moments as he wrestled with himself over how to answer. "Yes, I will. Now let's get out of here." They each dropped a couple bucks on the table and left. Neither of them realized they were being watched.

Chapter Thirty-eight

Miles returned to his apartment and got back to work. He often worked through the night when data struck him as interesting or was particularly elusive. Miles was glad to have connected with Morrissey. He concluded his report for Liz and forwarded a copy to her. Included in his report were references to specific links he had uncovered. He hoped Liz would grasp the details but he was used to having to interpret. Miles had accepted long ago that what was simple in his mind was confusing and complicated for the average brain not steeped in financial acumen or data research. He was prepared to guide her through it.

Satisfied with the work he had completed, Miles was exhausted. He stretched, yawned, and threw away the empty can that had contained the third energy drink he had consumed since early the evening before. He would take that over the café coffee any day. He locked down the system. He fell onto his bed and was asleep within minutes.

He woke abruptly about an hour later when there was a knock at his door. He was dazed by the intrusion into his R.E.M. sleep and staggered to the door. He checked the peep hole but saw no one. Miles opened the door, still more than half asleep. A sharp blow sent him reeling backwards into his apartment. He heard the door close before he passed out.

Liz woke to the smell of coffee. Besides the enticing aroma of fresh ground French roast, she knew Mike was still there because neither of the cats had urged her to get up. When Mike was there and up before her, Eddie and Little

Kurt didn't care how long she slept. They both enjoyed Mike's company as much as hers.

She crawled out of bed and slowly ambled to the kitchen. Mike was sitting at the breakfast bar, in running shorts and a tee shirt, scrolling through messages on his phone. The cats were sitting on the bar stool next to him. She walked over and dropped her head, face first, on his shoulder.

"Good morning, Sunshine," he said.

Walking around to the kitchen, Liz took a coffee mug from the cupboard, and poured herself a cup. She took a breath, taking in the aroma, then she sipped, barely believing how good it tasted. Mike always made great coffee.

"How long have you been up?" she asked as she took another sip.

"Not long. Just long enough for a cup of coffee and to have fed the boys."

"Are you running?"

"I am. It's not raining. Want to go?"

The clock told her she had about an hour to herself before getting ready for work. And there was plenty of time before the students would hit the track next door at the high school.

"Sure. But only if I get to finish my coffee."

An hour and a quarter later, they had finished running together on the quarter-mile track. They walked one final lap to cool down as the P.E. teachers started to appear. The teachers waved to Liz and Mike as they were headed back to Liz's apartment next door. Liz enjoyed using the track when it was empty. She felt lucky to have it available and the faculty at the high school didn't mind having the neighborhood cop around setting an example.

Another half hour later, they had both showered and were dressed for work. They had to hurry but had agreed that the run was worth it. The cats were slumbering on the sofa. Mike made more coffee for them and Liz toasted bagels.

"Look at me, domestic as hell," mumbled Liz through a bite of bagel. Mike shook his head in response, amused. He reached for a bagel.

"We should run in the morning more often, rain or shine," Liz decided. "I get lazy, I guess."

"Well," said Mike chewing, considering how best to share his thoughts. "It's good for me. Clears my head. Makes me less anxious. It was nice having you join me and I don't mind running on the track." Mike had taken strength from running since he had been in recovery. He knew that the physical exertion calmed him, kept the buzzing in his gut to a minimum.

Liz nodded, agreeing to run with him more often. "So, let's plan on tomorrow," she suggested. She noticed a couple of paperback books on the bar. They may have been there earlier but she hadn't noticed when she was focused on waking up and drinking coffee.

"What are these?" she asked, picking up a copy of Steinbeck's *Cannery Row*. "Are you taking them to Avalon?"

"I told Ty I'd bring them to him. He requested something he could get lost in, so I grabbed Steinbeck and *White Fang* by London. What do you think?"

"Great choices. Hopefully he won't be in jail long enough to finish them. Would you like me to drop them by? Might be faster for me with my clearance."

"Sure. Thanks, Liz. Tell Ty I'll see him soon. Oh, and I meant to pick up toothpaste for him. He asked for that too. Can you take him yours? I'll replace it later today, I promise."

"The custody officer won't let him have an opened tube. It could be used to smuggle something. But I have a fresh one I'll take him. Still sealed in the box."

Liz grabbed the toothpaste from the bathroom vanity. She placed it in her bag along with the novels. Service weapon and shield in place, she followed Mike out the door with a full travel cup of coffee.

The drive to the justice center complex took longer than usual. Even with decent weather, no rain but overcast, traffic was heavy on the commuter streets. The areas around the courthouse and the precinct were clogged with pedestrians. Finally, Liz made it to her office. After checking phone messages and holding a couple of impromptu conferences with detectives in the squad room, she found her way over to the jail with the items for Ty.

The custody officer manning the desk was an older fellow by the name of Murphy. Liz had known the man for years and knew him to be a decent guy. Murphy's job was to control the flow of official visitors into and out of the jail. Personal visitors were limited to certain times of the day, but investigators, attorneys, evidence gathers, et cetera, were allowed access on a more-regular, less-stringent basis due to their special clearances. They relied on access to do their jobs in a timely manner. Protocols were still followed to the letter because everyone's safety was the responsibility of the custody officer.

Liz approached the desk, which was secured behind a heavy metal grating and a locked entry.

"Hey, Murphy. How are you?"

Murphy glanced up with a half-smile when he saw Liz. "Lieutenant. Good morning to you. I'm well. What brings you over to my patch?"

"Can you clear these items for one of your guys? Ty Phillips," Liz told Murphy, as she handed over the two softcover books and the toothpaste. "I purchased the toothpaste myself. It's unopened. The books are from a friend of his. I'm just doing a favor and bringing them over."

Murphy looked at Liz, then nodded his head. He performed a cursory fan through the pages of both books, careful to position his bifocals to get the best field of vision. He placed the three items to the side and offered a sheet of paper for Liz's signature, which was customary as she was the person providing the items to an inmate.

"Phillips, you said?" asked Murphy, as he keyed the name into a database.

"Yes. Ty Phillips."

"Mr. Phillips is with his attorney at present. There have been some issues."

"Diana's here? What kind of issues? Is Ty okay?"

"There only so much I can say, Lieutenant." Murphy checked the data again. "I see that you were the supervising officer on the case." Murphy hesitated, looked at Liz over the top of his glasses. "Do you know Mr. Phillips?"

"Yes, we're acquainted. It's a long story, Murphy. Can you tell Ms. Harrison I'm here?"

Murphy studied Liz for a moment, thinking. "I can do that, Lieutenant." Murphy picked up a phone, waited for another officer deep in the fortress to answer. "Can you tell Diana Harrison that Lieutenant Jordan is here?" He listened for a few seconds. "Got it. Thanks. She's on her way." Murphy hung up the phone.

"Lieutenant, hang your shield, put your weapon in lock up, and you can go back. They're in room four," instructed Murphy. He placed a hand on the books and the toothpaste. "As you come through, you can take these with you."

Service weapon in a locked compartment and her Lieutenant's shield visible on a chain around her neck, Liz stepped through the door after a loud buzzer indicated that Murphy had released the lock. An officer signaled with a wave for Liz to head down the corridor and pointed to the fourth in a row of small meeting rooms. Stepping forward ahead of Liz, the officer opened the door.

Inside the small, bare, nondescript room was a gray, metal table and three chairs. Seated in one chair was Diana. Across from her sat a version of Ty that Liz had not seen before. Unkempt and unshaven, Ty still wore the orange jumpsuit. But there was more to be concerned with than his appearance. He looked small, withered; eyes barely focused on the table, his hands in his lap. Ty sat eerily still. The fact that another person had entered the room didn't seem to register with him. It appeared to Liz as though integral parts of his cognitive and physical systems had shut down.

Diana glanced up as Liz entered the room and indicated the empty chair next to hers. Diana and Ty seemed to be communicating on some level. Liz took the chair, making eye contact with the attorney. Ty had yet to look in Liz's direction. Diana gave Liz a nod, urging her to speak.

"Hey, Ty. It's Liz. Mike asked me to bring you a couple of things." Liz spoke calmly and slowly. She wasn't sure what kind of response to expect. Studying Ty with a cop's eye for detail, Liz alternated her focus between him and Diana. She hoped the attorney would clue her in as to what was going on with Ty.

His gaze resting on the paperbacks, Ty picked up the Steinbeck. His hand moved slowly and with great effort as though he could scarcely will his limb to do his bidding. He looked over and touched the toothpaste, seemed to realize what it was. Without looking at Liz, he simply nodded his head slightly. Liz watched as Ty slowly swallowed, like a thirsty man who craved water but had none. His breathing was barely perceptible.

"He remembered I like Steinbeck," said Ty. Liz was relieved that Ty sounded like himself except his voice was more quiet than normal. He sounded subdued, tired. Very tired.

"How are you, Ty? Is there anything I can help you with?"

After a few moments of silence, Ty lifted one shaking hand and rested it over his mouth. He looked at Diana and shrugged. She took the reaction as a request for her to answer for him.

"Ty hasn't been sleeping. I mean, at all. He hasn't slept since he was arrested. He's had headaches, stomach aches, and no appetite." Diana looked over at Ty, her face filled with concern. "The doctor we requested from the VA will be here shortly. I was able to stave off the contracted physician here at the jail from examining him because it's not an emergency. The custody officers wanted to have him seen by a doctor because of the tremor."

Again, Liz noticed the shaking of Ty's hand. There was a steady vibration.

"Is the tremor new, Ty?" Liz asked him gently.

He struggled to answer, swallowed again. "It comes and goes. Gets more pronounced when I'm tired. Or stressed." He shook his head, impatient with his own frailty.

"We've been talking, Ty and I, about the new evidence and how I'm working to have his charges dropped," said Diana. She looked from Liz to Ty.

Liz nodded. "Mike would like to visit you again. Let me know when you'd like to see him and I'll let him know."

A knock at the door was followed by the entry of the officer who had led Liz to the conference room. "Dr. Curtis from the V.A. is waiting in the infirmary. I will escort him over when you're finished."

Diana looked at Ty. "Are you okay with that?" she asked him.

Ty stood up, using the table to push off, moving slowly. "Yes, it's okay. Do what you can," he said to Diana, in a quiet, tired voice. He turned to Liz. "Give Mike my thanks. I'll see him anytime they'll let him in. Gary too. And thanks for these." He slid the paperbacks and toothpaste across the table to Diana. The small items appeared heavy as he pushed them away. "Could you hold on to these for me?"

A few moments later, Ty left the room with the custody officer, the books and toothpaste left with Diana. Alone in the room, Liz turned to her friend. "This is what I worried about. I was afraid of adverse reactions. So was Mike. What are you not telling me, Diana?"

"It's part of the trauma. The symptoms are exacerbated by the confinement. Being in jail limits Ty's feeling of control. No sleep, more stress leads to more anxiety. Ty told me the tremor means he's reached a critical point. It's his body's way of signaling overload."

"I feel for him. He's not looking good."

"He's suffering. I'm glad he knows and trusts Dr. Curtis and that the doctor knows Ty's history."

"The fact that he's in recovery makes it harder to treat him," said Liz. "Treatment to calm or relieve pain comes with concern because of his history of dependency."

"And none of this had to happen to him," Diana said with resignation, hands in the air. "I filed a motion to have Erica's statement submitted in evidence, providing Ty's alibi for the time of her son's death. McCarthy's agreed. My office is scheduling with her for later today. We need to have an officer present."

"I'll arrange to have Castillo there. She's familiar with the case. She was one of the first on the scene." Liz looked toward the door through which Ty had exited. "So, with an alibi on the record, Ty should be released soon. Maybe tomorrow?"

"We'll see but I have further news. The DA's office is moving to challenge Erica's statement on the grounds that she's not a reliable witness. Powell is citing her connection to the case and her addiction to alcohol."

"Connection to the case? She's the victim's mother. And as for her problems, how does he even know about that?"

"He knows why Erica was with Ty that evening. And he plans to make Ty's version sound like nothing more than a desperate move by a guilty man."

"Can he do that? Will McCarthy accept it?"

"I doubt it. But that doesn't mean Powell won't try."

"This is bullshit. We have reopened the case. We're looking for a killer, Diana. Ty can prove he didn't kill Colby and it doesn't matter?"

"I will make sure it matters, Liz. In time, we will iron it out and the charge against Ty will be dropped. But right now, I'm concerned about his health and his well-being. As soon as Dr. Curtis gives the okay, Ty's psych eval will be completed. A mental health professional named Tom Beckham will complete it. Ty requested him. Beckham leads recovery groups around town. He's a Licensed Mental Health Counselor. I'm hopeful that talking with Beckham will help him."

"Yes, let's hope so," responded Liz.

Chapter Thirty-nine

Within a few hours, Dr. Curtis' summary of Ty's physical state was submitted to Diana. The physician from the Veteran's Administration had examined Ty in the past so he had an established baseline of his overall health. As suspected, Ty was exhausted, unable to sleep. He had no appetite. His pulse was slightly elevated and he was exhibiting hypertension that was abnormal for him. In addition, he was lethargic but at the same time, overly sensitive to stimuli. The doctor noted a tremor in Ty's dominant hand, his right. He had seen it in Ty before and attributed it to exhaustion.

Dr. Curtis had talked with Ty about using a temporary aid to facilitate rest but Ty flatly refused. The doctor ordered his summary be made available to Beckham, the mental health professional, and requested that the counselor's evaluation be completed as soon as possible.

Tom Beckham had asked to conduct his evaluation in as comfortable an environment as possible. Behind the scenes, Captain Miller had stepped up in a break with protocol and provided a room near his office. There was a sofa and chair on one side of the room and a desk on the other. Miller insisted that Ty be allowed to wear his own clothes for his meeting with Beckham.

Publicly, Miller was saying little about the case other than it had been reopened due to the emergence of new evidence. Privately, he was outraged at the treatment Ty had received, not only as a fellow veteran but as a member of the community and one who had assisted the department on occasion. And Miller was angry that he had been used to make this happen.

Beckham had just finished reviewing Dr. Curtis' notes when an officer escorted Ty to their meeting. Miller had insisted that the officer remain at the door while Beckham met with Ty. Miller may have felt that the officer's presence would ensure their privacy or their safety. Beckham didn't feel the officer's presence was necessary and he didn't know Miller's reason but he went along with it.

When Ty entered the room, Beckham was surprised by his weakened appearance but was able to keep his reaction to himself.

"Hey, Ty. Let's have a seat," he said, as he placed one hand on Ty's shoulder and offered the other to shake.

Ty grasped the counselor's hand for a brief moment, greeted him with a silent nod of his head, the tremor evident. It had been hours since he had seen Dr. Curtis. Ty had eaten nothing, ingesting only water.

"It's good to see you, Ty. It's been a while." Beckham observed Ty with as much discretion as possible. The signs of stress and anxiety were clearly evident.

"It has, Tom. Thanks for agreeing to do this," Ty responded quietly. He hardly moved as if he was conserving sound and energy. He sat on the sofa.

Beckham sat in the chair nearby and began with an explanation. He spoke calmly, his words measured. "This meeting will serve, in part, as a formal evaluation, so allow me to get preliminary questions out of the way. Can you tell me which state are we in?"

"I'm guessing you mean Washington State," he replied. "But as of late, I move between states of confusion, agitation, and fear."

The counselor smiled to himself. The response told him that Ty's sense of humor was alive and well. "Okay, Ty. Can you tell me what day of the week it is today?"

Ty sighed. "That's harder to say. I'd wager it's a weekday but that's about all I know for sure." Beckham noted that Ty made eye contact but it was not sustained.

"Can you tell me where you are and why you're here, Ty?"

"I'm in jail. This room we're in must be somewhere in the bowels of the building since we didn't go outside to get here."

"Can you tell me why you're here?"

"I've been accused of killing a young man, the son of a friend. I didn't kill him and they know it. Someone wants it to look like I did."

"The deceased was the son of a friend, you say. Did you know him well?"

"Not well." Ty tilted his head back, looked up at the ceiling. "I've been in contact with his folks over the years. I rarely saw Dylan."

"The young man's name was Dylan?"

"Yes. Dylan Colby. His father and I were good friends. Doug passed a couple of years ago. I've kept in touch with Dylan's mother. Doug asked that I would."

Grasp of the situation and his surroundings. Understanding of his present and recall of past relationships, noted Beckham.

"I appreciate that you allowed me to see the notes from Dr. Curtis. So, you're not sleeping?"

Ty reached his hand back and rubbed his neck. He took a few moments, appeared to collect his thoughts before he responded. "There are a lot of guys who didn't see combat, and they're in worse shape than me."

"Yes, it's a syndrome including various factors and causes. Right now, I want to talk about you," said Beckham.

Ty sighed and nodded. "No, not sleeping. I can't close my eyes. Weird smells, weird sounds. It's so loud. There's a constant echo. Men walk by my cell constantly. When I try to close my eyes, I see the front line. Basra. Khafji. Bravo Two-Zero." Ty named off Gulf War battles he'd been involved in during his tours. "Strike that last one. I forgot we weren't there, at least not officially."

"Are you reliving the experiences, like they're real for you and you're there? Or are you remembering them, reminded of being there?"

"It's pretty real. At least it seems that way to me." Ty stopped speaking. He glanced at his hands resting on his lap. He held the right hand within his left, trying to hide the tremor. His focus returned to Beckham. "There's some poor kid in the cell with me. Tries to be tough but when he thinks I'm sleeping, he cries. Sobs. As soon as I hear him cry, I'm in Kuwait City. Remember what I told you about the airport, during the liberation?"

Beckham nodded. "I do remember what you told us, Ty."

Ty had shared his experience in Kuwait at a support meeting. During the liberation of Kuwait, the Iraqi resistance tried to hold the airport and was not notified of the retreat order. They continued to fight. Of course, many such facts were withheld from the general public back home.

"It was a bloodbath. It ended as it always does: wailing and crying. Then silence. I hear the kid sobbing and I'm there. It's happened on the street a few times. Someone in distress. It takes me back."

Reliving trauma provokes anxiety. Anxiety makes it impossible to sleep. Exhaustion recalls the trauma. The dreaded cycle.

"And you're not eating." Beckham noticed the tremor but wasn't ready to mention it.

Ty shook his head. "Staying hydrated is the best I can do."

"You have no appetite or you choose not to eat? There's a difference."

"Jail food isn't exactly appealing but I'd eat if I could. My gut knots up at the sight and smell of it."

"You feel unable to eat?" Beckham asked, to which Ty nodded.

"Tell me about the tremor, Ty."

"Started middle of last night. When the kid started sobbing."

"As you said, it's happened before. Dr. Curtis attributes it to exhaustion caused by anxiety."

"Yes, it's happened a few times." Ty studied the shaking limb lying in his lap. "In the past I've relieved the tremor by lowering my stress level. It takes quiet to do that, alone time, extra rest. That's not happening in here. Everything's too vivid and I can't get it out of my head."

"Okay, I understand what you're saying. The surroundings, being in jail, it's extremely stressful. I want to get back to the physical stress you're dealing with in a minute. Tell me more about the accusation you face. You mentioned that someone wants it to look like you killed your friend's son."

"I was with Dylan's mother when he was killed. We had no idea what happened to him." Ty took a deep breath, the inhale taking great effort. "Erica's been abusing alcohol for a long time, her whole adult life. She finally asked me for help. We were talking about it that evening. I didn't feel it was my information to share even though it proved I wasn't the one who killed Dylan."

Beckham understood what Ty was talking about and wanted him to know that. "You were honoring the privacy of someone seeking sobriety. We both know the sanctity of that commitment. But it's an alibi and it can be supported."

"Well, it's more complicated than that. I was in the wrong place at the wrong time. I have military training and I spend my time on the street. All those pieces have played into some local political bid."

Beckham listened closely to what Ty had to say. He had heard some of the recent news stories and made the connection. He knew of Jackson Powell. Beckham knew of Powell's political leanings. He knew that Powell's efforts made it harder for him to do his job helping people with substance abuse and mental health issues. Beckham wanted to keep his disgust at the situation from showing on his face. It required effort.

"You refer to the assistant district attorney who's running for mayor?"

"That's right. And this man thinks homeless people are some sort of scourge, something to rid the streets of. He's prosecuting this case. That's why I'm thinking he doesn't care whether I'm guilty or not. Dylan's death and charging me are his perfect storm."

Beckham agreed. But his thoughts were with Ty's immediate care.

"Stress and anxiety are common issues for you. You manage them well when you can control your environment and activities. Your arrest has made that difficult. I'm concerned that the stress and exhaustion that you're experiencing are compromising your physical health. I realize that you know this, Ty."

Ty attempted another deep breath. He looked Beckham in the eye and nodded.

"Might you be more comfortable in the hospital? At least it would be quieter. And private."

"I don't know, Tom. Seems excessive."

"I'd like to recommend it. You need rest, less anxiety. Your body needs nutrition. Until these charges are dropped it may be the only way to provide what you need. The truth is that if your condition deteriorates much more, hospitalization will be necessary anyway."

Ty nodded that he understood and agreed. A thought occurred to Beckham. "Do you think you would be able to rest on the sofa here while I complete my notes? It's quiet. I'll be just outside."

"I could try. And you don't need to leave."

Beckham took Ty's response to mean that he wanted him to remain in the room without actually saying so. He gave a slight smile and said he would stay. Ty stretched out on the sofa. Beckham covered Ty with his jacket. He dimmed the lights and sat at the desk on the other side of the office. When he glanced back for a moment, he saw that Ty's eyes were closed. Beckham was determined to take at least an hour to complete his report.

Chapter Forty

Diana had returned to her office. She was waiting for the psych evaluation. It would be included with notes from Dr. Curtis in the motion she was preparing for Judge McCarthy. Deep in the details, she was barely aware of the knock at her office door and that it was followed by Lynda, her receptionist entering the room.

"I'm sorry, Diana, I hate to interrupt you but these papers were delivered. I guessed you'd want to see them as soon as possible." Lynda walked toward the desk where the attorney was seated and offered a sealed envelope in her extended hand.

"It's fine. Thank you," said Diana as she accepted the parcel. "Continue to hold calls for me until I prepare this motion. When it's ready I'll need a court courier." Lynda nodded that she understood and left the office to return to the reception area. Diana glanced at the clock. She was always racing against the clock.

As her office door closed, Diana noticed the envelope had been sent from the Office of the District Attorney, specifically from ADA Jackson Powell. She felt her eyes narrow as she turned the parcel over to open the seal. What bullshit was Powell up to, she wondered.

The envelope contained two documents. The first was a motion already filed with McCarthy. Powell had petitioned to disallow testimony from Erica Colby in the matter of the *People v. Phillips* on the grounds that the woman was not only "unduly prejudiced" but was found to be an unreliable witness. Damn, thought Diana. The man had guts but she wasn't surprised.

The second document, however, took her very much by surprise. Powell was attempting to have her removed from the case as defendant's counsel. He was claiming an inappropriate connection between Diana and the investigative team, namely Lieutenant Jordan. The motion continued with the claim that Diana's "past work with the homeless community and women's advocacy groups would require her to withhold information which the prosecution had a right to obtain."

Powell was one sly dog. Diana read the document again to be sure she understood the ploy. Basically, Powell was proposing that because she had served as legal counsel for cases that were somehow connected to this one, her professional boundaries forbade her from disclosing information that may be pertinent in this case. He even cited a past ruling that he felt supported the contention.

It was ludicrous. What did he think? That the homeless in Columbia City were a united bloc who shared with her all the collective details of their lives? It was true that she had represented street people, especially young, indigent adults needing legal counsel. And yes, she often accepted cases pro bono. But the numbers represented a small percentage of her clients.

She could have laughed but she knew ploys like this sometimes worked. She needed to keep her head in the game. But this wasn't a game. The situation involved people's lives, Ty's life, Erica Colby's life, and the death of her son, Dylan.

Diana simmered over the information and its implications, attempting to calm herself. She picked up a pen, held it in both hands, and focused on the writing tip. It was a tactic she had learned in law school and often employed in the courtroom sitting at her table while her opponent had the floor. The action provided a means of calming down by appearing unconcerned when, in truth, she was deeply troubled.

An idea came to her. She pursed her lips as she reached for her office phone. Diana dialed Powell's direct line. *Fine,* she thought. *You want to reduce this to a game, Jack? Don't assume you're the only one with a strategy.*

"Jackson Powell," he answered. The phone had barely started to ring. Did he expect her call?

"Hey, Jack. It's Diana."

"Diana. What's up?" The rush in his voice told her he wanted her to think he was busy. She should feel special, he wanted her to think, that he would take time to speak with her. What a smug, self-important asshole.

"Just a couple of quick questions. Do you have a new hire in the DA's office named Rhodes? Xander Rhodes? The name came across my desk and it's not familiar."

Powell hesitated just long enough for Diana to know she'd caught him off guard. "He's not with the DA. Rhodes is working on my campaign."

"Oh, got it. That makes sense. Interesting name, Xander. Do you happen to know if Xander is short for Alexander?" she asked, trying to sound precise. She wanted Powell to suspect she was researching Rhodes.

"Uh, yes, I think so. Why?"

"Because I wondered if it was the same Neanderthal who bullshitted his way into a phone conversation with Captain Miller. Not very professional of him, don't you agree?"

"No, I don't agree, Diana. He simply asked the captain for a quote regarding a current case."

"Here's the deal though. Rhodes claimed to be you. That's how Rhodes represented himself and was put through to Miller. He told a bold-faced lie. Your campaign staff does not work for the DA's office. There should be very clear lines of separation between the two. This was strike one for your team, Jack. I'll look forward to meeting this cretin in court. Nice to know I can have papers served at your campaign headquarters. Bye, Jack, and thanks for the help."

Diana hung up the phone. On the other end of the line, Powell slammed down the receiver.

Chapter Forty-one

Liz returned to the precinct to find several messages and an alert that she had a priority communication from Miles. She was about to open the correspondence when her phone rang. The caller ID told her it was Kelly Denucci, outreach manager-slash-expectant mom. Liz didn't have time for a social conversation. She had work to do. She needed to find Connors for an update. The fact that Ty was languishing in jail was heavy on her mind, as well as the fact that the real killer was out in the community somewhere. Kelly's call may be important, she thought. Kelly wasn't one to waste anyone's time. Maybe she had had the baby. Liz reconsidered and picked up the phone.

"Hey Kelly, what's up? Are you a mommy yet?"

"Uh, not quite yet, but thanks for checking. I've been thinking about something. I couldn't get it straight in my head until last night. Am I correct that a couple of street kids claimed they saw Ty near the CSO around the time Colby was killed?"

"Yes. That's been part of the evidence against Ty. Why? Do you know something? Are they lying?"

"No...not exactly. But there's a chance they may be mistaken. Just follow my train of thought. I'm sure you've heard Mike talk about working with the county's accounting department. Gary and I have the same relationship with them. It's tedious work. Some of them are decent people, don't misunderstand me. But some of them make it difficult because they only see the bottom line. I try to tell myself they are only doing their job. Many are fine to work with, a few I don't care for. But there's one I don't trust in the least."

"Okay, I hear you," responded Liz, wondering where this was going. She really needed to move this along.

"This one person, he's bold. He's about my age. Most younger guys aren't so transparent with their opinions but he's bold. It's like the old joke: was he absent the day they taught common courtesy? At budget meetings, his attitude is that what we do, the services we provide, is a waste of time. He clearly feels that the funds allocated for services to the homeless community would be better spent elsewhere. It can be uncomfortable. Anyway, I saw him a couple of times with Colby."

"Okay, go on." Kelly had Liz's full attention at the mention of Colby. Liz felt her heart rate increase as her attention was piqued.

"I saw them together once near the park. It was a Saturday morning. It struck me as odd. I was talking to a group of folks. Checking in with them, you know, seeing how they're doing. I noticed Dylan and the guy across the street at the Java House on Beaumont. They tried to keep a low profile, I think, but I recognized them. I wouldn't have thought anything about it. I mean they could have been friends but I would have given Colby credit for having better taste. This accounting guy is a piece of work."

"You say you saw them together more than once?"

"I saw them together only one other time. It was in the evening about a month ago. I was driving home from an after-hours meeting. They were on Main near the CSO, Liz. They were parting company as you would at the conclusion of a meet. I had time to watch because the light on the corner was red. I can get the date if you need it because I remember the meeting."

"This guy works in accounting for the county? And you saw him with Colby twice, having coffee on a Saturday morning and again on the street near the CSO." Liz wanted to be clear for her notes.

"I did. That Saturday morning was about a month earlier than when I saw them by the CSO. I gauge everything by when I stopped doing field work because I was too far along in my pregnancy."

"What's the guy's name, Kelly?"

"His name is Marshall, Grady Marshall. He won't be difficult to find. He's a county employee. And Liz, this is what is most significant. When I saw them on the street in the evening, I thought for half a second that it was Ty that I was seeing with Colby. Marshall resembles Ty enough to be mistaken for him. Same build, same dark hair, only younger. And Marshall carries a backpack. It's not exactly like Ty's but the same size and it's a dark color."

"Okay, Kelly. Thanks. Let me look into this Marshall. Can I get back to you if I need to?"

"Of course. I'm sorry I didn't put the pieces together sooner. Pregnancy brain, I guess. At any rate, I'm glad I caught you in the office."

Kelly was relieved to have talked with Liz about Marshall. The information may not lead anywhere but she knew Liz would look into it. Kelly wasn't sure when she'd have another chance to talk about it anytime soon. Unbeknownst to Liz, Kelly was in early labor. She wanted work-related details out of her mind. She looked at the time and noted ten minutes since the last contraction and they weren't lasting long, about half a minute. That was a good start, she told herself. Pete would be home in a couple of hours. With luck, the timing could be just right.

Chapter Forty-two

Liz opened the email correspondence from Miles. It had been sent early that morning. Very early, in fact. The time stamp was hours before she and Mike had taken their morning run on the high school track next to her apartment. Checking the clock, Liz realized it had been a long day and it wasn't over. The email began with a greeting and an odd explanation:

Liz:

Nothing in the files that I was able to work with. They were too scrambled. Glad to hear when we talked earlier this evening that you had dumped the originals. There was no reason to save them. When you have time, check leave reports for your crew. I need you to confirm. They are under the usual file names. Thanks for putting me in touch with the guy at the *Post*. He was helpful. We're talking about a collaboration.

Miles

Liz read the email twice before she realized it was coded. To begin with, it didn't sound like it was written by the Miles she knew. He would not use a word like "scrambled" to define financial documents. She and Miles had not talked yesterday evening. And he had clearly told her to put the thumb drive in a safe place. They had not talked about dumping anything. And leave reports? Mikes didn't review them. That was the purview of the department's HR people.

He was steering her toward the files, the ones she had placed on the department server from Colby's thumb drive. And Liz had forgotten that she had asked Miles to look into the financial articles written by John Morrissey about Doug Colby's business.

Liz found the files in question and opened them. She could see that he had flagged certain fields as significant but she didn't know why. He had added brackets around certain numbers and had highlighted or bolded others. Liz knew that Miles had discovered something. She just didn't know what. She punched in the numbers for his desk. He didn't answer. If he'd worked all night, he may still be at home asleep. Liz didn't want to bother him at home unless she had no other choice.

She wanted help but Liz felt a need to be cautious about whom she approached. She could ask Miller. He may understand the accounting process. She'd told him that she had the thumb drive so he shouldn't be surprised. Liz called his office.

Clarice answered almost immediately, knowing the call was from Liz's desk. "What can we do for you, Lieutenant?"

"Is he in, Clarice? I could use a few minutes."

"He is. But let me check if he can be available. Hold on for a few moments." While she waited, Liz stared at the accounting files, trying to interpret something of value. Clarice came back on the line.

"Captain Miller will come to your office in a few minutes. He says he needs a walk and a change of scenery."

A short time later, Liz could hear a mild commotion coming from the direction of the squad room. She realized that Miller had chosen to stroll through and say hello to the team. When he made his way over to Liz's office doorway, he tapped a quick knock on the doorframe. Liz rose from her seat and walked out from behind her desk.

Miller waved both hands in Liz's direction. "Don't get up, Lieutenant. I'm fine taking a chair on this side. It's your office. I'm the visitor. I'll take the visitor's chair."

"Hello, Sir. Thank you for seeing me on short notice. There's something I need to show you. It's on the server. I'm hoping you can tell what some of it means. Please," she said, as she motioned to her desk chair. "It may be easier for you to see the document from my chair."

The Captain was confused for a moment but he quickly shook it off. "Okay, Lieutenant, let's have a look." His reading glasses were hidden in his shirt pocket. He pulled them out carefully with his thumb and index finger and put them on. He sat down in Liz's chair and studied the computer screen. "This looks to be a financial document. Am I correct?"

Liz stepped over to the door and closed it then took a seat in the visitor's chair. "Yes Sir, these are financial documents. I placed them on the department server for Miles Carey to analyze. These files were on the thumb drive obtained from Colby's partner."

Miller looked at Liz over his glasses for a long second, then he turned his attention back to the monitor, tilted his head back at an angle to look through the lenses. "This appears to be the same accounting software the department uses. May I assume these flags were added by Carey?" As he asked the question, Miller pointed to particular notations.

"Yes, Sir. Miles sent an odd email that directed me to the files you see here. The email was coded. He wanted it to sound like he had been unable to gain anything from the files but we can see that's not the case. Carey was trying to stay under the radar. I'm sure this file is connected to why Colby was killed."

Captain Miller looked at Liz over the top of his reading glasses again, his eyebrows raised. He returned his focus to the screen. Pointing to several numbers in particular columns, Miller explained to Liz what he thought he was seeing. "These are revenue sources. These numbers are lines with totals for allocations. The ones with Carey's flags seem to reconcile. I'm seeing dates, as well. This file covers a fiscal quarter. You say there are other, similar files?"

"Yes, Sir. Close to a dozen, if I remember correctly."

"Then we could be dealing with fiscal malfeasance going back a couple of years." Miller continued to study, commenting on what he saw. "Where is Carey? We need to know exactly what we're looking at here."

"He's not in his office. He may be sleeping, Captain. He pulled an all-nighter on this."

"Screw that. Get him in here. We're wasting time. We're most likely looking at data that got Colby killed. And we need to find his killer and get Ty Phillips out of jail. We need to clean up this damn mess."

Liz nodded. "You're right. I'm on it." Reaching for her phone, she tried Miles' desk again. No answer. "I'll get hold of him, Sir. I'll get him in here." She tried his cell phone. The call went to voice mail.

Chapter Forty-three

When Miles came to and tried to open his eyes, it was the taste of blood in his mouth that told him he wasn't dead. He was not able to move his body much. He was disoriented. The confusion he felt could have been from the hit, an injury, or a sedative. He didn't know which nor did he have the capacity to figure it out. He had a tremendous headache.

He thought he was in his apartment, lying on the living room floor. Miles wasn't sure if that knowledge was helpful or not. He wanted nothing more than to sleep. It was a long while before he was alert enough to begin figuring out what may have happened. He tried to make sense of the series of events but he kept losing his place and had to start over.

Miles had been asleep after working into the wee hours of the night. He thought he had finished and gone to sleep around dawn. Because he had been asleep, he was unsure what was a dream and what was real. He remembered talking with someone. *Morrissey, John Morrissey, the reporter. That's right, from the financial desk at the Post. They'd had coffee in that grubby café.*

He'd been awakened by the knock on his door. He thought he checked to see who was outside before he opened the door but he wasn't positive. *But why wouldn't I check? I always check. I must have opened the door.* Before he passed out again, Miles thought there was someone in his apartment with him. But he was too out of it to care and he lost consciousness again.

*"I need you in my office, Connors. As soon as you can get here," said Liz, leaving a message. She hadn't spoken with Connors since the previous afternoon, before dinner at UnderBar and running into Powell and his right-wing mouthpiece, Rhodes. With the investigation into Colby's death reopened, Connors was retracing steps, re-interviewing folks, and re-examining the evidence from the night of Colby's murder.

Liz knew that pieces were missing but she could feel them coming into view, but it felt like shadows that were not yet defined. Miller or a few of the other veteran investigators might relate to what she was feeling but it was hard to explain. It was even more difficult to teach this to the younger investigators on the team.

Connors had left a message for Liz earlier, about the emails on the dead man's work computer. IT had traced the IP address to a location in the city but it had taken some time. They were working to identify the account subscriber.

Liz grabbed her Cougars cup and headed to the coffee maker in the break room. She brewed a fresh pot from ground Robusta she'd forgotten she had in the back of her desk. It was probably too late in the day for the high level of caffeine in the Robusta but Liz wanted the boost. As the aroma of the brew started to filter into the squad-room she knew she'd only get one cup. Everyone jokes about cops and donuts but the truth is that strong, fresh coffee is what they crave.

She tidied up the table in the break room while she waited for the coffee to brew. The strong scent took Liz back to the scene of Colby's death and her conversation with Cheryl

Hamilton, Colby's boss at the CSO. Cheryl had been helpful to the investigation and they had shared a cup together. Liz wondered how the woman and her staff were handling their loss. Perhaps Connors had been in touch.

When Liz returned to her office with hot coffee, she had two new messages. Connors was on his way back in. With traffic, he was thirty minutes out. The second message was from Mike. He and Gary were planning to visit Ty. He said things were calm at Avalon. He assumed she was having a long day. If he didn't hear from her, he would feed the kids at the end of the day. Liz was grateful for the message. She was appreciative that Mike had thought to connect. She wanted to give him a heads up that Ty's stress and exhaustion levels had worsened. She settled for two minutes to send a quick text message:

"Delivered books this a.m. Ty more stressed. Not sleeping or eating. Dr. visit and psych eval today. Visit with you and Gary might help. I'll try to be in touch later."

Sipping her coffee, Liz saw the alert signaling recent updates from the IT department. They were on the trail of the last few emails sent from Colby's work computer. The last of them had been sent the evening he died, shortly before the time that forensics had estimated to have been the time of his death. The email had included attachments. It was sent to a personal email address belonging to a local reporter named John Morrissey. Liz recognized the name as the same journalist who had written articles about the Adams and Colby family businesses. And Miles made it sound like he had been in contact with Morrissey, as well. She really needed to talk to Miles.

IT had identified another account connected to Colby's work computer. Liz read the IT report stating that Colby had sent several emails at regular intervals from a personal web account over the past two years. It struck Liz that this was the same period of activity that Miller had mentioned regarding the files on Colby's thumb drive. There were only so many coincidences you could excuse before admitting that details were inextricably linked. IT had traced this recipient email account to Grady Marshall.

Chapter Forty-four

Liz quickly reviewed each detail that Kelly had shared about Marshall: dark hair, medium build, worked as an accountant for the county. Kelly was a good judge of character and rarely expressed distaste for a fellow human being. But Kelly was adamant that she didn't trust Marshall and he had made it clear he didn't respect the work she did.

Liz needed a visual, something to make sense of the details in her brain. On a legal pad she kept at her desk, Liz drew a circle. She placed a DC in the middle for Dylan Colby. No. That wasn't the visual she needed. She scrapped it and made a cross representing X and Y axes. At the top of the Y axis she placed DC for Dylan Colby. She knew now that Colby was connected to Marshall. She placed GM at the bottom of the Y axis. Collaboration. That was the word Miles had used in the coded email about his contact with Morrissey, the reporter. Collaboration was significant. On the left end of the X axis she placed an MC for Miles Carey and on the right, a JM for the financial reporter, John Morrissey. She traced both axes with the tip of her pen, deep in thought. These four men were connected and one of them was dead. Their shared area of expertise was finance. Liz stared at the intersection of the axes. Then it hit her. It was the data files.

A fast search through the county directory gave Liz the contact information for the accounting department. She put a call in to the supervisor listed in the directory. Instead of going to voice mail, a live person answered. A woman's voice said, "Accounting, this is Rollins."

"Hello. This is Lieutenant Jordan with the Police Bureau. Am I speaking with the department supervisor?"

"Yes, you are, Lieutenant. This is Marta Rollins. How can I help you?"

"Ms. Rollins, I'm looking for one of your staff, a man named Grady Marshall. Is he available?" While Liz was talking with Rollins, she searched DMV records for an ID photo of Marshall.

"Actually, he is not. Mr. Marshall is not in today. If this is regarding an accounting issue, might there be something I can assist with?"

Marshall's ID appeared on her monitor with his photo and vital stats. Short, dark hair and brown eyes, clean shaven. Medium height and weight. The driver's license showed an address near downtown. The date of birth put the man closer to Connors' age. Liz could see why Kelly mistook Marshall for Ty when she saw him on the street with Colby. The basics were similar. And like Ty, Kelly said he carried a backpack. Liz hit the print command.

"Ms. Rollins, I need to locate Mr. Marshall as soon as possible in connection with an active investigation. Do you know where he is right now?"

"My guess is he's at home," she responded, without hesitation. "He left a message for me very early this morning that he would be out today. I have not known him to miss a day of work before. Not one. And the message was hard to hear. He was calling on his cell."

"Ms. Rollins, I need Mr. Marshall's cell phone number." Liz jotted down the number as Rollins recited it.

"I guess you can't tell me what this is about," Rollins stated to Liz. It wasn't a question.

"As I said, it's regarding an active investigation. Should you hear from Mr. Marshall, under no circumstances are you to tell him I've been in touch. Are we clear on that?"

"Of course."

"And no one is to go near Marshall's work space either."

"I understand," said Rollins. Liz thanked the woman for her help.

"You're welcome. Whatever's going on, it doesn't surprise me."

"How do you mean?" Liz asked.

"Grady's a good accountant. He's young but he's precise with figures. The issue is he's not very skilled at social interaction. I'm sorry. I really shouldn't say anything."

"Anything you can tell me will help, Ms. Rollins." Liz hoped to play on the woman's concern for an employee. "Mr. Marshall may be in need of our assistance. We're not exactly sure of his situation. Now is not the time to hold back."

"Well, here's the deal: Grady tends to see the world differently. He's better with numbers than with people. He can be offensive. It occasionally causes a problem. Do you think he's in trouble?"

"Could be. That's why we need to find him. Ms. Rollins, if you see or hear from Mr. Marshall, call me."

"Oh, I will. Be sure about that," she said, and they ended the call.

Liz grabbed a communications tech specialist to locate Marshall's cell phone by accessing GPS. Even if he was at home, she wanted that information before knocking on his door. She had to hope he'd left his phone on. He had. The GPS locator in Marshall's cell phone placed him within one hundred yards of Miles' apartment. Liz figured there were only a couple of reasons Marshall would be near Miles' home and none of them were good.

Connors appeared at her office door. "Don't sit down," Liz told him, as she flew out of her chair. "Come on. I'll catch you up on the way."

Chapter Forty-five

No one had heard from Miles since the evening before. Liz's best guess was that he was being held in his home against his will by Grady Marshall. She had to hope he was all right until she knew different. It didn't help to assume the worst. Their plan was to surprise Marshall and take him into custody.

"We've connected Colby to Marshall, and Carey to Morrissey," explained Liz as Connors drove. "The commonality is the data files from Colby."

"And who is Morrissey?" asked Connors trying to keep up with Liz's process.

"He's the financial reporter for the *Post*. He's written articles about the Colby family businesses going back to when Erica Colby's father was mayor. I'll bet he's been looking at records for a long time and I'm sure he knows a lot. Connors, the last email from Colby's work station was to Morrissey. It included attachments."

"Colby's dead, Miles may be in danger or injured, and we suspect Marshall is involved." Connors was going over the basics for his own benefit. "So, where's Morrissey?" Connors and Liz exchanged a glance causing Connors to get dispatch on the line. He requested that a team of uniformed officers contact the reporter at his office to ensure that Morrissey was safe.

Miles' apartment was on the ground floor toward the back of a small complex with buildings arranged to afford privacy but not to allow neighbors to be intrusively aware of each other's comings and goings. As far as Liz could tell from the rear of the apartment, the residence appeared easy to secure. The shade on the sliding glass door was drawn and the small concrete patio was surrounded by an six-foot wall. Liz opted to enter from the front, doubting an escape from the rear was possible.

Trying to listen at the door was useless. Connors could hear nothing from inside. He looked up and saw that there was a small, fixed window high up and to the right of the front door. He was taking a huge chance of alerting Marshall but he climbed up and carefully peered inside.

Miles lay on the floor at the furthest point from the front door. Connors couldn't tell his condition but his hands appeared to be bound. Marshall was sitting in a chair, his right side toward the door. He wasn't armed, at least that Connors could see, but after he climbed down and relayed to Liz what he'd seen, they weren't assuming anything.

Connors kicked in Miles' front door with one hit and the blow sounded like a flash-bang. Liz entered the apartment first with her weapon drawn. Connors was right behind, covering her and scanning the room at the same time.

They had definitely taken Marshall by surprise. He was shocked. By reflex, his hands flew above his head as his body shrank away from the armed officers. He was soon shaking like a leaf, screaming, "Don't shoot me! Please, don't shoot!"

A quick search proved there was no one else in the apartment. Connors kept his weapon aimed at Marshall while Liz cuffed him. With the scene secured, Liz immediately checked on Miles. He was breathing, had a pulse, but was barely conscious.

"What did you do to him?" she yelled at Marshall, as she called for an ambulance.

"I didn't touch him!" Marshall screamed back.

"Liz?" The voice didn't register at first. She realized it was Miles calling her name but she scarcely heard him. "Liz..." she turned back to her hurt colleague.

"Yes, it's me, Miles. And Connors is here. It's probably best if you don't try to talk. We don't know how badly you're hurt. An ambulance is on the way."

"But, Liz, you need to know...there was another guy here."

The next couple of hours saw the day fade into evening. Miles had been taken by ambulance to the hospital. He was evaluated in the emergency room and found to be in better shape than Liz would have expected. He'd suffered a nasty blow to the head but would recover. He was admitted for observation and rest. An officer was posted outside his room.

Marshall would be arrested for felony assault, forced entry, and unlawful imprisonment. He may or may not have inflicted injury on Miles, but he had entered his home without invitation and kept him from leaving. In addition, Miles was obviously in need of medical care which Marshall had chosen to ignore. He had not yet been charged because they didn't want the information on the public record just yet. They hoped they could get him to talk.

Liz had only a few minutes with Miles. The ER doctors said no excitement, only rest and fluids. Liz promised to keep it short but it was important she speak with him.

"Tell me what you remember, Miles," asked Liz quietly. She didn't think he looked bad, just tired.

"I think I was asleep. I mean... I remember going to bed. I think a knock on my door woke me. I'm sure I checked the peep. I always do. There was no one there." Miles stopped. He closed his eyes for a moment, tried to lick his lips but his tongue was dry. Liz helped him take a drink of water. He thanked her then he continued. "I must have opened the door to look out. I didn't see anyone but something hit me. Hard. It was like an explosion. I felt myself fly backward." Miles winced, the memory of the attack making his head hurt more. "I don't know how long I was out. I must have been in and out for a while."

"What can you tell me about the other man who was there?"

"Only that there were two distinct voices. One guy, he was there first. It must have been him that hit me. Then they were both there. They argued. Then the first guy left. The guy who was there with me when you and Connors came in, sounded younger, nervous. He was totally freaked out by the first guy."

"His name is Grady Marshall. He works for the county as an accountant. Have you ever had contact with him before?"

"Marshall, huh? Shit, I don't know."

"What did they argue about?"

"The second guy, the nervous one, Marshall you said, didn't want to be there. The first guy told him he had to stay with me but this Marshall guy told him he wanted out. That's what he said, he wanted out. The other guy said that wasn't happening and he'd better not fuck up. He told Marshall the plan was riding on this. The older guy kept mentioning their plan...some plan."

"Would you recognize the other guy? The guy with the plan?"

"I doubt I'd recognize him. I didn't see him. But I might recognize his voice."

"His voice?"

"Well, yeah. I woke up one time, before the younger guy, Marshall came in. I could hear the guy trying to boot up my computer. He was really pissed, cussing. My system has a kind of failsafe on it. If it gets messed with, it goes dead...can't be restarted. Well...except by me. The asshole didn't plan on that. That's why I sent you the strange email. There is evidence of major corruption on those documents. I felt confident that the files on the server would be secure, but you never know with email. Even departmental email."

Miles paused for a moment. He closed his eyes and took in a ragged breath, but he wasn't finished. "And I wanted you to know I'd connected with John Morrissey. The guy's been reporting on local financial news for many years. He's familiar with the Adams and Colby families and he's been studying the documents that were sent to him by Dylan Colby. Apparently, they'd been in touch a few times. Morrissey was saddened and alarmed by Colby's death."

"Okay, Miles. Get some rest. I'll check back when the doctors think it's okay."

"There's one more thing, Liz..."

"What's that, Miles?"

"When the guy was cussing and angry, he sounded completely different, animated. It was weird. When he and the guy named Marshall argued, Marshall was freaked out. But the first guy? He was calm and cool. He sounded mechanical, like he'd been trained to stay in control."

Chapter Forty-six

They had discussed it together as a team. Liz thought it was better to have Connors question Marshall. She would observe and if she felt anything was missed, Liz could jump in. But she doubted Connors would miss a beat.

Marshall had been placed in a holding room. He'd been given time to think about his choices and what to do next. Whoever he was working with hadn't heard from him and may have figured out that they were in trouble. The place was being watched. Maybe they'd get lucky. If the partner returned to Miles' apartment, they would know the situation had soured for them when they saw the front door.

Marshall was already sweating. By now, his partner would have assumed what happened and was moving ahead on his own. Liz and Connors wanted Marshall to think about that and how he'd been told not to "fuck up the plan."

Connors entered the room alone and sat down, barely acknowledging Marshall, to see how he'd react.

"Hey, you can't keep me here," he yelled, pulling on the cuffs which were attached to the metal table. "I'm starving. You have to get me something to eat, man." He acted like a spoiled college kid, thought Connors and he would bet that Marshall had a tendency to gravitate to people who got him into trouble.

"Do you remember me, Mr. Marshall? I'm Detective Connors. I was the one who broke down the door and put you in those cuffs at Mr. Carey's home. You know Mr. Carey, right? He's a colleague of mine. The man who was assaulted and needed medical help in his own home, thanks to you."

"I did not hurt that guy. And yes, I remember you. How could I forget? I said I was hungry. How long do I have to stay here?"

"Well, that up to you. Mr. Marshall, we'll get you food. But you're wrong about the other problem. We can keep you here for as long as it takes. Until you tell us what we want to know." Connors gave a shoulder shrug, like it was beyond his control. It was all up to Marshall himself.

"I told you, I don't know anything."

"We both know that's bullshit. I'm aware that you knew Dylan Colby. Did you kill him?"

"No, I didn't kill Dylan! Yes, I knew him but I sure as hell didn't kill him. You have the guy who killed Dylan. A bum. At least that's what I heard."

Connors wasn't a violent man but he wanted to hit Marshall on the side of his head with the steel chair he was sitting on. Instead, he looked him in the eye. Connors wondered if Marshall knew how lucky he was that Connors was capable of self-restraint.

"Why were you holding Miles Carey? Against his will in his own home? And who was there with you?"

"I was just watching him, all by myself. To make sure he was okay."

"He would have been okay, if you and your buddy hadn't beaten the crap out of him. What was that about?"

"I don't know. I said that already."

Connors stared at Marshall, thinking of how best to get in his head. Nodding his head slowly, he had an idea. "You know, Mr. Marshall, I think you must be a smart guy. I know you're an accountant, a numbers guy. I know you work for the county. I also know that you received financial documents from Colby on a regular basis."

When Connors mentioned the files from Colby, Marshall grew pale; a worried expression crept onto his face. "What was going on between you and Colby? You should tell me, you know. We're going to find out anyway."

"I'm not saying anything, man." Marshall repeated the same line but he looked worried, the smugness slipping.

"So, you've gone from 'I don't know anything' to 'I'm not saying anything'. That's not the same thing. Let me tell you what I think is going to happen: Miles Carey is a forensic accountant. You know what that is. Carey can trace money, where it came from, where it went, the whole nine yards. And he's the best at what he does. But I think you already know what Carey does and that he's good at it. That's why you and your buddy beat him up. But you were too late. We have the files and they've been analyzed."

"You have nothing. You can't harass me into telling you things I don't even know." Marshall waved his free hand in Connors' direction for emphasis. "I want a lawyer. Now!" Marshall sounded like a grade school bully who enjoyed getting other kids into trouble.

"No problem. You haven't yet been charged but you can have your call. Don't get me wrong," said Connors, sounding sympathetic. "I don't think any of this was your idea. I think you're caught up in shit that you didn't bargain for, shit that got out of control. But you're in a lot of trouble. We have three charges pending against you, possibly others, including malfeasance and conspiracy to commit murder."

"No, no. You're crazy! All you have is a bullshit story you've made up. I didn't conspire with anyone. I didn't murder anyone. And I didn't beat your friend."

"Then who did?" Connors slammed his hand down on the table, the hollow metal causing the sound to amplify. "We know you weren't in Carey's apartment alone. I'm asking you once more, who was there? If you don't tell me, I'll have to assume you acted alone. You really want to carry this load by yourself? Fine." At that, Connors stood up as if to leave the room, pretending to give up on Marshall having any idea of self-preservation.

"Wait!" The panic in Marshall's voice was real. He paused for a moment to regain his bravado before he continued. "If I tell you what I know, what are you willing to do for me?"

Connors wasn't ready to sit back down. He wanted to keep Marshall flailing. But he figured he had him where he wanted him. "Here's how it works: you tell us what you know and then we'll decide what you deserve."

The wheels of decision-making were turning. Connor could almost hear them grinding behind Marshall's eyes as he pulled himself together and decided to save himself.

"Okay, okay. Listen. The guy that beat up your friend. His name is Rhodes. Xander Rhodes. He's like a mercenary. He scares the shit out of me. He's a freaking robot. He was in Afghanistan or somewhere like that. Thinks I should kiss his ass for that or something."

"What happened this morning at Mr. Carey's home?"

"Rhodes called me. Early. I wasn't even up. He said to get my 'worthless ass' to the address he gave me. When I got there your guy, Carey, he was on the floor. Rhodes said he had things to take care of and I was told to stay there until he came back. I told him he was crazy. He'd gone too far. I'd had enough. He basically told me to suck it up. He left."

"Do you know where Rhodes went? What he was up to?" asked Connors.

"I do not. I don't want to know. That's all." Marshall made a side to side motion with his free hand like an umpire calling a runner safe. "If you want to know more, you'll have to ask Rhodes yourself."

From the small room next door, Liz observed the interrogation. She'd been impressed with how Connors had handled Marshall. The young detective had come a long way. A few days earlier, Liz stood in the same room with Powell as Connors had questioned Ty about Colby's death. It had been only a few days but it seemed like a much longer time. And it had been a much different interrogation. Ty had been placed at the scene of a crime and had been reluctant to defend himself by betraying a confidence. But this guy, Marshall, was apprehended inside the home of a seriously injured man. He whined like a child, asked for food, and then betrayed his friends.

Yes, Mr. Marshall, Liz thought to herself. *We will ask Rhodes. You can be very sure about that.* And Liz was certain that the path would lead from Rhodes in one direction: straight to ADA Jackson Powell.

Leaving Marshall to stew, Liz and Connors retreated to Liz's office. Before they continued their search for Rhodes, they needed to learn whatever they could about him. Connors searched the man's personal information while Liz checked into Rhodes' finances. It didn't take long for them to realize that Rhodes tracks were well hidden.

"I've been unable to find anything much about the guy," Connors told Liz. "He has an address in town, works for Powell's campaign. He has a SUV registered in his name. What about you, Lieutenant?"

"I haven't found any financial data. His credit history is almost non-existent. He intentionally has no paper trail, Connors."

"Marshall mentioned that Rhodes had been in Afghanistan, that he was proud of serving and wanted Marshall's respect." A search of a VA data base yielded nothing.

"If he's a veteran, we should be finding details, at least dates of service, discharge information," thought Liz, aloud.

"Why would a former serviceman want his information kept secret?"

"Maybe Rhodes isn't the one keeping it secret." Liz reached for the phone and punched in Miller's extension. "The only person I know who can get sensitive information on armed forces personnel is the Captain."

Chapter Forty-seven

Liz was able to catch Miller between meetings, but he didn't have a lot of time. "I know you're busy, Sir. We're on to something that I think is significant but Connors has hit a dead end. According to this shitbag, Marshall, Xander Rhodes served in the military but we're finding no record of him."

The details had piqued Miller's interest but the look on his face as she finished her explanation was cautious, to say the least. The captain nodded slightly, eyes squinted as if looking at a distance, lips pursed. "Let's not assume that he's a veteran until we confirm. There are any number of imposters who create the mystique of having been in uniform. To those of us that actually were, it roils the blood."

Listening to Miller, Liz knew that her captain had shared something important, personal. Miller realized it too. He raised his left hand, palm up to Liz, and said. "I'm sorry for that, Lieutenant. But if Rhodes served, I think we both know there are only a couple of reasons his records would be sealed."

"That's what Connors and I thought, Sir. But we've run out of options at our level to dig any deeper. And, please, no apology necessary."

"Give me some time. I'll get back to you," Miller said, excusing Liz, as he picked up his personal cell phone. Liz noted to herself that whomever Miller was contacting, it wasn't an official call and there would be no record of it.

Diana was seated in the modest conference room at her law office. With her were Erica Colby and Officer Castillo.

Due to the sensitivity of the case, McCarthy had agreed to let Erica's statement be recorded in Harrison's office with an officer present to represent the department. Further, the judge found no basis for the claim that Mrs. Colby would be a prejudiced or unreliable witness. He had firmly explained to Powell that any official statement was considered admissible unless proven to be false. That was why, McCarthy reminded the ADA, that penalties were imposed for making a false statement to police. Also, McCarthy had balked at Powell's assertion that Harrison had a conflict. The judge's feeling was that Powell had the only conflict, he had created it, and that he had better keep his mouth shut.

"Mrs. Colby, before we begin let me express my sorrow for your loss," began Diana. "And I am also sorry that the court must ask you to record your official statement at this time."

"Thank you, Ms. Harrison. I know you mean that and I appreciate your kind words."

"The court and my client are grateful to you, as am I. The information you have to share is necessary to allow an accused man, whom I represent, to go free."

"Yes, that's why I contacted Lieutenant Jordan. I couldn't allow this mistake to continue even if the truth reflected badly on me."

"Is there anything you need before we begin, Mrs. Colby? I will need to be thorough but I will try to complete this process as quickly as possible."

"I understand. No, I'm quite comfortable and I want to be here. It's the least I can do."

"Would you state your full name and place of residence for the record, please?"

"Erica Adams Colby. Columbia City, Washington."

"Thank you. Do you understand that your statement will be part of the official record regarding the investigation into the death of your son?"

"Yes. I understand," responded Erica, confirming her knowledge of the process.

"Please explain how you are acquainted with Tyler Phillips."

"I've known Ty, Mr. Phillips, since high school, almost thirty years. He and my husband were best friends."

"We are interested in what transpired on the day in question between yourself and Mr. Phillips. You may limit your response to the period of time between five o'clock in the afternoon and shortly after seven that evening. Do you understand?"

"Yes, I do understand," said Erica, in response to the question. "But I feel the need to provide back ground as to why the evening progressed...uh...for Ty and myself...the way it did. Is that allowed?"

"Certainly. If you feel the information is relevant," said Diana.

"I had talked with Ty earlier that day and we spoke a few times in the days prior." The woman hesitated for a moment. "I...have a problem with alcohol abuse. My late husband wanted me to address my problem but I know now that he enabled me to avoid it. My son wanted me to address it but wanted the issue to be dealt with privately, at home. That solution wasn't going to work for me. Ty was going to help me by being a friend, as he's always been to my family."

"I know that was difficult to share, Mrs. Colby, Diana said. "You talked with Mr. Phillips leading up to that afternoon. Did you see him in person?"

"Yes. Ty suggested that I attend a support meeting as a first step. To listen, to be present in a community of people who understand how difficult that first step can be. He said I didn't have to speak until I was ready. He offered to attend with me as a support. He was aware of a meeting in a different neighborhood where he wouldn't be known, thinking I would be more comfortable. I was supposed to meet him there for the meeting from five o'clock to six. I intended to meet him there. I drove to the location and sat outside for quite a long while. But I could not do it. I couldn't go inside. I disappointed Ty and I disappointed myself." She reacted to her own statement with thinly veiled emotion.

"Would you like to pause for a few minutes?"

"No, I'm fine. Thank you." The attorney noted to herself how strong Erica sounded under the circumstances.

"What happened next?" asked Diana.

"I wanted to apologize to Ty, for wasting his time and effort. I knew he would be coming back toward the park after the meeting. I waited for him in the parking lot nearby. He sat in my car and talked with me. He said it would do me no good to attend a meeting until I was ready. But he urged me to admit I had a problem. Once I did that, he said, I'd place more importance on taking action. And he was correct."

"You talked with Ty while sitting in your car. Can you tell me what time that was?"

"I can tell you exactly. I know the time because my housekeeper ends her day at six p.m. unless I ask that she stay later. She called my cell phone because she had not heard from me. She asked if I needed anything else before she left my home for the evening. And she asked if I was all right. She thought I sounded upset."

"Is that in-coming call still noted in the call log on your phone?" asked Diana, although she knew that it was.

"Yes, it is. I took the call at six-fourteen pm. We talked for only a minute or two. Ty came walking up as I ended the call. He sat with me. We talked for quite a while. Possibly an hour."

"And you are sure, without a doubt that Mr. Phillips was sitting with you in your vehicle from approximately six-fifteen until after seven p.m. that evening?"

"Yes, very sure."

"And did you see the direction he went when he left you?"

"Yes. He walked across the street from the park. I saw him go up the steps and into Brooks House. I know the time because we checked it before he left my car. It was just after seven. He wanted to be sure how I was feeling before he left me alone. And Ty said he needed to eat something before it got any later."

"Thank you, Mrs. Colby. Unless Officer Castillo has further questions, I think we have everything we need."

Chapter Forty-eight

Captain Miller didn't disappoint. He called Liz back in less than an hour.

"This was a delicate subject for my contact. I confirmed that Rhodes did, indeed serve. Records are sealed unless you know who to ask. It seems that Rhodes was an exemplary soldier until near the end of his second tour. He was part of a team of Marines trained at Camp Lejeune. The team was referred to simply as The Squad. Apparently, this team was trained in a variety of controversial methods."

"Rhodes shares a similar background with Ty."

"Yes, and Rhodes was a Golden Boy until he started to spout less than tolerant views of many of his fellow teammates. At some point, he felt he was being passed over while other, less admirable men, in his opinion, were promoted or given key assignments. After receiving some disappointing news, Rhodes took a baton to a meeting room. He had to be restrained. He was placed in isolation and in the hospital for observation. Officially, he was discharged for medical reasons."

"Would Rhodes have been trained to take a man down in the way Colby was killed?"

"Are you asking if he have been trained to kill with his bare hands? Absolutely."

A warrant was issued for the arrest of Xander Rhodes. Finding him was another matter. Rhodes had not been seen at his residence. Connors and Liz would try his place of business, the newly acquired headquarters for Powell's mayoral campaign.

When they arrived at the campaign office, they were greeted by a staffer. The young woman had assumed that the officers baring their shields had stopped in to offer their support for Powell's campaign. Liz was happy to burst her bubble.

"We're here on police business. Is Xander Rhodes here?"

"Uh, no. Xander isn't here," she said, her face fell in disappointment that was quickly replaced by concern. "May I ask what this is regarding?"

"No. You can't," Liz told the young woman, keeping her response succinct. "Do you know where we can find Mr. Rhodes?"

"Uh, I do not. He...hasn't checked in lately. You can leave a message, uh, if you'd like."

"No, I wouldn't like. But thanks." As Liz and Connors turned to leave, Powell came bursting through the door. When he saw the two of them, his expression showed surprise tinged with suspicion.

"What are you doing here?" he asked them, glancing over at the woman who had greeted them, obviously looking for input. The round-eyed staffer didn't offer a word.

"We're looking for Xander Rhodes," she told Powell while she flashed the warrant. "Do you know where he is? And you'd better think before you answer, Jack. This is a police matter. If you bullshit us, we might take it as an attempt to obstruct."

"What? You are both mad! May I see the warrant, please?"

"Of course, as an appointed officer of the court, you're entitled," said Liz as she handed the papers to him.

Liz noticed that Powell didn't ask why they were there with a warrant, or what charges might be involved. Liz took that as a significant omission. Did he know something? Or had he merely anticipated trouble?

"Please notice the warrant was signed by Judge McCarthy," added Liz.

Powell perused the document, his jaw clenched. He exhaled quickly, as if frustrated. He had recalled Diana's threat and assumed the papers were regarding Rhodes' phone call to Captain Miller. He refolded the warrant and handed it back to Liz. "Can we speak privately?" he asked, gesturing to an enclosed area at the rear of the office.

"Absolutely, Counselor. But keep it brief. I don't have a lot of time." She and Connors followed Powell into a room at the back of the office. Powell closed the door.

"This warrant claims Rhodes assaulted a police analyst? When did this alleged assault occur?" Again, Liz thought it odd that he didn't ask where it had occurred, but he wanted to know when. Powell knew something, but Liz wasn't yet sure of what.

"Early today. Have you seen or spoken with Rhodes today? Keep in mind, Jack, you had better tell us the truth."

"I'm not going to lie to you." Powell acted like the idea was absurd. "Regardless of what you think of me, I'm not a complete idiot. I haven't seen Xander all day."

"Have you heard from him? Talked to him?"

Powell looked at Liz but he was silent. He appeared to be calculating how to respond, when he said, "Do you mind if I pour a drink?"

He was walking toward the liquor cabinet when Liz answered, "Actually, yes, I do mind. Please wait until we're finished here." Powell stopped abruptly, taken by surprise at Liz's response.

"You have a nerve, you know that?" he sneered. "You come into my place of business..."

"Answer the question. Have you heard from Rhodes today? Have you talked to him since this morning?"

"I have not talked to him. I've been busy doing my job. Remember? I have a job to do, too." He hesitated, thinking what to say next. He sat down on one of a pair of comfortable-looking armchairs and rested his forearms on his knees. "Xander left a text message on my phone. He said it was urgent that we meet as soon as possible. I messaged him back that I could not get away until the end of the day, that my schedule was packed. I told him to meet me here. I expected to find him here when I arrived."

"Do you know where Rhodes is? And I'd urge you to be very, very careful."

"I thought he was here," answered Powell, hands raised, fingers splayed in exasperation. "Since he's not, I do not know where Xander is."

"Forward his cell phone number to me, Jack. And we're going to look closely at the messages the two of you have been exchanging."

Powell stared at Liz for half a second then reached for his phone. He quickly punched a few keys, sending her the number. "I don't know if Xander's phone is even on. I haven't heard from him in hours." Powell placed the phone back on the nearby table. "But let me tell you one thing: if Rhodes doesn't want to be found, you won't find him."

Liz thought that Powell's statement was rather bold but she was careful not to react. Instead she exchanged a glance with Connors. The officer had been quiet but Liz wanted to know what was on his mind, what he wanted to do next, so she asked him. "What do you think, Connors? Do you believe this?"

Connors looked at him. "Listen, Mr. Powell. You're a man of the law, an assistant district attorney, for Christ's sake. To be honest, this is a pretty big mess. You might want to consider helping us here, if you can. Mind if I sit down?" With a look of condescension, Powell indicated the sofa opposite him. Connors sat down and posed a question.

"Mr. Powell, do you know a man named Grady Marshall?" The question came out of nowhere and hit Powell like a punch. He looked stunned. Shock was evident on his face. Powell struggled to recover his composure. Still red with anger, he tilted his head back with his chin raised a bit too much.

"I don't recall knowing anyone by that name. Why? Who is he?" Liz and Connors both picked up on the cue. Powell stared directly into Connors' eyes when jolted into shock at the mention of Marshall. But when the initial shock passed, so did the eye contact. They took the reaction as a sign that Powell was evading.

"Huh. Okay. Well, Mr. Marshall works for the county. He's an accountant. He was acquainted with Dylan Colby.

He says they were friends. He's been forthcoming about some recent events involving Xander Rhodes, namely the assault mentioned in our warrant for Rhodes' arrest. Are you sure there's not some information you could provide?"

Powell had lost his poker face, a critical skill for someone practicing law. He seemed mortified to hear that Marshall was talking to the police. Powell covered the lower part of his face with his hands. He closed his eyes and took a deep breath. It was sad to watch as he tried to maintain what was left of his dignity.

"I have nothing else to say. If we are finished here, I'd like you both to leave."

"Okay, we're going, we're done here," Liz said. If you hear from Rhodes before we find him—and we will find him—convince him to turn himself in. That's all you can do."

"Are you quite finished, Lieutenant?"

"Yes, I'm finished. Connors, let's go." At the door, Liz turned around. She couldn't resist. "Hey, at least you can have that drink now, Jack."

Liz followed Connors out to the front office. As they walked past the young staffer, Connors wished her a nice evening.

Chapter Forty-nine

Ty had slept for a full hour on the sofa in the small room where he had met with Beckham to complete his psych eval. He had needed the sleep badly and was grateful to Beckham for making it happen. When he woke, he was escorted back to his cell but not for long. Ty was moved to the hospital within a few hours. When he was transferred, there were no beds available on the general admissions floor, so Ty was placed in a room in that area of the hospital reserved for patients in a coma. At least it was quiet and comfortable.

It was well into the evening when Mike and Gary made the trek to visit Ty. Gary got held up due to a fight at Brooks over a pair of shoes and Mike wanted to wait for him. When they finally arrived at the jail, no one knew what was going on with Ty; at least no one was talking. Mike reached Diana and learned that following his psych eval, Ty had been transferred to the hospital. Although it concerned him, Mike was relieved to know his friend was receiving the care he needed.

There was a rather comfy arm chair, covered in soft vinyl, next to Ty's hospital bed. A nurse had quietly stepped in to see if he was awake and wanted visitors. When Mike and Gary walked in, he was sitting comfortably reading *Cannery Row* by a small, bedside light.

"Hey, guys," said Ty when they entered his room. Mike wanted to hug him but since Ty was seated it was awkward. Mike grasped his hand instead, alarmed at how weak it felt in his. Sitting or lying down was all the activity Ty had had.

"Good to see you, man," Mike said, as he shook Ty's hand.

"Good to see you," said Ty. "Thanks for coming." Mike thought his friend sounded tired but there was no tremor in his right hand.

Gary stepped over and placed a hand on Ty's shoulder. "How are you feeling? Have you eaten anything?"

"I had gelatin and chicken broth. That's what the nurse recommended. I need to take it easy on my stomach for a few days. The broth was good. The gelatin is all fat and sugar, which I guess is what I need. Maybe soup tomorrow. What kind of soup was in the pot tonight, Gary?"

"Your favorite, cream of potato. I should have brought you some, man. I wasn't thinking. Wild day." He stepped back. Mike was sitting on a small chair, the only other one in the room. Gary indicated the bed and asked Ty, "Do you mind if I sit?"

"Be my guest, please," Ty told his friend.

Mike stood up. "Here, Gary, take the chair." Mike didn't want Gary to have to haul himself up to sit on Ty's bed. It was an adjustable hospital bed that was high off the floor and hard to get up on. Especially for someone of Gary's age. It was the polite thing to do.

"Thanks, Mike," Gary told him, as he lowered himself to the chair.

"Sorry for being late," Mike explained to Ty, as he found a portion of wall on which to lean. "Gary had a little issue to deal with at Brooks and I wanted to wait for him."

"Yeah," added Gary, nodding his head. "We went to the jail first. Got the run around. Finally talked to Diana and found out you'd been moved over here."

"Nice, though," said Mike, as he looked at Gary. "We just walked in here like no one's business."

"It isn't anyone's business," said Gary, ready to protect his civil rights.

Ty grinned, listening to his friends. "So, what happened at Brooks?"

Gary looked up at the ceiling, scratched his neck below his beard. "You know Boyd, right? Well, he and Coot got into it over a pair of work boots. Boyd claimed they were his boots. I believed him but he didn't exactly conduct himself appropriately. But he's starting a job tomorrow, so he needed his damn boots. Coot said they were his, that he'd found them in the dumpster. Boyd was really pissed. It got out of hand. Now, Coot never accused Boyd of taking the boots from him, mind you. And he couldn't tell me which dumpster he found them in."

Ty listened, nodding his head. "Hey, a man's boots are a serious business."

"Yeah, they are. They surely are," agreed Gary.

"So, what did you do?"

"I found a pair of decent boots in the donations. Showed them to Coot. Told him he could have them. He was fine with them. Backed off. Good thing too, because I was close to asking them both to leave and I don't like to do that. Especially with Boyd starting the job in the morning. And Coot isn't safe on the street. When I left, Coot was asleep. Wyatt's there tonight. He's on top of it. He'll keep them apart.

If you'd been there you could have handled Boyd while I calmed Coot."

"Sounds like it worked out." He picked up the copy of his book. "Tonight, it's me and Steinbeck."

"And the gelatin," said Mike with a smile. Gary chuckled and shook his head.

"Mike, when this current episode is over, there's a favor I need from you," said Ty, sounding serious.

"Well, it should be over soon," Mike told Ty. "I understand Erica Colby's on the record about your having been with her the evening her son was killed."

"Yes, she's given an official statement, as the lawyers say. I'm grateful to her. Grateful to a lot of people, actually. Diana, Liz, Connors. The two of you," Ty said, through a pensive smile, his head resting on the back of the chair.

"What's the favor, Ty. I'm sure it's something I can handle."

"If I'm going to get my strength back, I need some time—weeks maybe—up at the cabin. I usually hitch-hike or take the bus as far and I can and then walk the last few miles but I'm not up to that. Could you give me a ride?"

Mike was caught off guard. He had no idea where the cabin was located, other than northeast of the city. But he was not going to disappoint Ty after the man had been through so much. "Sure. I can do that."

"I'll need provisions, too. I can't haul too much in the state I'm in."

"Make a list. I'll get the items together. No worries."

"Thanks, Mike. I very much appreciate it. I'll reimburse, of course."

With that done, he turned to Gary. "I'd like you to come along, Gary. The cabin is a place I've never shared with anyone. Mostly, for privacy but for safety, too. It's full of ghosts and memories, some I'm ready to deal with now. I'd like to share the place with the two of you."

"I'm there, Ty. Sounds like a road trip," said Gary, feeling honored. He gave Ty a fist bump. He turned to Mike. "We should let this guy rest and I need to get home. My bed is calling. I can hear it, I swear I can."

"Yeah, you're right and I'm ready for sleep, too," said Mike. "Ty, when these bullshit charges are dropped, you're welcome to use my place until you're ready to go up in the woods. It's small but quiet. I'm at Liz's most of the time."

Ty was touched by the offer and he told Mike so. "I'll consider it, I will. Thanks, man." Mike and Gary said goodnight and Ty returned his attention to Steinbeck.

When the two men exited the elevator on the first floor of the hospital, they ran straight into a tall, slender man in the corridor. The man was distracted beyond explanation and apologized for nearly knocking the two men over. The distracted man and Mike recognized each other simultaneously. They pointed fingers at each other, saying in unison, "Hey, aren't you Mike? Aren't you Pete?" The man was Kelly's husband, Pete Denucci.

"Yeah, yeah." They continued to speak in unison, heads nodding.

"Sorry, sorry," explained Pete. "Kelly's in labor. Our baby is coming. I have to get back in there. I had to move the car." He was a bundle of excited anticipation. Pete reached for Mike's hand and shook it. He reached for Gary's hand and shook it, saying "Hello, I'm Pete. Our baby's coming. It's nice to meet you."

"Best of luck to you," Gary told him. "Nice meeting you, Dad."

"Oh shit, you're right. Dad!" Pete looked Gary square in the eye and said, "It's happening. I need to go!" He took a few steps, then turned around. "Mike! Please tell Liz that our baby's coming. She's on the list of people Kelly wanted me to contact. But things were moving too fast. And I can't get hold of Kyle Connors either. Let him know, too, okay? Thanks!" With that last word, Pete headed down the corridor to the birth center.

Mike called after Pete, saying, "No problem. I'll let them both know." They watched as Pete headed down the corridor and out of sight.

Chapter Fifty

Neither Liz nor Connors felt any pity for Powell about the state of agitation he was in when they left him. Without saying it aloud, they were both thinking that at the very least, he had a lot of questions to answer. As far as Liz was concerned, it wasn't the philosophical differences. It was the lines crossed and laws broken. At some time in the near future, Liz hoped to learn what Powell knew and when he knew it.

"I don't get why people are so heartless," Connors stated, while Liz pulled the car into traffic. "Jackson Powell wants to be our mayor but he has no empathy for people experiencing homelessness, temporary, chronic, or whatever. All he sees is vagrancy. That campaign announcement speech made it sound like the solution is to lock people up or move them somewhere else. The court system has ruled over and over that experiencing homelessness is not a crime."

"Kelly told me that Marshall expressed a similar view. And when I met Rhodes at the restaurant the other night, I got part of the same manifesto from him," Liz said, stopping at a red light. She used the opportunity to adjust the wipers and the heat for the right balance. "He just assumed I agreed with him."

"We see the stats. People living on the street are victims of crime more often than they are perpetrators," said Connors with conviction. "When we get calls regarding folks on the street, most of the time they aren't bothering anyone.

They usually need something simple, like a phone, a meal, a safe place to rest."

"You know all this, Connors, because you actually talk to the folks on the street. Kelly and Mike too. And Gary's been doing that work for longer than anyone I know."

"Sorry, Lieutenant, for going on about it."

"Hey, Connors, we're all entitled to vent. My mom says it's healthy. When people see the homeless near their home or place of business, they see that as a problem. But the problem isn't that these people are there, it's that they have nowhere else to be. They are perceived as a threat even if they're minding their own business."

"People should ask themselves this question, Lieutenant: this person serving my lunch, delivering my order, or making my latte, is it possible they could be without a permanent address?"

"True," said Liz nodding her agreement.

"Okay, I'm done," resolved Connors. "My head needs to be around finding Rhodes. What's our plan?"

Liz handed her phone to Connors. "Contact the tech team with Rhodes' cell phone number. If it's on we can get a location on him. Check in for any buzz on Rhodes, possible sightings, bank transactions. Any word from anyone that can give us a clue to where he is. Everything is second to finding him. We've seen what he's capable of, what he'll resort to."

"Got it, Lieutenant," said Connors, as he prepared to make calls.

"And the reporter, Morrissey; I want to confirm that officers have had a face-to-face."

"At this point, we don't know what Morrissey knows or who he's been in contact with," said Connors, thinking out loud. His point was valid.

"True, Connors, but Miles mentioned him in the email to me regarding the data files. When Miles is well enough, we need details about what he discovered."

"Lieutenant, Miles must have learned more than he shared."

"Exactly. We know there was an organized effort between Rhodes and Marshall. Colby was either involved or found out. At some point, things turned really bad for Colby and it cost him his life."

"And Colby emailed Morrissey with attachments minutes before he was killed. It sounds like he was blowing the whistle, Lieutenant. Why else would someone send information to a reporter except to make it public?"

"And when Miles analyzed what we assume is the same data, he connected with Morrissey, and was attacked in his home."

Connors followed Liz's train of thought to the next step by saying, "So, Morrissey is either involved..."

"Or he's in danger, too."

Chapter Fifty-one

John Morrissey walked up the steps to his front door. He lived alone and liked it that way. Morrissey was good at his job and he enjoyed his routine. Now in his early fifties, he has no desire to complicate his life with on-going relationships. He found that they required too much of his time and energy.

Morrissey's forte as an investigative reporter was exposing corruption and the misuse of public funds. He took his responsibility as a journalist seriously. He believed that people should know when corporations were financially ethical and when they were not. Further, Morrissey wanted administrators of public funds to be held accountable because taxpayer dollars were just that, the taxpayer's dollars.

Key in the door, he thought of Miles Carey, the forensic accountant whom he had spoken with the prior evening. Morrissey's name had come up, Carey said, during the course of the investigation into the death of Dylan Colby. After Morrissey verified that Carey indeed worked with the police, he suggested they meet. Recently it seemed that they had been looking at the same data files. Morrissey had received the files in an email from Dylan, but Carey had known about that already. Carey didn't say how he had obtained access to them but Morrissey had a pretty good idea.

Morrissey had not known Dylan well, he told Carey. They had spoken a few times. Morrissey was familiar with the dead man's family going back to when his grandfather, Bill Adams, had been mayor. Morrissey was familiar with the

Adams-Colby business enterprises and had interviewed both the former mayor and Colby's father, Doug, for articles he'd written for the *Post* over the years. Morrissey explained that while he didn't always agree with their business practices, he had to admit that he had not uncovered anything illegal or unethical in their dealings.

As Morrissey stepped inside and closed the door behind him, he thought about having been contacted earlier by police officers at his office. Morrissey had not particularly minded and this wasn't the first time that officers had been seen in the newsroom. Their presence always got the place buzzing with possibilities.

Their visit had been to inform Morrissey that Carey had been assaulted early that morning. It was concerning to him, that Carey had been assaulted but he hadn't planned to tell the officers that he had met with him. As it turned out, they knew of the meeting already.

They were looking for a man named Rhodes in connection with the assault. Morrissey was not familiar with the name but the police considered this man to be dangerous. They had shown Morrissey a photo of Rhodes. Morrissey told the officers he did not recognize the man pictured. He promised to contact them if he saw this man. The police would be in touch again although Morrissey didn't feel he could help them. The officers confirmed Morrissey's home address and a number where he could be reached. The card with contact information given to him by one of the officers was in his jacket pocket.

Placing his keys, phone, and briefcase on the table in the foyer, Morrissey noticed how cool it was in the house. Had he left a window opened? Not likely, he thought. Two steps toward the living room, he stopped short, surprised to see a young man sitting on his sofa.

"Who the hell are you?" he demanded. But he already knew. He recognized Xander Rhodes from his photo.

Morrissey knew that surprise and fear had registered on his face. He realized now that the police had contacted him for assistance but they had also intended to warn him. Too late now.

"What are you doing here? How did you get into my house?" Morrissey's question was answered when he saw the broken window.

"My name is Rhodes but I think you know who I am. We need to talk, you and I, Mr. Morrissey." Rhodes was a distance away, maybe twelve feet. On instinct, Morrissey turned to run. Rhodes was on him before he could take a full step. He knocked Morrissey off his feet and had the reporter on his belly on the floor within seconds. Rhodes bound Morrissey's hands with a zip tie then leaned down, his mouth very near to the back of the man's ear.

"I said we need to talk. That's why I'm not going to gag you. But if you struggle or cause me more of a problem, I promise you, you will regret it."

"What do you want with me, Rhodes? I'll cooperate. If you tell me what you want, I'll do what I can. If you hurt me, I can't help you."

Rhodes hauled the man to his feet and dragged him to a chair. He pushed Morrissey into it and bound his feet using more of the zip ties. Now that Rhodes had him face-to-face, he saw a small trickle of blood from Morrissey's mouth.

He'd caught a tooth on his inner cheek when he went down. Rhodes pulled the bottom of Morrissey's shirttail and used it to wipe away the small amount of blood. He showed it to Morrissey as the reporter cowered. The reporter noticed that Rhodes wore latex gloves. Rhodes dropped the shirttail from his hand. He stepped back to the sofa and sat down opposite Morrissey, staring at the man.

"I am going to explain to you why I'm here, Mr. Morrissey, so listen carefully. Dylan Colby was an associate of mine. He betrayed me, the man we work for, and the objectives we have worked toward for a long time. Much effort and consideration have been wasted as a result of his betrayal. My task now is to minimize that waste, to stop the bleeding, you could say. In my experience, it's very important to stop the bleeding." Morrissey noted how calmly Rhodes spoke. His tone was chilling.

"What does any of this have to do with me?" asked Morrissey through the chill, reeling from finding his home invaded and then the body slam to the floor. The zip ties had begun to cut into his wrists. Morrissey told himself to collect his wits and stay as cool as he could manage.

"You're not dealing with an incompetent so don't play stupid." Rhodes still sounded calm but irritation was creeping in, putting his manner slightly off balance. "Colby was clear about his change of heart. He thought he could convince the rest of us that we were moving too much money too fast. He let it slip about contacting a reporter. From there it was a matter of simple research."

"Colby? Dylan Colby?" Morrissey tried to sound surprised as he mentioned Colby's name. "You're talking about the young man who just died. Listen to me, I don't know what's going on, but if you killed that young man, that decision will cause your undoing, not anything that may happen here with me."

The newspaperman was oddly cool under pressure and it caught Rhodes off guard. Rhodes didn't like being caught off guard. "You are starting to tire me, Mr. Morrissey. Whatever happens here, you can thank Colby for it. But it's up to you how this meeting ends. I want to know what you did with the financial data. I'm talking about the files Colby sent to you."

"Well, I certainly don't keep records here. I've been doing this a long time. Do you assume that you're dealing with an incompetent?"

Morrissey's doorbell rang. It was a pleasant tone, but under the circumstances it caused both men to jump with surprise. The bell was followed by knocking at the front door. "Mr. Morrissey, it's the police," called a loud, female voice. "If you're here, please open the door, Sir." The officer repeated words to that effect several times.

Rhodes' focus shifted to the window he had broken when he entered Morrissey's home. Then Morrissey's cell phone started to ring from the table in the foyer where he had placed it.

Rhodes pulled Morrissey up from the chair where he had sat him down. He hoisted the reporter onto his shoulder and carried him to the staircase, which was out of view of both the front door and the broken window. Rhodes dropped Morrissey into a sitting position about four steps up. "Make a sound and I'll crack your skull," Rhodes whispered to Morrissey. Rhodes removed the pistol from his ankle holster and crept into the living room, snatching Morrissey's cell phone from the foyer table. He disconnected the call to stop the ringing. He could hear radio transmissions from outside.

"No answer at the door," reported the patrol officer, speaking into her radio. "I heard a phone ringing inside. No sign of Morrissey and there's a broken window around the back of his house. It appears to have been broken from the outside." The officer on the radio paused, listening to instructions. "Roger that," she responded, and returned to the front of Morrissey's house where her partner waited.

Morrissey's cell began to ring again. The caller was unknown. Rhodes hit the accept button to answer the call but did not say a word.

"Mr. Morrissey? This is City Police. We have officers outside your residence. They need to confirm your location and your safety." The dispatcher waited a beat for an answer. "Mr. Morrissey?"

"Mr. Morrissey is unavailable at present," Rhodes answered. "I can confirm his location for you. He's here. I can also confirm that he is unharmed, at least for the moment. But unless those recruits back away from the house that will change, I assure you."

"Sir, who am I speaking with?"

"That is of no concern to you. What you need to know is that I want Lieutenant Jordan. Get her here. Get her here by herself and tell her to leave her weapon outside." Rhodes hung up the call.

Liz and Connors were notified by dispatch about a hostage situation involving John Morrissey. They were told to head to Morrissey's residence and a team would meet them. By this time of the evening traffic was light and the weather was on their side. It was dry, making for a quick trip.

"Tell me," said Liz to the response team leader when she and Connors arrived.

"Cole and Michaels arrived to make a welfare check on Morrissey," he said. "There was no answer at the door or by phone. Cole found a broken window at the rear of the house. Dispatch called again and the phone was answered by an unidentified male. He says he has Morrissey inside. He told us to back off. Dispatch said he referred to the officers as 'recruits.'"

"It has to be Rhodes," said Liz. She and Connors looked at each other, both of them feeling exhilaration and dread. But neither of them felt doubt.

"Rhodes? Who's this Rhodes?" the team leader asked.

"Xander Rhodes," Liz answered. "He's a Marine Corps vet. He's trained in tactical combat and he has an extreme agenda. He works for Jack Powell's newly announced mayoral campaign. He's wanted for the home invasion and assault on Miles Carey. Connors and I were attempting to locate Rhodes when we got this call. Our tech team notified us that his cell phone must be off." Liz let the info sink in then she added, "We now suspect that he killed Dylan Colby."

Cole and Michaels exchanged a look. "Lieutenant," said Cole. "This guy whoever he is, he asked for you."

"What?" The word flew from her lips. Liz stared at Cole as the officer's words sunk in. Before she could react any further, a car pulled up and out stepped Miller.

"Captain, what are you doing here?" asked the team leader, determined to maintain his authority. "We have the situation under control."

"I do not doubt that, Sergeant. But there's a hostage in that house. I was notified because the perp holding that hostage is demanding to talk with one of my lieutenants. That's why I'm here."

"Sir, I was just informed of those details," Liz said, then she hesitated. "I'm convinced the man who's holding Morrissey is Xander Rhodes." Her head was spinning, likely due to the increase she felt in her heart rate.

"Rhodes?" Miller expressed surprise at first, but followed his initial response by saying, "That's what I feared. Are we certain?"

"Almost certain," Liz confessed. Liz and Connors filled Miller and the others in on the recent developments. Liz explained that the information Miles gathered from Colby's data files had resulted in an attack in his home. Connors shared with the team about Rhodes' accomplice, Grady Marshall, that he was in custody and had implicated Rhodes. They let the Captain know they were looking to locate Rhodes and place him under arrest when they were alerted to what was happening here with Morrissey.

"Captain, might you and I step away for a minute?" asked Liz. Miller looked her in the eye then walked a few paces away. Liz followed. She didn't know what to say or how to say it, but she needed to figure that out and do it fast. "I'm not a trained negotiator, Captain. I'll go in there and talk, if that's what Rhodes' is demanding. I can verify that Morrissey is okay. I can hope to get Morrissey through this. I may make it out, I may not." She bent over at the waist, hands on her knees, trying to get a grip on herself. Liz couldn't believe this was happening. She stood straight again. "But he's a vicious asshole. It will take someone who knows what they're doing to deal with him. Rhodes might be planning to trade Morrissey for me." Liz stopped talking and shook her head. "But I'm not negotiating. I can't do that."

Miller looked over in the direction of the response team. His focus quickly returned to Liz. "You've received basic negotiation training. I would guess you know how these situations work."

"Basic, to say the least. A crash course with what I'd need to know as part of a team, not how to broker a deal with a murderer." Liz heard the panic brewing in her voice. It felt uncharacteristic, sounded alien to her ears.

"Listen, Liz. I'm not going to insist that you place yourself in the midst of this mess. But I know you to be a skilled communicator. Negotiation is establishing rapport, meeting no demand without receiving something in return, and achieving resolution. That resolution is to end the situation without force and without harm to a hostage. The use of force is an alternative. If the suspect is taken out, so be it. If it is Rhodes, as you suspect, then at this point, all he's asked for is to talk to you."

"And his bargaining chip is a man's life. Morrissey is in there."

"We're assuming that fact. And we're assuming the man is unharmed. We'll confirm that before we let him talk to you." Miller was calm and convincing. "Let's begin with a phone conversation between this man and myself. If it's Rhodes, I'll know. We've spoken."

Liz nodded her reluctant assent. She wanted to offer a strong sense of resolve to the team but the ruse was more than she could manage. Miller asked the team leader for the command phone, which had been programmed to ring Morrissey's cell. He put the call through. It was answered after a few rings with a curt, "Yes."

Miller knew that the voice belonged to Rhodes. "Mr. Rhodes, this is Captain Miller. We spoke a few days ago. You called my office wanting a statement about the Colby case."

"I know who you are. I said I wanted Jordan. Where is she?"

The team listened as Miller spoke calmly, with unmistakable authority. "I'd like to speak with Mr. Morrissey. The only reason we haven't taken the house by force is because you claim he's in there with you. Put the man on the phone."

"If I do, what do I get in return?"

"I don't know yet, Mr. Rhodes. You may get to have another conversation, possibly with Lieutenant Jordan. But that depends on how Morrissey's doing."

There were a few seconds of muffled noise, followed by a tentative voice. "This is Morrissey."

"Mr. Morrissey, this is Captain Miller. Have you been injured?"

"Not really. At least not yet. I'm restrained...they're starting to cut into my wrists..." There was more muffled noise as Morrissey was interrupted mid-sentence.

"There's your proof, Captain Miller. Now, where is Jordan?"

"Why do you want Jordan? She has no sway over the data files that contain the evidence against you."

"Because she's an arrogant, bleeding heart. I want to explain to her why our motives are justified, why our objectives are sound. The quality of life in this city will be markedly better when our plans come to fruition."

"To what plans do you refer?"

"Reclaiming our streets so decent, taxpaying property owners and businesses can thrive and feel safe again. We will begin with Jack as mayor."

Miller wanted to keep Rhodes talking, but he was abruptly interrupted. "Now get Jordan or the reporter dies." Rhodes ended the call.

Chapter Fifty-two

"Damn. I thought he was taking advantage of having a receptive ear. I was trying to keep him talking but maybe he doesn't enjoy the sound of his own voice as much as I suspected." Miller handed the command phone to Liz. "Make the call. Agree to nothing without something in return. It creates an atmosphere of cooperation."

"Right," said Liz as she accepted the phone from Miller. The captain had used the word "cooperation" but in Liz's mind, it was a bullshit term. They all knew that as long as Morrissey was in that house and that son of a bitch Rhodes was armed, it was Rhodes who was in charge.

Liz called Morrissey's phone, as Miller had done. When Rhodes took the call this time, it was silence he employed at his end. "Rhodes. It's Liz Jordan. Are you there?"

"Of course, we're here, Lieutenant. Why was my request to speak with you ignored for so long?"

"Your request wasn't ignored. I wasn't here. I arrived as soon as I was notified that you wanted to talk me," she lied. "How's Morrissey? Does he need anything?"

"You people are tedious. He's fine. Enough about Morrissey, Lieutenant. This is what you need to do: leave your weapon and join us inside."

Liz felt her ability for rational thought slipping. *Shit! You're a damn cop! A lieutenant!* She needed to get a grip and keep the panic at bay. Summoning the most cop-like manner possible, she asked, "Why do you want me to come inside,

Rhodes? What can we discuss inside that we can't discuss by phone?"

"Because I want to see you face-to-face. I saw the way you looked at me the other evening when Jack and I ran into you. You think you're some superior being because you're a public servant. I'm going to show you the essence of superiority."

"Your boss, Jack, is a public servant. Does Jack look at you that way?" Liz could tell she had hit a sore spot.

Rhodes made noises of irritation but didn't have a comeback. "Come inside, Lieutenant. We can have a conversation."

"Okay. I will come into the house." Liz recalled that Morrissey tried to tell them he was restrained. "But take the restraints off Morrissey. The man is no physical match for you anyway. Remove the bindings, I'll come in. No weapon."

"Fine. The front door is unlocked. Come in and close the door behind you. Only you, Lieutenant. And no tricks." Liz ended the call. She took a deep breath and handed Miller the command phone.

When she and Connors had arrived at Morrissey's home, the team on site had consisted of Cole and Michaels, the first officers at the scene, the response team leader, the tactical specialists, and a communications officer. Liz looked around and realized the team had grown to include Liz, Connors, Captain Miller and a few other response-team operatives. They had all been trained for this and were committed to neutralizing the situation.

"Rhodes still wants to talk with me. Inside. He says he will remove Morrissey's restraints." Liz handed her weapon to Miller.

"There is no way to get a shot into that house, Lieutenant," explained the team leader. "Without a camera or eyes in there, we don't have a line. But we are using a body heat scan and have positions for Rhodes and Morrissey. They appear to be right on top of each other. We can watch for that to change. We want you to carry a communication device, like a tiny microphone, in your pocket. We will be able to hear your conversation. Also, you'll wear an earbud to hear instructions from us. Listen carefully, Lieutenant," he demanded. "If we should get a line on Rhodes, we'll say 'Drop.' You hit the floor, got it? If you need us to take control tactically, say 'Butterfly,' wait a second and then hit the deck. Within seconds, we'll be in and it will be over."

"I hear 'drop' and I hit the deck. I say 'Butterfly' and cover myself and the team storms in. Got it." But Liz wasn't sure of anything. She questioned her skills, her judgment.

Liz stepped over to Connors where he stood nearby. She looked around to see if anyone might be close enough to hear then quietly asked him, "Depending on how this goes, will you call Mike for me?"

The officer was making a good effort of keeping a calm exterior. He blinked a few times as the full weight of the request registered. "I think you should call him yourself, when this is over, Loo. But I will definitely check in with him."

Connors had never before used the diminutive "Loo" when addressing his Lieutenant. None of the squad of detectives that reported to her had used the term except for a few off-hand times. Liz hadn't been a Lieutenant long and the simplified title was a sign of familiarity and respect. Connors didn't appear to have noticed he'd said it. But Liz did.

"Thanks, Connors."

"Um...if it was me going in there?" Connors offered, hesitating at first, not wanting his words to be taken as coaching a superior, "I'd try to connect with him about his armed forces career. Make a parallel between your commitment as a cop and his as a soldier. They both have to follow orders. And you're an officer. He may still respect that."

Liz looked Connors in the eye, trying to calm herself and give rational thought to what he said. *Connection. Parallel. Orders. Officer.* She nodded her head, thinking, eyes squinted.

The communications specialist outfitted Liz with the microphone and the ear bud and both devices were quickly tested. At the last minute it was suggested that Liz carry a second, tiny microphone into Morrissey's home and leave it wherever possible without alerting Rhodes. She donned Kevlar and Liz was as ready as she was going to get. She walked toward Morrissey's front door. It was only a few dozen yards from where she stood with Connors but it seemed farther because she approached the house alone. Liz couldn't shake the thought that her life and the life of a hostage depended on how she managed herself. She felt unequal to the task but she was going in anyway.

At the front door, Liz stepped to the side of the entrance, as she'd been trained to approach any dangerous location. She called out, "Rhodes. I'm here. I'm coming in." She opened the front door slowly, hearing the hinges creak. Rhodes must have heard them too.

"Close the door and walk forward. Keep your hands where I can see them." As she turned to close the door, she dropped the additional microphone on the mat in front of the door, where it landed silently.

Liz took a few steps forward. The entry was narrow. To the right, was the foyer table with Morrissey's keys and briefcase lying on top. There was a living room a bit further on the right. Liz turned to her left. A middle-aged man with dark, graying hair and beard sat near the bottom of a staircase. Morrissey. His hands were bound with what appeared to be black zip ties and the skin of his wrists had begun to bruise from the restraints. Rhodes had lied. He had not removed them.

Behind Morrissey sat Rhodes. His left arm was around Morrissey's neck. In Rhodes' right hand he held a service revolver that looked very much like Liz's own. The weapon was in his hand but Rhodes did not aim at anything. Other than the arm around Morrissey's neck, he didn't appear particularly threatening. Liz figured that was the look he was going for.

"Remove your jacket and toss it over there," said Rhodes, indicating the living room area. She did as she was instructed, taking a couple of steps into Morrissey's living room. Liz's jacket landed on the floor near the sofa. "Now walk over here. Turn around with your back to me." Again, Liz followed his demands. Standing with her back to them, Liz heard Rhodes moving behind her. "My gun is pointed at your head, Lieutenant. I am going to search you for weapons and wires. If you speak or move in the slightest, I will shoot you. Nod if you understand."

Liz nodded. She calculated that she had placed the first microphone near the door which was now roughly twelve feet away. The second was in her coat pocket, at a similar distance. Neither was on her person. She hadn't been instructed as to their range. She wondered if the team would be able to hear anything. Liz cringed as Rhodes ran hands over her body. Satisfied that she was unarmed and not wearing a wire, he stepped back and resumed his position behind Morrissey. The tiny ear bud was so deeply imbedded in Liz's ear that it had not been detected when he searched her neck, her upper arms and shoulders.

"Let me introduce John Morrissey, Lieutenant. He's a journalist. My guess is that you're familiar with his work. I was hoping he could help me with a problem, but unfortunately, I have discovered he is unable to do so." Liz made eye contact with Morrissey, who looked to be doing well, under the circumstances. His eyes didn't leave hers.

"Maybe I can help you with your problem, Rhodes. What is it you need?" Liz thought her voice sounded strong, clear. She was glad of it because her gut was a jumbled mess. "If I can help, you and I can handle things and Mr. Morrissey can leave us to it. But I want to hear from Mr. Morrissey that he's okay."

"He's fine. Tell her," urged Rhodes.

"Yes, I'm okay," answered Morrissey.

"We had a deal, Rhodes. You said you'd cut his restraints," said Liz, pointing at Morrissey's wrists.

"I removed them from his ankles," responded Rhodes, plainly, pointing the weapon down at Morrissey's feet, to indicate no zip ties.

Liz took a breath. It felt like her first inhalation since she'd entered the house. "So, what was it you wanted Mr. Morrissey to help with?"

"My former colleague, Dylan Colby, chose to share sensitive information with Mr. Morrissey. I was hoping he still had the information under wraps and I could retrieve it. But reporters are like jack rabbits, darting around for their stories, never considering the consequences."

"This information was about your operation. The plans and the objectives you're working toward. A large-scale mission," Liz said, borrowing a military term.

"Yes. Starting with Powell as mayor."

"And you were redistributing the city and county finances to better address the issues as you saw them. Dylan was helping you, wasn't he?"

"Of course, he was. Civic responsibility was in his blood. His grandfather, his father. Dylan had so much promise. But he turned his back on his legacy. Decided our objectives were 'too extreme,' he told us. All the runny-nosed, bleeding hearts he worked with had obscured his political vision."

"I understand duty. I understand how it feels to learn that a colleague isn't up to the task. But let me be of some aid to you. Mr. Morrissey can't help you. Let him walk out of here. You have me here now, as you requested."

"Fine. He can leave." Rhodes moved his arm away and gave Morrissey a push up. With his hands bound, the man reached for his banister and pulled himself up to standing.

"I will need to walk him to the door to let the team know he's coming out. Will you allow me to do that?" Liz asked Rhodes.

"Yes. But any error and I'll drill you both in the back. And I'll miss that vest, Lieutenant. Be sure of it."

Chapter Fifty-three

The team already knew that Morrissey was coming out because they heard the exchange between Rhodes and Liz. Both devices were transmitting every word. Liz's request to alert them was a ploy on Liz's part to keep the listening devices secret.

Liz returned to stand near the foot of the stairs. She looked at Rhodes, sitting a few steps up, making their faces parallel. "The information that Colby shared: were they financial reports?"

"Yes. He thought the files were some kind of insurance. They weren't."

"Dylan had been part of your operation and wanted out. He knew too much. You felt he had to die."

"Yes. He could have walked away but he felt foolishly obligated to bring us down. It was a betrayal of the worse kind."

"Rhodes, I have some further information of which your team may not be aware."

"What would that be? And why would it matter now?"

"Dylan placed the financial data on a thumb drive. It was found in his home after his death. We had the files before we knew that they'd been sent to Morrissey. It seems that Dylan had a back-up insurance plan."

Liz paused as the news sunk into Rhodes' mind, then continued. "Miles Carey had analyzed the files and connected them to the data Dylan had sent to Morrissey by email. They're both financial nerds. They realized they were looking at the same information. But tell me something," asked Liz.

"How did you make the connection to Carey? He's a consultant. He doesn't even carry a shield." Liz wondered if the distinction would be significant to Rhodes. It was.

"My colleagues assumed he'd be the one deciphering the data. It was a sensible conclusion, given his skills."

"Your colleagues. Would one of them be Grady Marshall?" Rhodes was irritated, but Liz pushed on. "That's my other piece of news, Rhodes. We have Marshall in custody. We found him at Carey's home. We know you couldn't get the data you wanted there. Carey is too savvy to leave his ass hanging out like that. And Marshall pins the attack on Carey totally on you. He's a whimpering coward who will probably tell us whatever we want to know."

"I'm disgusted by him. He's an embarrassment." Rhodes was deep in thought, or so it seemed to Liz. When he spoke again it was with resignation. "We were too late eliminating Colby. We were late getting to Carey, and to Morrissey. Failure on all counts."

"You can't place all the responsibility for failure on yourself, Rhodes," Liz told him, trying her best to sound empathetic. "We succeed or fail as a team."

Rhodes narrowed his eyes and looked at Liz. "Since we are sharing, Lieutenant, here's a couple of other details: your homeless crusader wasn't the first in our cross-hairs. In fact, we started out with a hands-on, street-wide effort and it was systematic. We selected vagrants to isolate and attack with violence. This served to keep them off balance with fear. Then we committed random acts of vandalism and placed blame in their direction. We even went so far as to frighten young people and convince families that the culprits were street dwellers."

Keeping quiet, Liz listened as Rhodes continued with pride. "The financial maneuvers were only a piece. Yes, we moved funds around, reallocated to better suit our plans. With Jack's campaign launched, we connected with wealthy donors, ready to foster our objectives. With their support, we've been investing in security firms to keep our city safe, self-supporting incarceration facilities to lock up vagrants, and private schools so families can control what their children learn. It was all part of the big picture. A revolution. We were going to reclaim our communities." *He's a mad man,* thought Liz. *A mad man with extreme views, like so many, but Rhodes chose to act on them.*

"I get that, Rhodes. On the face of it, a well-conceived plan," she lied. "Except that no one deserves to be incarcerated unless they've committed a crime and I'll be damned if anyone should profit from it. As for education, we can never control what kids learn. The best you can do is teach them empathy and to trust their own conscience."

Liz didn't know where the strength or the resolve had come from but she had recovered her voice was determined to continue. "But where's the honor? What about the pledge to protect people who aren't able to protect themselves? Shouldn't that be the true essence of power? That it's used to promote freedom, not control?"

"Freedom and control come with responsibility, Lieutenant. And both should be fully appreciated." Rhodes aimed the weapon at Liz. She felt panic in her gut but knew there was no time to deal with it. "I was unable to complete my objectives, as I was trained. I will not leave here alive, Lieutenant. You've failed too. Why should you deserve to live?"

Liz was about to yell the code word and hit the floor, but Rhodes was quicker. He took aim and squeezed the trigger of the pistol, firing a round close to Liz's ear. A noise preceded the weapon's fire by a split second. It was the ring of a cell phone. It was Morrissey's phone, which Rhodes had placed in his own pocket. Rhodes was stunned just enough that his aim was interrupted. Liz was given a momentary advantage. Her years of training kicked in.

She lunged for Rhodes, keeping her weight low, leading with her shoulder. Rhodes upper body plowed into the steps behind him. The gun he held in his right hand flew over the bannister and clattered to the floor of Morrissey's foyer. Liz used the ball of her right hand above her inner wrist to slam a powerful blow to Rhodes' face. She heard his nose break with a crack. Rhodes was injured and off balance enough for Liz to haul herself up. She clambered to where the weapon had landed.

Grabbing up the gun, Liz checked that there was, indeed, a round left in the chamber. Never trust an adversary's weapon, she'd been taught.

Rhodes had made it to the foot of the stairs. He wiped blood from his face with his sleeve. His face was a contorted mess but he looked oddly pleased.

"You're a stupid bitch but that was a well-placed punch," he told Liz. Rhodes sounded amused, almost impressed. Liz aimed the gun at Rhodes.

"This all stops here and now, Rhodes. You're an intelligent guy. You can make it out of here. Just put your hands up on top of your head, fingers clasped, and turn around."

"No Lieutenant. It ends here. And you'd better hope it's a kill shot."

Rhodes flew toward Liz, reaching for the weapon. Liz was faster. She aimed and pulled the trigger. The round pierced Rhodes upper chest near the shoulder. He flew backward and landed on the floor at the foot of Morrissey's stairs. Liz has stopped him just as she has been trained to do.

Within seconds, the response team came through the door. Minutes later, Liz exited Morrissey's home escorted by a member of the team. It was dark out. Drizzle was falling. Lights were blazing, flashing.

Not much time had elapsed since Liz had entered the house, but enough for Connors to have called Mike and explained what was happening. Liz saw Mike as he rushed toward her. She fell into his arms for a few seconds.

In her head, Liz knew it was over. She was safe, Morrissey was safe. But she had shot a man. She knew Rhodes would be taken into custody and arrested for the murder of Dylan Colby. Even knowing all those things to be true, she couldn't fight the reaction. She pushed Mike away, stepped to the side of Morrissey's front walk and vomited.

Chapter Fifty-four

The news all over town was that Xander Rhodes was in custody. The political operation working to see Jack Powell elected mayor was going to be dissected into the smallest possible pieces.

According to the files that Colby had kept safe before he died, Powell, Rhodes, and Marshall had systematically dismantled or rerouted scores of services for the disadvantaged that they had deemed wasteful. Their plan had been in motion for well over two years. As with most efforts in terror and deceit, they enjoyed reminders of their successes so they had recorded every move. Ironically, those records would provide the evidence to convict them.

The reaction everyone wanted most — the police, the community, the local news mongers — was the reaction of ADA Jackson Powell, whose campaign for mayor had been organized by Rhodes himself.

Unfortunately, Powell's reaction was tragic, as well. He was found in the very room of his campaign headquarters where Liz and Connors had left him when they were looking for Rhodes. The young staffer who had greeted Liz and Connors the evening before had found him the next morning. He had finished a bottle of scotch whiskey, placed the barrel of a revolver into his mouth, and pulled the trigger. Due to the alcohol in his system, his hand was unsteady. It was determined that the round entered under his left eye and exited above his ear. He died of hypovolemic shock due to extreme blood loss. Powell had not left a note. Had he been discovered sooner he might have survived. The staffer who found him decided that politics wasn't her calling after all.

A couple of days passed before Liz talked with Miller about what had occurred inside Morrissey's house. An official report of the incident was completed. Because Liz had discharged a weapon — and had a weapon pointed at her head and fired — she was required to speak with a department psychologist. The ring of the cell phone saved her life.

Liz and the captain sat in her small office. She made them each a cup of coffee, fresh-ground Kona in the French press Liz kept in her desk but rarely took the time to use. They sipped, each savoring the strong, hot beverages, barely cooled enough from the boil to sip without burning their mouths.

"You did an exemplary job in there, under extreme pressure. I'm proud of you, of the way you handled Rhodes."

"Thank you, Sir. Means a lot."

"You and Morrissey made it through the ordeal with your lives. And Rhodes is alive to face charges for his crimes. More importantly, you should be proud of yourself. Your instincts kicked in, and I don't mean the ones you were born with. I'm talking about the ones you have been trained to rely on as a police officer."

Thinking about the captain's assessment, Liz sipped her coffee, then replied. "I guess I'd have to agree, to some extent. But timing was on my side. The surprise of Morrissey's phone ringing gave me just enough of an edge. Rhodes must have forgotten the phone was in his pocket. It was the exact moment I needed to have the team make that call."

"The call was from an outside line. A business associate of Morrissey's. It wasn't us. Once Morrissey was out, the plan changed. It changed again when Morrissey confirmed for us that Rhodes was armed. We had a shooter at the rear of the residence, near the broken window. We were about to have you back away and to the left, giving them a shot. We knew it was risky but we decided it may be necessary. We wanted you a safe distance away and then we'd give you the drop signal. Before we could implement, Rhodes fired, the phone rang, and you had made your move."

Liz looked at Miller. "So, luck played a hand, as well."

"Lieutenant, it may have been luck, it may have been karma. My mother would have called it divine intervention. But whatever it was, you knew how and when to make the most of it."

"Captain, what do you think happened to Rhodes? Do you think he was a killer before he was trained as one?"

Miller sighed, looked into his near-empty mug. Liz noticed he held the mug in his left hand, the gold of his wedding band perfect against the brown of his skin. "Hard to say. Chances are that his life was on this trajectory, for whatever reason, long before he became a soldier."

"So, you don't see him as a troubled ex-warrior but as a man unable to rise above his disappointments."

"I don't know, Liz. I barely know the man. But I know one thing: the ability to manipulate others coupled with a lack of conscience is a dangerous combination, one that has created and fostered conflict for a long, long time. And we rarely remember to be vigilant of the signs."

Miller finished his coffee, placed the mug on the desk, then asked Liz. "So, have you scheduled your mandatory appointment with the department shrink?"

"No, but I will soon."

"Let me know when you've completed it. I'll note it in your file."

Miller wanted to acknowledge Liz's efforts with an official recognition of valor. She declined.

Chapter Fifty-five

When Grady Marshall found out that Powell was dead and that Rhodes had been arrested, he had more to say, as the charges against him started to mount. Connors listened and recorded as Marshall offered his account of Colby's murder and the last meeting between the conspirators.

"We met with Dylan every few weeks, Rhodes and I did. Sometimes it was just me. These weren't exactly business meetings, more like Rhodes telling us what he and Jack wanted done. Jack was the boss, it was his operation, but Rhodes liked pushing limits and Jack didn't stop him. His agenda got more and more extreme, more so than Jack ever planned on. Too extreme for me, believe it or not." Marshall waited for Connors to take the bait and comment on his effort in restraint. When Connors remained silent, Marshall sighed and stared at the table.

"I want to hear what happened the night Dylan Colby died, Mr. Marshall."

"Dylan had started barking back about plans, what he was ordered to do. We had a meet scheduled that evening. I knew Rhodes wasn't happy with Dylan's view of things. We looked like we belonged, you know? I had my backpack with me. No one looked at us twice. They never had. I was ordered to stay outside near the alley entrance. Rhodes snuck in, avoided the lobby camera, and waited in a conference room until the office closed. We'd made it inside without any problem before."

"What time was this?" asked Connors, wanting to be clear for the record.

"Rhodes went inside right before five p.m. Anyway, He was back outside sooner than I expected, just after six. Rhodes was breathing hard, sweating. The guy never broke a sweat, so I noticed it. I asked him where Dylan was because we usually would leave together. Rhodes said, 'He was expendable. He's not a concern any longer.' He took off the gloves he was wearing and looked at me. His eyes were so crazy. I started to freak out. He told me to get a grip on myself. Then he said, 'The data may be an issue but I tried to buy us some time.' Before I had a chance to ask him what he meant, he said we had to get out of there. Rhodes told me to head out to the street and walk downtown a few blocks before making my way to my car. He said he'd be in touch and walked down the alley in the other direction."

"When did you find out what Rhodes meant about the data?"

"Later that night. He told me later that he pummeled the hard drive in Dylan's office. He thought I'd be thrilled since the data led straight to me. Rhodes was angry when I told him that it was a dumb move, that it would just attract attention. I said, 'You think you're such a smart guy but don't you realize how easily those files can be accessed?' I was talking about the server. Shit, I had no idea that Dylan had sent them to that reporter. Rhodes glared at me like he was going to kill me. He said we needed to agree on what to tell Jack."

"Okay, Marshall. You're filling in a lot of blanks. Tell me what happened when you and Rhodes met with Powell."

"Jack was not happy that Rhodes had killed Dylan. We met in the campaign office. Jack was really frustrated. I was defensive, nervous, chugging beers to relieve it. Jack started to grill us immediately. 'I can't believe you've done this,' he kept saying. 'What were the two of you thinking?' Like I had anything to do with it. It wasn't my idea you have to believe me. But I wasn't going to irritate Rhodes."

"Okay, that was probably smart," said Connors. "Go on."

"We told Jack it was the best way to proceed. That we couldn't trust Dylan anymore. We reminded Jack that he had said as much to us. Jack's feeling was that he was controlling the damage. He said we had complicated things. Jack was drinking a lot that night. So was I, but it wasn't like him to drink so much. Rhodes thought so too, because we kept looking at each other. Jack felt that we'd made it impossible to achieve the objective. They both used that word all the time, 'the objective.'"

"Rhodes looked so calm. He wasn't even drinking. Just water. 'We made a decision. We were under threat,' Rhodes said. 'The threat needed to be neutralized.' That's how he put it. Neutralized." Marshall shook his head. "Jack just scowled at us he was so frustrated."

"I tried to tell Jack that Rhodes and I needed to hang low, maybe leave the city for a while. We could take a trip, make it look like work. No one would even notice. Jack said to forget it. We'd be leaving him here to deal with the fallout from our bad decision, that we should have thought of that before. He said he had enough to manage already."

"Rhodes was so cool, so calm. He said, 'There's been an arrest. We couldn't be in a better position here. What we have to do is make sure that the charge sticks,' he said."

"I asked him, 'You're talking about that bum?' I said that I'd heard he may have an alibi, that he's protecting someone. That's what I heard. So, I asked him, 'What if they come forward or he decides to talk?'"

"Rhodes got all arrogant. 'You're merely stating a problem, not forming a solution to it. That is not helpful,' he says. Such an asshole. If that happens, he said, we will have his alibi discredited. Like it would be so easy. Then Rhodes did the weirdest thing. He leaned over toward me and said in a low voice. 'Don't refer to him as a bum again in my presence.' It sounded like a warning, as cold as steel."

"I was shocked by his tone. 'Why would you defend him?' I asked. 'What is he to you?' As soon as I asked, I regretted it. But it was too late."

"You didn't like crossing Rhodes, did you?" asked Connors.

"Hell, no. And Rhodes was pissed, more pissed than I'd ever seen him. He glanced at Jack, waiting for a comment from him, but Jack said nothing."

"Rhodes said, 'He's nothing to me personally. But his situation and his background will prove useful to us. I've known hundreds, legions like him and no matter how low they sink the last thing they lose is their cunning. Don't underestimate him,' he said. Jack just stared at Rhodes, listening to every word, like he was so impressed. Then he tells us, 'No one leaves town. It will take effort from all three of us to continue with our original course, considering the setback you've caused us. Now we plan how to move ahead,' he said."

"What was the plan? What did you three decide to do?" Connors asked.

"Jack said he would make sure the charges against the homeless guy stuck. He could steer the police away from us. He said the situation would benefit his campaign, the effort to clean up the streets. 'What better way to get the constituency behind him than to convict a vagrant of murder?' he said. I understood that. Rhodes seemed okay with the idea, although he had some weird respect for the guy who was charged. I didn't get it."

"Tell me about the financial data. What was the plan?"

"Colby and I were both approached to assist with Powell's preliminary campaign plans. I'm talking long before he announced, back in his planning stage. Both of us liked his politics. We felt he could make things happen. We were both led to believe we would be respected members of a team. We figured out pretty soon they needed us because we could manipulate the money."

"How did it work exactly?"

"Budgets are set up on allocation lines, with each line a specific expense. Dylan could access the daily expenditures and knew how much was allocated to what service, because he was on the client end, see? I couldn't determine daily or weekly expenditures for services from my desk, like Dylan could, but I had the capability to reallocate. So, every couple of weeks Dylan and I would communicate which lines to take funds from."

"Ok. But to what end?"

"Sometimes we were told to place money on certain lines, things important to Jack, like school programs or transportation for old folks. But usually it was to shadow money, make it look like it was there, but it's really gone. I siphoned the funds on a quarterly basis to an account for the DA's office. It was a placeholder, you could say. The money went to Jack's campaign. Or whatever he felt it should be used for. All with an okay from Rhodes, who supposedly had the green light from Jack."

"And Colby got killed over it."

"Yes. Rhodes and Jack both thought they could hide the reallocations we'd made until all this mess blew over. I tried to tell them it didn't work that way, that we were screwed. They didn't believe me until your analyst got hold of the files. And then we learned the reporter got his hands on them, too."

"How much money are we talking about, Marshall?"

Marshall looked up at the ceiling, thinking, not wanting to answer. "We have the data," Connors told him. "We will know soon anyway. You may as well tell me."

"Over two years, close to one point five mil."

Connors stopped recording. He explained to Marshall that he may receive consideration for telling what he knew, but it might not help him much. He was looking at serious charges.

Chapter Fifty-six

With Miller's help, Liz uncovered as much as possible about Alexander "Xander" Rhodes. The sources the captain had contacted prior to the standoff had provided little else. One source, however, was able to put them in touch with someone who had known Rhodes before he'd joined the Marines, before he'd been a recruit, before he was sent to Camp Lejeune in North Carolina.

A young woman by the name of Quinn Hadley had been seen with Rhodes on many occasions. It took time, perseverance, and patience, but Liz was able to track down Ms. Hadley, who, luckily, was still using the surname. Hadley was living in Seattle and Liz thought it worth her time to make the three-hour drive north to talk with the woman.

The day was beautiful, crisp and cool, the kind of day Seattle didn't enjoy often this time of year. Liz had considered the restaurant at the top of the Space Needle with the tremendous views it offered but it was hard to get reservations. Also, Liz grew anxious at the idea of being many flights up above the Seattle waterfront and at the mercy of three little elevators to get back to the ground.

They met for lunch at an oyster bar on Elliott Bay. Hadley had told Liz that her black hair was cut very short and she'd wear a leather coat. Liz was sitting at the table against the window sipping coffee when the woman arrived. Quinn Hadley looked to be in her late twenties. She was tall, close to Liz's height, slender and fit. Her hair was very short and jet black against a pale complexion. She wore the promised leather coat over a shorter-length dress. Heavy tights covered shapely legs and she wore serious ankle boots. Dramatic makeup and artisan jewelry completed a look best described as Pacific Northwest urban-chic. And Hadley pulled if off extremely well. Marjorie would have approved.

Hadley looked around for a brief moment. She saw Liz and raised a hand in a slight wave, then approached Liz's table.

"You have to be Lieutenant Jordan. You described yourself well," she said offering an outstretched hand. "I'm Quinn Hadley. Please, call me Quinn."

Shaking the woman's hand, Liz confirmed, "Yes, I'm Jordan. Join me, please." She indicated the chair on the other side of the table.

Under the circumstances, Liz had expected some degree of nervousness or anxiety, but Hadley seemed calm, collected, even pleasant. "How was the drive up, Lieutenant? Nice day for it."

"The drive was fine. You're right. Great day for it," answered Liz. "And I like to drive I-5."

The server approached and Hadley ordered tea. Neither woman was interested in a menu. Hadley went right to it. "Lieutenant, you called about Alex Rhodes. But you know him as Xander. He was called Alex years ago and I can't think of him as anything else."

Hadley adjusted in her chair for more comfort, moved the messenger bag she had carried to the other side. "Anyway, after we talked, I searched news stories." She paused for a moment but maintained eye contact. "I think I'm up to speed," she said with a shaking head. "I want to help but I haven't seen Alex in years. You can ask me whatever you'd like."

"I want to start by thanking you for agreeing to talk with me," said Liz. "I'm guessing it was a surprise when I called." Hadley nodded, slight smile under big, dark eyes as Liz continued. "In return, you can ask any questions you have of me. I'll answer whatever I can as long as the information is not withheld due to our investigation."

Hadley nodded again. "Anything you could share was probably released to the press, but thank you."

"Let's start with this: how long have you known Rhodes."

She sighed. "I've known Alex since we were kids, teenagers here in Seattle. I'm originally from Lakewood. Alex is from Aberdeen."

"Aberdeen," said Liz. "Cobain's hometown,"

"Yes. Another tragic native son."

"Quinn, have you had much contact with Rhodes, since you knew him in Seattle as a teenager?"

"I haven't seen or talked with Alex in ten years, when he turned eighteen. He's actually a few months younger than I am. If I remember, he's a June Gemini and I'm February Aquarius."

"When was the last time you saw Rhodes?"

"I saw him right before he enlisted in the Marines. We all tried to talk him out of it."

The server returned with tea for Hadley, who made eye contact with the server. She smiled and thanked him. "By then, Alex had had enough. His birthday opened up some possibilities, not all of them good, but better than what he had." She checked that the tea had steeped long enough, then poured the hot beverage. The steam rose from her cup. The server refilled Liz's coffee.

"Did you and Alex attend high school together? Is that where the two of you met?"

Hadley sipped her tea. She placed the cup on the saucer and clasped her hands in front of her, taking a deep breath. The slightly pensive smile returned as she looked at Liz. "Let me start at the beginning. Lieutenant, are you familiar with the term 'gutter punks'?"

"Sure," said Liz. "Street kids, usually teens or young adults, often runaways. There's a theory that most kids who identify as such choose to live on the street and panhandle. In my experience, I'm not sure that's true. Fifty years ago, they might have called themselves hippies or flower children."

"You have a good grasp on the idea. I'm not surprised. You have a community of street kids in Columbia City. Seattle does better than most urban areas with addressing the issue of homelessness, and whatever reasons people have for experiencing it. Teens and young adults included. Actually, that's what I do for a living. I work for the City of Seattle. I run a youth shelter. Gutter punks are part of my life. Lieutenant, I was a gutter punk. So was Alex."

"I ran away when I was sixteen," continued Quinn. "I was tall and could blend in pretty well. People thought I was older which came in handy, to be honest. I never say I 'ran away from home' because I had not really had a *home*, a place of safety. When I was ten, my stepfather started grooming me for abuse and my mother looked the other way. She was too afraid of losing out on his paychecks from Boeing. I kept a backpack ready for weeks. One night he tried to rape me and I fought the asshole off. I took a baseball bat to the side of his head and ran before the ambulance arrived. I heard he didn't press charges."

"Rough life, Quinn. I'm so sorry to hear all that."

"Thank you, Lieutenant. Anyway, I ended up downtown. In the university district for a while, then the parks. You keep moving, you know how it is. I won't go into how I survived or how I passed the time. You've heard the stories. You know that kids do what they have to do to live. It's not pretty. But it made me who I am. My experiences prepped me to help lots of other kids. I see myself so many times over at that age, on any given day."

Liz thought of Mike and Kelly and the commitment they shared to people existing on the fringes. "I have friends who do similar work with the community, Quinn. Their backgrounds may have been difficult in some respects but nothing compared to yours. Except for one man I know." Liz thought of Gary as a young man, living on the streets in the Haight-Ashbury district.

"Experience is often relative, at least what we do with it certainly is, in my opinion," she answered between sips of tea. "And I don't mean I deserve any special honors. I think my feisty personality served me well. Anyway, let's talk about Alex. We met up at a warming shelter. It was the middle of a cold spell. I'd been on the street a year by this time. Alex must have been seventeen."

"He's a pretty fit adult. Was he as a teenager?"

"He was strong, able to hold his own. Looked older than his age. I guess we had that in common. His home life had been like that of so many kids. According to Alex, his father was killed in a drug deal gone bad. He was eleven. His mother was a drunk. That's why Alex doesn't drink or do drugs. He used to pretend, if getting messed up was part of the gig, but I won't go into those details. It all became a way of life anyway."

"No need. I understand," said Liz.

"Alex said he got into a fight at school. Tenth grade. His loving mother kicked him out. Told him he was a train wreck like his dad. Nice, huh?"

"Great." Liz shook her head in disgust.

"Alex hung out in Aberdeen for a while, down on the harbor. The waterfront area can be rowdy and he got beat up a couple of times. Pretty bad, I guess. Eventually, he made his way to Seattle."

"You were both older teens by this time. Did you stay friends for the next year?"

"More like family. You have to understand, Lieutenant, when you're on street, you find a crew and you stay together. You look out for each other. No one can make it alone. There were six of us that hung together like a pack. Myself and one other girl named Misty. There was Alex and three other guys."

"You all took care of each other."

"We did. Alex was a great friend to have. He acted like the enforcer, a bodyguard. But he also took the brunt of the damage because he protected us. One night, Alex took a job for one of the guys who was too sick to show up. Alex was assaulted by a twisted couple, a man and a woman, who paid him for a threesome. He wouldn't let us go to the cops even though we knew where the assholes were staying. He said it was his own fault. He spent a day in the hospital. He told the ER doctor that he was eighteen and that the incident was consensual. No one questioned it. None of us carried ID anyway."

Liz listened attentively, but her mind kept thinking back to the arrogant man she'd met at UnderBar, whom she knew as Xander. She thought of the man who had killed Colby and assaulted Carey. The man she'd shot in the line of duty in Morrissey's home. Despite her best efforts, Liz found herself feeling pity. Not for the adult Xander, but for Alex, the abused street kid. The gutter punk.

"Alex changed after that," said Quinn. "He became angry. Always angry. Not that I blame him, he'd had it as rough as anyone. But it wasn't the cause or even the situation; he was angry at himself. Alex didn't even blame the sadistic slime-bags that hurt him. It was hard to understand. Still is."

"Around this time, we started seeing Armed Forces recruiters coming around to the parks and the places we hung out. They zeroed in on Alex, of course, like some trophy. He soaked up all the accolades, all the promises. I think Alex needed a new tribe, one that could defend him, for once. The recruiters helped him get his ID. That's all he needed. They had him committed before his birthday and grabbed him right up." Quinn snapped her fingers for emphasis.

"That's what you meant when you said 'all of you' tried to talk him out of it. The five of you. Your crew."

"Yes," Quinn gave a sigh. "I lost track of Misty and one of the guys. But I stay in touch with Liam and Howie. They're in Eugene. They're a couple, married and they have a daughter. They probably were a couple then but they weren't open about it so we didn't ask. We loved them, that's all that mattered."

"Good to know. I don't know why I feel relieved you've kept in touch but I'm glad for them. For you."

"Thanks, Lieutenant. Me, too. And until yesterday when you called, I had no idea what had happened to Alex. Unfortunately, now I know. It's awful. But he was a good friend when we needed him. I'll always be grateful for knowing him back then."

"Should I tell him I talked with you? Would you object?"

Quinn didn't hesitate. "I don't mind. Tell him. In a way, it's my story, too. I won't ask anyone for permission to share it. Lieutenant, I might even be okay with talking to him but he needs to take responsibility for his crimes. Nothing excuses what he's done. But maybe he can remember a piece of himself from his past, when he needed others. Maybe find some reason, some explanation for it all."

Liz finished the meeting with Hadley. The two women decided to keep each other's contact information. They split the check, said goodbye, and parted company. They never ordered lunch.

Chapter Fifty-seven

Xander Rhodes was in a hospital bed under twenty-four-hour guard. He'd been placed under arrest for the murder of Dylan Colby, the assaults on Miles Carey and John Morrissey, and for dozens of counts of conspiracy to misappropriate public funds. His left arm was cuffed to the bedrail, a condition of his arrest.

He had survived the shoulder shot but the damage had required surgery to repair bone and cartilage. His injured right shoulder and arm were immobilized and the arm was suspended from a support above his shoulder. He was in a lot of pain and not talking much. Right-handed, it was doubtful he would shoot a rifle, roll a bowling ball, or row a boat again. Thanks to the punch to the face, Rhodes also sported a broken nose and black eyes.

Liz had a conversation with Rhodes the day following her visit to Seattle. Miller had insisted an attorney be present to represent Rhodes' interests. The Captain wasn't accommodating Rhodes. He was being proactive. And smart.

She entered the room to find a male nurse taking vitals. Rhodes was tolerating the process but he didn't engage with the health provider in any way. A young public defender was standing near the window on the other side of the room.

"What do you want?" Rhodes asked, sounding as though the persecution was trying his patience. "You broke my damn nose. You shot me in the shoulder. Just ask your inane questions and get the hell out."

"Well Mr. Rhodes, I broke your nose to keep you from shooting me, remember? You called me a bitch, not that you were the first. That was right before you complimented my punch, the punch that broke your 'damn nose.' Then you said you weren't planning to leave the scene alive. Sorry to have disappointed you on that point, but you're not the first in that regard either. Then you lunged at me while I had your weapon trained on you. That's why you were shot in your shoulder."

The public defender didn't look excited to be there but wanted to sound useful. "Lieutenant, did you have questions for Mr. Rhodes? He's clearly not up to banter."

"Actually," answered Liz, "I don't have questions at this time, Counselor. Instead, my intent is to inform Mr. Rhodes of a few things. First, we've conducted extensive interviews with Grady Marshall, who's provided us with a wealth of information. We're going to hold you responsible for everything, Rhodes. Now, trust me, you won't go down alone. Many heads will roll, as they say. Except for Jack, of course. In case no one told you, Jack took the easy way out. He killed himself.

The news about Powell's suicide didn't cause any discernible reaction. Liz could have told Rhodes about some mundane detail, for all the news seems to mean to him. He was pretending to ignore her, but Liz wasn't having it.

"You might be interested in knowing that I had a conversation yesterday with someone you probably remember. She certainly remembers you, Rhodes. Except she knew you as Alex."

"No one has called me Alex in years," he sneered like she was too dumb to know this.

"I believe that much is true. But I'm betting you remember her. Quinn Hadley?"

Rhodes reacted to the name. There was no mistaking the surprise. His eyes darted in Liz's direction then quickly looked to the other side of the room. His breathing accelerated and his jaw muscles grew tight. But he stayed silent.

"Quinn and I spoke for quite a while. She told me about how difficult it was on the streets of Seattle as a gutter punk. She said it's been ten years but she shared a lot with me. How she came to be on the streets, how she and her friends managed to survive."

At this, Rhodes briefly glanced at Liz but then closed his eyes. Still, not a word from him.

"Quinn and I discussed how our pasts, and how we deal with what we've been through, can have so much impact on what we become. You must know what I'm talking about, Rhodes. Take Quinn, for example, she chose to take all the shit she lived through and uses it to help kids who are on the street. She runs a youth shelter in Seattle."

Rhodes was undoubtedly hearing everything Liz had to tell him. He tried to stay calm, slow his breathing, and minimize reactions. His color had paled but then returned. He was perspiring.

"Quinn had a lot to say about the hell that some street kids go through, how they have often been abandoned before they even end up in the street. The street becomes a refuge for them. She talked about blame, about blame and anger. How reactions can destroy a person. That's why she does what she does with kids; she doesn't want any kid to blame themselves for what the asshole adults in their lives do to them. It's not their fault. She's doing great, by the way. And she wanted me to let you know that we spoke. I have her business card for you. She's not averse to talking with you, if you should want that."

"Does this story have a point, Lieutenant? Or a purpose?" Rhodes' attorney finally asked. "If you have no questions, my client needs rest."

"Your client gets my point, as well as my purpose." Liz said, staring pointedly at the public defender. She placed Quinn Hadley's business card on the bedside table. "See you in court, Rhodes. Good day, Counselor." Liz turned and walked out into the hospital corridor.

A few evenings later, Liz and Mike attended a party at UnderBar in celebration of the birth of Henry Cyrus Denucci, Kelly and Pete's newborn son. Kelly and Pete were not in attendance, however. They were home with little Hank, as he would be called, each of them trying to get some sleep. Diana was there, so was Gary, and several of Kelly's staff from the outreach program. Connors got some video of the event and, keeping with tradition, the establishment collected contributions in honor of the family.

Chapter Fifty-eight

The three men traveled for an hour and a half, east from the city on State Route Fourteen, before they stopped. They passed though Camas and Washougal, and the small communities of Skamania and North Bonneville, before they reached the winding, rural roads that took them further up into the hills. They passed a small craft winery, horse stables, and fallow fields.

Mike drove. Gary rode shotgun. Gary tried to insist that Ty sit in the front passenger seat but Ty was adamant about preferring the back seat. He said he liked the vantage point.

Neither Gary nor Mike knew what to expect on the trek. They weren't sure whether the conversation would flow easily or if Ty would prefer quiet. As it turned out, Ty was relaxed and well rested, had regained some strength and stamina, but shared few of his thoughts about recent events.

Ty's mettle had been tested. He'd been accused, incarcerated, then vindicated. His physical and mental wellbeing had been stressed to the point of collapse. But Ty had persevered. He had been forced to widen his circle of allies, accepting help from others. Now he was heading to the place he loved best in the world in the company of the two people he trusted most. They stopped at a small diner in the city of Stevenson. Mike and Gary each ordered ham on rye while Ty stuck with a stand-by favorite, a steaming bowl of beef stew.

From Carson, they headed north up the Wind River Highway into the Indian Heaven Wilderness. The area was in an expansive national forest that had become a checkerboard of publicly owned lands, commercial logging properties scalped to clear-cut, and private holdings owned by families for generations. When they reached the point in the trip where pavement gave over to dirt road, Ty asked Mike to pull over. "I want to show you both something," he told them, as they scrambled out of the car.

The three friends stood by the side of the road, looking up an expanse of hillside. The dirt road was obscured by woods on either side. They watched red-tailed hawks glide in graceful circles, heard the occasional chipmunk screaming his nervous chatter. Ty pointed to a spot in the distance. "The road ends just beyond that big Douglas Fir. The cabin is one hundred yards or so further. I usually hike from here. Nice to have a ride. I appreciate this."

"I've enjoyed this. It's a great drive," Mike answered, looking at the landscape. "Good weather today."

"Glad I could come along," said Gary. "Beautiful up here. Besides, you're stocked up with provisions. You can't haul all that on foot."

"I'll be back in a week just to see how you're doing," Mike reminded Ty. "It was Dr. Curtis' idea. You agreed to it."

"I did. I'm fine with that. It might be good to have some company."

The three had spent a few minutes enjoying the view when Ty said they'd better finish the trek up the hill. "We're wasting daylight," he said. "Let's do this."

They climbed back in the car. Mike turned onto the dirt road Ty had directed him to take, although there weren't any other options that Mike could see. The road wasn't in bad shape, but narrow and with only a few turn outs in case vehicles needed to pass. They came to a posted warning that they had entered private property and no trespassing was allowed. "The warning has been posted since Doug and I were in high school," Ty said. "There's only one other property owner that uses this road."

A wide spot at the end of the dirt road provided barely enough room to turn a vehicle around. "This is it," Ty announced "The cabin's a short walk through the woods."

There was a decent trail leading through the woods but if you didn't know where to look, you would miss it completely. They left the car, Mike and Gary each carrying a box of food and supplies. Ty hauled his backpack and a heavy sleeping bag. Within a few moments' walk, the rustic cabin came into view. Further ahead, was a large, rotting, ramshackle structure. The weed barn from years before.

At first sight, it looked like an abandoned shack that had fallen into disrepair. As they walked closer, they realized that this impression was by design. Effort had been put into discouraging anyone coming across the place from thinking there was anything worth exploring. There was a shuttered window facing their trail on what was actually the back wall of the structure.

As they came around the side to the front of the cabin, Gary and Mike were amazed by what they saw. Three broad, sturdy steps led up to a narrow, covered porch that extended the length of the place. A large, wooden chair and a small table waited on the porch below two more shuttered windows. In addition to a deadbolt, Ty had installed a heavy hasp for a padlock. He unlocked the door and Mike and Gary followed him inside.

The interior of the cabin was one large room, nearly twenty-feet square. To the left of the door was an ancient, steel basin with a hand pump for drawing well water. Open shelves nearby held a few precious items. To the right was a small wooden table and chairs. In one far corner, a rocking chair stood near a wood burning stove with a cooking plate. There was a bed and a footlocker in the back corner near the window. To the side of the bed was a bookcase where dozens of books were neatly stacked.

"Here it is," said Ty. He looked around at the interior of the cabin like he was greeting a long-lost love.

"The place is great, Ty," Mike told him. "I see why you love it up here. How long since you were here?"

"A while. I leave the place set for extended absences. I try to make it back every few weeks but I never know for sure. You can leave the boxes on the table there," Ty said as he tossed the sleeping bag and backpack onto the bed.

"Have a seat, guys. Or feel free to avail yourselves of the woods should the need hit you," Ty told them.

Ty went outside and opened the window shutters. He returned with an armload of kindling which he placed in a bucket. Then he brought in larger pieces of wood to burn. Soon he had the stove lit along with a kerosene lamp. Chores complete, Ty sat down.

"Erica and I talked when I was still in the hospital. She came to see me. She offered to have the place put in my name. Tried to tell me it's what Doug had wanted to do. I believe that may be true. But I'm no property owner. I'm not sure I ever want to be back on the grid. We agreed that the place will continue to be mine to use, as always. That's good enough for me. Erica insisted on having papers drawn up to that effect. Nice of her."

"How's she doing?" Gary asked him.

"She's okay, under the circumstances. She's trying to deal with what happened to Dylan, what he got himself mixed up in. She knows that he did the right thing in the end. Even though it got him killed."

"Tough days ahead for her," said Mike.

"Yeah. She's going to meetings though. She and I plan to be in touch once in a while. And she sees Jayson, Dylan's partner, often. I'm glad for that."

Ty walked over to his footlocker. He opened it and removed a cardboard container the size of a shoebox. Inside were several items, envelopes, and the like. He reached inside one of them and brought out a stack of photographs.

"This is Doug and I as seniors in high school." The kid on the left was undoubtedly Ty, as a younger man. Dark hair, silly grin. But the young man in the picture had not yet gone to the Persian Gulf to fight in a terrible war as a trained killer. He hadn't suffered the consequences of needless bloodshed and tragedy. He was just a kid standing next to his buddy, who bore a striking resemblance to Dylan Colby. Ty studied his younger self for a moment then replaced the photograph in the stack.

"This is Erica and Dylan. Doug sent this to me when I was in...well, I don't remember where I was."

Erica was a young woman in the photograph, not much more than a teenager, and as attractive in the picture as she was now. The years had been good to her. She held a toddler in her arms. Both smiled happily for the camera. It was bittersweet to see the photo of Dylan as this sweet, young child, knowing the man he had become had died recently at the hand of another.

"It was a favorite photo of Doug's. Erica said she doesn't remember it. She should have this."

Ty reached further into the box and pulled out what appeared to be two small medallions on a chain. They were his military ID tags. "I haven't looked through this stuff in a long time. Too long a time."

"Maybe we should leave you to it. Some memories aren't meant to be shared." Mike looked from Ty to Gary as he spoke, and Gary nodded. Mike continued. "We can give you your privacy."

"Listen, Ty," said Gary, "Years ago, I had a friend named Jocelyn. She was an incredible woman, truly an Old Soul. Anyway, one day she told me something so profound that I've never forgotten it. She said that there are those who make their own candle burn brighter by blowing out the flame on someone else's. Those are the Jack Powells of the world. She was talking about our inner light. Our soul. Jocelyn said the kindest, wisest of people are the ones who understand that our inner light is to be shared. The light we share enables us to see and understand. You, my friend, have had a hell of a time keeping the flame burning on your own candle. We need your light, man. We all need your light."

Ty felt tears in his eyes as he looked at the ID tags he had hidden away in shame. He inhaled deeply as he nodded to his friend.

The End

Acknowledgements

There are many people deserving of my thanks for their help in the writing of this novel. My thanks go to the friends who contributed their time by reading the manuscript and offering feedback from a variety of perspectives. Thank you to Wayne Seeley for his views regarding particular details related to our armed forces. Thanks to Jac VerSteeg for once again sharing his skills in line editing and plot hole detection. Thank you to Rey at ReyzArt.com for a killer cover design. A tip of the hat to Kendra Zorn and Kurt Van Orden at UnderBar, for allowing me to include their inspiring establishment within these pages. Thank you to my husband, Dave Conine, for surviving a read-aloud of the manuscript while driving on the 10 between Palm Springs and Phoenix. To those of you after whom characters were named, you know who you are, and I thank you all. Lastly, thank you to my editor, Matt Love at Nestucca Spit Press, for his honesty, his encouragement, and for sharing his expertise and his love of fiction.

Keeping reading for a peek from

Runaway*, City Streets Trilogy, Book One*

Chapter 1

When the shelter residents returned from searching for housing, work, help, whatever—they were told the girl was dead. But when asked by the investigators, no one had noticed whether she was not at breakfast, nor could they remember if the girl had been around the night before. No one noticed. It was the story of her life, as they say. No one noticed whether she was around unless it was some degenerate Fagin-like creep who saw her as a commodity. But they noticed her now, now that she was dead. The shelter where she was staying was called Avalon, a temporary shelter for street folks who needed a place to stay.

Mid-November was wet from the incessant rain and cold at night. Avalon was busy. Families with children or single women can stay at Avalon for thirty days. Then they have to move on—to permanent housing, to in-patient treatment, to transitional housing, to another shelter, back with relations or friends, or back on the street. Avalon has a dorm, one large room, known as The Suite. The space is made available for up to four women at a time. The unnoticed girl had a bed in The Suite and had been there three days before she was found dead in the alley. Mark Twain was quoted to say that the rumors of his death were greatly exaggerated. Not so with the girl. She was gone. Had the girl been able, she would have told them what happened, how it felt. She would have told them that dying was less painful than many things she had encountered in her young life. At least her death had been quick and of that she was grateful.

The first one to notice the girl in the alley was Ty. A decent sort, Ty returned from the Gulf War a different guy from the one sent. Ty never blamed anyone else for his situation. He had simply heard, seen, and smelled more than anyone should have to in this lifetime and he was haunted by what he'd been through. He tried to work, tried to relate to people, tried to quell the nightmares, but the memories defeated him and he toppled down like one of Saddam's statues. Ty was a regular at Brooks House, the men's shelter down the street. Actually, Ty was a fixture there. And because he was a decent guy and he didn't have a temper, the staff liked him.

Ty walked from the bus stop to Avalon every Sunday at five p.m. because Mike worked the Sunday evening shift. Ty looked forward to seeing Mike on Sundays. Mike treated him like a man instead of some wasted shell person. Mike didn't divert his eyes when Ty looked him in the face and he greeted him when he saw Ty approach. Days could go by on the street without that happening. Ty and Mike would have a cup of coffee and visit like old friends.

But on this Sunday, as Ty walked past the alley, he smelled it. He knew what it was. For a few seconds he was there in the smoke and the stink and the fire. He made himself approach the lump at the side of the alley entrance and saw that it was the girl. *What was her name? Had he ever heard her name?* he asked himself. He must have. Ty took in the ugly gash at the side of her head. It was just above her right ear but more to the front. Something heavy had slammed into the side of her head, cleaving skin, tissue, and part of the skull. There was a lot of blood producing the sour smell that had brought Ty to her. The blow or blows had missed her open right eye. The girl stared into hell without seeing or caring that she had arrived.

Two others came along minutes after Ty. It was Marco and Genevieve, known as the seniors. Marco spoke with an accent although he had been in the States forty years. Having never learned to read and write and with no driver's license or Social Security number, Marco was like a ghost in that he was only seen in shadows. Marco's friend, Genevieve had been married at one time with a family. She had four children with her husband and "functioned well" until the voices started to dictate how to raise those children. At some point, Gen's path crossed with Marco's. Marco didn't mind that Genevieve heard voices because she helped him keep a stash of meds handy for his back pain. The arrangement worked for Genevieve, as well. Marco kept the street predators at bay and reminded Genevieve to eat.

Marco and Gen had followed Ty from the bus stop. When they saw him enter the alley, they followed like lemmings. Ty called to Marco, "Hey man, go get Mike. Now, man, get Mike." Ty didn't consider whether Marco knew who Mike was or if he'd know where to find him. Marco and Gen had been on the streets long enough and folks on the street knew that Mike was the guy at Avalon.

The pair stopped short of approaching the girl. *Too intense, too much,* they thought. Marco's back hurt since he hadn't had a pill since mid-day. Marco ambled toward the alley entrance and yelled for someone to get Mike. Gen was looking but not really looking. *Don't do it,* she told herself. They both took cues from Ty's demeanor. Marco and Gen could tell a hard rain had fallen. The Fates told them in their souls to be reverent because a fellow traveler had met with a bad end. Death, they knew, even of a disenfranchised soul, was sacrosanct.

Marco yelled again for Mike while heading down the alley toward Avalon. Residents appeared and wandered into the alley, stopping short when they realized that Ty had discovered tragedy. Soon, the buzz filtered to the shelter. Mike came running into the alley with cell phone in hand. "Who is it, Ty? Is it bad?" he asked.

"Yeah, man. It's the girl," Ty answered, then paused before adding, "and she's dead. What's her name, Mike?"

Mike dialed 911 and waited for dispatch to pick up. "Hell, Ty, I don't remember. I'll have to check her intake card." By then an emergency dispatcher was on the line. "Yeah, this is Mike Dwyer at Avalon. We found one of our female residents lying in the back alley." Mike paused to listen to the emergency dispatcher. "No, there's no doubt." Mike listened again, said, "Yeah...I know."

Read further to enjoy a sneak preview of

Gutter Punk*, City Streets Trilogy, Book Three*

Prologue

"We need to get out of here, Pooki," whispered Elle. "We've been here for, like, two days."

"Yeah, I know," answered Pooki. "I'm sick of these dudes too. I'm sick of their faces, and I'm sick of them beating on us for kicks." She wanted to cry. Pooki was tired and in pain. But she was too angry. Angry, physically hurt, and scared. "I hope they don't hear us talking, Elle. Do you think they can hear us?"

"I don't know. They're pretty sauced. If they keep drinking, maybe they'll pass out," said Elle. She was as exhausted and achy as her friend. She had bruises on her face, arms, and shoulders. The least the men could do was to offer the kids some of their whiskey to take the edge off the pain.

There were two of them. The younger one was a skinny dude. He had offered Pooki food and a place to stay. They met up in the alley behind Dahlia's Asian Café where Pook was searching the dumpster for something to eat. Pooki had asked Elle to come along so there would be two of them. The skinny guy seemed okay at first, but he turned weird. He got mean and he enjoyed it too much when things became violent. It crossed Elle's mind that he may have been a spotter with the West Coast Track, looking for young bodies to sell for sex up and down I-5 between Canada and Mexico. If he was, Elle knew that she and Pooki were done. Neither of them would be seen or heard from again.

They didn't know about the other guy until they got to the address they'd been given. This second guy was older—old and kind of dumb. He was a big guy. He could hit hard and he liked to hit. It was too late for Elle and Pooki to wonder if they had been overheard. They heard the assholes coming back from the other room.

It was the old, ugly one who spoke. "Forget it, you little shit! You're not going anywhere. You still owe me for food. What about the movies you been watching? Who paid for that, huh? I even let you take a shower and clean up your scrawny ass." He grabbed Elle by the hair and started to shake her. It was the guy's version of foreplay. The attacks had been going on since yesterday.

Elle had had enough but didn't know how to make the jerk leave her alone. "Please, man, I can't take anymore. You gotta give me a break, okay?"

"We gave you a break, you freeloading freak!" He shouted at Elle. "Here's all the break you get, now shut your mouth!" He hit Elle so hard on the side of her head that she saw stars.

The old guy went after Elle again. He wasn't taking no for an answer, and his buddy was laughing at the show, enjoying it, like it was staged entertainment. Pooki grabbed the closest thing she could—a dinner plate. It was heavy, thick, ceramic. She smashed the plate into the guy's head. He went down on his belly, his pants around his knees. He was stunned, but he wasn't knocked out. Elle climbed out from under him, eyes wide.

"You little fuck!" screamed the skinny guy, sticking up for his moron friend. Then Elle and Pooki saw that he had a knife in his hand. He started slashing the blade around, in wild motions, fueled by whiskey and outraged that two street kids would dare to defend themselves.

Pooki tried to move a safe distance away from the swinging knife. Elle was faster. She had just enough of a head start. Pooki was right in the path of the crazy asshole's blade and before she could back away, the knife cut into Pooki's side. Blood spurted and Pooki's hand went to her wound. She sat down on the floor, wide-eyed.

The skinny asshole looked like he couldn't believe what he'd done. He stared at the knife for a moment, then he tossed it to the floor. Elle didn't think twice—she reached down, grabbing the blade from where it had landed on the floor and held it out between her and the two creeps.

"Stay the fuck where you are!" Elle screamed at the creeps. The older one had pulled his pants up by now. He started to make a move toward the knife. Elle looked at him and said, "Go ahead you crazy asshole, you think you're faster than me? I owe you some pain and some shit right about now!" It was a surprise to Elle that her words stopped the guy in his tracks. The big, tough brute didn't say anything. He must have been too drunk. Apparently, the sight of blood hadn't sobered him up.

Keeping the knife out in front of her, her eyes peeled on the creeps, Elle reached for a dish towel that had been left on the table. She scooped Pooki up off the floor and pushed the towel into the side of Pook's abdomen. Elle tried to pretend that there wasn't as much blood as it looked like. She put Pooki's arm around her shoulder and they backed out the front door. Elle and Pooki stumbled down the front walk of the crummy place. Elle tossed the knife into a rhododendron bush and they headed down the dark street to find help.

Don't miss out!

Visit the website below and you can sign up to receive emails whenever Susanne Perry publishes a new book. There's no charge and no obligation.

https://books2read.com/r/B-A-TQXL-FMDJB

About the Author

Susanne Perry is the author of the City Streets Trilogy, a series of crime mysteries set in a fictional urban area in southwest Washington. Previous to writing novels, Perry worked with public programs serving children and families. Future writing projects include short stories, children's books, and of course, mysteries. A voracious reader of who-done-its and historical fiction, Perry resides in Arizona and Washington.

www.ingramcontent.com/pod-product-compliance
Ingram Content Group UK Ltd.
Pitfield, Milton Keynes, MK11 3LW, UK
UKHW042005190726
13854UKWH00005B/2166